FALLEN MESSIAH

A Vampire Novel

S. G. Hardt

The characters and events portrayed in this book are fictitious. Any similarity to real persons, living or dead, is coincidental and not intended by the author.

ISBN-13: 979-8-218-04248-6

Printed in the United States of America

Have a sense of humor for small problems,
and faith in God when confronting big problems.

RWG

You'll be somber,
Even weak
Moments of silence,
When one should speak.

Yet greater are days
When strength is replete,
Confidence, passion, soul complete.

Regardless of high or low,
There is but one way to go.

Fortuna favors the bold

PROLOGUE

52 BC

Iron swords brandished overhead, a hopelessly small band of Germanic warriors ride to their besieged village. With the thunder of galloping horses filling the air, they break from the mist of early morning as they approach their huts on the edge of the woods.

Screaming, "Protect the women and children!" the German warlord's long black hair cannot disguise the fear so evidently emblazoned on his chiseled features. *The slaughter has begun!*

Attention drawn to the approaching warriors; the Gallic invaders cease their assault to form a mass line the breadth of the village.

Outnumbered thirty to one, the young warlord leads a charge into the flank of the enemy with the hopes of breaking the stout formation. Swinging swords with deadly skill, the Germans slash and chop at the impenetrable wall of death, riding ever deeper into its ranks.

No sooner does one Gallic soldier fall, than another takes his place, each seemingly bigger and stronger than the last. Amid screams, and gasps of death, the warlord prods his horse forward, moving ever closer to the heart of his village.

Breaking through the line, he jumps from his horse with an energy born of terror, in search of his pregnant wife.

Desperately sprinting to his hut, a band of blood-soaked invaders slowly encircles him.

Fear all but forgotten, he steadily approaches the snarling devils, deftly wielding his sword in figure eights. Taking a bead on the nearest Gaul, his sword crashes down, splitting the invader's skull. Yanking the impeded sword from its anatomical vice, he feverishly seeks a new victim. Stepping to his left in preparation to strike, a burly invader attacks from the right, clubbing the back of his head, sending him to the ground, unconscious.

* * *

Spread-eagled, and face-down in the dirt, he wakes to find his limbs staked to the ground. Through a haze of double vision, he prays the sight of women being raped, and children murdered within mother's view, to be nothing more than a nightmare planted by an evil demon. Among the chaos, he methodically twists and pulls at the ropes binding his wrists and ankles, blood pouring forth as flesh wears thin. Frustration supplanting clandestine action, he flails wildly, hoping to jerk a stake from the hard, dry earth.

Catching glimpse of his futility, a nearby Gaul screams, "He's awake!"

With hungry determination, the invaders gather around in anticipation of what's to come.

Cursing threats of retribution, the teenage warlord demands, "Cut me free! I will kill you all!"

"There will be no cutting you free!" the Gallic leader bellows, "I have a surprise before your death."

Hearing a familiar voice plead for life, he yanks mercilessly at the stakes, ignoring the pain of rope on bone.

Crowd parting, his young, frail wife is thrown mercilessly

to the ground.

"Please, I beg of you! Spare her life, and you may do whatever you wish with me!"

Crawling to him for protection, she receives a swift kick to her pregnant belly, force flipping her onto her back. Laughing heartily, the Gallic leader relishes the look of terror in her soft green eyes as he begins his planned assault.

Five men break from the crowd, four grabbing hold of her limbs, as the fifth cuts every shred of clothing from her body.

Screaming, "By the grace of Wotan, I beg you not to harm her!" the warlord watches the ugly, blood-splattered leader of the Gaul's remove his clothing and smile menacingly, as he strokes himself to erection.

Flailing and screaming, she fights the rapist as best she can before a punch to the gut lays her flat.

Disgusted with his inability to fight, he wishes nothing more than to look away, but his love would never allow such betrayal. Her agony shall be his, so long as they live.

Forty barbarians later, her dirt and sweat-covered body is nothing more than a rag doll for her captor's abuse. Once tearful eyes, now hazy and dull, hollowly peek through locks of disheveled black hair.

"Enough, bring her to him!" the Gallic leader commands.

The words spark hope in the restrained youth, and he eagerly lifts his head as she is thrown before him. As best he can, he stretches out to kiss her one last time, but before the softness of lips can meet, her neck is slit from ear to ear. Eyes peeled wide, her blood runs across the hard ground, pooling under his head.

Amid roars of laughter, two Gauls grab her feet, and drag her away. Her lifeless head bounces across the unforgiving ground, leaving only a trail of blood to connect him with his departed love. Flipping her onto her back, they throw her limp legs wide to continue the assault.

"No, I beg of you! Take my life and let her rest in peace!" he cries, searching the crowd for acceptance.

Smirking with pride, the Gallic leader offers reply by way of plunging his sword into her pregnant belly, skewering the unborn child.

Drained of every reason to live, his head falls to the bloody ground. *ALL IS LOST!*

✻ ✻ ✻

Restrained in an ox cart full of pigs, the Gauls bring him to their village for a triumphal torture, followed by an all too slow, punishing death. The swine accompanying him nip hungrily at his bloody ankles, hoping a morsel will be surrendered, while every bump of the cart causes the binding ropes to tear further into his wrists.

They will rip at my flesh and shatter my bones, a well-deserved penance for leaving my village unguarded.

With night encompassing day, the aggressors set up camp at the base of a hill, merrily feasting while regaling in tales of heroic action and lustful degradation.

Ignoring the revelry, the warlord turns his gaze to the stars, wondering how Wotan could have abandoned him at such a desperate time. Cursing him, and the heavens where he resides, he pities himself for having foolishly put faith in a false god.

The stars lie!

Consumed with hate, he looks to the heavens and catches glimpse of a falling star. Following the streak of light, he soon sees another. Unable to believe his eyes, the very stars he cursed, begin to fall. Flaming balls drop randomly about the camp with increasing ferocity, sending the drunken Gauls into a frenzied panic. Attempting to fight, they run for their weapons, but it is futile, Wotan has come for them, and death is at hand.

Through the haze of smoke and chaos, the young warlord sees a god-like figure approaching on horseback, the noble purple of his cape shimmering in the firelight of burning tents and wagons.

It is Wotan, come to save my life!

Standing high in the saddle of a brilliant white horse, Wotan roars, “What tribe do you hail from?”

In awe of the majestic figure, he cries out, “I am Cheruscan. They have killed my people!”

“Join me in defeating the Gauls or die with them!”

“I shall follow wherever the battle may lead,” he pledges, with vengeful exhilaration. “So long as my sword may taste Gallic blood!”

Smiling broadly, Wotan raises his sword to the stars, commanding, “Stay clear, young German, for Caesar’s blade shall cut your fetters!”

ONE

PRESENT DAY

"It's a lot bigger than it looked in the pictures," Sierra notices, crouching behind a large bush on a bright, moonlit night.

"It looks like Chambord in the Loire Valley, doesn't it?" Weston asks, leaning out from the cover of the bush. Scanning the expansive grounds for signs of life, his bright blue eyes and pretty-boy features belie a sinister soul.

"I suppose," she offhandedly replies, long black hair tied back, revealing wide green eyes, set in a cute, softly featured face.

"We're gonna go through that window on the near-corner of the house, follow me when I say, go."

"Wait, wait, wait!" she directs, glaring at his shoulder-length blonde hair shining like a beacon in the moonlight. "You forgot your mask!"

"It doesn't matter. They don't have any cameras and no one's home. Look, the lights are out, just like they've been all week. Whoever lives there is on vacation, at their summer cottage, or some other damned place."

Always nervous before a heist, she wonders if they might be forgetting something. *We're both dressed in black, night vision goggles and knives to cut out paintings are in his backpack, and I have empty duffel bags to hold the stolen goods.*

"C'mon, everything looks good. You ready?" he prods, an easy smile accentuating his cockiness.

"You're sure we're not moving too fast? Usually, you stake places out a lot longer than this." Biting her lip nervously, she leans out from behind the bush to take another look.

"We're fine. We haven't hit a house in this part of Connecticut for over a year, so the cops won't be on the lookout. And judging by the size of the place, they've probably got a ton of priceless art in there. Besides, you couldn't ask for a better night to get rich!"

He's right about that. The breeze and crisp air are invigorating compared to the oppressive humidity of the last few days. "Okay," she responds, with trepidation. "Just tell me when."

"When!" Darting from their cover, he makes a steady run for the distant house.

Caught off guard, she yelps, "Wait!"

The distance being greater than visualized, pushes his physical stamina, and upon reaching the corner of the house, he gratefully leans against it with outstretched arm. Coming up from behind, she pants heavily, attempting to catch her breath as she unzips his backpack to remove a pocketknife.

"Look, it's open already," he exclaims, in between breaths.

"What?" Not sure she heard him correctly, she leans closer.

"It's open. The window's open."

"How?"

"Who knows? Maybe the housekeeper forgot to close it."

Looking like two black statues silhouetted against the gray stone of the French styled mansion, they stare blankly at the partially opened window.

"I don't like this at all! If they were out of town, they wouldn't leave a window open. Let's postpone. Come back after more surveillance," she advises, as he snatches the knife from her outstretched hand.

"No way. No turning back until we've done the job." Cutting the screen open, he pushes the window up enough to squeeze through.

Anxiously watching his careful movements, goosebumps cover her arms. *Something's not right. It's too easy!*

Reaching out to stop him, his T-shirt slips through her fingers as he jumps up onto the windowsill, belly-first, and crawls into the house.

With a roll of her eyes, she tosses the empty duffel bags through the window. *No going back now.*

Stretching her arms out, he takes hold of her hands, pulling her up through the window, into the house.

Unzipping his backpack, she removes the night vision goggles. Clenching her teeth, she cautiously sets them in his open hand. *Careful, don't let them drop!*

The large square room has built-in bookcases on every wall, and each shelf burgeons with books, magazines, and assorted papers. A round, ornate table surrounded by six leather chairs occupies the center of the room, with an antique globe perched artfully in the middle.

"This looks like the library. Where should we start, the living room?" she whispers, knowing most people display their most expensive pieces where they can be admired by guests.

"Yeah, follow me." Putting on the goggles, he exits the room, entering the adjoining hallway.

Following his lead, she surveys the paintings adorning the walls, all the while, glancing about for signs of life. The hall is longer than she can make out in the darkness, and the stillness of the house makes her breathing seem magnified, almost excessive.

They pass open-doored rooms until Weston comes to a stop before a wide opening on the left side of the hall. Moonlight pours through a wall of windows into the expansive two-story room, highlighting an extensive collection of paintings and sculptures, with a massive stone fireplace on his right-hand wall. He remains still, examining the room, before gingerly stepping off the hardwoods of the hallway onto the travertine tile of the great room floor. No longer concerned with creaking wood, he moves quickly, setting a determined pace for a large painting hanging above the fireplace.

Barely having gotten her feet on tile, Sierra hears a faint noise. A whisper on the wind. Taking long, quiet strides, she reaches out, firmly grasping his shoulder, the predetermined signal to *stop and listen.*

Frozen in the center of the room, he points down, signaling, *kneel.*

That fuckin moon may as well be the God-damned sun, he thinks, pulling the goggles down around his neck. Looking around the room, he squints and blinks repeatedly, eyes slowly adjusting to the moonlight.

Remaining still, they listen intently for the faintest of sounds.

I know I heard a voice! I wonder if someone heard us and got out of bed to look around, she wonders.

Tired of waiting and resigning it to be no more than her nerves, he signals, *rise,* with an upright finger.

Admiring the large impressionist painting above the mantle, he asks, "What's it worth?"

"It's too high, you'll never get it!" she cautions, looking back to make certain that no one is sneaking up on them.

"I didn't ask for your opinion, just the price."

"Maybe five million with the right buyer, but you'll never get up there. It's too high!"

Five million? I want it! Scanning the room, he searches for a chair that is tall enough to use as a ladder.

Grabbing his T-shirt to pull him close, she puts her lips to his ear. "I'm going back down the hall. With those five or six paintings we passed, we could easily get the same amount, and it'd be a helluva lot easier."

Eyes fixed on the painting, he nods, letting her slip away so that he may ponder the Monet.

Shuffling down the hallway, she recognizes the first painting to be a Picasso, and knows she's off to a good start. Walking further, she sees a dark figure out of the corner of her eye. Heart skipping a beat, she instinctively turns to get a better look, but whatever it was, it's gone.

It had to be someone! My eyes have never played tricks on me like that. Heart pounding, she ducks into the nearest open room. *God, please don't let me get caught! I swear, I'll never do this again!*

After a brief stint of fearful listening, she peeks into the hallway with bated breath. *Maybe it was nothing . . ..* Foolish optimism trumps logic, when her inner voice whispers, *Nobody could move that fast. I'm only freaking myself out.*

Having had enough for one night, and the Picasso being enough to net a decent profit, she stealthily creeps back to the great room to inform him of the easy grab-and-go in the hallway.

Finding him carrying a chair to set on a coffee table, she can't believe her eyes. *It'll never work!* With quick steps, she races up behind him. "Let's go, there's enough in the hallway to more than make up for this."

Spinning his head back, she recognizes the look on his face. *I want it all!*

Wrinkling her brow, she's about to admonish his foolishness, when a dark figure rushes past the great room entry in a barely perceptible blur of motion.

"What the fuck?" he unwittingly blurts, knowing it couldn't have been a person moving that rapidly.

"I knew I saw somebody when I was in the hallway. Let's get out of here!" she hisses, heading for the hallway.

Getting one foot on hardwood, the blurry figure rushes past, followed by a loud thump. Nearly jumping out of her skin, she turns back to find Weston pinned to the floor by a woman with cropped, platinum blonde hair. Reaching out, attempting to pull him free, the girl menacingly opens her mouth and bares two long fangs, causing Sierra to stumble back in fear.

Regaining her balance, she steps forward to lunge at the girl, but is frozen by the sight of teeth piercing flesh. Blood spurts from his neck, onto the girl's face as she repositions herself to gain better access to his jugular. Instinct screams, *RUN! RUN! RUN!* as flight overrules fight, and she sprints for the hallway.

Moonlight shines through the distant library door, and with every step forward, the sound of heavy footsteps approach from behind. Wondering if Weston has freed himself or if the girl is in hot pursuit, she turns to glimpse the figure of a towering man. *Not Weston! Get to the window and jump!*

With every stride, his footsteps become more pronounced. *Don't look back . . . almost there! HE'S SO CLOSE!*

Glancing over her shoulder, the man can't be more than ten feet behind as she clears the doorway. Lungs burning, she heads for the window, only to find a tall woman blocking her exit. Long, curly hair highlighted by the effervescent moon, shines in a golden streak, as the woman comes straight for her.

Receiving a sharp thud to the chest, Sierra flies backward, hitting the floor, headfirst. With cat-like ease, the golden-haired woman jumps in the air and lands squarely on Sierra's midriff, pinning her down.

Struggling to break free, she thrashes about, feet and elbows knocking against wood floor. In the light of the moon that highlighted Weston's hair so brilliantly, the woman's fangs glimmer as they approach with such speed, they form a blazing white streak to her neck.

The pain of the bite is a strike of lightning to the jugular, and her heart pumps feverishly as the woman lovingly sucks her blood. Arching her back, Sierra feebly twists in defense, until inexplicably, her body relaxes, giving into the woman's will.

Moans of ecstasy fill the room as the man steps near, preparing to tear into the other side of her neck. With a downward glance, he catches Sierra's eye, and screams, "STOP!"

TWO

The morning sun pours through the window, illuminating the deep blue eyes of the petite platinum-blonde woman, causing her to hold a hand to the light. Seated behind a large desk with his back to the window, the sunlight accents the long, wavy black hair of the thirty-something-year-old man.

"Take care of him, Eve," he instructs. "Push as much of your emotions into the both of them as needed. If they have time to think about their true feelings, they may become frantic and try something foolish."

"It will be a pleasure, the cute one's always are," she coolly shines.

Smiling, his stormy grey eyes show a glint of pride in her response. "Abah is bringing the girl as we speak, go to him before he wakes."

Having barely finished his sentence, Sierra is escorted in by the golden-haired, caramel-skinned woman that drank so voraciously from her the previous night.

"What have you done with him? You can't keep us here!" Sierra shouts, mustering all the energy she can, in her nervous, blood-depleted condition.

With a sly grin, Eve steps close, fearfully close, and meets her eye. "We do whatever we please. In fact, I may go have a little fun with your friend, right now."

Happy to hear Weston is alive, she gains confidence, threatening, "We'll be missed! People know where we are and who to call if we go missing!"

"I do not believe that to be true," the man calmly replies, in a deep, gravelly voice, demanding attention.

"Do you really think we're so stupid that we haven't planned for something like this?" *How could we have been so stupid not to plan for any possible event!*

"Yes," he gloats, elbows resting on chair, with fingers tented. "I believe you were too worried about being turned in to the police or blackmailed to have ever told anyone you are a thief. Am I correct?"

Fearing her expression will only confirm his assumption, she blinks, and looks away to examine her surroundings.

The room is expansive for an office and formally decorated. Large windows look onto the estate, and wood paneling covers the walls except for a bookcase to Sierra's left and a fireplace to the right. Two leather chairs rest comfortably in front of the desk, giving the room an elegant, yet cozy feel.

Eve, sensing Sierra's anxiety, leans in, blowing lightly on the two puncture wounds on her neck. "Ooh, that looks painful. Did it hurt?"

Doe-eyed and trembling, Sierra looks down on the slightly shorter Eve, only to look away before getting locked in a stare-down.

"Eve, that is enough," he admonishes. Attempting to assuage Sierra's fear, he mentally transfers emotions of tranquility into her. *Relax, there is no need to fear us.*

Examining her from head to toe, he inquires, "Tell me why you broke into my home."

Sierra looks at the devilishly handsome man and knows she should be terrified, but feels relaxed enough to confidently spout, "Why should I tell you anything!"

Eve smiles at her defiance and runs a fingernail down her neck. "Because if you don't tell him what he wants to know, I'll kill your friend."

Shaken, she rattles, "My name is Sierra and my boyfriend's name is Weston." *Damn it! Toughen up! Don't reveal things so easily!*

"We already know your name," Eve snickers. "I found your Jeep outside our security wall, with the registration in the glove box. Smart thinkers that you are, I'm surprised you didn't have your phones in there as well."

Surprised her car has been discovered so quickly, she stammers, "Wh-what are you going to do with us?"

"Please, sit down and relax," he gestures, with outstretched hand. "You need not be frightened. If we were going to harm you, we would have done so last night."

Eyeing him suspiciously, she gives a half-hearted nod. *I suppose that's true.*

"Since you may be staying with us for a period of time, I think it best you know our names. I am Altus, the girl to your right, is Eve, and if she did not introduce herself earlier, the girl on your left is Abah."

Getting an eyeful of the classically featured Eve, she examines her blue, see-through top and tight black skirt, showing off every inch of her thin, subtly curved body. *Tramp . . . may as well be naked.* With a cautious toe-to-head motion, she checks out Abah. Dressed in black tights and a white T-shirt, her athletic, curvy frame is evident without the need for excessive revelation. *Pretty . . . and tall as hell. She's built like a track star, with the tits of a porn star.* About to make eye contact, she quickly looks away, too fearful to meet the gaze of her attempted killer. The initial rush of fear dissipating with her adrenaline, a feeling of light-headedness overwhelms, so she steps forward to sit in a chair.

Leaning across the desk, he hands her a glass of juice, specially prepared for her arrival. "Please, drink this. You will feel better if you stay hydrated." Looking up, he tells Eve, "Check on Weston. He lost more blood than Sierra and will require a great deal of attention."

Eve blinks with affirmation, then leans over the back of the chair, running her hands across Sierra's tense shoulders. "Your boyfriend tasted so good! Does he like blondes?"

Jerking forward, she angrily retorts, "Not cheap, slutty ones!"

Joyously, Eve giggles, "Ooh, she has a temper!" Turning to Abah, she asks, "Did she taste good?"

"Like a ripe berry, bursting in my mouth."

Seeing Sierra hunch in fear, Altus pushes more feelings of tranquility. "Eve, take care of Weston. Abah, please prepare the guest suites, Xi will be arriving soon."

"Xi is coming? When!" Eve jumps, forgetting all about Sierra.

"Very soon. Now please, attend to our other guest."

Smiling happily, Eve leaves the room with Abah close behind.

"How do you feel?" he asks, with piercing stare.

"Why are you keeping us here?" she demands.

"For now, I think it best you do not ask too many questions, but instead, focus on what I have given you."

"And what is that?" she challenges.

"Your life," he justifies, with upraised brow.

Not sure how to respond, and feeling a burst of energy from the juice, she sets the half-empty glass on the desk and walks to the fireplace. Pretending to admire the hand-carved, marble mantle, she gives herself time to think. *Are they going to kill me . . .? Maybe I should play along until I can talk to Weston.* Resting a hand on the mantle, she inspects the artwork hanging above.

"Eve's hair is longer in the painting," she observes.

"That is not Eve. Though the resemblance is quite remarkable, is it not?"

"Who is it, then?" she asks, unaware his transference of emotion is keeping her from feeling the true fear of her predicament.

"Are you familiar with the history of the Sade family?"

"As in the Marquis de Sade?" Turning, she catches him

studying her. *Why is he giving me that smug look?*

"Yes," he answers, analyzing her every movement.

"I never took much interest in him. From what little I know; he was quite fond of S&M." *God, I'd love to smack that look off your face!*

"He was quite fond of all things sexual, to be more accurate."

"So, who is she?" Feeling light-headed again, she steps away from the fireplace to plop back in the chair.

"That is Laura de Noves. She wed Hugues de Sade, or as he was also known, le Vieux, in the year 1325. She has often been thought of as the most beautiful woman to have ever walked the earth."

"I might agree if she didn't look so much like Eve."

Grinning for the shortest of moments, he thinks, *She has spirit!* "From what little is known about Laura, she was a bit more endearing than Eve."

"Wouldn't take much. . .. What's known of her?" she asks, his transference and her love of art taking her focus away from where it should be.

"Most knowledge of her comes from Francesco Petrarca. He first saw her in 1327 at the church of Sainte-Claire d'Avignon, where she awoke in him a burning passion, which he celebrated in his book Rime Sparse. Though they had little or no personal contact because she was married, her presence brought him unspeakable joy. Unfortunately, upon her death, he found his grief as challenging to live with as was his former despair."

"Too bad for him, huh." Locking onto his stormy grey eyes, framed in chiseled features, she finds it hard to look away. *My God, he's hot. And cocky. And conceited. Typical asshole.*

"Later in life, in his Letter to Posterity, he wrote: 'In my younger days I struggled constantly with an overwhelming but pure love affair - my only one, and I would have struggled with it longer had not premature death, bitter but salutary for me, extinguished the cooling flames.'"

"It sounds as if he loved her." *He seems awfully young to have so much money. Is he a drug dealer? Oh God, did Weston pick a drug dealer to rob?*

"His love was true, but was it only from afar? She was written to be of great virtue; thus, it is quite likely he was merely a voyeur."

"Voyeur makes it sound a little creepy," she accommodates. *Just my luck. We rob a drug dealer that plays vampire games!* Swiping her hair behind an ear, she shifts uneasily about the chair.

"Do you think he should have revealed his feelings to her?"

"I guess," she breathes. *Why does he keep staring at me so intensely? Is he some kinda perv? Holy fuck, that's it! He and his sluts get high and pretend to be vampires! Ugh, Weston. Why didn't you stake this place out longer?*

Letting out a sigh of desperation, she does her best to conceal her thoughts, murmuring, "Did you pay a lot for it?"

"It was given to me at a most fortunate time. Donatien, or the Marquis as he is so widely known, was in hiding after I helped him escape from the Citadel of Miolans."

"Wait!" Sierra exclaims, hand upright, palm out. "I know you and your friends like to play weird vampire games, but don't treat me like an idiot. At least give me that much respect!"

"I know it may seem hard to believe, but I would not lie to you. I do not waste time with games or trickery, and I would greatly appreciate the same from you."

Seeing doubt etched across her face, he states, "Maybe this will convince you."

Reaching into a drawer, he takes out a knife and holds it in the sunlight to display the gleaming metal blade. Before she can realize what's about to take place, the blurred motion of the knife slices deeply across his forearm. Grimacing slightly, blood spurts out of the open wound, showering the fine mahogany desk.

Jutting back, she huddles into the chair as far as the cushion allows. From the corner of her eye, she watches the gaping wound slowly heal from its ends. Curiosity peaked, she leans closer, mouth falling open as the skin miraculously pulls together. As the scab flakes away, and the skin returns to its unmarred appearance, she mutters, "It can't be! It just . . . can't . . . be! I know what I saw last night, but this can't be real!"

"It is most definitely real, and this is but the beginning."

Taking the napkin from under her glass, he wipes up the blood.

"What are you people!" Head spinning with jumbled thoughts, she leans back, increasing the distance between them.

"If you believe in folktales, we would be referred to as vampires. Though, personally, I have no fondness for the term."

Vehemently shaking her head, she justifies, "There's no such thing as vampires!" *He's a rich, drugged up, demented fuck, that's what he is! It was all a trick!*

"I wish I could have been more tactful, but no one believes until they have seen." Sensing that she is wrestling with incomprehensible thoughts and a healthy dose of fear, he pushes more of his emotions into her. *Relax . . . open yourself to me.*

"I've seen, and I still don't believe! How can it be real?"

"Did you not see the wound heal?"

"Yeah," she scoffs, "but that and being a vampire are two different things."

"They are one and the same. We have a disease that infects our bodies and continually renews our cells, making us strong. Much like cancer mutates healthy cells, leading to death, this disease brings eternal life."

With continued transference, she relaxes further, arms resting on chair as she tilts ever so slightly forward. "Where does this disease come from?" *Could this be real? No way!*

"No one knows, other than it has been passed through the blood for more than four millennia. Not even Khaba, the oldest of our kind, can answer that question. But, for that matter, can you tell me how cancer, Alzheimer's, or Parkinson's originated?"

"I suppose not," she readily admits. "Who is Khaba?"

"He was a Pharaoh in the third dynasty of ancient Egypt. He knows more than anyone about the history of mankind, as well as our species."

"What is your species?" *What am I gonna do? This is the craziest fucking thing I've ever seen!*

"I am the same as you, only infected with a virus that perpetuates my entire being."

"What about daylight? I thought vampires died if they're out in the sun."

"Folktales. Though it is true our vision is not as good as a normal human's in the light of day, which keeps many of my kind out of the sun, it is more than made up for at night, when our eyes operate much like an animal's, in that we see with incredible clarity."

"Is that the reason people believe vampires sleep in the day and hunt at night?"

"Most likely, for it is under the cover of darkness when we normally seek blood."

I wish Weston were here, he'd know how to handle this. Maybe I can find a weakness and let him know. "Why do you need blood if it's a disease?"

"The disease demands it to survive. If you took your greatest loves and joined them with your deepest lust, then multiplied it one-hundredfold, only then would you begin to understand our craving for human blood. In my hungriest moments, I can feel the blood rushing through those around me. It is intoxicating! When the virus needs to be sated, there is nothing that can stand in its way. The taking of blood is our lust, love, and passion. And there is no other blood that will keep us alive. Some of my kind went so far as to drink animal's blood, but it only brought on sickness."

"Not death?"

"No, they were cut open, drained, and replenished with

human blood."

The thought of it horrifies Sierra, causing her to cringe, before regaining her composure. "So, if you don't drink blood, you die?"

"Eventually, yes, but it takes time."

"How much time?" she asks, a little too eagerly.

She searches for a weakness. "If I did not replenish within the next four to five weeks, I would become slightly weaker, somewhat less exuberant, and appear moderately older."

"You don't need to drink blood every night, then?" *Could vampires be real? Never . . .! How much longer should I play along with this?*

"That is a myth." *Does she worry I will kill her?* "I want you to know that I would never harm you."

Unsure, she meets his impregnable stare, hoping to find a glimmer of truth. "How was Eve able to overpower Weston?"

"We are much stronger than the average human."

"How much?"

"Four to ten times stronger, and faster. Plus, it increases exponentially with age."

Can't be! She must have surprised Weston, that's how she held him down. "I don't remember things very clearly from last night, but I swore I saw fangs on Abah, and today, nothing. Are you putting fake fangs in your mouth to play vampire games?"

"They protrude when we need them," he answers, "much like a cat's claw extends from its paw."

"Show me," she demands. *I have him now! They're putting in fake fangs to go along with their drugged-up charade!*

Opening his mouth wide, his canine teeth gradually extend an inch from their original length. What once appeared to be a handsome and intelligent man, suddenly appears a devilish freak of nature. Sensing her fear, he retracts his teeth, and closes his mouth.

OH . . . MY . . . GOD! They really are vampires! They really do exist! Grabbing the glass of juice, she gulps the last of its contents, wishing it were spiked with vodka. "Then, all you need to live forever, is blood!" *Incredible! Never dying!*

"The need for blood is but one necessity. Humans need only eat and drink to survive, whereas we require the infusion of blood as well."

"Then, you're not really human?"

"It may not seem that way, but we are." Not entirely sure he has explained himself adequately, he offers an analogy. "Think of it like this. We require blood to treat the disease much like a diabetic would require insulin."

"I suppose that's one way to look at it." *How long before they kill us? A day, a week, a month?*

"How is it so different?"

"Because what you have is eternal life, the greatest gift of all. Diabetes is a debilitating disease. "

"Yes, it is a gift." *She is intrigued. Does she desire it?*

"What about God? How could he let creatures like you exist?"

"Which god? There are many religions."

"Christianity." *I must be dreaming! How could there be vampires, and no one knows they exist?*

"To begin with, I am not certain where my place would be with any god. Regardless of my immortality, I have done things that would appease only the most Pagan of gods. And I am most certainly an abomination to any of the gods being worshiped today, with the exception of one."

"Which god is that?" she frowns, knowing no righteous god would condone killing.

"The religion that grows greater every day. The religion that will eventually replace all gods."

"What are you talking about?" *We not only rob a vampire, but we also pick a bat-shit, crazy one.*

"Science. It is mankind's new god. Man is coming to understand his past and what makes him unique. In another hundred years, he will no longer require ancient myths to explain his existence. He will see his significance and grandeur in being a species that picked itself up from the jungle floor to plant its foot firmly upon the universe."

"You think mankind will disregard religion?"

"Tell me of Mithraism."

"I've never heard of it," she exhales, hopelessly. *What am I going to do? How are we going to get out of here?*

"At one time it was more popular than Christianity and Judaism combined."

"You think Christianity will be forgotten in the same way? It's been around over two-thousand years. I don't think it will disappear in a hundred years."

"Man has come far in the last one-hundred years. Soon, mankind will see that fictional beings created out of fear and desperation in his ancient past, are no longer worthy of worship. The age of humanism is upon us."

She ponders, wanting to refute his beliefs, but the thought of evolution being taught in schools, and governments constantly siding with atheists, makes for a hopeless cause. "But that doesn't make it true," she counters, half-caring, half-pondering her dire situation. *How do I explain all this to Weston? He'll think I lost my mind!*

"I have seen and read much in my life, and there is no god. Nor is there a heaven and hell."

"And if you're wrong?"

"There is only one way to know, and I may outlive any real or imagined gods. What does that make me?"

After a silent pause, she looks at the painting over the fireplace. "So, when you tell me that you helped the Marquis de Sade escape from prison, you're actually telling the truth?"

"I would not lie. What benefit would it serve me?"

"I don't know, maybe you're nuts," she scoffs.

Slowly, a smile crosses his face.

At least he has a sense of humor. Maybe I'll keep playing along to win his trust. "What was he imprisoned for? Sexual deviancy?"

"Truth be known, it was more his mother in-laws wish, the Madame de Montreuil, that he be incarcerated. Though, it was undoubtedly his own actions that paved the way."

"How did you become acquainted with him?" *Could I really be talking with someone over two-hundred years old?*

"Through mutual friends in Paris. You must realize that Donatien was a victim of the times in which he was born. In this era, his acts of indecency would be written off as the acts of a sexually adventurous person." Carefully examining her every movement, he continues transferring emotions, striving to keep her calm.

"Were you good friends?" she asks.

"Enough that when he needed my assistance to escape from the Citadel, I supplied him with fifteen soldiers to aid in his quest for freedom."

"And in return, he gave you the painting?"

"Not exactly. He was in hiding for several months after his escape and required money. While he was in Italy, I loaned him an amount necessary for survival, and when he secretly returned to his chateau in La Coste, in the Fall of 1774, he repaid me with this painting. It was fortunate that he gave it to me, for only two weeks later, the police would raid his home and destroy much of its contents. Luckily for him, I learned of the raid early enough to send him a letter, forewarning him of the imminent danger."

"How did you learn of the raid?"

"The Madame de Montreuil obtained an order from the King to arrest Donatien, and my contacts in the royal court duly passed the information on to me."

"It pays to have friends in high places, doesn't it?" she remarks, never having been able to count on anyone for anything. "Have you known many historically famous people?"

"I suppose I have. While residing in different cities of the world at varying times, it was nearly impossible to avoid some of the people that have since become celebrated figures."

"Which explains the painting."

"Exactly, but that is only the tip of the iceberg. Come, I

would like to show you my gallery, it is filled with my most prized possessions."

Walking around the desk, she gets her first good look at him. Tall, muscular, and lean, his athletic physique is perfectly outlined beneath a fitted white dress shirt and crisp black pants. With his wavy, black locks pouring past his collar, he looks more like a movie star than a bloodthirsty vampire.

Following him down the hallway, past the great room where Weston was attacked, she feels diminutive. *Damn, he's tall. Six-six? Six-seven? But the way he acts . . . too cocky. I hate him!*

Entering the expansive gallery at the end of the hall, her eyes are immediately drawn to the ornately decorated ceiling, gilded in gold leaf. *This is the treasure chest; Weston picked the wrong room!*

Paintings and sculptures fill the massive room, easels and statues forming aisles up and down its length. At the far end of the room is a wall of windows with French doors leading onto a veranda, which overlooks an Olympic sized pool.

"Wow!" she gasps. *There must be millions of dollars in artwork in here!*

"What do you know of the Masters?"

"Quite a bit, I was an art history major in college."

"You have the love of art," he smiles, appreciatively. "Do you collect?" *There is more to her than I realized.*

"I wish. I don't have that kind of money."

"What of the paintings you steal?"

"We sell everything. I wish I could keep something for myself, but I have to survive."

Softening his stare to a friendly glance, he asks, "Do you visit many museums?"

"God, yeah. The emotions that can be represented in a single piece of art has me visiting museums fairly often."

"We are similar, I make a point of visiting museums all over the world."

"You're fortunate, I would love to travel like that. How long has it taken you to collect everything?"

"It has been my life's work."

"Which is your favorite piece? Or is it even possible to have a favorite?" she inquires, feeling more comfortable with their shared love of art.

"I treasure them all, but I hold one more precious than all others combined."

Looking at the paintings, she doesn't recognize anything of historical significance. "I'm not familiar with any of these. Are they your favorites for personal reasons?"

"Look closely before you judge. I think you will be extremely impressed when you realize what you are looking at."

Leaving his side, she examines one of the paintings.

"Since you are a scholar, I will let you study in peace. Please, take your time, I will be on the veranda to answer your inevitable questions."

Watching him pass through the doors and rest in a chair, she contemplates escape. *Run to the road and hitch a ride to the police station! Yeah, sure, and tell them what? I was robbing a house of vampires and they made me stay for breakfast?*

Gazing around the room, she sighs, "Look closely before I judge . . . like I can't tell what I'm looking at. Ha!"

Focusing on the nearest painting, she analyzes the use of color and brushstrokes, slowly making her way down to the artist's signature. Unable to believe her eyes, she spouts, "No way!" and sprints out to the veranda.

"Leda!" she exclaims. "It can't be real!"

"You saw Michelangelo's signature on it, did you not?"

"And that's supposed to mean it's authentic?"

"Do you really believe I would own anything but an original?"

"It's impossible! That painting and the cartoon for it disappeared over three-hundred-and-fifty years ago."

"I am impressed, you are very knowledgeable."

Walking back into the gallery, he holds the door for her.

"Did you see The Battle of Cascina? It is just to the right of Leda. Unfortunately, it is only the cartoon."

Rattling off titles of long-thought disappeared artwork, she follows closely in tow, a pointed finger accentuating his words. "Giorgione's self-portrait as David, Titian's portrait of Charles the first, as well as his paintings of the twelve Caesar's. I also have artists from the T'ang dynasty school of art, such as Wu Tao-tzu, along with masterpieces by the ancient Greek artists Apelles, Zeuxis, Protogenes-"

"It's not possible!" she interrupts. "No painting ever survived from ancient Greece or that period of Chinese history!"

"Yet, you see it before you," he smiles, proudly.

Halting before a pedestal, he points to a gold vase encrusted with precious stones. "This is one of my favorite pieces. It is the Jane Seymour Cup, made by Hans Holbein the Younger for Henry VIII."

"For his marriage to Lady Jane in 1536," she interjects. Studying its intricate design, she reads the inscription aloud. "Bound to obey and serve."

"It was Lady Jane's motto."

"How is all this possible?" *Someone needs to pinch me; this is beyond a dream!*

"In time, I will answer all of your questions. But first I would like to show you my most prized possession."

Following him down another aisle, she attempts to soak up the brilliance of every piece at a glance. Reaching the fourth of five aisles, he stops before an iron stand with a glass encasement resting on top.

Leaning over the case, she finds a gold necklace, armband, and bracelet with peridot gemstones set in every piece.

"Would you like to look at it?" he offers.

"I would love to!" *If curators saw this place, they'd think they'd died and gone to heaven!*

Lifting the glass from the case, he leans it against the stand. "Please, help yourself."

Eagerly picking up the necklace, she instinctively examines the quality of the work, silently appraising its value. *There must be at least thirty, one-inch pieces of gold shaped into ivy leaves forming the chain. The attached gold pendant looks to be about three inches around, and it's formed into a snake curling around a one-and-a-half-inch peridot gemstone, with the head of the snake engulfing the tail. Damn, the extensive detailing is spectacular. Clearly made for someone of considerable means. Very impressive!*

Carefully setting it back in the case, she picks up the snake armband. *Definitely Roman. While these were common throughout the empire, the detail on this is like nothing I've ever seen. The snake's head is accented with a small eye of peridot, and the body forms the infinity symbol, head engulfing the tail, similar to the necklace.* Running her fingers over the snake's body to feel every scale, she can't help but exclaim, "Fabulous!"

Putting the armband back, she hastily grabs the bracelet. *Two thick gold wires intertwine to form a series of loops. An ornamental disk connects the wires, and it's a smaller version of the pendant on the necklace, with a smaller peridot, but the same great attention to detail. God, I could retire from these alone!*

"What do you think?" he asks, watching her carefully set the bracelet back in the case.

"Where did you get them?"

"It was a gift from Julius Caesar to Cleopatra, shortly before he was murdered. The finest craftsman in the empire were commissioned, and they were intentionally adorned with peridot, her favorite gemstone."

She hears what he's saying but is too caught up in her thoughts to comment. *This can't be real . . . what the fuck is all this about!* "Why are you keeping us here!" she demands.

Folding his arms across his chest, he looks into her eyes with a seductive glance. "I do not believe in gods, but I do believe in destiny."

What does he mean by that? How long does he plan on keeping me here! Terrified, she blurts, "You can't keep me here! If I don't get out, I'll destroy your precious artwork! What do you think of that?"

"I do not intend on keeping you here by force or restraining you against your will. In time, you will be free to go."

"How much time?"

"Do you enjoy these masterpieces?"

"Yes . . . so!" she shouts, anger boiling.

"Study my collection as long as you like. In my library are biographies of many of these very same artists. Most historians would give their life to view these treasures for a day, and I am giving you all the time in the world."

"What makes you think I'm so interested that I'd gladly remain a prisoner?"

"I do not want you to feel as though you are a prisoner, because you are not. I want you to appreciate the beauty of the pieces, possibly even understand the emotion that went into creating them. For many of the artists I cannot offer any more information than you will find in my books, but for others, I can tell you what they were like, as well as their inspiration. Once you have studied all that you desire of these treasures and your friend has healed, you are free to go."

"That simple! I study some paintings, read a couple books, and you'll just let us go? After revealing so much. I don't think so!" *Is he keeping us around until he needs blood?*

"Yes, you will be free," he gently implores. "I am a man of my word."

"Liar!" she spits, then wisely thinks, *Pull it together before he kills you! Play his game.* "Okay, let's assume we stay here until Weston recovers. What makes you think you know more than any other scholar as to what the artists felt when they created these pieces? We've all studied the same biographies. Besides, even if you are being truthful about living since the time of the Marquis de Sade, that's only a couple-hundred years ago. These pieces are far older than that!"

Staring deep into her eyes, he soberly explains, "The set of jewelry you examined. It was given to Cleopatra on the evening of 15 March, 44 BC. Caesar intended to give them to her days later, at a party celebrating his departure for the Parthian war, but Brutus and his co-conspirators put an end to his life."

"How could you possibly have that much detail?" she counters, turning away as if the sight of him alone were too much to bear.

"Because I was the man that gave them to her. When the light of our lives was extinguished, I went to Caesar's garden villa and presented them to her, as she wept."

Gawking, with utter disbelief, she theatrically throws her hands in the air. "You're completely fucking nuts, aren't you? You expect me to believe you're over two-thousand years old!"

"If you believed me to be over two-hundred years old, only moments ago, then why is it so hard to believe that I am over two-thousand . . .? I fear I have given you too much to think about. I believe it best you spend some time alone, relax, and think your situation through. Should you have any questions, please feel free to ask me anything you wish. I will be in the library, that is where you broke in last night. If you feel yourself becoming weak or tired, I encourage you to rest before dinner this evening. You will find that Eve has placed some of her clothing in your bedroom. You two are similar in stature, it should fit well enough."

Walking away, he stops and pivots. "Need I say, do not leave the house? It would lead to great misfortune for you, and your friend. That unpleasantry aside, please enjoy yourself."

Watching him leave the gallery, she listens to his footsteps until they are no longer audible. Arms crossed, she breathes, "Oh my God, Weston. What have you gotten us into?"

THREE

The morning nearly over, Weston lays sleeping in a dimly lit room. The sun peeks through a crack in the drapes, dividing the bedroom, showering its full intensity on Eve, sitting at his bedside. If not for the lack of wings, any human in a half-awakened state would believe her to be an angel illuminated by the light of God.

With a soft lullaby caressing his ears, he slowly rouses from his blood-depleted sleep. Too tired to decipher the words, he smiles at the sound of the angelic voice, burying his head so deep in the pillow, not even a glimmer of light may invade his slumber.

Softly, she rubs his back and shoulders. "Wake up, baby. Mommy's here."

Exhaling, he rubs his head in the soft pillow.

"Yes, that's my baby boy."

Groaning in appreciation for the massage, he mouths into the pillow, "That feels good."

Slowly lifting his head, he opens his eyes to the strange room. Jerking upright, he comes face to face with Eve. The sudden movement makes him light-headed, and with rolling eyes, he falls back into the pillow.

Attempting to alleviate his bleary-eyed confusion, she goes to the window, flinging open the drapes.

Fingers splayed haphazardly over his eyes, he pulls them

away, one by one, dilated pupils slowly adjusting to the light. With clearing vision, the beautiful angel with Barbie-esque features comes into focus. Displaying a stripper's eye for fashion, she is clearly bestowed upon all men as a portent of what heaven holds for lusting, moderately upright souls.

Returning to his bedside, she grins, "Do you have issues with your mommy? Possibly an Oedipus complex? Freud did say that every little boy wants to fuck his mother."

Her sarcasm befits no angel of heaven, so he shoots a disparaging glance in her direction, then surveys his surroundings. *Period room, decorated with Louis the 14th furnishings, and hand-frescoed walls. More than a few valuable antiques in here. Somebody's got some cash!*

"Didn't your mother return your affections?" she snickers, sticking her chest out to give him a good look at her perky tits, clearly visible through the sheer blue top. "If you like, you can suck on my tits and call me mommy. Would that make you feel better?"

"Fuck off," he snaps, in no mood or intellectual capacity for witty retorts.

"Whoops, I see I touched a nerve," she replies, sarcasm filling every word. "Well, now I know where not to tread, don't I? I'll just make a mental note that mother jokes are completely off-limits."

"What happened to me! Who are you?" he demands, searching his memory for bits and pieces that may help him understand why a mean-streaked angel chose this morning to torment him.

"I'm Eve, don't you remember our date last night?"

Squinting his eyes, they slowly open with astonishment as it starts coming back to him. "Where's Sierra!"

"Don't you worry, she's safe."

"Where am I?" he begs.

"You don't remember? After you brought me home from our date, you tried to take advantage of me. And being that I'm a good girl, I tried to push you away, but you became forceful and threw me to the floor."

Furrowing his brow, he slowly shakes his head as she rambles on about their mythical date. With every beat of his heart, the paltry blood makes its way to his numb brain, and with oxygen firing axons, details come back with ever greater clarity.

"And since you had me spread out like an easy prom date, I thought it best to give you what you wanted," she chirps.

Ignoring the endless chatter, he puts a hand to his neck, cringing as he touches the swollen puncture wounds. Face contorted in disbelief, he opens his mouth to speak, but with a finger to his lips, she keeps him silent.

"Then, when I tried to give you a kiss, you turned away. Which, to be perfectly honest, hurt my feelings, and pride. I've always thought I was a stunningly beautiful girl. At least my father always said so." At which point, she poses, giving him an innocent, yearbook smile.

"I-" he begins, but is quickly cut off by her hand covering his mouth, pushing him into the pillow.

He attempts to fight back, but his weakened body instructs, *Lay back and relax, bro. You ain't got the strength.*

"And since you didn't want a kiss, I thought a little hickey would be more appropriate." Opening her mouth wide, canines elongating into fangs, she leans over, inches from his face.

He tries to scream, but with mouth covered, all he can do is close his eyes as a means of escape.

As quickly as the fangs came out, they retreat, and she laughs happily, relishing her wit and strength.

Blinking his eyes open, he prays the fearful devil is no longer in sight. *What the fuck! How did she do that!*

"You've been such a bad boy; I shouldn't even be bringing you anything to eat."

Walking to the dresser, she grabs a tray holding a pitcher of orange juice, glass, and assorted food. Setting it on the nightstand, she pours a glass of juice, hands it to him with a look of assured superiority and sits on the bedside.

Overcome with fear, and what he perceives to be an unstable girl, he hesitantly sits up, accepting the glass. As the sweet juice runs through his body, waking his tired muscles, his inner voice warns, *She's crazy! Get outta here before she kills you!*

"But you know, like lots of girls, I do always seem to fall for the bad boy," she confesses, placing a hand on his leg, fingertips rubbing against his shaft.

Anger surfacing, he yells, "I want to see Sierra. Now!"

"Why? I thought we were having a good time."

With every caress of her fingers, his engorged member reveals itself with greater clarity, tenting the sheet.

"You shouldn't be so mean to me. I'm the only nurse you have. No one else wanted to take care of you, not even Sierra! She's too busy being the scholarly art student. I mean, I like paintings just as much as the next person, but don't you think music is a much more soulful expression of art? Just the way it gets into your soul, you know?"

"Don't toy with me. You're fucking with the wrong person!" he shouts, hoping to intimidate.

"But I thought you enjoyed me toying with you? Look how hard you are? I'm surprised there's enough blood left in you to fill that thick prick."

Angry, yet hornier by the second, he considers rolling over, but before he can budge, she pulls the sheet back, taking hold of his rod.

Narrowing his eyes, he considers fighting her advances, but his tightly squeezed head feels intoxicating, and he finds it impossible to look away from her perky tits, enticing him behind the deliciously see-through fabric.

Stretching out, her nipples become hard, begging to be fondled. With growing passion, she transfers her emotions, taking him deep into the ocean of lust.

"Relax, baby," she purrs, lifting her skirt to reveal a neatly trimmed bush with drops of passion forming on the lips.

Sierra fades from memory as his eyes wash over her skinny body and drop-dead gorgeous face. “You’re incredible,” he moans, unaware that her transference has overpowered his ability to think clearly. “I love your tits. Can I feel them?”

“That’s a good boy. Ask nicely, and mommy will give you anything you want.” Gently removing her top, she turns, giving him a side-view of her pert, upright nipples.

“Anything?” he hungrily wishes, gazing into her lusty, blue eyes.

“Anything, baby,” she breathes, leaning in close to let him suck on her taut nipples.

“That’s it, sugar. Flick your tongue on my nipple . . . mmm . . . now take all of it in your mouth and suck hard. Ooh yeah, I like that! Now blow on my wet nipple . . . yeah, just like that. You’re so good!”

“Damn baby, get on top and ride me.”

“You’re not being nice enough.” Putting a hand between her legs, she pulls out her honey covered fingers, and sticks them in his mouth, to lick clean.

“Please baby,” he suckles, licking up every drop of the incredibly sweet juice.

“Maybe if you beg.” Grabbing him by the hair, she gently forces his head into the pillow.

“I’m begging, baby. Please, give it to me! My cock is aching!”

“That’s better.” Letting go of his thick blonde locks, she runs a finger around his baby-blue eyes, and traces his pronounced cheekbone, down to his full lips. Almost too full for a man.

“I need you more than any woman I’ve ever had!”

“More than Sierra?”

“Much more! I’ve always loved blondes, and I’ve never seen a woman as beautiful as you. Please, baby . . . I need you more than my cock can stand. It’s gonna explode if you don’t ride me!”

“That’s what I wanted to hear.” Throwing a leg over him, she works herself down his thick, throbbing shaft. “Ooh, you have a nice one. That feels so good . . . give it to me hard!" Squeezing his hard, pumped chest, her fingernails tear at his skin, causing blood to trickle. Lapping up the nectar of life, she moans, "Tell me what you'll do for me."

"Whatever you want, baby. Just ask."

"That's what I like to hear, and you'd better be good."

"God, yeah . . . I'll be good!"

Loosening her grip on his rod as she squirms down, and tightening as she rises, she squeezes him harder than he could in his own fist.

"Your pussy is so hot and tight. How's that fucking possible?"

"Cuz, I'm really fucking hot. Say it!"

"You're so fucking hot!"

"Hotter than Sierra?"

"Ten times hotter!"

"Mmm, you know it."

"Fuckin' hell, bitch" he screams, climaxing into her heavenly sex. "You're squeezing the cum right out of me!"

With his load spent, and energy depleted, he lays back, attempting to catch his breath. "Fuck, you're incredible!"

With lids half open, and a sideways grin, she boasts, "I am, aren't I."

FOUR

ONE WEEK EARLIER

Bits of rhythm, to strings of melody, followed by screeching guitars. The beckoning sound of music becomes clearer with Weston's every step through the woods. Finding the rope hanging from the high stone wall, he slings the camera strap over his shoulder, climbs the rope, and perches atop the wall before gingerly jumping onto the roof of Sierra's Jeep, discreetly parked on the other side. Stepping onto the hood, he leaps to the ground, and unties the rope from the front bumper.

"We may be headed for retirement, baby girl!"

"Promise?" Sierra giggles, as he throws the rope in the back seat, and squeezes his six-foot-frame behind the wheel.

"It's not getting to be too much is it?" he asks, not really wanting to hear the answer.

"It's just that I'd like to stop for a while. Relax a little, you know? There always seems to be one more job after what should have been the big score."

He couldn't deny that. For her, robbery was a means to an end, but for him, it was a way of life. Not just the money, but the rush of pulling off a difficult job. From the initial excitement when finding a target, to the thoughtful planning of the means-and-ways, followed by the adrenaline pumping fear when first setting foot in a forbidden place. It was a high that was better than any drug. Not to mention the easy payout from the stolen goods.

Growing up privileged, he never had much to worry about, and his father was quick to lay out his future before him. The *stagnant life*, as he referred to it, was more than he could bear. *Doing time* at his father's company. *Mere existence until your time is called.* No, that was not for him. Right or wrong, good or bad, this was living. No killing mind you, just liberating artwork from one party and putting it into the hands of another. Pieces of art that were gathering dust and more than likely over-insured, netting a nice profit for everyone.

Cheerfully, he turns down the radio and starts the Jeep. Head cranked to the rear, he backs out of the trees toward the road. With a quick glance in either direction, he drives onto the empty street, careful not to leave tire marks in the dirt, or dirt tracks on the road.

"Did it really look that good?" she asks, brimming with energy.

"It looked great from the outside, and if the inside compares even slightly, we're about to retire." *Stop saying, retire! She takes it too literally.*

The chance of scoring big and leaving their crooked ways behind, brings hope that this may be the payout that finally satisfies him. Gazing out the passenger side window, she admires the bright summer foliage as the black Jeep winds its way out of the Connecticut countryside, back to New York City.

With ample time to ponder the events of the past year, she analyzes their relationship to the mind-clearing whistle of the wind, blowing through her torn door seal. It was a party her then-boyfriend, Jeff, was throwing for one of his friends moving to the left coast. In retrospect, she wonders why she hadn't stayed with him. She was a Long Island girl of average height, blessed with a cute face and figure, but what stood out more than anything, were her middle-class values. She had never cheated on any of her boyfriends, let alone leave one for another man. That was until Weston walked into her life. 'Sierra, come here! There's someone I want you to meet,' Jeff yelled from across the room. 'It's my old roommate from Harvard.'

'It was all sparks when I met Weston, and we have so much in common,' she recalls telling a friend. 'Jeff is too busy with his career as an investment banker to care about my love of art, but Weston and I can't get enough. And he's so charming! Not to mention the sex, wow!'

His place, her place, cars, and bars. Anywhere they couldn't be seen, and sometimes where they could. They were a match made in heaven, at least it seemed that way in the beginning. As time passed, his love of art waned, and she couldn't help but feel his love for her had too. There was a lot of sex, and a fair amount of theft, but no commitment to anything beyond the next job. On top of that, the constant research into the market value of relatively obscure painters was daunting, compared to the payoff. Not to mention the risk of getting caught. But worst of all, a woman couldn't walk within twenty feet of him without a leering look, or worse, the incessant flirting with everything female.

Doesn't he care about my feelings? she thinks, followed by a heavy sigh.

"What's the matter now?" he asks, recognizing the familiar sound.

"Oh, nothing," she mutters.

Irritated that it may be the same old subject, he huffs, "Spill it."

"Alright. . .. I was just thinking how ironic it is that you come from one of the wealthiest families on the east coast, but you rob from your peers to make ends meet."

Touching on a sore subject, he growls, "Are you really bringing that up again? You know how I feel about that!" *She's pushing me to go straight! She did date Jeff, after all, the straightest arrow ever. Deep down, could she really be that different? Jeff mentioned they had a lot in common, and he was considering proposing. He probably would have too, if I hadn't stolen her away. I suppose I shouldn't have, but how often do you run into someone that knows the value of so many paintings, and has a great pair of tits, to boot?*

Fortunately, for Weston, Jeff had filled him in on her encyclopedic knowledge of artwork before going to the party, giving him just enough time to brush up on historical high points, and obscure painters. Days thereafter were spent at museums, which made her fall even harder. A quick read-through on paintings displayed at museums they would be visiting proved beneficial, for after spouting a few boring facts, she was head over heels in love. Luckily, she was in such desperate need of money to support her ailing father, it didn't take long to turn her into a thief. But now, the money wasn't enough. She wanted him too, and he didn't belong to any woman. Especially not this one.

FIVE

PRESENT DAY

The jeans are too tight and the floral-print blouse more revealing than what she would typically wear, but Sierra is resolutely determined to carry herself with the utmost strength and dignity. Coming down the grand staircase, into the foyer, she takes stock of the paintings covering nearly every available inch of wall space. It never ends. His collection is better than most museums.

The sound of Altus's voice draws her into the dining hall with its plush Persian rug, and expansive dining table. Keeping par for the course, historical artwork lines the walls, and windows at the far end of the room offer expansive views onto the estate.

Try being nice, maybe that will sway him, she thinks, laying the seed for a yet to be devised plan. Finding him residing at the head of the table, she resolutely sits in the corner chair beside him, offering a well-rehearsed plea. "Please, I'm begging you! Just let us go, and we'll never tell anyone what's happened here!"

Soaking up her flowing hair and sparkling eyes, he takes in every drop of her alluring beauty, only turning away as Abah walks to his side. "How did everything go?" he asks.

Observing Abah's movements, Sierra sizes her up. *She*

doesn't seem to have the arrogance that exudes from Eve and Altus. Is she the one I should be prying information from?

"The loose ends have been tied up," she answers, her soft, whiskey voice, giving off a sensual vibe.

What did she mean by tying up loose ends? Was she referring to Weston and me! "What have you done!"

"It's not what you think," Abah replies, almost apologetically.

"Then what is it?" Breathing rapidly, she sits ramrod straight, gripping the arms of the chair.

"Relax, Sierra," Altus advises, transferring emotions to calm her down.

"Abah, please pour her a drink."

Picking up a bottle of wine from the table, she fills a glass, and hands it to Sierra, bloodlust filling every thought. *So tasty, my young love. Another bite, and your soul will be free as a dove.*

Sierra raises the glass, and pauses, examining the dark red liquid. *Would they poison me . . .? I suppose if they wanted me dead, I'd already be six-feet-under. Bottoms up!*

"I want you to feel comfortable while you are here," he reassures. "I have no intention of harming you, or Weston, and I relish the idea of getting to know you better. You may find we have more in common than a love of art."

Sighing loudly, she lays back in the black, silk-lined chair. "There's just so much going through my head, and at the same time, my heart is sinking without Weston."

"You will see him soon enough. He requires a great deal of rest."

"That's only one of my problems. Why are you keeping us here? We have nothing you could possibly want. Or use!" *You narcissistic fuck.*

"Do not worry about leaving here. I would never hold anyone against their will."

"But you are! I don't want to be here!" Turning from his stare, she instinctively looks to the freedom of the sunlit outdoors.

"You forget, it was not me that brought you here. You broke into my home. Would you rather I call the police?"

Definitely not prison! Maybe I should try and make the best of this until Weston's back on his feet. "Phew," she exhales. "I've just seen so much, and I'm still not sure I believe. Logic and reason fight everything I see, and I'm left trying to make sense of the impossible."

"I know you have many questions, and I intend to answer all of them to your satisfaction. All I ask, is that you be open-minded and honest with me, and I will offer the same in return. But should you lie, disrespect me, or try to escape, I will be forced to either inform the police or take more drastic measures. Your destiny is in your hands."

Looking back and forth between him and Abah, she purses her lips. *I suppose things could be much worse. Anyone else would have turned us in or shot us on sight. Maybe I should keep digging. See if I can find something that might help us get out of here.* "How many are there like you, and how did it happen? Can you really live forever? How old are you?"

Seeing that his emotions are overriding her fear, his eyes gleam. "I would venture to guess that approximately one-thousand of my kind exist. Though it is possible that there are more, I sincerely doubt it. As for how it happened, it was much like what you may have seen in vampire movies, simply the exchanging of infected blood. And living forever, while it is conceivable, very few make it past the age of one-hundred eternal years. As for my age, I was born in the year 68 BC."

Hoping to have found a crack in his facade, she shakes her head and throws up her hands. "How can this be real?"

"I would like to tell you a story. It is of a man that exists today but was a completely different being long ago. So much so, it is impossible to say that they are one and the same. The years that have filled the space of time have removed the essence and fire of that which made him unique, yet the warmth of that once intense fire still fuels his desire for life. In this story, I believe you will find the answers you seek."

"It sounds like it may give me more questions than answers, but go ahead, my brain's already mush."

Sitting directly across from her, Abah represses a smile. *She's funny. And cute.* Moistening her lips, she advises, "For right now, listening is best. In time, things will make sense. You'll find that once you open up and accept the impossible, there's so much more to life than you've ever imagined."

"It is true," he confirms, "the doors we open in our lives make all the difference. Opening yourself to alternative thoughts and desires may help you rise above the simplicity of good and evil, revealing the true meaning of life."

"And you've found the true meaning of life?" she ridicules.

"When I was young, survival was the meaning of life. I was born into a Cheruscan tribe that resided along the eastern shores of the Rhine river. Our lives were simple, for we were only slightly more civilized than nomadic hunters, searching for food, and fighting enemies to protect our lands. But that was no small task, war was always at hand, and weather could decimate our small crops and herds in an instant. If conquered by enemies, we expected to be killed, our women raped, and survivors made slaves. Everything we did carried heavy repercussions if not performed correctly. I learned to ride a horse at a young age, and soon after, trap animals and hunt game. My father being warlord and tribal leader, groomed me to fill his place, and when I was but seven took me into battle. I still recall the rumbling of the ground as the Gauls approached on horseback. I could not see them due to the hill before me but could feel them with every fiber of my being. Fear growing, every hair stood on end as they flooded over the hilltop. Hundreds of them, wielding axes, swords, and arrows. I was terrified, but my father remained calm, commanding, 'Attack!'

"I had never seen anything like it! As I watched from our base camp atop a nearby hill, I saw barbarity of which I could never have imagined. Limbs and heads were lopped off, and men run through with swords, yet there, in the center of the carnage, I saw my father, a pillar of strength and leadership. With his painted face and great height, he looked to be the devil himself, taking life with the swing of his sword. I could not have been any prouder. The destroyer, conqueror, and most powerful man in the world, was my father. From that moment on, I was his devoted follower.

"As time passed and I grew into manhood, I believed myself to be a seasoned soldier and competent leader. On the day of my fifteenth birthday, we learned of an attack being mounted against our village and rode off to meet the Gauls in battle. Riding no more than ten miles, they ambushed us at a break in the forest. I do not recall how many directions the arrows came from, only that they filled the sky, falling on us like rain. My father roared, 'RAISE SHIELDS!' but for him, it was too late. No sooner had the command been issued, than an arrow caught him below the jaw. I watched in horror as blood spurted from holes in the front and back of his neck. He gripped his throat, attempting to speak, but made only gurgling noises as blood spewed from his mouth. Tumbling from his horse, I attempted to catch him, but his weight was too great and I was pinned to the ground. Screaming for help was fruitless since everyone had ridden off to engage the enemy, so, with strained effort, I rolled him off my chest and knelt at his side. I screamed, 'You will live!' but he knew it was over, just as well as I did. I begged the great god Wotan to spare his life, but, as with all gods, it fell upon deaf ears. He pulled me close, and with dying breath, choked, 'Carry on!'

"To this day, I cannot recall mounting my horse nor riding into battle, only that I entered the fray filled with single-minded purpose. Stabbing, slicing, and beheading every Gaul in sight. I was invincible! The pure fire of hate gave me strength and clarity above all others. We were outnumbered four to one, but quickly had them on the run. I ordered, 'No prisoners!' and we viciously slaughtered everyone in our grasp. After the battle was over, my fellow soldiers, or witan, as they were called, appointed me the new warlord and tribal leader.

To commemorate my leadership and memorialize my father, I ordered every Gaul beheaded."

Looking away from the glass of wine he swirls in hand, he finds Sierra slack-jawed in horror.

"You must understand, those were vastly different times. It was a time when martial fame counted for much, and human life comparatively little. That is why Caesar was regarded as a god when he killed over a million people in his Gallic campaign, compared with the butcher, some call him today."

Nodding weakly, she feigns understanding, but wide eyes and frowning brow reveal disgust.

Knowing that no person of the modern age could fully comprehend the ways of ancient man, he continues, "Once appointed leader, I thought it time to take a wife. We had been arranged to be married since I was a child, and I felt her to be the most beautiful of the girls in our village. Soon, she became pregnant, and I looked forward to the possibility of having a son to follow in my footsteps. Life was good. Too good. Bordering on arrogance, my edge for battle had dulled."

Pausing, he stares at the table. When he resumes, sorrow fills his voice. "A new year brought drought and consequentially poor hunting. With my people hungry and horses malnourished, it was imperative that we find new lands. Believing the Gauls would never cross into our territory after suffering such a humiliating defeat, I took my witan into Belgae lands to search for better domains, leaving only a small contingency of soldiers to guard the village. After two hard-won skirmishes against Belgae tribes, we found our new home. Overcome with joy, I and twenty of my witan headed back to the village, leaving the main body of the fighting force to protect the new lands. We rode at the speed of lightning, resting only when our horse's demanded food or water, but it was not fast enough, for the village had fallen under siege. By the time we arrived, most of the villagers were dead, and those alive were either seeking refuge in the neighboring forest or being tortured. The Gauls sought retribution, and they were getting it. They killed my wife and unborn child, then took me prisoner."

The wine and Altus's transference has given Sierra a mellowing buzz, and her growing curiosity eclipses any thought of Weston. "What did they do to you?"

"During the trek back to the Gaul's village, Julius Caesar and his army happened upon us, and killed them in a surprise attack. When he found I was their prisoner, he granted me clemency, and I joined his legions.

"Was it clemency since you were fighting the Gauls too?"

"Most definitely. Rome was at war with many Germanic tribes, as well as the Gauls. Clementia was a common cry from Caesar's defeated enemies, but it was not always granted. It depended on his mood and current need for soldiers."

"I assume he was in no great need since he killed the Gauls," she reasons, all the while watching Abah grasp the wine bottle in her aristocratic hand, and gracefully fill Altus's glass.

Stretching to fill Sierra's glass, Abah bites her lip with protruded fang. Heart pumping feverishly, she gazes upon the raw, swollen wound. *Come to my embrace, avail one last taste.*

No longer frightened by her presence, Sierra takes a long look at Abah. *Her caramel skin, golden hair, and black eyes are so exotic. It's like the best of two races came together and created a goddess.*

"He was most definitely in need of soldiers," Altus protests. "All of the Gallic tribes were uniting under their common leader, Vercingetorix, who was hoping to push the Romans out of Gaul, and though Caesar was terribly outnumbered, he felt no Gaul could be trusted."

"And that's why he saved you. Even one sword can make a difference." With a sideways glance, she catches Abah's lustful gaze. *He analyzes my every move, and she looks at me like she wants to date me or dine on me.*

"Yes, but I was not one sword, I was four-hundred strong. You forget that the remainder of my soldiers were only a week's ride away. After camp was set that night, I informed my new

Roman comrades of my witan lying-in-wait, and a centurion took me to Caesar's tent. As I waited at the entrance, I watched him dictating to his scribes. It was amazing! The clarity and directness he had for even the simplest of matters was awe-inspiring. Dictating letters to seven different people, he would address the scribes in order, telling each a paragraph, then move onto the next, never once pausing to reflect as to where he had left off minutes earlier. His train of thought was as concise as his iron will. Jumping from letter to letter, he wrote Cato, Pompey, Calpurnia, and the Senate, among others, yet, not once confusing what he had said to whom, nor what he meant to achieve with each letter."

"He never paused to ask where he left off?"

"Never, he picked up with each scribe exactly where he had left off."

"How did you keep up?"

"I could only focus on a few at a time," he admits, still awed by the feat. "Only when the letters were read back, did I come to appreciate his incredible intellect."

Leaning back in the chair, Sierra relaxes, analyzing his every feature. *He looks like a Greek God, fallen from Olympus. Unfortunately, all the ego too.* "What was Caesar like?"

"Supremely confident. Though not as tall as me, he was tall for the times. With dark hair, intense eyes, and a gritty determination, one could not be in his presence without being impressed. As I walked before him, I could not help but feel I were the one looking up. He did not dally in our conversation, only wanting to know how many men I had and how long it would take to acquire them. I tried to thank him for saving my life, and tell him of the greatness of my horsemen, but by putting a hand on my shoulder, he quieted my youthful ramblings, and said, 'By actions, you will prove your words,' at which point he motioned to the centurion, and I was escorted out. I felt alive again, for, with the next battle, the might of Rome would help me slaughter the hated Gauls. When the sun was but a glimmer on the horizon, I went in search of the centurion, not wasting a minute of the day."

"Did he send troops with you for protection, or in the event you might use your army to escape?"

"Surely both. Though it would be pleasant to think it was only for protection, he did not know me well enough to put his trust in me. But soon, he would see how faithful I was to his cause. Upon telling my witan of the atrocities done to our families and village, we would become the deciding factor in Caesar's Gallic campaign. Returning to the Roman camp, we were trained in Roman tactical warfare, then assimilated into his army as a separate cavalry division."

"You didn't fight alongside the Romans?"

"No, but it was because of that, we made ourselves indispensable. It was our autonomy, if you will, that we brought victory to Caesar in Gaul."

The sight of Eve coming into the room with dinner distracts him. "Have you prepared something for Weston?"

"Yes, I'll take it to him after I finish serving your dinner."

"When will I be able to see him?" Sierra asks, with anticipation.

"In the morning," he assures. "He is extremely fatigued and needs all the sleep he can get. I am afraid you visiting would only exacerbate his condition, and the emotional stress prolong his recovery."

Nodding, with dejected affirmation, her inner voice warns, *If he doesn't let you see him tomorrow, they're up to something. You can't take no for an answer!*

"Thank you for all your hard work," he tells Eve, "I know it has been a rough day."

"It's not so bad when you know it's temporary." Angered by the sight of Sierra wearing her clothes, Eve sneers at her, menacingly bearing her fangs after Altus looks away.

Whoa, what the hell! Momentarily shaken, Sierra quickly regains her composure, quipping, "You mean, Eve's not the maid?"

"No!" Abah laughs. *I like her more all the time.*

Sierra flashes Abah a smile, appreciating that she got the joke. *She seems nice enough, it's hard to believe she's the same person that attacked me.*

Sensing the tension, Altus hopes Eve didn't pick up on the slight, remarking, "It takes a good deal of servants to keep the house and grounds in proper order. To put Abah and Eve through the mundane drudgeries of life would be cruel. We live far too long to struggle with simple burdens."

As Eve serves the dinner of Cordon Bleu, she sets plates softly in front Altus and Abah, then haphazardly drops Sierra's before her.

"Eve!" Altus reprimands.

"Oh, I'm sorry, it must have slipped," she flippantly apologizes. *Why is this girl having dinner with him? She should have been dead last night!*

"It's completely understandable," Sierra chimes, "I sometimes lose my grip on things too. Hopefully, I won't spill any wine on this beautiful outfit."

In a flash barely perceptible to the human eye, Eve grabs Sierra by the throat. Fangs bared and eyes narrowed to slits, she slams her into the back of the chair, sending it sliding backwards.

Jumping to his feet, Altus picks up Eve and throws her across the room. Like a cat, she lands on all fours, crouched to strike, fangs bared for a fight.

"Enough," he fumes, fangs bared and chest out, preparing to repel the attack.

Standing upright, Eve points to Sierra. "She does not belong here!"

"It is not your decision! Know your place!" Taking a deep breath, his fangs recede. "Take dinner to Weston, I will see no more of you this night."

Watching Eve slink away, Sierra attempts to catch her breath. *Holy fuck! She was gonna kill me!*

"I am truly sorry, it will not happen again," he apologizes, smoothing back his disheveled hair. *Sierra stands her ground.*

Very impressive!

Wide-eyed and trembling, Sierra nervously rubs her lower lip. *She's out of her mind! Is Weston safe with her?*

SIX

Filling Sierra's glass, Altus transfers a healthy dose of calming emotions. "As I was saying, it was my cavalry that would become the decisive factor in the war against Gaul. At the time, Caesar was losing control of the whole country. His allies were deserting him, and he had recently lost the town of Noviodunum, where he kept his grain, baggage, fresh horses, and the state chest. If this were not bad enough, he also kept his Gallic hostages there, and once freed, they pressured Caesar's remaining allies to join their cause.

"While marching eastwards to secure alliances, we encountered Vercingetorix's army. He divided his cavalry into three divisions, one on each flank, and the third blocking the road ahead of our vanguard. Caesar broke up his cavalry likewise and engaged the enemy. It was immediately apparent that the Roman cavalry was outmanned, so much so, a contingent of Gauls on a nearby hill broke off and attacked the transport column. Seeing that his soldiers were dropping under the heavy advance, Caesar ordered the entire column to form a hollow square, encircling the transport for protection. By sheer manpower, the Gauls hacked deep into the lines, causing heavy casualties. Even with Caesar's reserves covering the embattled flank, it was clear to me that they could not hold out. On gut reaction, I ordered my witan into battle before being commanded by Caesar. We rode to the heart of the enemy's army, stationed atop a nearby hill, and I exploded, 'Revenge is at hand, coat your swords in blood!' We were overflowing with hate, and revenge was ours for the taking. No one would stop us from carving the hearts from every man on that hill. As we hacked our way through the forest of men, I saw only my wife before me, pleading for her life as the Gallic pigs assaulted her. Looking like demons from hell with our painted faces and voices crying of vengeance from Thor, we shook their confidence, sending them into a hasty retreat. With the even breath of my horse and his steady trod in tune with my command, I rode through their ranks, taking life as if I were God, on judgment day. As we chased them down, slaughtering at will, I looked back at the column to find the Gallic squadrons had witnessed my victory and begun retreating. As they fled, it became a complete rout, and slaughter was prevalent. Upon reaching the Suzon river, I commanded my men to break off and return to camp. If Wotan was ever in his heaven, he was surely on our side that day.

"Upon returning to camp, two Centurions escorted me to Caesar's quarters. I was exhilarated by my witan's execution in battle, but became worrisome as I approached his tent, thinking I may have broken up his battle plan by attacking so impetuously. As I neared the opening, I stiffened for the possible reprimanding of acting with such insolence.

"Barely having had time to push back the flap of the tent, Caesar joyfully threw his arms around me, gushing, 'You have most heartily proven your allegiance, my young comrade. Your actions have spoken very clearly this day!' My mind was no longer racing from battle, for I was beaming with confidence. We talked for hours about his campaign, and he inquired into my ancestry and fighting history. When I told him my father's name, he instantly knew who I was. It turned out my father had outwitted him in battle before I was born, and a truce had been reached between our village and Rome. Seeing the greatness of my father in me, I became drunken with admiration. To have such an esteemed commander of men look upon me with gratitude, only made me want to please him further."

Altus softens his tone and, with a sense of admiration, tells Sierra, "That is the kind of leader he was, you wanted to fight for him! Men gladly laid down their lives for his. After conversing the better part of the night, I thanked him for saving my life, and brashly told him I would one day return the favor. He looked at me with a broad smile, exhorting, 'I do not doubt you, my young friend.' Leaving the tent, I heard him say to Mark Antony, 'Fortuna has delivered the hand of Mars, in an angelic Germani princeps.' I stood tall with pride as I headed back to my camp, but upon seeing my men, the memories of my wife and village drug me back to the depths of depression.

"The next day, I was informed that Vercingetorix believed the Romans to be leaving Gaul and wanted to inflict a heavy blow before their departure. With his error in judgement, we marched to the walled town of Alesia, hoping to crush him and his troops. The town was on the summit of a hill, so it was impossible to take by storm, and the walls made it nearly impregnable. He had at least eighty-thousand men in town, so our only option was to starve them out by building a siege wall and digging trenches. It sounds ordinary enough until realizing we had to build two walls and would reside in between them. One for besieging the town, the other in the event Vercingetorix received reinforcements. The two walls totaled over twenty-five miles in length with twenty-three forts as strongpoints, and we dug three trenches that encircled the town, varying in width from fifteen to twenty feet. Adding to the enormous workload, we filled one of the trenches with water by creating a diversion in the nearby Ozerain river."

Pausing, he continues with a note of sorrow. "It may seem strange, but I do not recall the incredible amount of labor it required to dig the trenches nor build the walls. Too deeply haunted by my wife's agony and the damage done to my people, I did not care about a thing."

"My God, that seems like a monumental amount of work to

do without machines," Sierra interjects.

"It was the only possible course of action. We had to starve the townspeople into submission while protecting ourselves from possible reinforcements. The biggest problem we faced was not the labor, but the repeated sorties by the Gauls as we obtained grain and timber. It was because of these attacks that Caesar asked my witan to patrol the area between our wall and the town, offering protection to the soldiers as they worked. They were digging pits with sharpened stakes sunk in the bottom, covering them with twigs and brushwood, and calling them *Lilies* due to their resemblance to the flower. In front of those, foot-long logs with iron hooks were sunk into the ground and named *Spurs*. Caesar stressed that we were working for our lives, which was most definitely shown to be true when Vercingetorix's reinforcements arrived. I had never seen so many men on one field of battle in my entire life. There were at least two-hundred-and-fifty-thousand on foot with more than eight-thousand horses at their disposal, not to mention the men in town."

"Weren't you terrified knowing you had to fight so many men?"

"At the time, I welcomed death. My wife filled my every thought, and the likelihood of joining her calmed my tortured soul. My enemy's lives meant nothing, and mine was not worth a great deal more. It was only time spent with Caesar that cleared my head and lifted my suffering. We talked at length of ambition and what any single man might achieve in the short span of a lifetime. He gave me papyrus scrolls that detailed Alexander the Great's battles and asked my opinion as to what I might have done differently if given the same parameters. We analyzed the upcoming battle endlessly, looking for unseen possibilities and other variances that might occur in the haze of battle. At the time, I thought I was helping him create a battle plan, but with reflection, realized he was only analyzing my mental capabilities. Seeing if I understood the minute details that win wars."

"And did you?"

"Not at his level, but enough to impress him with my knowledge. For when he informed me of his plan for the upcoming fight, he asked me to be the hammer that would smash the Gauls. He felt my men could cut through enemy lines and create enough confusion that his cavalry might deliver the decisive blow."

"What do you think he saw in you?"

"Hate. I had the dark fire in me, and it was unquenchable."

"There had to be more than that," she justifies. "After getting to know you, he must have seen something great and good in your character."

"Great, possibly. Definitely not good. None of us had any good in our souls during that era of butchery. My greatness lay within the ability to think clearly under the most barbarous conditions ever asked of man. War in ancient times was hell on earth! There was no luxury of shooting guns from a distance. We stabbed, hacked, and disemboweled our enemies at arm's length. Tell me, what good is there in the bloodlust that permeated my soul?"

He abruptly stops, seeing the familiar look of disgust on her face. "I am sorry, I should not go into such detail, for it is irrelevant. It was my affiliation with Caesar that changed my life, not the barbarous acts which I performed. Let me continue with the forthcoming battle, for it was at Alesia, where my fate would be sealed. As the campaign took shape, the Gauls within town ventured out and began to fill the first trench with hurdles and dirt. Seeing this, Caesar sent out his cavalry, but the Gallic archers exacted a heavy toll on the horsemen. When their cavalry came out, it looked as though they would rout the Romans due to sheer numerical superiority, but the Romans fought bravely, and we watched intently from our fortifications as the battle raged on. I waited with anticipation for Caesar to wave the red flag, signaling my attack, but nothing came. As the day wore on and the body count grew, I was certain he had either forgotten us or changed his plan of battle. But just when it looked as though I would spend my night replaying guilty memories, I saw the blood-red flag waving wildly beside the setting sun. Calling upon my witan, we attacked in mass formation, my two most competent horsemen at my side, Segimer, and his brother Segestes. With the wind at our backs, we sliced into the heart of the Gallic line, sending fear and panic with our painted faces and bellowing screams. With every swing of our swords, a Gaul lost his life, and their cavalry quickly broke ranks and fled. Seeing their retreat, Caesar sent the remainder of his cavalry out to assist in chasing down the fleeing squadrons before they could rally. Running for the safety of town, they closed the gates behind them, confused and frustrated as to how they could have lost the battle with such a large force.

"Passing back through the gate of the siege wall, the welcoming cheers of the Romans put me in high spirits, and I went in search of Caesar to congratulate him on his victory. Finding him outside his tent, speaking with Antony, he turned to me and smiled, 'Did you think I had forgotten you?'

"'Indeed, for a time I did,' I confessed. 'Were you wearing them down to shock them with a mass attack?'

"'You learn quickly, my young friend!' he affirmed, waving me into his tent, with Antony in tow. We spoke endlessly of the battle, drinking well into the night. When I left, the moon was full, and I rode slowly to my camp, hoping to find reason to deviate from my destination."

"Was it really that hard to be near your people?" Sierra probes, finishing her glass of wine, only to be filled again by Abah.

"Yes and no. They were my people, and I loved them. They had sacrificed just as much as I had, or more, some losing sons and brothers in the recent battles with the Romans. Yet . . ., seeing them was a constant reminder of what was once good and had since been ground into dust. We congratulated each other on our triumphs and spoke of great bravery and heroism, but when all was said and done, there were too many painful memories to pretend our bond was not broken.

"And after the most recent battle, it was evident to all. Some spoke of starting their lives over near our old village, while others became distant and isolated, walling themselves off emotionally, only to explode with rage during battle. A sword being their only means of communication. And I? I was no better. I spent every possible moment with Caesar, meeting only briefly with my men to inform them of new plans, or when the time came to join in battle. We were coming to the end of our road, and I began hearing whispers that it was my fault we were in our current situation. Had I not tried to move our village or left more soldiers behind to stand guard, we would have remained contentedly secure."

"It wasn't fair to second guess you. How could anyone have known your village would be invaded?"

"That is true, I suppose. But as leader, I took full responsibility. Good or bad. And it turned out for the worst."

"I understand what you're saying, but how could none of them see your position?" she implores, pushing her empty plate away to bring her delightfully inebriating wine front and center.

Seeing that she has finished eating and Altus is merely picking at scraps, Abah rises from her chair. "I'm going to clean up and let the two of you continue talking."

"Thank you," he replies. "Would you mind bringing a bottle of bourbon for Sierra and me?"

Admiring his striking profile, Sierra draws his attention away from Abah. "You were saying, your men wanted to leave?"

"Yes. But at that moment, we were completely surrounded. The only way for anyone to leave was either through death or victory. As the days passed, I found I preferred victory when accompanying Caesar, and death when residing in my encampment. That is why I chose to spend my time with Caesar. We went over battle plans regularly, and I also rode with him when he encouraged the soldiers to keep up the fight.

It was uplifting to be with someone so confident and inspiring!

"When the fighting resumed, the Gauls tried a different type of attack. Instead of using cavalry, they shot arrows, and stones flung from slings to assail us in the night. It was so dark, it was impossible to see anything coming at us. If it were not for the lilies and spurs impeding their advance, our archers surely would never have been able to halt their advance. It was only upon the sun's rising; did we see the heavy casualties taken by both sides.

"As the days passed and we waited for the next assault, I came to be friendly with the brutish and seasoned Mark Antony. He was a complimentary second in command and an outstanding leader of men. Though Roman in the same sense of the word as Caesar, his devotion to pleasure went hand in hand with a severe lack of attentiveness for greatness. Unfortunately, it would be those very flaws that would bring about his ultimate demise. But, regardless of what was to come, I found him an enjoyable person to be around and highly regarded by his men. One afternoon, while buoying troop spirits, he told me of Caesar's great admiration for me, and that Fortuna, the Roman God of destiny and good fortune, was undoubtedly smiling upon me. Thrilled to hear such things, I pressed for more details, but he would reveal none. Then he told me something that has stuck with me to this day, 'Fortune favors the bold, do not be meek while your heart still beats. The path you walk, may lead to a land of dreams.'

"I do not think he could have ever imagined how prophetic he was that day. Things were about to change for me in ways I could have never fathomed, though at the time, not quickly enough. One morning while speaking with my witan, Caesar rode into camp and praised them for their gallantry. He said it would not have been possible to be where he was without them and that when the war was won, it was they who would be responsible for its victory. My men cheered, thanked him for the opportunity to have revenge upon the Gauls, and promised to kill twice as many in the ensuing battle.

"Caesar exhorted, 'I trust you will, Altus is fortunate to have such worthy men under his command!' He bid them good fortunes, then asked me to meet him in his tent. My troops were happier than I had seen in weeks, and I prayed this would pull them out of their malaise.

"As I rode to meet Caesar, I felt better than in recent memory and wanted to thank him for the encouraging words. When I arrived, he welcomed me with a hug, and Antony joyously slapped my back, but when we sat down to talk, Caesar's tone became serious. 'I came to visit your men this morning because I hear of troubling news. Antony's soldiers have picked up word that your men are angry with you. They blame the destruction of your village on your youth and inexperience. I fear your life may be threatened.'

"I tried to convince him that things were better and that I had control of the situation, but he would not listen. He knew then what I know now. The hate my men had for the Gauls was fierce, but it did not match their hate for me. I was the cause of their misery, and only my death would cure it . . . or so they believed. Emotional scarring that deep never heals, it only gets buried, and dug up on occasion to remind us of the hell life has to offer.

"It was Caesar who saw this more clearly than me. He knew that if he didn't separate me from my men, they would kill me in the chaos of battle. At that moment, he made me his singulare, a personal bodyguard, and I would study under Antony, the code of the Roman citizen and soldier. I asked him if I could lead my men once more, but he maintained that it was too dangerous. They would be partially assimilated into the Roman cavalry, whereupon with the defeat of the Gauls, they would be free. I was somewhat relieved not having to confront their whispers of treachery, but I was also deeply hurt that it had come to such an unseemly end. The people I had lived my life amongst were no longer friends, merely bitter acquaintances."

"How did your men react when you told them they would

be assimilated into the Roman cavalry?"

"They were jubilant at the prospect of being free, yet some begged me to fight one more battle together, finalizing our revenge upon the Gauls. Especially my closest ally Segimer. It was a strange feeling though, for, I was not sure who longed for comradery, and who desired my death."

Raising his palms, he shrugs, "I will never know, for I was no longer a part of their lives. Looking back, it was an abrupt end to my previous existence, and I was happily sucked into the Roman way of life. I gave up the Germanic ritual of face painting and cut my hair short, resembling my new countrymen. When the final battle for Alesia began, I looked more Roman in my centurion's uniform than I did German. Vercingetorix was finally able to concentrate his forces from within the town and our outer wall to attack simultaneously, and I had the supreme honor of riding next to Caesar. We joined the battalions at the heart of the campaign and pushed the Gauls back until our cavalry approached their rear, at which point, they broke formation and fled. We chased them back into town, where Vercingetorix realized the hopelessness of the situation and offered his surrender. It took the death of one million Gauls, and another million enslaved to turn Gaul into a Roman province, but it had finally been achieved. And as for myself? I watched from a distant hill as my men mounted their horses and rode off to begin new lives. Just as surely as I had begun mine."

"It must have been a relief that the war was over."

"Even after the conquest of Vercingetorix there were still minor battles to be fought before Caesar's consulship came to an end."

"Was it soon after, that he crossed the Rubicon?"

"Yes, partly because he was forced to do so, but mainly because it was his first step towards world domination. It was the actions of his opponents, Cato, Pompey, and a faction of the Senate, which he referred to as the inimici, that forced his hand to battle his brethren. If they had allowed him back into

Roman politics, there would have been no cause for war, but Cato repeatedly swore he would prosecute Caesar for pursuing the war in Gaul, once stripped of his consulship. He argued that only Caesar or the Republic could exist, not both."

"Why would he strip him of his consulship?"

"The only way they could prosecute him was if he were a citizen of no political standing. Caesar knew that without official title, they would imprison him, and without troops, Pompey would become the supreme commander of Rome."

"The Roman soldiers didn't mind marching on their own people?"

"His army and the people of Rome loved Caesar, and he knew it just as well as the inimici. Besides, Caesar had been leading his troops in this direction all along. He did not want peace, nor did he want to advance his career through elections and political turmoil. He wanted to rule the world, and there is only one way to do that, militarily. To an extent, we were all pawns in his self-absorbed game, even the inimici. They thought they were upholding the honor of the Republic, but knowing what their actions would be, Caesar used it to his advantage. He always saw much further afield than the rest of us. While we dwelled upon the prospect of civil war, he was devising a method by which he might become dictator of Rome, yet still have the populace believe he was the savior of the Republic. He was a genius in that regard, and the time had come to realize his ambitions."

"How do you have so much reverence for a man that you said yourself, was self-absorbed?"

"All men of great accomplishment are self-absorbed. They force their will upon the masses. To conquer men, you cannot have their best interests at heart, only your deepest aspirations. Thus, on the morning of January 10, 49 BC when a courier brought news of the Senate's reluctance to meet his demands, Caesar proclaimed, 'They have given me what I always desired,' and sent the thirteenth legion to Ariminum while summoning his other legions out of winter quarters.

That night, he instructed Antony, me, and a few other centurions to meet him on the edge of the Rubicon River.

"When we arrived, he was staring silently at the rain-swollen river, deep in contemplation. With a look of fierce determination, he exalted, 'It has been a journey of monumental proportion up to this point, and I fear it is only a trifle of what is to come. The inimici have rendered their decision and put all of Rome's destiny in my hands. My only misgiving is that to refrain from crossing will bring me misfortune, whereas crossing will bring misfortune to all men. It is, therefore, of the greatest necessity that we go forth from this point as the true saviors of this greatest of civilizations. For without our honorable determination, the subjugation of the inimici shall forever ruin Rome.' Then, he raised his sword to the skies, thundering, 'The time is now, the die must be cast!' And with that, we rode through the frigid waters of the Rubicon onto the lush soils of Italy, outlaws of the Roman Republic."

"He started a war under the premise of being arraigned before a Roman court, didn't he?"

"Yes, Fortuna was by his side in directing the inimici, inadvertently laying the path for his success. If ever there was a man befriended by luck, it was surely him. As we advanced through Italy, we increased in numbers, so much so, Pompey and the rest of Caesar's opposition had no choice but to leave Italy. We spent the next year and a half in pursuit of Pompey and his legions, until finally engaging them in battle in Pharsalus. When Pompey's legions took to the field, it was evident we were outnumbered two to one."

"How many men did Caesar have?"

"Twenty-two-thousand, compared with Pompey's forty-five-thousand. It was not as bad as the numbers we faced in Alesia, but then, the Gauls were not as impeccably trained as Roman soldiers. Though I did believe to know the Roman soldiers one weakness. I told Caesar I found Roman cavalry to be more dandies than warriors, and suggested we spear their horsemen in the face instead of throwing our spears from a distance. He thought me mad but said I may lead the charge if I felt so confident in my beliefs. I knew I was correct, and I quickly proved it. I led the charge into Pompey's cavalry, and when we struck at the horsemen's faces, they turned and fled. Attacking the archers and slingers, we slowly circumnavigated the enemy's battle line and attacked from the rear. By midday, the battle was won. Pompey's troops had surrendered, and he took flight. Surveying the dead scattered across the battlefield, he confided, 'They would have it so, I, Gaius Caesar, after so much success, would be condemned had I dismissed my army.'"

"Was the war finally over?"

"No. Pompey had escaped, and he still ruled the seas, so we had to go in search of him. Immediately after the battle, Caesar sent a letter to the Senate informing them of the outcome and ordered them to make him dictator for one year, to which they had no choice but to grant."

"Meaning, he was the ruler of Rome, for all intents and purposes. Very shrewd," she nods, unaware that alcohol and transference numb her senses.

"Most certainly, it was only Pompey who stood in his way, and we pursued him across the Mediterranean. We heard rumors that he was in Cyprus, and surmised he was on his way to Egypt to fortify his relations with the Royal Egyptian house of Cleopatra and Ptolemy XIII. We sailed with two legions to Alexandria, and upon landing, an Egyptian greeting party welcomed us with the head of Pompey. Sickened at the sight of his dead friend, Caesar turned away. When they presented Pompey's signet ring, he began to weep, overcome with sorrow. To make matters worse, the Alexandrian's felt it was an insult to the dignity of their king that Caesar be afforded such authority upon entrance to Egypt, and a mob formed around us as we marched to the Royal Palace. Upon reaching the palace, the inhabitants greeted us with such hostility, we thought about leaving, but the prevailing northwest winds made it impossible to sail. Over the next few days, there were riots in the streets, and Caesar openly expressed his contempt for Ptolemy XIII tricking Pompey."

"How did he trick him?"

"Pompey sent a message to Ptolemy XIII, reading, 'I implore you to help me in this hour of my distress. I ask it in memory of your father, who was once my host as well as my close friend.' Ptolemy replied, 'Yes,' it would be possible for him to reside in Alexandria, but he wanted to meet with Pompey first. When Ptolemy's attendants arrived in a small boat to ferry Pompey to Alexandria for the meeting, they killed him on the trip to shore."

"There was so much treachery! Could anyone be trusted?"

"Surely not Caesar, especially when he was angry. For it was the very rioting of the Egyptians that he would use to conquer Egypt. He told the courtiers of Ptolemy XIII that he was sending for two legions of reinforcements to halt the rioting, when in fact, he would be using them to conquer Alexandria, followed by the rest of the country. While waiting for the reinforcements, he thought he would find out the state of his enemies under the pretense of concluding a quarrel between Ptolemy XIII and his sister Cleopatra."

"Why would they listen to him, he was Roman?"

"During Caesar's previous term as consul, a treaty had been signed with the late King Ptolemy XII. His elder son and daughter were to be joint heirs to the throne, and a clause invoked the Roman government to carry out his wishes. Once more, Caesar had luck on his side, giving him the jurisdiction to plant the seeds of his eventual conquering. He requested that both parties dismiss their armies and meet before him to present their cases, but this proved difficult for Cleopatra, since Ptolemy XIII's troops occupied much of Alexandria."

SEVEN

"On a hot, sun-scorched afternoon, while discussing the repayment of Egyptian debts to Rome, a Greek man entered, holding a long, rolled-up rug.

Caesar demanded, 'Who are you, and what is this you bring before me!'

"The man introduced himself as Apollodoros of Sicily, bowed before the rug, and began unraveling it. Upon reaching its end, we could see that someone was wrapped within. I raised my sword to strike, but as the rug unfurled, it fell to my side, and I stood hopelessly enamored of the radiant goddess before me.

"With a bow, and sweeping gesture of his hand, Apollodoros proclaimed, 'The Goddess Isis, Queen Cleopatra.'

"Rising from the rug, she sauntered before Caesar, declaring, 'Under more peaceful circumstances, I would have made a more dignified entrance, but meeting you was more important than the means by which I arrived. Do you agree?'

"'Very much so, Queen Cleopatra,' Caesar chuckled, 'though, I do believe if your rug had been any longer, my friend Altus would have greeted you with the tip of his sword.'

"Approaching, she looked me up and down, noting, 'You are different from these men. You dress as a Roman but have the ferocity of a barbarian.'

I tried not to stare, but her naked body, barely concealed

beneath a sheer white dress, made it impossible to look away. She smiled seductively, 'You are the most beautiful man I have ever laid eyes upon. In time, I shall fulfill your dreams.'

"But it was not the words that shocked me, it was that she spoke them in my native tongue.

"'What does she say to you?' Caesar questioned.

"I was not sure how to answer, but luckily, I did not have to. She quipped, 'I simply informed him that patience yields great rewards.' And with those words, she ran a fingernail across my chest and walked back to Caesar.

"'Meaning what?' Caesar asked, inquisitively.

"Ignoring his question, she flirted, 'I dismay to think I might never have been afforded the great honor of meeting the man who conquered the world.'

"Knowing she was trying to win him over, he played along happily. 'Ah, but I have only just arrived in Egypt, and have no intentions of making it a Roman province.'

"She eyed him shrewdly. 'You tell me what I long to hear but if I were in your place, I would gladly run a sword through the heart of Egypt and make her my own.'

"She had seen right through him, and he was instantly enchanted with her brazen confidence, spouting, 'If only I were as ambitious as you, I would not have been of such advanced age before accomplishing what I have thus far.'

"Sensually running her hand down his arm, she put her lips to his ear, purring, 'She is a very tempting mistress. Wealth unknown, even to Rome, and the splendor of her palace is beyond compare.'

"Grabbing her arm, he smiled, devilishly, 'I do believe she would enjoy a master such as myself.'

"Leaning close, lips nearly touching, she seductively grinned, 'Indeed she would, my king . . . indeed she would.'"

"Did she really conquer Caesar so easily?" Sierra asks.

"It was more along the lines of being kindred spirits. Both ambitious, proud, and self-sufficient. While she was born into divinity, and Caesar had to rise up from a once distinguished family, they were soulmates in ruthlessness. Both grasping at self-assigned destinies. That being said, she did conquer him to an extent, with her insight, affection, and grace."

"What did she look like?"

"I found her strikingly beautiful, but it was her soul and mind that made her unique. She was decisively aplomb, with a tenderness, once revealed, any man would traverse oceans to win her love."

"She was taken with you, wasn't she?"

"No more than I was with her."

"Why did she tell Caesar that she spoke to you of patience?"

"I suppose she knew what Caesar wanted to hear, or she was speaking to me under the guise of answering him."

"How well did you come to know her?" *Flirting with him like that, she must have liked him.*

"In the beginning, not well at all. They became lovers after that first encounter and spent every waking minute together. Once Ptolemy XIII realized they were a couple, he marched his army into Alexandria, and once again, we were at war. Looking back, it's strange to think we were fighting during that period because I only recall the parties Cleopatra hosted until dawn. It was a time of merriment for all those close to Caesar, and after enduring hardships for such an extended period, we threw ourselves into the arms of drunken debauchery most willingly. We did not realize it then, but those were to be Caesar's happiest days as well."

"Did you become close with her during those parties?"

"We did not come to know each other better until the war was over, which was in the spring of 47 BC, while sailing up the Nile on her three-hundred-foot barge. Ptolemy XIII had drowned in the Nile as he tried to escape after an ill-prepared battle, and Cleopatra was so happy, she insisted on showing us the grandeurs of Egypt. Though I do not believe she was quite as exuberant when Caesar appointed her younger brother, Ptolemy XIV, coruler."

"Why would he do that when he could have easily

controlled Egypt through her?"

"He had to make it look as if he were fulfilling the will of the late King, not starting another war for personal reasons. He had been elected consul a little over a year earlier, along with his title of dictator, and did not want any comparisons from the Senate on this war being disturbingly similar to his Gallic campaign."

"Makes sense. By fulfilling the will, he appeased Rome and kept control of Egypt. Do you think he also did it to remind Cleopatra of who was in charge?"

"I am quite certain of it. But as long as Cleopatra held onto power, she was not bitter. And to justify his prior actions to the Senate, he worked with his scribe during idle times on our journey, assembling details of the Gallic and Civil wars for their review."

"I take it the Senate, or at least Brutus, never cared for what he had to say."

"Some did, most did not. Most Senators cared only about their own security and wealth, much like politicians today. Nevertheless, he left a wonderful account of his life and times for future generations. If only he had written more about his personal life, it would have offered incredible insight into what makes one man reach for greatness, while most reside happily in mediocrity."

"Do you think he considered himself gifted or divine? I mean, if you don't believe in yourself, how can you expect others to believe in you?"

"You are correct in your thinking, no one follows the weak and indecisive.

"Did you become closer to her on the trip up the Nile? Since she flirted with you the day you met, there must be some juicy details," she smiles, alcohol making her far-too-confident with an all-too-dangerous vampire.

"I see we have not deviated from your earlier question," he smiles, happy that his transference has vanquished her fear. "On the periodic days Caesar spent with his scribe, she would take me on tours of the ancient temples. One afternoon, as we walked the ruins of the temple of Queen Hatshepsut, she opened up to me."

"Were many temples ruins back then?"

"In comparison to present day, they were pristine. Much of the vandalism and destruction took place at the hands of the Christians, followed by art collectors. The Christians being the primary culprits, they were excessively unruly and destructive. Rioting, burning down temples and destroying all forms of Pagan statues and monuments. That is why they were persecuted by the Romans, they believed their religion to be superior to Pagan beliefs. It is terrible what atrocities have befallen mankind in the name of religion. From the destruction of ancient art to the slaughtering of innocent people, it is difficult to fathom the savagery inflicted by man, and upon man, in the name of God."

"Did you ever believe in God?" she probes, wondering if something caused him to doubt his faith.

"You are too concerned with religion. Gods come and go, much as people do. I once believed so deeply in the Persian sun-god Mithra, I established a temple in Memphis so that my fellow soldiers and I would have a place to worship. But as time passed, I came to realize that my kind are the only eternal beings in this universe, and to be perfectly honest, the only gods you need put faith in."

"I'll take that as a no," she scoffs. *What a fucking ego! God, I hate him!*

"I am sorry, I did not mean to be callous or egotistical. I forget that you have been brainwashed for so long, you see religion as your only reason for existence. Created by God, tested by God, then cross your fingers, nurtured by God in everlasting peace."

"Is it wrong to believe that?" she counters, narrowing her eyes at his pompous audacity.

"It is not. It is just that when you have seen religions come and go, as I have, one does not put faith in the imaginations of men. You must understand, modern religions are nothing more than outlandish stories created by ancient man, and with time, the utterly fantastic and less rational aspects were either disposed of or transmuted into a rational, positive theology. Simply put, they are nothing but stories that got better with time. Each religion borrowed freely from the other, adapting and improving the story to increase followers. If Egypt were not a theocracy, then Israel surely never would have been. And it cannot be ignored that Parseeism had a very distinct impression on Judaism in its formative stage, and subsequently on Orthodox Catholicism. Thereafter, Christianity started when a sect of Jews and gentiles took the messianic aspects of the Torah, as well as other Jewish stories, and created an amalgamation of the writings on the Eastern religions of Krishna, Mithra, Osiris-Dionysus, and even the Egyptian god Horus, to personify Jesus. In this syncretism, the Christians did away with the rigorous demands that justify entrance into heaven by creating Jesus's teachings of infinite mercy and absolute forgiveness. Do not believe egomaniacal minds are only in world conquerors like Caesar and Alexander, they are also in the creators of so-called messiahs. After all, if Jesus really did exist, did he fulfill the Jewish prophecy of the messiah? Any Jew will be more than happy to tell you that Shimeon Bar Kochba was the closest thing they have ever had to a messiah, not Jesus.

"It is important to remember that ancient people were predominately illiterate and terrified of a world that offered unimaginable cruelty at the hands of both man and nature. They needed something greater than the physical world to bring solace and meaning to their lives. They yearned for a supreme being who offered an afterlife devoid of suffering to believe that their lives were worth more than a sixty-year struggle with futility."

"It's so depressing when you put it that way." *Could he be right?*

"Religion is such a personally held value," he consoles, "it can only lead to conflict. Let us return to my time with Cleopatra."

She bites her lip, softly holding back, but inside, she can't help but question the origins of Christianity. *Could it all be fiction?*

"To get back to the juicy details, as you put, we spent the better part of the day at Queen Hatshepsut's temple. When she finished telling me the history of the Queen and her temple, she subtly interrogated me as to Caesar's plans. I informed her that if he did have any plans to conquer Egypt, I surely did not know of them. When I thought she had befriended me to gain information, I turned the conversation away from Caesar and asked what she hoped to achieve by seducing him.

"Looking me in the eyes, she revealed, 'I want nothing more than to keep control of Egypt. I feel secure with his alliance, but we both know his wife and ambition will take him back to Rome. And if that is what destiny demands, I only hope to maintain my crown. That said, we are both at a point in life where we desire each other's presence. He needs my affection to fill his aging soul, and I require his wisdom and strength as a mentor.'

"I understood her feelings perfectly, for I knew Caesar expected nothing more. She asked how I came to be in Caesar's army and went on to tell me of a Greek tutor that taught her the German language." Pausing, a gleam comes to his eye. "She was a fascinating woman! Her intellect was unmatched when it came to philosophy, and history. I would listen to her endlessly, only to remain in her presence."

"You cared for her very deeply, didn't you?"

"Like no other." Altus stops for a moment, not wanting Sierra to think his wife wasn't as important to him as Cleopatra, and explains, "It was not that she replaced the feelings I had for my wife, it was that I had become a different man by that point in time. The boy that was the leader of that long since disbanded tribe no longer existed. If that makes sense."

"I think I understand, you experienced so much in the years spent with Caesar, you grew to be a different person."

"Yes, and Cleopatra only made me want to grow further. I was captivated by the civilized world and everything it had to offer, and she was the incarnate of all its trappings. When she was near, my heart raced. When she spoke, her sensual voice calmed my soul and aroused my senses. And when we touched, I felt passion as never before. That is why, on that very afternoon, without a word spoken between us, we wantonly tore the clothes from each other's bodies, making love upon the altar in the Chapel of Amun."

"Didn't you feel guilty, betraying Caesar?" *Typical hot guy. Can't keep it in his pants.*

"Yes, and I felt my betrayal deepen with every word I spoke. After a period of torturous days, I informed Caesar that I wished to sail with the cavalry on one of the barges that trailed us. He asked if something was wrong, commenting that I seemed distant, but I explained it away under the pretense of being envious of the other men's time spent exploring the ruins on horseback. Knowing that I loved the freedom of riding, he said, 'It is selfish of me to keep your nomadic spirit chained idly at my side. Go explore this land with your comrades.'

"I felt as if I were being pardoned from a death sentence. When we docked at the next port and I began packing, Cleopatra entered my room, begging me to stay. I told her I could not, and that the two of them were tearing me apart, giving me no choice but to leave. But I was only kidding myself, whenever we were near each other our passion was uncontrollable. We need only look in each other's eyes, and our hands would intuitively rip the clothes from each other's bodies. Before she could finish her pleas, we were madly making love, thoughtless to Caesar, or any other that might happen upon us."

"Did you end up staying?"

"I could not. Luckily, Caesar was working with his scribes

when I departed, for the tears that streamed down her face would have given him clear evidence as to our affair."

"Did it help not seeing them?"

"I suppose." Hanging his head, he shrugs, "In the beginning, anyway. As the days passed, I needed to see her. I longed to smell her perfumed hair and feel her body move beneath my touch. It became so unbearable, that as we neared Philae Island, I persuaded the soldiers to petition Caesar to stop our journey and return to Alexandria before losing favor with Rome."

"And did he?"

"He asked my opinion, and since we had not been in contact with Rome for nearly five months, I felt it imperative that he not lose ground with the Senate. Especially as of late, since his course of action looked as though he were courting a woman, a foreigner at that. The Senate would crucify him for such disregard of Roman principles."

"Hmm, you shortened their time together." *Treachery, in the name of love.*

"You talk as if I were breaking up Romeo and Juliet. True, they needed each other politically, but she was a young woman full of passion, searching for her first true love, whereas he was an older man, deeply touched by a younger woman's affection. They served each other's purpose, but Cleopatra's heart belonged to me. I did not force her to love me, it was of her own free will!"

Realizing his passion is getting the better of him, he lowers his voice. "Nevertheless, we sailed for Alexandria, and I did not see her, nor Caesar for the remainder of the voyage. The barge I sailed upon reached port before theirs, and I hastened my exit so as not to be near when they disembarked. I spent the next week wandering the maze of streets that made up Alexandria and sleeping in the cavalry's camp. In a city of over half a million people, it made for a cultural mix that heightened my senses and alleviated my emotional torment. That is, until I was summoned by Caesar. Was he wondering what became of me, or had Cleopatra betrayed our love?

"I anxiously climbed the red granite steps of the palace, wildly contemplating his fury. When I found him at the columned entrance, surrounded by centurions, he embraced me, announcing, 'The time has come to depart, the world is coming undone around us! The remaining Pompeian legions are amassing in Africa and Spain, my legions in Italy are threatening mutiny, and Pharnaces II has set out to regain his father's kingdom, causing all Roman rule in the Eastern provinces to collapse.'

"I was not surprised by Pompey's legions gathering, nor startled by the actions of Pharnaces, but I was shocked to hear that his legions were considering mutiny. I asked how that could be possible when Antony was leading them, and he rubbed his chin, disclosing, 'The more control I give to Antony, the harder I find it to control my men. I am starting to question with whom Antony's allegiance lies. Me, the Senate, or himself. But that, we will discover in due time!'

"I was forlorn at the thought of leaving Egypt and never seeing Cleopatra again, but my place was at his side. So, I asked how soon we would depart.

"'Immediately,' he answered, 'but you will not be joining us.'

"I was floored and began to question his decision, before he cut me off, explaining, 'You have brought luck to me as I have never known, and it is with a heavy heart I leave you, but Cleopatra has begged that you stay for her personal protection. There is no other I would put my faith in as I have with you, therefore, I am leaving three legions at your disposal under the command of Rufio. If Fortuna turns her back on me, I will surely beckon. Keep a close eye on Cleopatra, for she is bearing the future ruler of the world!'"

"Hold on!" Sierra interjects, vehemently waving her hands.

Knowingly, he clenches his jaw, mouth set straight. "It was not my child."

"How do you know?"

"The timing. It was not possible."

"How can you be so positive?"

"She was already with child when we consummated our love. It was not mine, let us leave it at that."

"Okay," she acquiesces. *Men, they never really know.*

"I hugged him as I would my own father and we bade our goodbyes. Shuffling through the palace, I made my way to the balcony that overlooked the palace entry and watched him kiss Cleopatra farewell. Despondent, I drug myself back inside. My mentor, inspiration, and second father was leaving. I was a rudderless ship, adrift in a strange land."

"I thought you loved it there, and didn't you want to be alone with Cleopatra?"

"I did love Egypt and I yearned to be with her. But at that moment, I could only think of how Caesar was responsible for everything I had become, and the pain of never seeing or speaking with him again was suffocating. I sat for what seemed an eternity, thinking how he had become the measure of how I defined myself, and now, it was up to me to forge my own path. Then, Cleopatra walked in, more beautiful than Isis. It was then, I realized everything I had ever hoped or dreamed of, was standing before me."

"Was Cleopatra upset at his leaving?"

"No, she came to me as quickly as he rode away. And I must admit, for how much I missed him, I was thrilled at having her to myself."

"She gave birth to a boy, didn't she?"

"Yes, not long after Caesar departed. He was named Ptolemy Caesar, or as I came to call him, Caesarion. I raised him as my own from the day he was born, and I think Caesar knew I would, for that is why he left me there. I was a foreigner, so I could not challenge for power, and he knew my love and respect for him would carry on to the child."

"He was politically motivated leaving you there, wasn't he?"

"It would be foolish not to think so. He saw all possible outcomes and did what was in his best interest."

"Did you ever feel as if he were using you?"

"Aren't we all guilty of using those around us at one time or another?" he asks, rhetorically. "Besides, how could I have felt taken advantage of when he laid so much opportunity before me? If it were not for him, I would never have been to Rome, Egypt, or, more importantly, met Cleopatra. And our life together was just beginning. We spent our first year together making love and sailing in the private royal harbor, taking rest only to eat, and be bathed by servants. It was a paradise of which I had never dared dream. We were young, rich, powerful, and in love. No other lovers ever had Fortuna smile upon them so heartily, and residing in the world's most beautiful and civilized city made it that much sweeter. Rome, which I had previously thought of as a pinnacle to man's achievement, seemed no more than an overcrowded slum in comparison. The imposing monuments of marble, limestone, and red granite struck awe into all who had the fortune of walking Alexandria's streets. And the women? They were different from any I had ever known. They wore make-up and perfumes to accentuate their femininity to much greater skill than either their Roman or Greek counterparts."

"What did they use for makeup?" she asks, feminine curiosity peaked.

"Plant and seaweed extract for rouge, ochre to tint their lips, ground-up minerals such as galena to darken their eyelids, and some even went so far as to rub white lead powder into their skin to appear fairer. They also stained their nails, palms, and soles of their feet with henna. It was a joy to be in their presence."

Leaning forward, he meets her eyes. "As beautiful as you are, you would have been revered a goddess!"

Taken aback, she turns away. *Is he flirting with me? Wow, his arrogance knows no boundaries!*

"I was enthralled with the beauty of the architecture as well. So much so, when Cleopatra was needed for political matters, I roamed the five sections of the city, visiting the Pharos lighthouse, Public Gardens and, most importantly, the

Library of Alexandria to learn all I could of the modern world. The library was in the Beta section, which included the Royal Quarter, which made it a quick stroll from the palace."

"I read that Caesar burned the library," she says, meeting his gaze. *Is that why he stares at me so intently? Does he honestly think I'll have sex with him? Ha!*

"During the battle with Ptolemy XIII there was a fire that spread from the docks, and unfortunately, burned a small wing of the library. It did not affect the overall operation of the library, for while it was being repaired, I continued to study from the more than four-hundred-thousand scrolls in the library's collection. Cleopatra possessed a hunger for learning and, recognized it in me as well. She assigned scholars to teach me different languages along with the works of Homer, Hesiod, Sophocles, and Euripides, to name a few. I grew exponentially during those times, both intellectually and emotionally. She was the sun that lit my day, and the moon that aroused my passions by night. We cherished our time together and plotted endlessly to keep Fortuna on our side. Which would prove to be impossible, for our fortunes were tied directly to Caesar's."

EIGHT

Senses impaired from the evening's alcohol abuse, the paintings that captivated Sierra earlier in the day are no more than blurry images passing imperceptibly.

Steadying her gait, Abah hungrily eyes the bite marks on her neck. *Just one drop, maybe two. Quench my thirst, and you'll be through.*

"Howdya meet 'im?" Sierra slurs.

"It's late, and you've had a lot to drink. Besides, my life before Altus wasn't very exciting or enjoyable."

"Why's zat?"

"In my time, being black was a curse."

Entering Sierra's Louis Seize bedroom with its vanilla-colored walls and intricate paintings, Abah guides her to the bed and sits beside her. *Stop wasting time. Suck her dry!*

"Ya don' mean slavery? Do ya?" Exhaling lightly, the drunkenness lessens to a heavy buzz, and with a deep breath, holds her head steady.

"Unfortunately, yes. I was born in South Carolina when racist beliefs such as those of the Baron de Montesquieu, were considered to be inevitable truths."

"Who's he? Wha'd he say?"

Pursing her lips, she sighs, "'One cannot put oneself into the frame of mind in which God, a very wise being, put a soul, above all a good soul, into an entirely black body.'"

"Ugh. Did it bother you?" Head teetering slightly, it jerks instinctively upright.

"Not when I read it, later in life, because I knew he was ignorant. But if I had heard it when I was a slave, living as I had been, I would have undoubtedly believed it. When you're berated daily, made to feel stupid and worthless, it doesn't take long before you convince yourself of the same. And that was how I felt most every day."

"Did you live in Charleston?"

"Just outside the city. Though I did get into the city somewhat regularly on shopping trips with the lady of the house."

"Are you okay talking about this? I don't wanna make you uncomfortable." *Why should I care if she's uncomfortable? I'm a prisoner!*

Resting a hand on Sierra's thigh, she caresses her. "No, it's okay. It's so far behind me, I don't think about it very often."

Comforted by her touch, she feels correct in having sensed a softness not found in either Altus or Eve. Taking hold of her hand, she fails to realize it's Abah's transference of lust that she reciprocates.

"Did you believe what he told you this evening?"

"I suppose so. I mean, I did when he was telling me. But now . . . how could it all be true? Then again, he cut his arm open, and it healed in seconds . . . it's all so confusing! Yesterday, I was looking forward to putting an end to our life of crime, and today, we're prisoners in a French chateau."

For the first time in hours, Weston crosses her mind. Letting go of the enemy's hand, she drunkenly staggers about the room.

"He'll be okay, Eve is looking after him," Abah assures, pushing calming emotions.

"Eve! She's the one that nearly killed him!" she spits, anger growing, yet quickly snuffed out through transference.

"You need to rest. Can I find something in the closet for you to sleep in?"

"All you'll find in there are hooker clothes."

"That's Eve's wardrobe," she muses. "You looked to be closer to her size than mine."

"Does she always dress like a slut?" Feeling tipsy, she sits again.

"She definitely leaves nothing to the imagination."

"I suppose she has a nice figure," Sierra admits, grudgingly.

"If you like, I can bring you some of my clothes."

"Can I get something from my apartment?"

"No, you're officially gone from the world. None of us can be seen there."

"Gone from the world? Altus said he would let us go when Weston felt better!"

"Oh," she mumbles, sheepishly.

"He will let us go, won't he?" *Did he lie to me?*

"I'm certain he will," she confirms, attempting to sound more definite. *I'd better get off this subject before I say something I shouldn't.* "Would you like to hear how I met him?"

"Yeah," she gulps. *Does she know something, and she's not telling me?*

Placing her hand on Sierra's, Abah squeezes firmly, soaking up the heady sensation of blood pumping through hot flesh. "I was twenty-six. A house servant on a plantation. I had more privilege than the field slaves, though being a slave under any condition is misery at best. It was 1851 when he came into my life, though at the time, I couldn't honestly say if I knew that or not, for I was not only disinterested in my world, but I was also illiterate. And that's how they liked it."

"The owners of the plantations?"

"It would probably be more accurate to say all white people, regardless of what part of the country they resided in. And while it was a curse to be born black, it was even worse to be mixed. I was black enough to be excluded from white society, yet far too light-skinned to be accepted by my own people. I was the effigy of two opposing races. Neither wanting to see any part of themselves in me."

"What about your family?"

"My mother died giving birth to her first and only child, and my father died of tuberculosis when I was very young. It was only my grandmother and me, and she died when I was ten. The only information I have about my history is what my grandmother used to tell me, which was primarily about how the Benin tribe of Africa captured her village and sold everyone off to slavers. She was only thirteen at the time, and because the Benin were armed with rifles supplied by the slave runners, they stood no chance. Chained together, the people of her tribe looked to the heavens, crying for mercy, but instead, were granted a two-week march to one of the five slave rivers of the Bight of Benin. There, they were loaded on boats and sailed to the Dutch trade castle Elmina, situated on the Gold Coast. At Elmina, she was purchased from the Benin for an assortment of copper pots and cowrie shells, then assigned to a waiting camp.

"When the Dutch slavers started walking through the camp, screams were heard everywhere. Not sure of what was happening, my grandmother frantically looked about, only to find they were separating families and tribes to reduce the likelihood of revolt. In a desperate attempt to thwart the forced disbanding, my grandmother, her sister, and their parents embraced tightly, in a group hug of sorts."

"Oh, my God! Did it work?"

"No, they were whipped until the flesh pulled from their backs and blood pooled at their feet. They had no choice but to let go. My grandmother was the first to be loaded on a ship, and once put below, was overtaken by the smell of death and vinegar."

"Vinegar?"

"That's what was used to clean the ships. If not for that, disease ran rampant, killing the white man's *precious cargo.* Pregnant women were assembled in the back cabin, then children packed into the first entrepot like sardines. Which is where my grandmother was placed. Then, came the women in the second entrepot, followed by the men taking up the remainder. If anyone needed sleep, they had to lay on top of one another. As the days progressed, the odor became fouler with people relieving themselves where they laid, dunghills abounding throughout the cargo hold. The food of yams and bread didn't sit well in their stomachs since it differed from their regular diet, and many had diarrhea from the outset. Every few days, an allotment of slaves would be taken on deck to dance to the rhythm of a drum, an attempt at keeping spirits high. This would happen more frequently when it rained because dampness would sink into the boards on which they slept, and disease might take hold.

"After fifteen days, with at least ten slaves thrown overboard due to death or sickness, my grandmother was brought up on the main deck. Dancing to the beat of the drum, she looked over the rail to witness groups of sharks swimming alongside the ship. Since the dead were thrown overboard, sharks knew where to find their next meal. Never having had the chance to observe white men so closely, she snuck looks at their fair skin and differing hair colors with every beat that allowed a spin of her head. Upon being ordered to return below deck, a girl not much older than her refused, and promptly had her hand cut off - nothing like a show of strength to keep others in line. They heated an iron, sealed the wound, and threw her below, screaming in pain."

"I'd rather be thrown to sharks than go through that," Sierra frowns.

"There were plenty of them. Herman Melville wrote in Moby Dick, 'Sharks are the invariable outriders of all slave ships crossing the Atlantic, systemically trotting alongside, to be handy in case a parcel is to be carried anywhere, or a dead slave to be decently buried.' You may think it strange, but after hearing my grandmother's story, tales of sharks have always fascinated me."

"I can see why. How long was she on the boat?"

"About two months, she reasoned. Upon reaching America,

they put into Sullivan Island, which was essentially a pesthouse to monitor for disease, and if fortunate enough to be free of smallpox, they were cleared to leave. After ten days residing there and having lost about twenty percent of the slaves to disease, they set sail for Charleston. Which, at the time, was the largest port of entry for slaves in North America. While preparing to disembark, she saw a group of decrepit slaves chained to each other near the docks. They were called *refuse* because no one wanted them. Even when sold door to door."

"Slaves were sold door to door?"

"Yes, can you believe it? The ones that couldn't be sold on arrival were chained together, bargain priced, and walked door to door to be haggled upon. And if that didn't work, they ended up on the docks, like those my grandmother witnessed, waiting for death to take them home."

"How did your grandmother fare?"

"After disembarking, she and the others were instructed to clean themselves, then branded on the left shoulder with the mark of the Dutch West India Company. This proved legal importation. The women were given a blue flannel dress, the men, blue cotton trousers, and all were lined up at the open-air exchange behind the post office at the foot of Broad Street. Once the prospective owners arrived, the slaves were forced to remove their clothing so that they could be inspected for signs of sickness, strength, or for men, a deformed or minuscule penis. It was crucial that they be able to impregnate the female slaves, thereby cutting down on future expenditures. Luckily, if the word applies, my grandmother was purchased for the sum of ninety-five gallons of rum. She was taken to the plantation, branded on her right shoulder with the initials, SRP, then schooled in her duties by the other house servants."

"SRP?"

"Stone River Plantation. It's where she lived out the rest of her life."

"That's so sad." Eyes welling up, she is unaware that Abah is inadvertently transferring painful emotions.

"Not as sad as my mother's story, she never knew what freedom was. My father was the only one that ever experienced real freedom, and he was cut down by TB when he was no more than thirty."

"Do you remember much of your father?"

"A little. He oversaw the gin house and was quite tall, with blonde hair that shined like gold," she smiles, softly. "I recall him walking through the master's garden once, singing and whistling as his hair blew in the wind. I don't know if he always sang, or whistled, though I like to think he did because it makes me happy. He found me playing in a flower patch, softly patted me on the head, and said, 'There isn't a flower in this garden as pretty as you, but the master doesn't allow slaves to pick flowers.' He picked me up, asked me if I liked to sing, and sang rhyming verses as he bounced me in his arms all the way back to my little brick cabin. There were twenty-seven of the one-room slave cabins that lined the entry road, and mine was the closest to the master's house. He kissed me on the forehead, called me 'Little Princess,' and walked away. That's the only vivid memory I have of him. Little Princess," she repeats, staring blankly at the floor, ghosts filling every thought.

Noticing a tear forming in Abah's eye, Sierra can't help but feel for her. "It sounds as if he loved you very much."

"Do you think so? I like to think so. Sometimes, it's the only thing that makes me feel human. He was my one connection to this world, besides my grandmother, and at the time, I didn't even know who he was. I've often wondered if he and my mother were secret lovers, unable to be seen together due to the times, and one day planned on running away to the North, but . . . I ended her life."

"It's not your fault she died. It was common in those times to experience complications during childbirth."

"Who knows, maybe I'm just romanticizing the whole affair. It's just as likely he raped my mother and was justifiably stricken with that deadly disease."

Visibly jarred, Sierra searches for a comforting word, but finds none.

"Altus tells me it doesn't matter either way because he loved me that day in the garden. But Altus doesn't understand, or more to the point, he doesn't want me dwelling on the past. That is our greatest enemy, you know. The past. There's so much of it! So many people, so many things done, and seen. It haunts our souls! Altus tells me not to think of such things, and that dwelling on it will surely bring about my end, but I can't shake it. It has taken hold of me as surely as tuberculosis took hold of my father. It flows through my mind like a virus, infecting my every thought. My present is consumed by it, and my future pays the inevitable price. Strange, isn't it? I have a never-ending future to agonize over my past."

Not sure how to answer, Sierra gently rubs her leg, hoping to ease the pain.

The caress fuels Abah's bloodlust and she leans over, kissing her on the cheek, before running a fingernail in figure eights around the scabs on her neck. *Just one flick, and the blood will flow. Just one flick, and down you will go.*

Instinctively, her fangs pop out, and she rapidly clenches her jaw. Fighting the urge to kill, she jumps up, pacing about the room until the desire ceases. "I don't suppose that is what you wanted to hear. My inability to come to grips with who, or what I am."

"I don't mind, it keeps my mind off my predicament." *Why is she kissing me?*

"Sometimes, I think I rushed into it too fast. My situation was bleak, and any path seemed better than the road I was on. When I realized what Altus was, I begged him to make me the same. The power. The freedom. It was beyond everything I had ever wished for! For the oppressed, those are the true gifts of life."

"You don't feel those things any longer?"

"It's not that I don't have a great deal of power or freedom.

It's that with time, everything becomes monotonous."

"I suppose in time, all things fade or burn out." *Just like Weston's love.*

"All but us."

"I havta get sum sleep," Sierra slurs, the drunken lightheadedness returning. "I'd like ta think when I wake up tomorrow, this'll all have been-a bad dream."

The thought makes her happy, and she lies back, fluffing a pillow under her head. Rolling over, she lets out the softest of sighs. *I wonder where they're keeping my faded lover?*

NINE

FIVE DAYS EARLIER

Scrolling through images on his laptop, Weston turns to Sierra as she walks into the den of their pre-war, robbery-funded, Westside apartment.

Pulling up a chair, she affirms, "You were right about one thing, the place is big. I think I've stayed in luxury resorts smaller than that."

"I know, imagine what's inside."

Randomly glancing at him as he studies the pictures, she can't help but wonder if he's biting off more than he can chew.

Looking up, he catches her eye. "You look terrible, what's with the circles under your eyes?"

"I couldn't sleep last night." *Why does he always comment when I look bad, never when I look good?*

"You're not worried about an elaborate alarm system that I can't get around, are you?"

"No, it's not that. I've just been having a strange dream."

"Oh yeah, is there any nudity involved?"

Rolling her eyes, she shakes her head in frustration. "Do you want to hear about it or not?"

"I'm only joking, relax."

"There's this group of blurry, faceless people around me, except for a dark-haired man who stands out clearly. He keeps talking to me like he's waiting for an answer, but I'm unable to speak. Finally, I force myself to say something, but when I do, the dream ends."

Weston wrinkles his brow, unsympathetically asking, "You been eating anything weird before bed?"

"Other than you? No," she joyfully retorts.

"It's a big meal. It would give any girl strange dreams."

With a hesitant smile, she anxiously rubs a finger across her lower lip, a habitual reaction when deep in thought or worrying excessively. "Have you thought about when we'll do it?"

"I'm not sure. I'm still putting everything together." *Rubbing her lip again . . . so annoying.*

"Soon?"

"I've been driving out there the last couple nights, and no one's ever home. I think it best we do it in the next few days."

"That leaves us a couple of days. Let's go to some art museums, like when we first met." *We were so close then. I miss that!*

"We could. I suppose." *Fuck, if I have to listen to her endless ramblings on brush strokes, use of color, or inherent meaning, one more time, I'll shoot myself.*

"Remember how we used to discuss the Masters, then sneak off into that quiet corner in The Met? That was so hot, the idea of someone seeing us make love."

"Yep, that was pretty hot." *But was it worth all the bullshit beforehand?* "I don't think so, baby, we may end up doing this much sooner than I anticipate, and we still need to go over the details. Besides, after this job, we'll be on an extended vacation."

"I thought you said retirement."

"Yeah, that's possible, too," he dismisses, shifting his eyes back to the screen.

"I'm going to make some coffee. I'll be in the kitchen if you need me." *It'll never end. Unless the police end it for us.*

"That sounds good," he replies, cheerily. "Make mine Irish."

Pulling the photos from the printer, he examines each one carefully, then places them in one of two piles. Good shots, or unusable crap. Reaching the last of the pictures, he picks up the good shots and heads for the kitchen.

"If you want more whiskey, just let me know," she offers, lovingly.

"It's fine," he mumbles, thumbing through the pictures.

"Are you planning anything differently since they look to have more money than the people we usually hit?"

"The house is bigger, and they obviously have more money, which probably amounts to a few more cameras and motion sensors, but to be perfectly honest, there's been no great advances in home security that makes me feel any differently about this house from any of the others we've hit."

"That's true," she acknowledges. *Maybe I'm overthinking the whole thing.*

"Don't worry your plump little ass about nothing, baby. There may be a few more obstacles, but the payoff should be incredible."

"What if the payoff is as big as you think it might be? Could we please retire? Like you said!" *God, I'd love to stop. Please say yes, the pressure is killing me!*

"If we score big, sure. If that's what you want."

"I do," she sighs, the weight of the world falling from her shoulders.

On the surface, he shows a pleasant facade, but inside, he cringes with those two simple words, *I do.*

"If that's what you want, I guess it's okay by me," he murmurs. *Well, this is it, one last time, and she's done. Fuck!*

Not wanting to deal with the aggravation, he pushes it out of his mind and focuses on her nipples protruding from the tight T-shirt. "But before the big score, I've got something big of my own to give you."

Tired and anxious, she apologetically replies, "I'm not in the mood right now, honey. Maybe later, okay?"

"Come on, loosen up." Leaning closer, he cups her breasts.

Stepping back, she pushes his hands away. "Not now, I really don't want to."

"If you don't want it, there's plenty who do," he crows.

"You know, if you ever cheat on me, I'm gone!" Studying his reaction, she looks for a crack in his expression that offers a clue to his being unfaithful.

"Yeah, yeah, I know . . .. Why don't you let me stick it in. Once we start, you know you'll love it. All the girls do, once they loosen up."

"I don't want to hear about other girls you've fucked! Do you really think that's going to turn me on?"

In no mood to argue, she picks up her coffee and leaves the room. *I know he's cheating on me! Jeff told me I'd regret leaving him for Weston, and he was right.*

"Why do you have to be such a fuckin' prude," he snarls, hastily assembling the pictures. *Women, they're all the same! God forbid you ever sleep with someone else. I thought she might be different. Not bogged down by the ridiculous morals of the world. She's become a drag, just like the rest of 'em.*

TEN

PRESENT DAY

The opening of the bedroom door causes Sierra to wake, tired eyes opening to the disappointing sight of the Louis Seize bedroom.

Holding a glass of water and a few aspirin, Abah instructs, "Take these. You'll feel better."

"I appreciate that," she yawns, "my head is throbbing."

"Did you sleep well?"

"Yeah, I think all the drinks made for a good sleeping pill."

"Is three enough?"

"Perfect, thanks."

"About last night . . . I didn't mean to depress you with my problems. Things aren't as bad as I made them sound. I'm just going through a tough time."

"I'm sure it's not half as bad as what I'm going through."

"We're at opposing ends right now." Sitting on the edge of the bed, Abah informs, "My time has come to leave. Altus thinks it's time for me to be on my own."

"He's kicking you out?" she gasps, slightly surprised.

"No, it's not like that. I've been with him over one-hundred-and-seventy years. Most of the others left around a hundred."

"What do you mean by others? Is this some kind of a breeding ground for vampires?"

"He teaches us to be immortal. To ride upon the ocean of life without experiencing the swells that wear you thin over time."

"And how does one do that without becoming a stone?"

"That's precisely the problem. When you feel too much, like I do, the world is destined to wear you out."

"Where will you go?"

"I haven't given it much thought. It's not happening immediately, so I have time to think about it. Maybe I'll return home for a start. From there, who knows?"

"Charleston?"

"No, the plantation," she muses. "Wouldn't that be ironic?"

"More creepy than ironic."

"I suppose I couldn't buy it anyway," she laughs.

"Not enough money?"

"Money is the least of my problems. Altus's departing gift will make me one of the wealthiest women in America."

Damn! How much money does this guy have? Mouth dropped, she probes, "How much?"

"It's not important. Besides, didn't you want to visit Weston?"

"Yeah!" she yelps, jumping out of bed to get dressed. "Is he feeling better?"

"Yes, but it takes time. Don't push him to the point of overexertion. He needs a lot of rest."

Throwing on the top and jeans from the previous evening, she follows her into the hallway. "I was thinking about you last night. What happened after you became a vampire, how did you explain it to your friends?"

"For me, it was easy. Since I was a slave and berated by everyone, it was a gift never having to see any of them again."

"Did you want to be like him?"

"God, yes! He was an eternal angel, free to do as he wished, whenever he pleased. I begged him for his blood when he told me what he was."

"How long did you know him before you found out he was a vampire?"

"It couldn't have been more than a couple weeks."

"How did you meet him?"

Smiling softly, she reminisces, "One day, Master Sullivan, ordered two mint juleps be brought to the parlor, and there he was." Somewhat giddy, her exuberance accentuates the story. "I only looked at him momentarily, but I thought he was the most beautiful man I had ever laid eyes on. When I handed him his drink, he looked me in the eyes and smiled. I nearly melted; I was so bashful!"

"He is pretty hot," Sierra admits.

"It wasn't just his looks, though. There was an energy that emanated from him. The whole time I was in that room, I knew he was staring at me, and my body felt hot and alive."

"What did you say to him?"

"Nothing." Catching the inquisitive glance of Sierra's alluring eyes, the bloodlust returns. "I just kept doing my job. If I'd have spoken to one of the master's guests, I'd still be getting whipped."

"That's horrible!" Eyes cringed, she's shocked by the senseless brutality.

"That's just the way it was. We didn't question orders. 'You don't think. You do,' the master used to say."

Feeling empathy, Sierra takes hold of her hand.

Squeezing firmly, Abah stops near the doorway to Weston's bedroom. Breathing heavily, she pulls her close, close enough to kiss. "After about a week of seeing him around the estate, he approached me at the smokehouse. We were on the creek side, so no one from the main house could see us. I don't recall what we talked about, only what I felt when he was near. Comforted, safe, strong. Sexy! I wanted to give him everything I was and ever could be."

Looking deep into Sierra's eyes, she wantonly transfers her lust. "If he had told me I'm going to rip your neck open and suck every last drop of your blood, I would have gladly bared my neck. I knew he wanted me, and I wanted him even more. We made love in the long grass, the rushing water from a nearby creek muffling our passion."

"Was he your first?" *Her eyes are so black . . . they're mesmerizing.*

"No, but with Altus, it was so much more than I had ever experienced." Her eyes fall slowly from Sierra's glittering green eyes to her full, luscious lips. "To this day, when he looks at me, I still feel him in my soul." *Altus couldn't be angry with me for having one little taste.* Putting a hand on Sierra's waist, she pulls her tight, and kisses her, starting the seduction that will end her life.

Running her hand through the soft, golden curls of Abah's hair, Sierra returns her kiss.

Wrapping Sierra's silky hair in her fist, she retreats from the kiss, licks her lips, and pulls her head to the side, gaining access to the healing wound. *Oh, pretty girl, so young and true. You really shouldn't let me, have bite number two.* Brushing her lips against the subtly scented suppleness of her neck, her fangs protrude, viciously eager to consummate the kill.

Stop! Stop! Stop! Abah's inner voice wails.

Pushing Sierra against the wall, she steps back, shaking her head to clear the bloodlust. *Fuck, that was close. Altus would have killed me!*

Head bouncing off the wall, Sierra is stunned by the sudden turn of events, and gently rubs the back of her head. *Damn, that hurt! What the hell's with her?*

Looking up and down the hallway for signs of life, Abah steps close, whispering, "Be careful of your emotions when you're near us. They may not be your own!"

"What do you mean?" she questions, terrified of what she is about to hear.

"We are strong in many ways. When you are alone, search your feelings, for they may be the only true feelings you have."

"What are you saying, I can't think clearly when I'm near you?"

At the sound of Weston's door opening, Abah abruptly changes the conversation. "Give him time, he's lost a great deal of blood."

Left hanging, Sierra's mouth drops, desperately hoping to finish the conversation.

"Rest is what he needs, don't keep him awake too long," Abah announces.

No sooner does she finish her words, than Eve walks out of the open door. Wearing a thin, cotton halter-top, and skin-tight jeans, she sneers, "Well, if it isn't my new best friend. I see you kept a grip on your wine glass."

Rooted, Sierra stands fearfully still.

"Not very talkative this morning, are you? What I don't understand, is how such a beautiful outfit can be made to look so ugly. I suppose the old saying is true - you can't make a silk purse out of a sow's ear."

Gliding past Sierra, she purposely brushes against her. "Do you like them?" she glares, confidently.

More fearful of Eve, than Altus and Abah combined, she steps back, increasing the distance between them. "Like what?"

"My tits. You stared at them as you bumped into me."

"I didn't bump into you, you pushed them into me. And if I looked at them, it was probably due to their unremarkable size," she counters, half-heartedly, refusing to back down, but not wanting a fight.

With curled lip, fast becoming a smirk, Eve proclaims, "I know someone who finds them quite remarkable."

Knowing that she's referring to Weston, Sierra plays innocent, not letting her get the best of her. "Yeah, I thought I heard the garbage men discussing you this morning when they took away the rest of the trash."

"Ha, ha, ha. Aren't you funny?" In the fraction of a second, Eve closes the distance between them, and with lips lightly brushing her ear, whispers. "One of these days, you won't have Altus or Abah around to protect you. And I'll drink so deeply, I'm going to cum, cum, and cum again." Running her hot tongue under Sierra's jaw, ear to chin, she closes her lids, then slowly opens them to look her square in the eye. “Mmm, so good!

Turning pale, beads of sweat breaking out on her neck, Sierra takes a step toward Abah.

“What? Nothing to say?” Eve giggles, with wolfish smile.

De-escalating the situation, Abah grabs Sierra’s hand, pulling her toward the bedroom. “Go to Weston, he needs to see a friendly face.”

Nearing the open door, she lets go of Abah’s hand and rushes in. The room is nearly a mirror image of her bedroom, only colors and furniture differing.

“West!” she yells, jumping on the bed to kiss him.

“God, it’s good to see you,” he bursts, uncertain he’d ever see her again.

“Remember what I told you,” Abah interrupts, “give him lots of rest.”

“Thanks, Abah,” she bubbles, “for everything.”

“I trust you, so I’m not going to lock the door. But if you two try anything, you know Altus will only make things hard on you.”

“I know,” she answers, “thanks again.”

Watching to make certain the door has closed completely; she waits to speak. “How are you? I’ve been so worried!”

“I’m so lightheaded I keep drifting in and out of sleep. What time is it anyway?”

“It’s about ten o’clock." Looking into his soft blue eyes, she fixes his messy locks. "Do you need anything?”

“No, just you.”

Not used to hearing nice words, she smiles, and lays next to him, affectionately rubbing his chest. *He missed me. Maybe things are better!*

“What’s been happening?” he asks.

“I don’t even know where to start,” she whimpers, eyes open wide.

“Do you know what they are!”

“I do.”

"You think it's true?"

"I've seen some pretty unbelievable things. I don't doubt it."

"Eve drank my blood, can you fuckin' believe that? She even flashed her teeth at me over breakfast yesterday. It was like her teeth grew when she opened her mouth. She scared the shit outta me!"

"Has she been mean to you?"

"Not at all. In fact, she said she'd bring some medicine later that would help me feel better."

"Maybe you shouldn't be taking any pills right now," she cautiously advises.

Never having thought they might drug him, he concurs, "Maybe you're right. I thought she seemed somewhat trustworthy, but who knows?"

Sierra frowns, appalled by his judgment. "I think she's the worst of the bunch, don't trust that bitch!" *Does he like her? That would be just like him!*

"You're probably right. My head's spinning so fast, I don't know who to trust."

"What are we going to do?" she squints, hoping he's devised a plan of escape.

"I don't know. To tell you the truth, I haven't even thought about it. The only thing I know is that she's strong as hell. She tackled me, pinned me to the floor, and I couldn't do a damn thing about it. . .. You know," he asks with vigor, "I was thinking about your dream. Is this guy, Altus, the one you dreamt about?"

"No. He looks nothing like him."

"Are you still having that dream?"

"Yeah, every night," she confirms, and switches the subject to more pressing concerns. "I talked to Altus yesterday."

"And?"

"I tried to find out about them dying, but he wouldn't give me much information. I think he knew what I was getting at. He did say we'd be free to go when you get better, but when I spoke to Abah about it, she sounded doubtful. I don't think we can rely on his word."

"You think there's anything to the old Dracula movies? You know, making the sign of a cross to keep them away."

"Not from what he told me."

"Would he tell you the truth?" he justifiably counters.

"Think about it, West. It's the middle of the day, and they're not sleeping in coffins."

"I suppose not. What about a stake through the heart?"

"Even if that did work, you said yourself you couldn't overpower Eve, and she's the smallest of the three."

Gazing at the ceiling, he discloses, "I don't know, babe. I just don't know."

"Me neither," she exhales, hopelessly. "I was hoping you'd thought of something." *He needs a plan to get us out of here. That's the one thing he excels at. Being devious.*

Rubbing his eyes, mouth open wide, he yawns.

"Are you tired? I can leave and let you rest."

"No, I want you here with me."

Cuddling close, she pulls the sheet up to their necks. "Just close your eyes and sleep, honey. I'm going to stay right here."

Turning his back to her, he casually remarks, "Since we can't overpower them, we'll just have to outwit them."

Arm slung over him, pulling tight, she thinks, *He's got no clue how far out of our depth we are.*

ELEVEN

Relaxing in a chair across the desk from Altus, Abah sits in reserved silence, vacantly staring at the painting of Laura de Noves.

"How is she feeling?" he asks.

With a tilt of her head, she looks softly upon the only man she has ever loved. "Surprisingly well, all things considered."

"Excellent, do not transfer any more emotion into her than necessary. I want her to feel comfortable and safe without clouding her thoughts."

Strutting through the door, chomping on gum, Eve carries the confident aura of a high school cheerleader having spent the previous night in the backseat of a car with the co-captains of the football team.

Watching her sit, proud as a peacock, he inquires, "How is Weston?"

"Typical man. He only thinks with his dick."

"Do you think he is faithful to Sierra?"

"Uhm . . . what?" Eve pauses, looking perplexed. *Does it really matter? Soon, I'll be draining that bitch and her boyfriend too.*

"I need to know if they are in love."

Love! What does he care? Curiosity peaked, Abah asks, "What is it about her that we must go to such lengths?"

Eyes narrowing, he admonishes, "You should know better

than to question me."

"She only wants to know why we didn't kill them. I must admit, I'm curious as well," Eve concurs.

"Because it is not my wish for her to die. Need I explain myself further?" he bellows.

Realizing she has gone too far, Eve bites her lip, reluctantly apologizing, "I'm sorry. It's a little strange, that's all." *He's going to offer her the disease! I've played second fiddle to Abah for almost a century, there's no way I'm letting this bitch get in my way!*

Looking from Eve to Altus, eyes crinkled, Abah justifies, "It's all happening so quickly, neither of us can wrap our heads around it."

"It is not for either of you to pass judgement. Now, I will ask again. Do you believe they are in love?"

Disparagingly blinking her eyes, Eve defeatedly exhales, "It shouldn't be long before I find out if they're in love." *Once Sierra finds the present I left for her in Weston's room, I'll have the answer.*

"Is he opening up to you?" he asks.

"To an extent." Elbow resting on chair, Eve rubs her temple, a headache coming on from talking about Sierra. "Would you like me to move more quickly?"

"Yes, but do not push your emotions. I want him to give you a clear answer as to whether he loves her or not."

No longer chipper enough to chew gum, Eve plucks it out of her mouth and eyes him coolly. "I'll take care of it." *In my own way.*

TWELVE

Standing over the sleeping figures of Sierra and Weston, Abah thinks about Altus's last words, 'Protect this girl with your life.'

What is it about her that he desires so? How could he replace me when I haven't even left?

The thought alone makes her cringe, and with clenched teeth, she pushes back the pain.

The crazy part is, I like her. . . . But why?

Pulling back the hair covering Sierra's neck, bloodlust turns from trickle to torrent. Kneeling beside the bed, the flow of blood beneath the soft, penetrable skin, causes her to breathe heavily. Running her tongue in circles over the tip of a fang, lust permeates her soul, and she becomes moist with anticipation.

I want her naked when I take her life!

Reaching down, she rubs her sex, the crotch of her jeans getting wetter with every experienced movement of her hand.

Carefully pulling the sheet down, her body writhes with approval at the sex and blood to come.

With a muffled moan, Sierra rolls over.

Startled, Abah grinds her teeth, driving the fangs back in.

Opening her eyes, she wakes to Abah's soft smile.

"Dinner will be in an hour. You should get ready and let Weston sleep." Unable to control the bloodlust, Abah heads for the door before doing something she regrets. *So close! God, why couldn't you let me have one small drop?*

Sierra leans over, lightly kissing Weston on the cheek. Climbing out of bed, she notices that the sun will soon be shining on his face, and steps lightly around the bed to close the drapes. In the light of the sun, a familiar blue garment peeks out from under the bed. Letting go of the half-closed curtain, she kneels to get a closer look. *Eve's shirt . . . you fucked her! You son of a bitch! How could you?*

"What is it?" Abah asks, noticing a change in her demeanor.

"Nothing, he just left his shirt on the floor." Walking around the bed, she stomps to the door, no longer caring if her footsteps wake him. Before leaving, she looks back at the sleeping bastard. *I can't believe you would do this to me. Especially now!*

THIRTEEN

Lounging in a bubble bath, contemplating a means of escape, Sierra pauses to admire the ornate, fully appointed bathroom that adjoins her bedroom.

I feel like I'm staying in a billion-dollar resort in the Loire Valley. Weston said that, didn't he? Seems like weeks ago. The cheating fucktard even found a girlfriend in our fucked-up, prison resort.

Tears flow at the thought of Eve with Weston, and she briskly rubs them away.

"No more," she sniffles, "I've cried enough to fill this bathtub."

I'm hungry. I suppose I should get dressed and go have dinner with the freak show. Or should I say, shit-show, that's a better description of my life.

Wearing the least revealing clothes she can find - jeans, and a white silk blouse with modest heels, she pulls her hair forward, concealing her breasts.

If I see that fuckin' bitch, I'm gonna stick a fork in her eye. The thought alone brings a smile to her face, and she holds her head up proudly, ready to tackle whatever comes next.

The grand, curving staircase stretches down into the foyer, and her heels click loudly on the marble steps.

Alright Mr. Demille, I'm ready for my close-up. Evoking a smile, she steps seductively down the stairs, the day's problems momentarily forgotten.

Opening the front door, Altus looks up at her smiling face and seductive walk. *I cannot believe she walked into my life!*

Embarrassed at being caught in *her moment*, the smile disappears, and she plods down the last few steps. *Not gonna entertain the jailer.*

"You are magnificent! Any man would be lucky to have you."

"At least there's one man in this house that thinks so." *Damn, shouldn't have said that!*

"How is Weston?" he queries, with wrinkled brow.

"Doing as well as can be expected, I suppose." *For a lying, cheating, son-of-a-bitch.*

"He will improve greatly as the days progress. Do not expect him to be his normal self for some time."

"I'm afraid he already is."

"Is everything okay?" *If he hurts her, I will kill him!*

"I'd rather not talk about it." Prying her gaze from his towering presence, she looks up at the foyer ceiling, painted with renaissance angels. *Even devils can't deny the beauty of heaven.*

"Are you hungry?"

"Famished, nothing sounds better than a big dinner and a stiff drink." *Find out more about him, maybe there's something I can use to get out of here.*

"That, I can promise you. May I escort you?"

Charmed with his manners, she takes hold of his arm. *At least he's a gentleman.* "Will Weston be joining us?" *I want to confront that S.O.B.*

"I do not believe so. It will take a great deal of rest before he regains his strength. I will have Eve take dinner to his room this evening."

"She'll be having her dinner with him?" *Isn't that wonderful? A romantic meal in bed . . .. Fucker!*

"Yes, I thought it would be best if Eve was not in your presence."

"I appreciate that, but I don't feel entirely comfortable with her getting so close to him."

"Eve is focused on someone else. We have a guest arriving that is very much her kindred spirit."

"Was that the person you spoke of yesterday?"

"Yes, her name is Xi."

"I assume she's one of your kind."

"You are correct, she is a very old and dear friend."

"Is she as old as you?"

"Not quite, but close."

"Where did you meet her?"

"Let us discuss it over dinner, I will continue where I left off with Cleopatra. I did not meet Xi for another seventy-five years, and I would rather not jump ahead since you may have questions as to how I became immortal." Looking down at her breasts swaying as they walk, he pulls her closer. *Perfection! Just a slight push of lust to bring her close.*

Pulling out her chair at the dining table, he leans forward, catching a scent of her perfumed hair as she sits. "You are so very beautiful, and the perfume is intoxicating."

"Thank you. The perfume wasn't really a conscious choice. It just smelled better than the others I had to choose from."

"Amazing, you picked my favorite scent. It is an ancient mixture I have specially created in Egypt." Pulling his chair close, he takes hold of her hand and sits.

Smiling softly, she meets his eyes. *It's nice to have someone appreciate me. Even if it is an egotistical vampire.*

"You need not be afraid of me or anyone else in this house. There is nothing I would not do to protect you. I only want your happiness, and if I am lucky enough to have you share that with me, I would be eternally grateful."

Touched by his words, and aroused by the transference of lust, she catches a soft glint in his eye, the mysterious, impregnable shroud of grey broken.

Leaning forward, he kisses her softly. *Give yourself to me.*

As if his kiss were filled with adrenaline, her heart skips, then races, as she runs her hand through his soft, wavy locks.

Give her more time, you fool! his thoughts cry out.

Abruptly, and to her dismay, he retreats, leaning back in his chair. "I am sorry. I did not mean to be so forward. It has been an eternity since I have been near a woman so lovely. I lost my head, and my manners. Please forgive me."

"I want you. There's nothing to be sorry about." *Whew, that was hot!* The sound of footsteps entering the room distracts, and she turns to find Abah entering with a bottle of wine and glasses.

"Dinner should be ready in a few minutes. I thought you two might like a drink." *He's transferring his lust. It won't be long now, and I'll be forgotten.*

"Thank you, I would," Sierra swiftly replies, embarrassed that Abah may have witnessed their private moment. Watching her fill the glasses, her arousal slowly dissipates, fading completely as Abah tops off the last glass. *Did I really just say, I want you?* Rubbing her lower lip, she watches Abah leave the room, too embarrassed to connect with his indescribably haunting eyes.

Moments of silence pass as she looks uncomfortably around the room. "When I said, 'I want you,' what I really meant was, I was okay with you kissing me. You don't have to be sorry about anything." *Why am I kissing the man that has me held captive? Is this what Abah meant by, 'Don't trust your feelings?'*

"I understand. Sometimes things come out the wrong way. I think it best we forget about the whole incident. Would you like to hear more about how I came to be?"

Wanting anything besides talking about the kiss, she readily answers, "Yes." *Watch yourself. Talk to Abah about this 'trusting your feelings' thing, before doing anything crazy like that again.*

Seeing that she is caught up in her thoughts, he picks up where he left off the previous night. "If you recall, Caesar had left for battle, and I had fallen in love with Cleopatra during his absence."

Looking up at him, she can't stop analyzing the situation. *Is he playing with my feelings now, or is it only when I feel passion? What is he after?* Perplexed and wanting answers, she demands, "What is it about me that you didn't kill me the other night? I mean, that is what you usually do. Right?"

"I have seen many women in my lifetime, but you are unique. It has been my honor to have you with me these last two days."

"Thank you," she relaxes, dropping her guard.

"They are only my true feelings. I am sorry I could not have expressed them more poetically."

"It was Shakespearean compared to what I'm used to." *I think he's said more complimentary things in one day, than Weston has in a whole year.*

Softly, he offers an apologetic smile.

"This whole thing has been more than a little strange," she confesses. "I feel terrible about breaking into your home, and this whole vampire revelation has only confused things further. I guess what I'm trying to say is, I appreciate you not calling the police . . . and not killing us." Leaning back in the chair, she exhales, "It sounds stranger coming out of my mouth than it did thinking it."

"I appreciate your honesty and I understand your confusion, but I do not want you to feel bad about trying to steal from me. Had you not broken into my home, I would never have come to meet you, and as I mentioned previously, I believe we were destined to cross paths."

"I don't know about that. We live in two vastly different worlds. This is more of a fluke than destiny."

Looking deep in her eyes, he puts his hand on hers. "I want nothing more than for you to feel safe and comfortable during your stay. Anything you need, I am most willing to accommodate."

"I appreciate that and I'm very flattered that you're attracted to me, it's not every day a girl meets a man like you.

But, truth be told, I can't make heads or tails of your kindness. To be perfectly honest, I have doubts that you will ever let me leave. And that terrifies me."

"I understand that you may be questioning my intentions, but you must believe that I will let you leave if that is what you desire. Soon, Weston will recover, and I fear we may never speak again."

"Will you really let us leave?" she questions, searching his eyes for the truth.

"I would not lie to you. When the time comes, you will be free to go."

Sensing his honesty, she lets loose of his hand and takes a drink of wine.

"Are there any other questions you would like to ask me? I am sure this must be a very confusing time."

"You have no idea," she rolls her eyes. "But, since you ask, what's it like to live forever?"

"Glorious. But for others, it can be hell. The past is an anchor that drags them to the depths of depression, and the boundless future feels more like a hopeless eternity."

"Is that Abah?"

"Possibly. Though she is not as bad as some I have seen, she most definitely carries the weight."

"What will become of her?"

"Sometimes all it takes is a small memory or feeling to change one's whole viewpoint."

"I don't mean to offend, but that sounds a little simplistic."

"She has lost the fire in her soul. I do not know why, but it has gone. At one time, all she needed was my presence to make her happy, but that is no longer the case. The weight of living brings her to the depths of despair, no matter what I do to alleviate her suffering. I hope, or should I say, I pray, that when she is on her own, a spark will ignite that fire. Who, or what that spark will be, and how long it will take to occur, is my foremost concern."

"And Eve?"

"She is the other side of the coin. Her strength and sexuality fuel her desire for life. She has been with me a fair amount of time, and for the better part of it, she has been prepared to leave. She yearns to experience everything the world has to offer."

"Inflicting herself on the world is a more appropriate term," she declares, tartly.

Sensing her anger with Eve, he explains, "Whatever you feel about Eve is irrelevant. One-thousand years from now, when you are but dust, she may still be here. Possibly tormenting your progeny."

Visibly upset, she is about to reply, before he points out, "You are not that different from her."

"I think you're wrong," she scoffs, folding her arms about her chest.

"You fight Eve, yet you are a mortal being. Many of my kind fear to even look at her for fear of raising her ire, but you, you do not back down. Your beauty and strength have me mesmerized."

"I'm not so sure it's strength, it's more along the lines of anger."

"I have been in many battles, and have come to know anger, fear, and strength intimately, and you have the strength of a warrior. Strength resides within, and those that speak the most of strength are usually the weakest. Regardless of personality traits, you, Eve, and Abah, are all the same. You can see the differences in their character, can you not?"

"Yes."

"Who do you think wanted the virus more?"

"My head tells me Eve, but I know what Abah was trying to get away from. It was Abah, wasn't it?" Anger dissipating, she rests her arms on the chair.

"Yes, she pleaded with her entire being. And when the disease did not kill her, she was ravenous."

"What do you mean by the disease did not kill her? I thought it brought eternal life?"

"Not everyone survives the sickness. Like any virus, one becomes ill, and once the virus has run its course, the body recovers. But with this virus, only a third of the people infected, survive. Those weak of character, or of little strength, do not stand a chance. But you . . . you fight me. You still seek a way out of here, I can see it in your eyes. Your strength would pull you through!"

Is he offering it to me? Could I be a vampire?

"Are you ready to eat?" Abah asks, breaking the chain of conversation as she enters with a tray holding three plates of prime rib. After setting the plates before each of them, she sits across the table from Sierra.

Watching Sierra anxiously rub her lip, he knows what occupies her mind. *She contemplates eternal life. The seed has been planted.* "To return to my story, I did not see Caesar for another year. He requested our presence in September of 46, to celebrate his Triumphs as well as the dedication of the Forum Julium, in Rome."

"Did he know of your relationship with Cleopatra by then?" *Could I kill other people, so that I could live forever . . .? No way! Not me.*

"He had no idea we had fallen in love. And with every passing day of our journey, I became more anxious. I worried that things might have changed between us, or that word had gotten back to him about Cleopatra and me."

"Did you tell him when you arrived?"

"I could not. From the moment we entered Caesar's secluded Garden residence, I reluctantly became a voyeur of the two people I loved more than life itself. I wanted to hate him for causing our separation, but when I saw his smiling face, my hate turned to guilt. When he embraced me, and spoke the words, 'I knew I could count on you,' tears welled in my eyes, and he laughed joyously as he pulled from my embrace to see them running down my face."

"You felt that guilty?"

"It was everything. The anxiety that had built up prior to

seeing him, my anger, my love for Cleopatra . . . all of it. But with one hug, he put me at ease. When he called out to bring wine for, 'The mother of his son, and the son of Fortuna,' I knew nothing had changed between us. We had a bond that was stronger than any woman's love could break."

"Did you still feel like a voyeur?"

"Yes, but it was not as bad as I had feared. Caesar had to attend the festivities with his wife, Calpurnia, whereas I only had to march with the soldiers in the processions celebrating victory over Gaul and Egypt. And whatever free time Cleopatra had, which was a great deal, we found a way to be together."

"What about the times when they were together, and you had no commitments?"

"I wandered the city, enjoying the festivities. There were gladiatorial games, theatrical performances, bloody reenactments of battles, and even an artificial lake on the Campus Martius, where two fleets met in battle to show citizens how war is waged upon the sea. So many people attended from all parts of the empire, the streets and squares were burgeoning with tents. Never before, or since, have I seen such a celebration. Twenty-two-thousand tables were set up for feasting, but not even that could seat more than a fraction of the people."

Pausing briefly, he reminisces on past days.

Noticing him lost in thought, she asks, "What do you miss the most?"

"The people," he declares. "Not only those close to me, but all of them. There was a spirit to the times not found today. We were simple people that did not require veils to hide our desires and sexuality, as modern man does. Perhaps it was because we were surrounded by death and knew that every moment meant something, or maybe we were anticipating the arrival of a messiah."

"Wasn't the messiah a Jewish prophecy?"

"Many religions believed a messiah was at hand. It was to be the time of milk and honey. Crops would no longer need tending, fruit would endlessly bear from the trees, and animals would give themselves peacefully over to slaughter. And for the Jews, the messiah would re-establish worship at the temple, found a government in Israel that would be the center of all world government and proclaim Jewish law as the law of the land. It depended on your religion, or what you desired that dictated your choice of messiah."

"What was it that you wanted?"

"No god or messiah could have given me what I desired. I wanted each day to offer fulfillment and new opportunity. I wanted Cleopatra at my side for eternity, and to rule the world as a Triumvirate. Caesar, Cleopatra and me . . ." His voice suddenly goes from exuberance to despair. "But those were the foolish wishes of a young man, unable to fathom the true reality and hardships of life."

"I thought you enjoyed immortal life?"

"I do, for opportunities continually arise. It may take decades or even centuries, but the flame of passion always reignites. With eternal youth and limitless funds at my disposal, I have found that in time I have always been given what I need to thrive."

Abah glares at him suspiciously. *Is Sierra what you need now?*

"What makes you thrive?" Sierra inquires.

"New beginnings. And this time, I believe my deepest wishes shall be fulfilled," he reveals, gazing upon her with heartfelt desire.

Uncomfortable that Abah may have picked up on his advances, Sierra looks away, taking a sip of wine. "What did you do after the festival ended? Didn't Caesar wonder why you weren't around?" *He comes on so strong. It's kinda flattering.*

"He had assigned me the duty of having a statue of Cleopatra carved in the personification of Isis so that it could be installed in the temple Venus Genetrix, honoring her for the birth of their son, and what other free time I possessed, I spent touring the city and visiting the public baths. But I was soon to have Cleopatra to myself, for weeks after the festival ended, he was called away by an uprising of Pompey's old forces in Hispania."

"And with him leaving Rome, you were free to do as you wished with Cleopatra."

"Yes, but I also found myself aching to return to battle. I missed the intensity of the fight, and more so, I missed him. After reuniting, I could not imagine having to say goodbye again so quickly, and to make matters worse, I felt as if he recognized my intentional absence from his presence. It was the timeless paradox, unable to be with or without someone. While he prepared for his departure, I tried to spend every waking moment with him, regardless of how my feelings for Cleopatra clouded the issue. I begged him to take me along. I even tried to convince him that I could rally some of my old tribesmen to aid in his cause."

"Do you really think they would have followed you? The way you spoke of them, it didn't sound like they would have done anything for you."

"Deep down, I knew that just as well as he did, but I was desperate. Looking for any means possible by which he would take me along."

"But he didn't, did he?"

"Holding my head in his hands, he confided, 'Your words tell me you want to fight, but your heart holds you to Cleopatra, and that is where you will stay. You are my closest confidant, and the only one I trust with my son's life. I still require your devotion, so it is with them you will stay.'"

"How did he find out about you and Cleopatra?"

"I suppose I made it evident with my absence, or perhaps I acted suspiciously when the three of us were together. Regardless of the method by which he discovered, he in fact, did not mind. So much so, he encouraged our love by telling me to remain with her."

"Do you think he did it out of protection for his son?"

"Possibly. As I mentioned, he saw all outcomes to every situation."

"Did you stay in Rome and wait for him?"

"No, the three of us departed immediately for Alexandria. The atmosphere in Rome was hostile to her and the boy, so I thought it best we retreat to safer environs. I had no troops at my disposal, and we were vulnerable to all types of treachery, not the least of which might come from Calpurnia."

"It must have been nice not having to hide your love." Taking a glance at Abah, she finds her beaming at Altus. *She cares for him so deeply. No wonder she doesn't want to leave.*

"It was bliss. Much like the previous year, I spent my free time studying in the library. Euclid to learn geometry, Hipparchos for astronomy and trigonometry, and Archimedes' works in hydrostatics and astronomy. The more I learned, the more I realized how little I knew. I dove into religion, studying the history of man and how his need was so great for a god, he came to create one. It was a wondrous year of intellectual growth, and I believed it would perpetuate until we grew old and satisfied with our accomplishments. That year passed so quickly, had I known what the next year had in store, I would have enjoyed my days at a more leisurely pace."

His tone suddenly grim, he mutters, "But good times never pass slowly, they race past us, crashing into the unforgiving future. Never fully appreciated until they have slipped from our grasp for eternity."

"Ah, yes. The Ides of March," Abah interjects, hoping to garner attention from Altus.

"Yes," he confirms, with a nod to Abah. "But something was lost before then. When we returned to Rome in 45 BC, Caesar had become absolute ruler of the world. It was no longer a matter of conquering foes on the battlefield, but a matter of healing Rome's many ills. Which proved to be a monumental task hindered greatly by the hatred he endured from the aristocracy. Though all were subservient to him, they would not be convinced of his social reforms and political agenda. They fought him on even the most moderate of improvements, making the most minute of tasks monumental.

"One evening as we walked among the gardens of his villa, he remarked, 'I am undoubtedly the most hated man in Rome.' I tried to explain away the pettiness of the populace, and how the Senate would in time follow his lead, but he bitterly remarked, 'Whatever I do, they do not care for me. I may as well do as I see fit.'"

"I read that he abused his power, was that true?" Sierra asks.

"The people themselves once sent a petition to him that read, 'By the Gods, look after the Republic and walk straight through all the difficulties, as is your wont.' And that is exactly what he did.

"As December closed and the month of Janus began, I could see that stress was wearing him down. When it came to physical activity, his energy was boundless, but when confined to endless mental activity and psychic struggle, he became tired and morose. At dinner one evening, he uttered, 'I have lived long enough for both nature and fame.' Hearing this, I pushed him to get out of Rome. I reminded him of the axle breaking on the triumphal chariot in front of the Temple of Fortuna during his festival, and how it was surely an ominous sign."

"Where could he possibly go? Rome was the seat of world government, and he was its leader."

"To the battlefield, it was his only true home. The Parthians had killed Crassus and his legions almost a decade earlier, so it would have been a noble fight to avenge the Battle of Carrhae."

"Did he take your advice?"

"He was already considering it himself, which to me, meant he would go. I begged him to include me among his forces, to which he replied, 'Though Fortuna may be turning her back on me, I need you to look after Caesarion. If I were to perish in battle, there would be no one to protect him, save Cleopatra, and she would surely be slaughtered as well. It is for this very reason I have named my nephew, Gaius Octavius, as my adopted son. He is older and of pure Roman blood so he may form alliances among the optimates and maintain the dictatorship until Caesarion comes of age. Then, when the time is right, you must fulfill Caesarion's birthright as ruler of the world, for his future is brighter than the Star of Isis.' I asked if Octavius could be trusted to relinquish his authority to the boy, and he said that it had been agreed upon prior to his will being written."

"That didn't account for much, did it?"

"It did not, Octavius visited Cleopatra and me to show good faith towards Caesar's wishes, but in the end, it was not to be. Octavius had us so focused on Antony's attempt to crown Caesar king, along with his connection to a foiled murder attempt on Caesar, we believed him to be faithful to our cause."

"Did Antony really try to murder Caesar, and why was it so bad that he tried to crown him king?"

"There was an attempt on his life, and the assassin was captured, but there was never any concrete evidence linking Antony to the assassin. But being crowned king, that would have surely brought about Caesar's death. Rome was a republic at the time, not the empire it would become under Augustus, it would be as if someone tried to make the president of the United States a king."

"Do you think he was involved in the assassination attempt?"

"At a minimum, he was aware of the plot and told no one. That alone made him guilty. No one is to be trusted when so much power is at stake. That was a lesson I had yet to learn. Since my allegiance to Caesar was noble, I believed everyone else's to be as well. Obviously, I was wrong.

"With the approach of the Roman new year, in Mars, or March as it is called now, plans were laid for the Parthian campaign, and Caesar's spirits were higher with every day he came closer to departing. The Senate was showering him with honors, and we came to believe that they were gradually accepting him as their undisputed leader. Things seemed to be going well, so much so, that after Cleopatra's statue was placed in the temple Venus Genetrix, he had me procure the most skilled artisan in Rome to create a jewelry set with the Egyptian serpent goddess, Uraeus, and the richest of peridots to match Cleopatra's eyes."

"The jewelry set! Did he see it before he died?"

"Yes, they were completed on the fifth day of March, 44 BC, and I took them to him that very day. He commented that the peridots shined as if they were taken from the glint of her eye. He was happier than I had seen him in years, and everything seemed to be coming together. He would be leaving in a matter of weeks, and a party for Cleopatra was to occur the night before his departure, at which she would be presented with the jewelry. His spirits were so high, he brazenly told me, 'No one would dare kill me now, my death would be the death of the Republic.' So certain that luck was on his side, he dismissed his bodyguards, proclaiming, 'I am superior even to death.'"

"Pride always comes before the fall," Abah declares, soberly.

"And there was no one prouder. Upon reaching the steps of the Senate, Artemidorus of Cnidus handed him a scroll warning of the assassination plot. Still, Caesar ignored him, as he pleaded, 'Caesar, you must read it, alone and quickly. It contains important matters of special concern to you!'

"He even scoffed at the augur Spurinna who had prophesied that misfortune would befall him on the ides of March. At the entrance to the Curia of Pompey, he shouted to Spurinna, 'The ides of March have come, and still Fortuna smiles upon me.'

"To which Spurinna replied, 'They have come, but they are not yet over.'

"And with those words ringing in his ears, he entered the Senate, unwilling to see that the cowardly acts of men can far outweigh the fickle hand of fortune. No sooner had he entered, than the assassins attacked. With twenty-three dagger-blows, the Republic, my mentor, and dream, lay dying on the Senate floor."

FOURTEEN

"Do you like it when I feed you?" Eve smiles.

"Sure, why not," Weston shrugs, laying back in bed.

"Would you like to see my tits?" she coos, nudging closer.

"Maybe later, right now I'm only interested in seeing Sierra," he bluffs, striving to appear disinterested.

"That doesn't sound fun at all. Don't you like me anymore?"

"Sure, I guess. I'd just rather see Sierra."

"I'm afraid that's not possible. She went out to dinner with Altus and Abah."

"What are you talking about? She left the house!"

"It's true, baby. You and I have the whole house to ourselves. If you wanted to, you could do me on the kitchen table. Would you like that?" she tempts, firmly squeezing her tits.

"Meh, you were just another one-night stand. Now that I've had you, I've lost interest," he nervously quips. Hoping beyond hope, she won't lose her mind.

Cheerfully, she giggles, "You're not playing hard to get, are you? Because I love a challenge! Would you like to play a little game?"

"What do you mean?"

"Just a quick game. You're not scared of little old me, are you?" she taunts, smiling seductively as she runs her hand over his naked chest.

"I think you know the answer to that. I wouldn't be in this bed if it weren't for you."

"I suppose you have a point; I can be a little bitchy at times. But that's just something you're going to have to deal with if you want to be friends."

"I never said I wanted to be friends." Raising his voice, he hopes to end the game before it begins.

"Ouch, I was a one-night stand?" Putting a hand to her mouth, she feigns surprise. "And I thought you were a nice boy. I should have listened to my mother about boys like you."

Running her long fingernails delicately down his lean stomach, she teases the stream of hair that leads to his manhood.

"Look . . . can we just get to the point. I'm tired," he pleads.

"Oh, but I am getting to the point. Just this one last game, and I'll never ask you to do another thing. Is that fair?"

"Whatever . . . just get on with it." Eyes rolling in frustration, he looks away.

"Here's how it goes. I'm going to show you everything you've ever wanted, and if you can keep from fucking me, I'll let you spend the night with Sierra. If not, you spend the night with me."

Removing her halter top, she pinches her hard nipples, causing him to unconsciously lick his lips.

"You're not *that* much prettier than Sierra, so this won't be as easy as you think."

"Hmm, you think so?" Standing up, she grinds her hips provocatively. "I know one thing for sure, I'm a lot more fun than her." Running her hands through her hair, she closes her eyes, moaning, as if nearing climax. "These jeans are so tight. Do you mind if I take them off?"

Undoing the buttons one by one, she turns her back to him and seductively gyrates her hips to push down the skin-tight denim.

"Do whatever you like," he snorts, pretending not to notice her bending over. *Holy shit, she's not wearing panties!*

"Mmm, that feels so much better." Kicking the jeans from around her ankles, she sticks her butt out and parts her legs. "I'm getting moist just thinking about how hard you get. Do you see me dripping, baby?"

Her grinding hips make him swollen and firm, yet he's determined not to be caught checking her out. *If she doesn't see me looking, she'll think I'm not interested and give up. Oh my God . . . what a fuckin' body!*

Putting Vegas strippers to shame, every sway of her hips puts him further into a trance, and with a quick turn of her head, his gaping mouth gives her the answer she craves.

Damn, she saw me looking!

His rod forms a hefty tent in the sheets, bringing a confident smile to her face as she returns to the bedside.

"Ooh, that's a good boy. So big and hard for mommy." Roughly running her fingernails down his torso, she catches the sheet, just above his sex, and throws it to his feet. "Mmm, that does look yummy. I bet you make all the girls cum."

Throbbing with lust, his rod ticks with every beat of his heart.

"You want it, don't you, baby," he pants.

"Mmhmm, you were made for me. Such a pretty boy, with such a meaty cock. Can I stroke it for you?"

"Fuck yeah . . . stroke it good and hard!" *Forget Sierra, I'm gonna make this bitch cum.*

FIFTEEN

The full moon brightens the night sky when Sierra bids good night to Altus. Though not having drunk as much as the previous evening, Abah escorts her in the event she requires a helping hand.

"Would you mind answering a question?" Sierra asks.

"No, go ahead."

"Does Altus always surround himself with beautiful women?"

"I suppose so, but no one meant as much as Cleopatra. That's why, when he told me that you touched her jewelry, I was shocked, to say the very least."

"It's because I studied art in college," she dismisses.

With probing eyes, Abah examines her expression. *Is it that simple? Am I reading more into this than I should be?*

Entering the room, she guides her to the bed, and they sit, bodies touching.

"You might be interested to know that Eve and I have only been allowed to wear them once or twice in the entire time we've known him. And it took years before that happened." Wrinkling her brow, she bites her lip before apprehensively admitting, "It makes me a little jealous. I know it's only a matter of time before he asks you to join him in eternal life."

Confirming prior suspicions, she glares absently at the wall, deep in thought. *Would he really offer me eternal life? Could I survive the disease? What if I turn him down, will he still let me go?*

Consumed by the throbbing vein of Sierra's wrist, Abah closes her eyes and breathes deeply, sucked in by the deafening sound of Sierra's pumping heart. *Oh, so young, oh, so tight. Just one kiss, to whet my appetite.*

Gently pushing Sierra's hair back from her face, Abah kisses her virgin neck, cheek, then mouth, where lips meet with unabated passion.

Every kiss tugs Sierra's heart in a new direction, and when tongues meet, bloodlust brings out Abah's fangs, causing her to break the kiss and prepare for the assault.

Shocked by the deadly teeth, Sierra jerks back, falling into the headboard.

"Relax, it'll feel good. I promise," Abah assures, pushing so much lust, Sierra can't help but return to her side.

Pulling her own hair back, she offers up the virgin side of her neck, breathing heavily in anticipation of death's kiss.

Innocent flesh succumbing to desire, sends shivers through Abah as she opens wide, gently running her fangs across the velvety, protective layer encasing the sweet nectar. *God, yes! Let me finish what I started.*

No sooner does the point of one fang break skin, than Altus's words fill her head. *Protect this girl with your life!*

Reluctantly coming back to reason, Abah turns away, clenching her teeth. *I can't take it anymore. If I don't replenish soon, I'll kill her!*

Longing for her touch, Sierra runs her fingers through the long curls of hair cascading down Abah's back. With transference stopped, the lust fades fast, and she begins to question her actions. *She almost killed me . . .. And I wanted her to do it!*

Realizing she's gone too far, Abah turns back and transfers as much serenity as possible, staving off the inevitable panic. "I'm sorry! I lost my head!"

Panting, Sierra pulls her hair forward, covering her neck. "That was what you meant by not trusting my emotions, wasn't it?"

Ashamed for not controlling herself, she confesses, "Yes . . . but don't be afraid. I would never hurt you, nor would Altus. Sometimes our lust for blood can momentarily overpower our judgment." Shaking her head, to clear her thoughts, she explains, "This probably won't make much sense, but just thinking about drinking blood is like the physical act of making love. It's not just lust, there's an actual physio-emotional response that takes place in our bodies. It's a craving and need that's intertwined with lust and love."

Calming down, Sierra forgets her well-warranted fear. "Like passion during sex?"

"Infinitely better. There's nothing humans could ever experience that would bring one-tenth of the emotional and physical gratification we receive from replenishing."

The passion I feel when I'm around them is so intense, it would be amazing to feel that all the time!

Seeing that she is consumed by the prospect of a new emotion in a drab world, Abah probes, "It's tempting, isn't it?"

"It is, but I could never kill anyone. I know that for a fact!"

"I never thought I could kill anyone either, but it's not the same once the disease takes you. It's like not eating for a long period, and your body demands nourishment. You don't think about where the food came from, or who prepared it, you simply dive in, fulfilling the body's needs. The rush is so profound, you don't think about the person any more than you do about the cow that gave its life for the steak."

"Are you saying your viewpoint on killing changes after you take the disease?" *Maybe I could do it. Eternally young and ridiculously rich. Who wouldn't jump at the chance?*

Sighing, Abah wants to tell her everything will be fine, but feels she should know the absolute truth. "The killing bothers some of us more than others. As the blood dissipates in our bodies, we become more prone to depression and doubt, followed by guilt. Unfortunately, this happens during the same period our bodies need blood the most. For the most compassionate of our kind, it becomes a war with oneself every time the body needs replenishment. The hunger is overpowering, so it usually wins out, but after many years of giving into the hunger, some view it as an addiction and would rather end their life than take another's."

"Where do you stand?"

"I haven't replenished for nearly a month, so I'm feeling exceptionally low. Not to mention, when I get to this point, I consider the religious implications of killing."

"That's why I could never kill anyone. If the hunger pushed me to it, I could go through with it once, but after that, my religious guilt would prevent me from ever doing it again."

"Don't be so sure of that. After you feed for the first time, you'd be amazed at the confidence and strength that fills your soul."

"Is it really that great?" she queries, hoping to be convinced of how much better it is than normal life.

"You couldn't possibly fathom the exhilaration."

"What's it like to be invincible?" *I'd love to be strong and fearless!*

Noticing that she is becoming too taken with the positive attributes, she attempts to keep her grounded. "In the beginning, it was glorious, but to tell you the truth, it can be mundane at times. There is nothing that can stand in my way, except other vampires, of course, which means there are not many challenges to rise above."

"But Eve and Altus seem to love it."

"They do, and so did I, at one time. I still recall begging Altus for his blood. I wouldn't take no for an answer."

"How did it happen?"

"On a dark, moonless night, he came to my cabin and put his hand over my mouth, rousing me from my sleep. He led me to the plantation dock house where the cotton bales were loaded on barges, and there, in the dark of night, revealed his secret to me. He had always been gentle with me, so when he showed me what he was, I was dumfounded."

“Did he cut himself?”

“Yes, as well as baring his fangs. Which scared the hell out of me! The knife in the arm freaked me out, but the fangs . . .? Whew, if the village voodoo priestess had seen that, her head would have spun in circles.”

Giggling at her depiction, she asks, “What did you say?”

“What could I say? He offered so much more than the freedom I craved. He offered me an eternity of domination over the types of fools that spat on me daily. Even more to the point, he offered himself. I loved him more than I ever dreamt possible of any man, and the idea of being with him forever was far sweeter than any atrocity this world could ever shower on me.” Hanging her head, she soberly imparts, “So, I begged him for the disease. . ..” Suddenly quiet, she considers her future. *Am I about to lose the only man I’ve ever loved? I don’t care what Altus does to me. I’m not going to be replaced so easily!*

Looking at the sorrow on her face, Sierra asks, “You regret it now, don’t you?”

Carefully crafting her words, she artfully replies, “I do have regrets, but given my circumstances, I would undoubtedly do the same, over and over again. You have no idea the hell and humiliation I lived with during that time. Besides, no one in my situation could have turned from that devil’s kiss. The spell he put over me was unbreakable, and it was all hidden behind that alluring demeanor. When you look at him, you know deep in your soul, that anyone or anything that beautiful could never harbor evil. But your wrong, dead wrong. People always think of the devil as an unbearably ugly creature, but they’re amiss. The devil appears beautiful and harmless, and that is how he draws you in. You don’t feel for a moment he could, or would betray you, but it’s with purpose he gives you that false sense of security. For when he desires your destruction, it’s with ease and casual abandon that he condemns your soul.”

“Are you trying to scare me?” she jitters, shifting about uneasily. *Forget about the whole thing. Don’t make a deal with the devil!*

"I only want you to realize it's not all happiness and riches. There's a reason most vampires don't live past one-hundred eternal years. Immortality sounds wonderful at first. To be eternally young, strong, beautiful, powerful, and wealthy, is every human's wish. But it doesn't take long before the wish becomes a curse. Killing other people is not something we all adjust to readily. For Altus and the other ancestors, it was a fact of their times that killing was not only accepted, but approved of. But for those of us raised in a Christian world, taught that killing is abhorrently wrong, it can be an unbearably heavy weight to bear. At times I feel as if I have ingested the soul of every person I ever killed, and in turn, they are tearing at mine, ripping it to shreds as penance."

Ew, that sounds horrible. "Why do you think Eve has taken to it so well?"

"It's possible that through her own feelings of superiority, she justifies killing those she deems less worthy of life than herself."

"Have you ever spoken to her or Altus about it?"

"Oh yes, this is an openly discussed topic among vampires. There is a survival rate that gets slimmer with every passing year."

"How so?"

"Only about twenty percent live past one-hundred eternal years, and of those that do, they tend to remain strong until about one-hundred-and-fifty to two-hundred years of age. But after that, there's a steep drop-off for these centenarians, where only ten percent will make it to three-hundred."

"You only have a two percent chance of living past two-hundred?"

"No, I have a ten percent chance of surviving. You, if you decided to take the disease, would have a two percent chance of making it past two-hundred."

"My God, those are terrible odds."

"And it only gets worse. The odds of making it to five-hundred are similar to winning the lottery."

Sierra hangs her head, quietly murmuring, "It's all a waste of time then, isn't it?" *I want nothing to do with the disease!*

"I've given you too much to think about, haven't I?"

"I guess I only considered the positive attributes. I know you've mentioned that you've been having a hard time, but I suppose I'm optimistic when it comes to my perception of how I might fare."

Afraid she may have gone too far and incur more of Altus's wrath than she bargained for, Abah accentuates the positive. "It's possible you may outlive me. Statistics don't mean a thing. Much like winning the lottery, the odds are infinitesimally against you, but someone seems to win every couple of weeks. Plus, Altus is much more taken with you than he was with either Eve or me. If I had his love and support, I wouldn't be having these doubts."

"Regardless of his feelings for me, I'd rather not gamble with my soul."

"That's *if* there is a God. What if there isn't? What if, when you die, your soul is no more real than Zeus? Maybe betting on eternal life with Altus, who you know to be immortal, is a statistically safer bet than rolling the dice on an unverifiable God, in an imaginative heaven. Who, even if he does happen to exist, will quite likely condemn you to hell because you strayed from his narrow path."

Unsure of how to answer, she rubs her lip, deep in thought.

"I think part of the reason the ancestors have lived so long is because they're completely certain that there is no God. They believed in mythical gods when they were human, and they were also there at the birth of Christianity, so they know for a fact that religion is man-made."

"Even Judaism?"

"It was founded upon the most ancient of all religions, Zoroastrianism, or Parseeism, as it's known today. Zoroaster, the focal point of the religion, was borrowed and given the name Abraham by the Jews, thereby founding Judaism. The religion of the Parsis was dated as far back as seven-thousand

BC by Aristotle and Eudoxus, and it still has almost one-hundred-thousand followers today."

"Interesting, I've never even heard of that religion."

"Well, that's where it all started. But more to the point of all religions, it's the mystery that makes them viable. This goes along with what you said about the nature of optimism. Deep inside, we all feel that somehow or someway, everything will work out for the best, and that's exactly the premise of heaven. It's dangled before the masses like a carrot, saying all will be justified in the end if they devoutly toe the line."

"It's funny, I've never considered myself to be very religious, but when it comes to doing something truly evil, I find myself looking to heaven for guidance."

"Can you really consider us evil? After all, isn't it written in the bible that all sins are equal?"

"That's true, but still." *Killing just seems so much worse.*

"Isn't it also true that by sleeping with Weston out of wedlock, and stealing from people like Altus, you're in the same boat we are?"

"I know that's what the Bible reads, but don't you think murder is the worst of all sins?" *Am I already condemned for stealing? No matter how I justify it as helping my father?*

"Now you're twisting the words of God to justify your so-called lesser sins. Can't you see, we're all victims to it. It's no more than organized fear. Have you ever noticed that preachers are always condemning those that don't follow their interpretation of what's *right*? It's never the forgiveness of Jesus they preach about, it's the fire and brimstone of hell. Think about it. Are you more concerned with burning in hell or being close to God in the afterlife?"

"I've never thought about it like that. If there were no hell, I probably wouldn't even care if I were distant from God in the afterlife, or if there were no afterlife at all."

"Fear. Be it God or government, it's all the same. They only mean to mold you into what best serves their needs."

Considering her viewpoint, Sierra vacantly turns away. *Is*

it possible that my fear of hell is the only thing that makes me religious?

"I brought something earlier when you were speaking with Altus. He gave it to me years ago when I was wrestling with religion, and he wanted me to show it to you." She walks to the nightstand on the far side of the bed and brings back a thick binder. Holding it before her with outstretched hand, she says, "It's a list of inconsistencies in the Bible. They show that man was the creator of the scriptures, not God."

Cautiously taking it from her, Sierra gazes warily at the cover. *Is it right to even read this? Should anyone doubt the word of God?*

"It's not going to bite you," Abah taunts.

"It's-" Unable to justify her fear, there are no words.

"They're only passages taken from the Bible. There's no more sin in reading this than there is in reading the Bible."

"I suppose that's true." Opening the cover, she is astounded at the hefty stack of pages. "There's so much!"

"Yes, there are many fallacies. Just read, and you will see."

Apprehensively, she runs a finger down the page, as if touch alone will bring eternal damnation.

GENESIS 1:3-5 On the first day, God created light, then separated light and darkness.

GENESIS 1:14-19 The sun, which separates night and day, wasn't created until the fourth day.

GENESIS 1:11-12, 26-27 Trees were created before man was created. GENESIS 2:4-9 Man was created before trees were created.

GENESIS 1:26-27 Man and woman were created at the same time. GENESIS 2:21-22 Man was created first, woman at a later time.

GENESIS 4:4-5 God prefers Abel's offering and has no regard for Cain's.
ROMANS 2:11 God shows no partiality. He treats all the same.

GENESIS 6:4 There were Giants before the Flood. GENESIS 7:21 All creatures other than Noah and his clan were annihilated by the Flood. NUMBERS 13:33 There were Giants after the Flood.

GENESIS 10:5, 20, 31 There were many languages before the Tower of Babel.
GENESIS 11:1 There was only one language before the Tower of Babel.

GENESIS 16:15, 21:1-3 Abraham had two sons, Ishmael and Isaac. HEBREWS11:17 Abraham had only one son.

GENESIS 17:8 God promises Abraham the land of Canaan as an everlasting possession. GENESIS 25:8, ACTS 7:2-5 Abraham died with the promise unfulfilled.

DEUTERONOMY 23:1 A castrate may not enter the assembly of the Lord. ISAIAH 56:3-5 I will give castrates, in My house and within My walls, a memorial and a name better than that of sons and daughters.

MATTHEW 1:17 There were twenty-eight generations from David to Jesus.
LUKE 3:23-38 There were forty-three generations from David to Jesus.

DEUTERONOMY 24:1-5 A man can divorce his wife if he finds indecency in her, and both he and his wife can remarry. MARK 10:11-12 Divorce is wrong, and to remarry is to commit adultery.

EXODUS 12:13 The Israelites have to mark their houses with blood in order for God to see which houses they occupy and pass over them. PROVERBS 15:3, JERE-MIAH 16:17, HEBREWS 4:13 God is everywhere. He sees everything. Nothing is hidden from God.

EXODUS 20:14 God prohibits adultery. HOSEA 1:2 God instructs Hosea to take a wife of harlotry.

NUMBERS 15:24-28 Sacrifices in some instances, can take away sin. HEBREWS 10:11 Sacrifices can never take away sin.

"I can't read anymore!" she exclaims. "Is it really just a collection of fabrications?"

"If it weren't for Constantine having a dream of the Christian symbol Labarum and adopting it before he defeated Maxentius at the Battle of the Milvian Bridge, there wouldn't even be a Bible. Just a collection of short stories from the different tribes of Jews and Gentiles." Letting out a sigh, Abah bites her lip, wishing she were as confident as she purports to be. "The truth is, there's no definitive answer. I've spoken with Khaba about it too. I thought that after five-thousand years, he would be the one to talk to, but all he can say, is that it's fictitious. He said there never was an Exodus from the land of Egypt, nor any man by the name of Moses in the Egyptian palace. When I ask him for proof, he chides, 'Show me of God's benevolence among the sick and poor, for it is those he claims are his children.'"

Taking in the blank look on Sierra's face, she jokes, "That's the same look I gave him."

Sierra chuckles in amusement, then becomes serious. "Is it only your fear of hell that keeps you alive?"

Giving it serious thought, she frames her words carefully. "Yes, the greater part of my decision is based upon the existence of God. For if there truly is a hell, it makes my current unhappiness look like heaven in comparison."

"Then, you're ruled by fear as well, not from government or man, but God."

"Yes, the unknown is what makes fear such a potent weapon."

"And vampires fear God?"

"It is our only fear. If we could rely on my observations, it seems that women fear God more than men. The men become so inebriated with their own strength, they feel they are gods, whereas women, except for Eve and Xi, remain caring and thoughtful as has always been our tendencies. I think it has something to do with men trying the shape the world to their will, whereas women adapt, taking a more metaphysical, or spiritual view toward life and what it has to offer."

"You think there's a correlation?"

"All I know is, I've had more conversations about heaven and hell with women, than I have men. Yet, neither sex fares better in the survival rate. I think women are just more open about the fear. Men bury it, until it consumes them."

"I suppose every man has a God complex." *Especially that bastard, Weston.*

"You're probably right, and becoming a vampire throws fuel on that fire," she chortles.

Laughing, Sierra confides, "You're easier to talk to than the others. I like that about you."

"I think it's because we're similar. I'd like to think there's some quality in me that Altus sees in you."

"Do you feel as if he's abandoning you?"

"Yes and no. He's done so much for me, I can't be angry, but I also can't help but feel terribly alone when I consider my life without him."

"You can visit. Can't you?"

"Yes, but it's not the same. You must understand, from the moment I stepped into his carriage and rode off that plantation, he's been my entire existence. I don't think he realizes how deeply I love him. If he knew, he could never let me go so easily."

"That's why it bothered you when he let me touch the jewelry."

"Yes," she replies, shamefully. "Though it was not you that made me feel that way, it was him. I felt as if I were no more than another girl in his endless parade of women."

"I'm sure he still loves you as much as ever," she petitions, nobly.

"That's nice of you to say, but I know it's not true."

"What was it like when you first took the disease?" Taking hold of her hand, she looks softly into her eyes.

"It was heaven," Abah glows. "We lived in Charleston, in the largest home overlooking White Point Gardens. It was such a scandal," she radiates, "and we loved every minute of it! The most prosperous man in town, courting a slave girl. You should have seen the women gawk!"

"I'm surprised Southern society didn't shut you out."

"Some tried, but most everyone was beholden to Altus in one way or another. Regardless of what the women thought, their husbands forced them to be polite. I was the belle of the ball in those days. It's hard to believe it was even the same South I'd lived in as a slave."

"It sounds wonderful."

"It was, up until the war started. I still remember the exact moment it began. We watched with bated breath, hoping the Union's Major Anderson would surrender Fort Sumter, but at 4:30 in the morning, we heard the explosion that affirmed our worst fears."

"I would have thought you wanted the war, having been a slave."

"The end of slavery, yes. War, no. I hoped against hope that with the election of Lincoln, a compromise could be reached that would appease both sides. But, looking back, I was blinded by false hope. Southerners would never have agreed to the abolition of slavery, and Lincoln would never have settled for anything less. Altus knew the South didn't have the manpower or the manufacturing to beat the North, so we departed for New York City. What everyone thought would be a ninety-day war, slowly escalated into a four-year hell. Altus was right about that too; he said the tenacity of the Southern people would prolong the war until the North's numerical and industrial superiority would eventually bring the South to ruins. That's the thing about him, he's always right. I hate him for it, but I can't deny that he knows what's best for all of us. Looking back, that explosion on the morning of April 12th could easily have signaled the change in our relationship too. That's not to say times were bad once we arrived here, just, different. The honeymoon wasn't over per se, he just spent a great deal more of his time amassing land and investing in businesses, instead of focusing on me."

"I'm surprised he cares so much about money when he's so wealthy."

"That's easy to say when you only have another fifty years to live. He may live for hundreds-of-thousands of years. How much money will it require to do that?"

"I never thought about it like that." *Could he still be here in ten-thousand years? Could I still be here!*

"And what if the global economy collapses, inflation running rampant? Currency as useless as toilet paper, much like Germany after World War One. It's because of that, I never felt slighted when he spent time on business. But Eve . . . that was an entirely different matter. It was because of the time he spent investing, that I traveled to Tibet in the first place, and on my return, found her here. It was a complete betrayal!"

So that's why they're frigid around each other! "Did he ignore you after she arrived?"

"No, and it wasn't the sex either. For us, sex and replenishing go hand-in-hand. It was the act of turning her into a vampire that hurt me so deeply. I thought it was a precious gift he had given me, not a cheap trick to be handed out to any common whore."

"I understand your feelings." *It's no picnic with Weston, either.*

"I felt as if I were back on the plantation again. Overlooked and underappreciated. Eventually though, I found that wasn't the case with Altus, it was Eve making me feel that way. After I revealed my feelings to him, he explained the reason for her being here."

"What did he say?"

"He expressed his undying love and told me why he created Eve. It wasn't love, or lust, for that matter, he was simply making an eternal living portrait of the Marquis de Sade's long-dead ancestor."

"The painting in the study!"

"Yes."

"Did that make you feel any better?"

"To an extent. still couldn't believe he would be so fickle with such a precious gift."

"You're confusing me. You call it a curse one minute, then a precious gift the next. How am I to decide if you can't?" *Is she trying to dissuade me from taking it? She already said she was jealous of Altus and me. Does she think I'm the next Eve?*

"It's a lot like life, I suppose. You go through bad times, then suddenly, something turns your whole perspective around. I guess what I'm trying to say is, being a vampire is like anything else, it's what you make of it. But the problem we face, is an eternity to dwell on mistakes and bad judgement, whereas human's problems are finite."

Shifting her gaze, Sierra squints, justifying her desire. *Why shouldn't I take it? That list in the binder shows inconsistencies that could only result from people creating stories. Not one God.*

"I've given you too much to think about, haven't I?" Getting up, Abah walks to the door. "I'll let you sleep, it's late."

Feeling they've made a connection, Sierra quietly pleads, "Would you mind if I visited Weston before I go to bed? I promise not to try anything, and I'll come right back after I check on him." *Maybe I'm wrong about Weston and Eve. She's such a bitch, maybe she left her top there knowing I would see it, and he never touched her.*

Feeling a bond after sharing so much, she acquiesces, "Yes, just come right back. You know better than to try and escape, right? Altus would never forgive you . . . or me!"

"I know," she smiles, brightly. "I'll come right back."

* * *

Turning the corner to Weston's room, Sierra finds the door ajar. Pushing it open, Weston is nowhere to be found. Looking in the bathroom, she finds it empty as well.

Oh my, God! Did he fall off the far side of the bed?

Running around the bed, she finds a woman's halter top and jeans. *This is what Eve was wearing when she bumped into me earlier!*

Plopping onto the edge of the bed, tears rain down. "Never again!" Desperately crying, a voice pops in her head. *You always knew! You just didn't want to see it.*

The flood of flirting, late-night returns, and perfume-scented clothing invades her thoughts. Eventually, anger overtakes sorrow, and she resolutely wipes away the tears as she rises to her feet.

Looking at the clothes on the ground, she narrows her eyes, preparing for a fight. "I'll get you, you fucking bitch! If it takes till the end of time, I'll get you. Somehow! Someway!"

Surveying the room, she finds a steak knife on the empty tray. *I could stick it in her when she isn't expecting it,* she thinks, before the thought of Altus's cut healing reminds her of what she's dealing with. *It'd never work, she'd only kill me.*

Grasping the knife firmly, she raises it overhead, and drives it into the pillow. Over and over, she stabs and slashes, sending feathers about the room like snow.

"You fucking asshole! I'm through with you!"

SIXTEEN

TWO DAYS EARLIER

Stressed out from the recurring nightmare and the upcoming heist, Sierra takes the afternoon off to visit her father in a nursing home on Long Island.

Sitting in a chair by the nurses' station, she stares at the checkerboard design of the white and black floor tiles. Noticing a wheelchair approaching, she lifts her head, smiling softly at the frail old woman being pushed along by a nurse. *They all look so lonely. I wish there was something I could do to help them.*

Knowing that getting old is just a part of life, she wonders, *How long before I end up here? Family visiting only on holidays or birthdays. Then again, the way things are going, no one will ever visit. Mother and brother killed by a drunk driver, father near death, and a boyfriend that will most likely dump me with my first grey hair.*

"You can go in now," the nurse behind the counter informs her. "They've finished changing him."

"Thank you."

Trying to remain optimistic, she smiles, and says, 'Hello', to the patients dotting the hallway, knowing they seek only the most minute form of recognition to feel alive.

Reaching her father's room, a Filipino nurse walks out with dirty diaper in hand. "He's not going to recognize you today," she apologizes, her round forgiving face, and short mom-cut hairstyle accentuating her pleasant demeanor. "I'm not sure how much longer you have with him. The dementia is reaching its later stages."

Knowing the nurse from her father's residency over the past year, she somberly asks, "That bad, huh? How much longer before he forgets me entirely?"

Not liking to convey bad news, she shifts about uneasily in her white vinyl nursing shoes. "Hard to say. Maybe today, maybe a month. No one knows for certain."

"But, from your experience, what do you think?" *Please, don't say soon!*

Hesitantly, she reveals, "I think he's reached the end. Any bits and pieces you get from here on out, you should treasure."

Worst fears confirmed, her eyes begin to water. Closing her lids, she staves back the tears.

"You've been a wonderful daughter. You should be proud. Most children and spouses visit a lot in the beginning, then only come once or twice a year. You're the only one that visits regularly in this whole place. And don't think it went unnoticed, he's always told us how fortunate he is to have such a caring and beautiful daughter."

Listening to the words, tears pour down Sierra's cheek. "I-"

"That's okay, honey. I know," she comforts, gently rubbing her arm. "You should go see him."

Walking past the first bed with its upright patient, she wipes her tears, avoiding eye contact with the hollow-eyed, disheveled man.

Passing the divider curtain, the deafening volume of her father's television is too much to bear, so she turns it down as she passes the dresser opposite his bed. Oblivious to the change, he continues staring out the window at the clouds drifting carelessly by.

"Hi Dad!" she chirps, wiping away the last of her tears.

The impossibly thin, white-haired man looks at her with a suspicious squint, then turns his attention back to the clouds.

Sitting in a chair at his bedside, she rests her arms on the aluminum safety bars of the bed. Even though the once-proud, tall man, is a shell of what he once was, she still sees the strong pillar that was her father.

"I just spoke with the nurse, she said you're feeling better."

Offering no response, he shifts his head to look at a different cloud.

"Things are going well for me. I'm making more money than I ever have, so you'll be able to stay here as long as you like. In fact, things may go so well, I might be able to afford a private room. Would you like that?" she asks, more to herself, than the living ghost. "I put flowers on Mom's grave the other day, it was her birthday. I put a bouquet there for both you and me, you know how she loved flowers."

Suddenly more aware of his surroundings, he yells, "Who turned down the TV? I can't hear the damn thing!"

"I'm sorry, Dad. You want me to turn it up?"

"Who are you to come in here and touch my TV!"

Reaching out, she attempts to shape his tousled hair.

"Don't touch me," he screams.

Offering an apologetic glance, she pulls her hand away, pleading, "Dad, it's Sierra."

Eyes opening wide, a pleasant smile crosses his face. "How's my girl?"

"I'm great, dad," she tears up, happily.

"You look a little tired, are you sleeping okay?" he lovingly inquires, always overly concerned for her welfare.

"I'm fine. Are they taking good care of you?"

"I can't complain, honey, I've lived a long life."

"I put flowers on Mom's grave the other day, as well as Peter's."

"You always were her pride and joy. And Peter always thought the world of you too. I can't believe it's been almost ten years. . .. I know you've carried a lot of anger because of that, but you must let it go. You need to open up to the world again."

Thinking about the senseless tragedy, tears run down her

face.

With a shaky hand, he wipes them away. “Soon, you’ll be alone. I just want you to know that your mother and I always loved you very much. And no matter what you do, we’ll always be proud of you.”

Unable to stop the tears, despair forces her to silence.

“Just remember. In life, you must have a sense of humor for the small problems, and faith in God for the big ones.”

Forcing a smile, she stops crying long enough to kiss him on the cheek. Pulling away, she watches his expression go from compassion to fury.

“Did you turn the TV down!”

With a defeated spirit and tear-streaked face, Sierra shuffles to the TV, and cranks up the volume. Returning to her chair, she clasps her hands to pray, then loosens them as she watches a cloud dissipate in the wind.

What’s the sense in living? Is there really anybody up there, anyway?

SEVENTEEN

PRESENT DAY

THIRD DAY OF CAPTIVITY

Carrying a tray of juice and light breakfast fare, Abah opens the door to Sierra's bedroom. Greeted with piles of shredded clothing, her lids peel back. "Holy hell, what a mess!"

Kicking torn fabric out of the way, she makes a path to the bed and sets the tray on the nightstand.

"Sierra, what have you done?"

Eyes riveted; she offers no sign of acknowledgment.

Kneeling, Abah looks into her bloodshot eyes. "Have you been crying?" Putting a hand on her shoulder, Sierra jerks away.

"Is it something I've done?" she begs.

Steely-eyed, she accuses, "You knew, didn't you!"

"Knew what?" she answers, innocently. *I'd better transfer my emotions and calm her down.*

"Don't treat me like an idiot. You knew!"

"If you're referring to Weston and Eve, yes. I mean . . . I didn't know until this morning that she'd seduced him. I'm so sorry."

Tears drip from her eyes, and she buries her head in the

pillow. *I have to stop this. I can't keep going back and forth between anger and tears. It's time to move on!*

Looking up at Abah, she sniffles, "You know, deep down, I always knew he didn't love me."

"It's not your fault, he's the type of guy that's too selfish to truly love anyone. Except himself."

"It hurts so bad. . .. And of all the people in the world, why did it have to be Eve!"

"I don't think this will make you feel any better, but she doesn't really care for him. She's just a manipulative bitch. And believe me, you hit her where it hurts. When she sees what you did to her clothes, she's going to go completely crazy!"

"Good, I hope they were the bitch's favorites!"

"Why don't you get up and we'll get some clothes from my room. You can't lay in bed all day, letting them get the best of you."

"What am I supposed to do? This mansion's my prison. I can't see how walking around it one more time could possibly make me feel better."

"Let's get out of the house then," she suggests. "Do you know how to ride a horse?"

"Hardly, my father took me once when I was twelve and I was scared to death."

"I'll put you on the tamest horse in the stable. It'll be like a pony ride at the circus."

"Do you have a short horse? It'll be a less painful fall."

Abah smiles, fixing Sierra's hair as she sits up. "There, you look better already."

"I know we haven't known each other very long, but you've made my time here easier. That must sound strange, me being a prisoner and all. . .. I must be suffering from Stockholm syndrome."

"It's not strange at all. To let you in on a little secret, you're making my last days here more enjoyable as well. It's nice having another girl to talk to."

"You don't talk with Eve?"

"She's not like you and me. She's more of a man in a woman's body. That's not to say she isn't feminine, it's that she's more like an egomaniacal man with all her ambition and control issues."

"I guess that helps me understand where she's coming from, though it doesn't make me feel any better."

Lifting her brows, confirming there is no reasonable explanation for Eve's behavior, Abah tells her, "I didn't think it would. Let's go to my room and put on some riding clothes. I know you'll feel better once you get outside. I always do."

Frowning, she puts on the clothes she wore the previous day. "Anything's better than crying all day."

Sullenly following Abah, she no longer cares about the hallway paintings or their historical significance.

"I've been wanting to finish our conversation," Sierra declares.

"Which one?"

"The one where you told me not to trust my feelings."

Signaling *hush*, with a finger to her lips, she whispers, "When we get to my room."

Entering the large, luxuriously appointed French decor room, Abah shuts the door behind them and motions her to follow. Walking into the immense closet, they sit next to each other on a pink, velvet chaise.

"It's important not to get too influenced by your feelings when you interact with us."

"Like, when we kissed last night?" Sierra asks.

"Yes, but it's more than that. How can I explain this . . .? Did you ever watch those old Bela Lugosi vampire movies where he would stare into his victim's eyes and wave his hand?"

"Yeah?"

"Do you remember how they went into a trance?"

"You can put me in a trance!" she gasps.

"No, bad example. That may have been a bit too cliche. It's more like we have a touch of ESP. We project our emotions into people."

"How?"

"What do you feel when you're with me?"

"Hmm. Comfortable, yet sad."

"And when you're with Altus?"

"Whew! When I hear him talk about his life, I go through a range of emotions. Sometimes I feel a deep emptiness that I've never experienced, and other times I feel as if I'm the most powerful person in the world. Capable of doing anything I set my mind to."

"Are you starting to see?"

"I think so. Are you saying that I'm comfortable with you because you're comfortable with me?"

"Kind of, yes. Let's try this. Look into my eyes and concentrate on your feelings."

Though she already knew Abah's eyes were black, she never noticed how dark and endless they truly are. *Ink, in a well, hauntingly deep.* Pondering the unimaginable darkness, she is overcome with sadness and desperation, feeling the urge to cry. As quickly as tears well up, she feels jubilation, and smiles, not a care in the world. Happiness quickly turns to lust, and she is overcome with desire, placing a hand on Abah's thigh.

Turning aside, she stops pushing emotions, giving Sierra a moment to gather her thoughts.

"Ready?" Abah asks. "You felt disheartened and despondent when I thought about my childhood, but when I began to think of my early years with Altus, it quickly turned to excitement and happiness."

Oh, my God. She influenced my feelings!

"And lastly, you were overcome with passion and desire."

"Exactly! So, I feel what you feel?"

"Yes, but without rationale or reason. I need only transfer my emotions, and we form a link. It's like staring at someone across the room, and they suddenly look back at you through the crowd. There's a link between humans, only we have the ability to expand that link and push emotions through."

"And when I touched you, am I reacting to you, or whoever

is in my vicinity?"

"The link is strongest one-on-one, but it can definitely pour into other people if I push hard enough."

"If you can do this to me, does that mean Eve is doing it to Weston?" *Maybe it's not his fault, after all!*

"Yes and no. Eve is most likely projecting her lust, but we can't make people do anything they don't want to do. The truth is, Weston wanted her. It's as simple as that. He may not have done it as quickly without the transference, but eventually, he would have slept with her of his own volition."

Hope falling as rapidly as it rose, she confesses, "I suppose I'm a hopeless romantic. I always want to think there's something there. Even when there isn't."

Emotionally beaten down, Sierra leaves the closet, walks across the bedroom, and steps out onto the balcony for fresh air. Taking a deep breath, she clears her mind and looks across the expansive grounds, before turning toward a balcony fifteen feet across from where she stands.

When Abah walks out to join her, she asks, "Is that another bedroom over there?"

"Yes, you wouldn't believe how many there are."

"Whose is it?" she digs.

With a great deal of hesitation, she replies, "Eve's, but don't think about doing anything crazy. She's much too strong for you."

"That's not what I was thinking. I only want to return her clothes," she grins, sprinting out of the room.

✻ ✻ ✻

Returning with arms full of tattered clothing, she peeks over the top to safely navigate her way onto the balcony. Dropping them at Abah's feet, she grabs one, and throws it onto

Eve's balcony. One by one, she makes her way through the pile, covering every inch of the distant balcony with torn, designer clothing.

"What the fuck is this!" A voice echoes from the distant room.

Hearing the familiar voice, Sierra balls up a pair of jeans, and throws it with all her might toward the open patio door. In a perfectly timed throw, Eve steps onto the balcony, catching the denim projectile squarely on the side of her head. Turning to see the culprit, she finds Sierra tearing her favorite Dolce & Gabbana dress in two.

"You. Fucking. Bitch!" Eve screams, baring her fangs. "I'm going to rip your throat open!" Looking down to gauge the distance between the balconies, she considers leaping across.

Smiling proudly, Sierra picks up a Giorgio Armani blouse and tears it in two.

"You've no idea the hell you've put yourself in!"

Smirking, Sierra puts one hand on hip, and flips her off with the other.

Sensing that her rage delights Sierra, Eve takes a deep breath, calming herself. "Your days are running short, girl. Or would you rather I let you grow old and have a family before I come for you. Killing your children as you beg for mercy!"

Wondering what the commotion is about, Weston casually saunters out onto the balcony. "Sierra! Baby you-"

Hand clenched tightly around his throat, Eve picks him up, toes franticly searching for ground.

Sensing fear rise in Sierra, Abah interjects, "You assume she will stay human. She may be one of us soon."

With a venomous sneer, Eve warns, "You take the disease, he dies! Your death, his death, it means nothing to me."

Releasing her iron grip, he falls to his knees, gasping for air.

Anger faded and facing the possibility of either her or Weston being killed, Sierra's face turns pale, and she rushes for the safety of the bedroom.

Following close behind, Abah gushes, "Wow, that was

something! Are you okay?"

"I'm fine." Hands trembling with fear, she wrings them nervously as she paces about the room.

"The war is definitely on!"

"You don't think she'll kill me, do you?"

"No, Altus forbids it."

"I don't get the idea she cares what Altus forbids!"

"She does, believe me. She wouldn't do anything to you in this house."

"What about when I leave? What about Weston? She's so crazy I could see her killing Weston. I may hate him, but I don't want him dead."

Hoping to calm her fears, she confidently assures, "You're both safe. Altus instructed us not to harm either of you." *At least not you, anyway.*

Looking down at her shaking hands, it reminds her of her father's deteriorated condition. "Wow, I'm really wired!"

"Instead of riding, would you like to stay in my room and relax?" she asks, pushing tranquil emotions while massaging her shoulders.

"I think a ride might do me good. I'll be so worried about falling off the horse I won't be able to think of anything else."

"It's just what you need. I've been riding a lot these last few months and it always clears my mind."

Anxiety rapidly dissipating, she considers Abah's comment about becoming one of them. "I have to ask you something. You know how you're leaving, and I've just arrived. Is this a normal pattern with him? Does he have a constant stream of women coming and going?"

"No. I've been with him about one-hundred-and-seventy years, and Eve a little over ninety, but there were times when he was completely alone. Sometimes longer than a century."

"That seems like a terribly long time to be alone."

"He rarely finds someone he cares enough about to grant eternal life. You must realize what an awesome opportunity he's giving you. That is, *if* he offers it to you."

"You think that after holding me captive, he may send me home? Even though I know about this whole vampire society?"

"It's possible, but doubtful. He seems to like you very much. And I've never heard of anyone refusing eternal life."

"After talking with you, it doesn't sound as if it's always been wonderful."

"Has your life always been wonderful?"

"Not that I'm aware of . . . especially of late," Sierra admits.

"That's what I thought. Everything won't change when you take the disease. Some things, yes, but you are still you. You can't hide from what you are, no matter the amount of money, or length of time. But the disease can make you free. If freedom is what you crave, then it's a godsend. Just look at your new friend Eve. From the day I met her, she has never looked back. In fact, quite to the contrary. She speaks to me endlessly, wishing it were her that could leave instead of me. She can't wait to bleed the people of this earth dry."

"Altus said she didn't want the disease as much as you."

"She didn't, at least that's what I've been told. I wasn't here when it happened. Like I said, I was with one of the ancestors at the time."

"Who are the ancestors?" Sierra probes, yearning for more information.

"They are the oldest of our kind, and there is only a handful of them. Altus is one, and Khaba another. To tell you the truth, I was shocked when he told you of his existence. I was never informed of Khaba until I was with Altus for nearly thirty years." She wrinkles her brow in jealousy. "What else does he tell you?"

"Not much. Only that you have a disease that affects your blood, and there is a sickness that comes on when you become infected."

"Hmm." *Why does he give so much information to a human? Especially his life story?*

"How many ancestors are there?"

"We shouldn't talk of this in the house. Let's go riding, we can speak freely outdoors."

EIGHTEEN

The expansive grounds stretch thousands of yards in every direction before reaching a thick wall of trees. A few-hundred yards downhill of the house sits a stone barn with a grey slate roof, matching the home in its architectural style. Behind it lies an expansive horse pasture surrounded by white fencing.

The riding clothes are slightly baggy, but Sierra is happy to be free of the house and relaxes more with every step toward the stables. "Are we far enough away that we can talk?"

Worried she may have revealed too much, Abah purposely avoids the topic of the ancestors. "Yes, we're fine. As I was saying, when I was in Tibet, Altus created Eve. When I returned, I came to find that she thought of herself as queen of the castle."

"She was always a bitch, wasn't she?"

"Pretty much," she chuckles. "Altus said he met her at the Cotton Club. Do you know much about the twenties?"

"Some, not a lot."

"There was a women's empowerment movement burgeoning, and Eve was a devoted follower. She was a headstrong flapper who wanted equality, yet still wanted to maintain her sexuality. Or more accurately put, she wanted to use her sexuality to get what she wanted. I don't think she realized the two can't go hand in hand. But then, that's Eve, she's always made up her own rules. When I came back from Tibet, I didn't think much of her being here, because I thought she was a traveler."

"A traveler?"

"Yes, it's a term we use when visiting the homes of other vampires around the world."

"How come Altus doesn't like the word vampire?"

"He thinks it's ridiculous. He prefers to think of us as humans with an incurable disease. I think it's all the same. Besides, I've heard him use the term every now and then. In my opinion, it's a lot easier to say vampire than to tell the drawn-out disease story. Anyway, I think she's staying with us temporarily until she tells me how she met him at the Cotton Club, and how he fell in love with her at first sight."

"Sounds like something she'd say," Sierra comments.

"Jumping to the heart of the matter, it didn't take long before she started in with how prominent her family was, how much money they had, and all these other ridiculous things I've chosen to forget. You know, just trying to convey her sense of superiority. Then she went on and on about how well she came through the sickness, even though she wasn't certain she wanted it - since she wasn't as desperate as I was."

"She said that? Unbelievable!"

"Typical, huh? Well, it didn't take long before I'd had enough of her treating me so disdainfully. One day in the kitchen, she made a remark about cooking up fried chicken or some other racial epithet, and I took a knife and stuck it in her jugular."

"Oh my God!" Jarred to the point of breaking stride, she's surprised by the casual mention of such vicious brutality.

"When she fell to the ground, I held her down and kept moving the knife back and forth so that the wound wouldn't heal. Fortunately, or unfortunately, depending on how you feel about her, Altus walked in just before I drained her. Another minute or two and she would've never recovered."

"You can bleed to death?"

"Most definitely. When the heart stops pumping, we die as surely as anyone. Altus's scientist informed us that the human body has ten pints of blood, and after four pints are gone, it shuts down completely. I bet she was only half a pint away from joining her beloved ancestors that stepped off the Mayflower."

Sierra laughs heartily before realizing how morbid it is. "I suppose it's not that funny, she almost died."

"I would've thought you of all people would appreciate the humor. Besides, after that, we got along fine."

"If you push back hard enough, she respects you?"

"It worked for me, but she wasn't as sure of her place then, as she is now. The best thing you can do is stay clear of her. She knows Altus will kill her if she touches you, so you don't have to worry about that, but it's still best you ignore her. At least for the time being."

"It does make me feel safer, knowing Altus is protecting us." *But what if I don't take the disease? Would she really hunt me down? And if I do take it, will she kill Weston?*

"If you want my opinion, I think she's jealous. She knows Altus cares for you deeply."

Uncomfortable talking about Altus's feelings for her, she switches the subject. "You said Altus has a scientist working for him. Why?"

"Not exactly working for him, he's one of us. He became a scientist about thirty years ago in hopes of discovering more about the disease."

"Vampires go to medical school?"

"That's only the tip of the iceberg, we're everywhere. Technology, banking, law, even acting. Though I don't know why anyone would be foolish enough to draw attention to themselves when they are going to stay young forever."

"What happens to someone like that?"

"I suppose they'll either walk away or stage a tragic death. Either way, they won't be able to surface again for centuries. Even then, they take a chance of the ancestors killing them for putting us all at risk."

"Has the scientist made any discoveries?"

"Other than the cells of the disease being pyramidal shaped, nothing significant. He knows the disease requires an abnormally high amount of oxygen to survive, which means our red blood cells must work harder than a normal human's to transfer oxygen. The human body produces two-hundred-billion red blood cells a day, and they normally live for one-hundred-and-twenty days. With us, the disease's demand for oxygen is so high, our cells only live twenty to forty days, so we need to make up that difference, or the disease will no longer repair the deterioration of our cells, and we'll age at an even more accelerated rate than humans. In addition, he's also found that we may require the lymphocytes present in plasma."

"What's a lymphocyte?"

"They're the B and T cells that fight off toxins in the body. To give you an example, people with HIV have incredibly low T-cell counts. One of his hypotheses is to create a synthetic vaccine or pill that would increase the red blood cell count as well as raise lymphocyte production, thereby replacing our need for blood."

"Couldn't the low red blood cell count be treated like anemia, simply by increasing iron intake?"

"That was his initial diagnosis, but it didn't work. To be honest, I'm not so sure the most intelligent vampire chose to go to medical school."

Sierra finds this amusing and begins laughing uncontrollably.

"I didn't know I was so funny," Abah giggles.

"I pictured Bela Lugosi in a dunce cap, examining blood samples to no avail."

"That is funny. It sounds like a Far Side cartoon."

"Exactly!" she grins, walking into the stable.

Larger than a football field, the stable has a riding track in the center with stalls lining its sides. While most of the stalls are empty, ten horses reside in the middle stalls on the right-hand side.

Abah puts saddles and bridles on horses in adjacent stalls, and holding them by the reigns, walks them to the pasture. Letting go of the reigns to the smaller horse, she says, "This one is yours. I'll help you up." Picking Sierra up like a feather, she lightly sets her in the saddle.

Sierra adjusts herself and grabs the leather reigns firmly, holding on for dear life.

"You don't have to do a thing; he'll follow my lead."

Walking to the other horse, she jumps high in the air, her six-foot frame landing comfortably in the saddle, graceful as a ballerina.

Awed by her strength and dexterity, Sierra can't help but feel a tinge of jealously.

"Khaba has a different view. He professes that people must die so that we may live. I suppose that's the hard truth of the matter, and there's a ritualistic beauty to it. It's our burden that we must experience their suffering, so that we may be forever young. It's a trade-off you must accustom yourself to, if you wish to survive."

Nudging her horse to begin walking, Sierra's follows suit. After a few short yards, she brings the horses to a slow trot.

"Then why have him try to cure it?"

"It's Altus. He worries about future technology. He's concerned that in another hundred years, all of mankind will be implanted with microchips, making it easy to monitor everyone's whereabouts and vital signs. Every time we replenish, the police may be immediately notified of someone's death. Even worse, they'll be able to view the exact location with global positioning satellites, and cameras."

"It's a valid point. Do all of the ancestors have the same concerns?"

"The other two live in countries that aren't as advanced as America. Altus is bombarded with new technology every day, and he paves the way for us. It's always been that way."

"Who are the other ancestors?"

"You must not repeat any of this to Altus. He'd be furious."

"I would never say anything, you have my word."

"Khaba is one, the other is Xi. You will meet her soon."

"Altus told Eve that Xi was coming and she was almost giddy. Are they close?"

"They are similar in some ways," Abah admits. "Though Xi is not frivolous like Eve. When you meet her, you'll see. Xi possesses a strength that is not seen in most women. I think it's that very quality that attracts Eve."

"Do the three of them tell all vampires what they can and can't do?"

"No, the Triumvirate, as they are known, keep mainly to themselves. Most vampires don't even believe there is a Triumvirate. They know of Altus because he makes himself accessible, but they think the others died eons ago."

"Is Altus the leader?"

"I think so, but he would never admit it. If it were not for Altus, none of us would be as wealthy as we are."

"How rich is Altus?"

"He's the world's richest man by untold hundreds of billions, if not trillions. Only Khaba and Xi come close to matching his wealth. The Triumvirate controls vast amounts of money and land, as well as having the power to influence governments. Which creates something of a dichotomy, since our strongest precept is not to interfere in the ways of man. That would surely bring about a quick death from the ancestors. We're instructed to be spectators, for lack of a better word. Though I do know Altus interfered during the siege on Tibet."

"Really, why?"

"Xi has a massive complex in Tibet, called Shangri La, that was once an ancient monastery. During Mao Zedong's fabled Long March that took him through Tibet, Xi came to meet and talk with him about his rural revolution. She found he embodied many of the same ideals that her father not only ascribed to but tried to implement during his reign thousands of years ago."

"Xi's father ruled in ancient times?"

"Her father was Wang Mang, the Usurper Emperor. But don't ever call him that around her, your life will be over before you draw another breath. She thinks of him as a visionary. A selfless reformer that strived to create the perfect Confucian state."

"I've never heard of him."

"He ruled China from the year 9 AD to 23, when he was killed during a revolution. It was Xi's marriage to the child, Emperor Ping, in the year 4 AD that made her Empress of China, and she still views herself that way. But, getting back to my point, she befriended Mao and pointed to the 1920's socialist state of Russia as being a good model for what China could become, since it was remarkably similar to her father's ideals."

"She influenced Mao's allegiance to Russia?"

"Yes, but the idealistic Russian socialism of the 1920's was far from what it evolved into."

"Does she feel guilty about the effects of Mao's leadership and how it affected all of Tibet? Not to mention the disastrous effects of the Great Leap Forward."

"I doubt it. Even though they talk of not interfering, it's obvious that Xi is trying to make China the world's leading superpower by whatever means necessary. And judging by the way things are going, it's hard to argue with any influence she's wielded up to this point, because China will undoubtedly rule the world in another fifty to one-hundred years. Very impressive when you think of the century prior to 1950, when China was plagued by civil war, intrusions by European powers, republican revolution, regional warlordism, and Japanese invasion. Which brings me back to my original point. Altus talks extensively about not interfering, but when I saw what was happening in Tibet, I begged him to get the Americans to help."

"And did he?"

"Yes, but only after a great deal of debate. It was just after World War II, and he was incredibly adamant about not interfering. He bordered on the obsessive whenever the subject came up. He mentioned countless civilizations that that were crushed, lecturing, 'It is the progress of man. You do not know what the inevitable outcome will be.' He was so hard-headed about it! But, in time, he changed his mind. Probably due to my endless pestering. Or maybe he just felt guilty about not doing more to end World War II. I'm not sure."

"How did he end up helping?"

"He directed his government contacts to aid them, sending CIA operatives to Saipan where they trained the warlike Tibetans."

"I didn't know there were warlike Tibetans, I thought they were all peaceful people."

"They are, for the most part, except a tribe called the Khampas. That's why the CIA picked them. They were given millions of dollars to undermine the Maoist revolution, that is, until Nixon inaugurated a policy of rapprochement with China in 1969, and the CIA was forced to pull out."

"How did Xi survive the onslaught?"

"She didn't have to survive it, she instigated it. As long as I've known her, she's spoken openly about uniting the provinces of China. Though I have no proof, I think the destruction of nearly all the monasteries was her doing as well."

"Why would she do something like that?"

"The monastery she lives in was once considered the most holy and beautiful in all of Tibet. When she acquired it in the 17th century, it was nearly abandoned, falling to pieces, so she liberated it from the few remaining monks residing there."

"Liberated?"

"I think she either bought it or built another monastery for them to live in. Whatever the case may be, it seems to me, she pushed them out."

“Why would she want a run-down monastery?”

“She’s been a teacher of her own style of Buddhism for the better part of her life. She lived in a Buddhist city that was the starting point of the Silk Road, heading west out of China, and while living there, she exported silk.”

“What do you mean by her *own style* of Buddhism?”

“She created her own Buddhist religion, if you can call it that. The premise is, it’s acceptable to act upon whatever you feel necessary to enhance one’s own well-being, as long as you remain true to the central tenet that the external world is a product of one’s own consciousness.”

“Isn’t that saying, do whatever you like, and don’t let your conscience bother you.”

“Pretty much,” Abah concurs. “It seems crazy, but Altus says it’s enabled her followers to exist longer than most vampires, so he’s okay with it.”

“She has followers?”

“Oh yeah, and they’re all vampires. When she gives them the disease, they must give themselves over to her religion. She calls it, ‘The Way of Xi.’ She even went so far as to try and sway other Buddhists into following the Way about eighteen-hundred years ago. She went to the ancient city of Taxila and spoke at a Buddhist university about how she had redefined Buddhism.”

“Was she successful?”

“She found some followers. How many? I don’t really know. I studied under her tutelage for the short amount of time I spent in Tibet but saw through it right away. Or more truthfully, my conscience got the better of me. I couldn’t justify using the world and all its people as my playground of puppets. But that’s what created the rift between her and the Tibetan monks. They knew what an abomination it was of true Buddhist philosophy, so they tried to overtake her monastery with a corps of fighting monks in the late 1800s. Of course, when she and her followers quickly decimated the soldiers, the remaining monks retreated and informed the others of her god-like powers. Unfortunately, instead of heeding the warning, the remaining monasteries pressured the thirteenth Dalai Lama, Thubten Gyatso, to create an army to wipe out Xi and her followers. He went to Shangri La to meet with Xi, and she told him, 'I could drain your spirit now, thereby affirming myself the Dalai Lama,' to which he put his butt in high gear and made for the nearest monastery that would offer protection. From there, he sent out word that he could create an army to fight Xi, but all monasteries must pay a tax to support the soldiers. When the monasteries realized it would cost them money to do away with XI, they adopted a live and let live mentality. But it was too late, Xi had had enough.

"Thus, years later, when Mao met with her, and spoke of how the Tibetans had made things hard for him on his march, Xi planted the idea in his head that they should be assimilated into the Chinese Republic, and not be the autonomous wild card in China's new future. I think Xi also threatened the thirteenth Dalai Lama, because on his death bed in 1933, his very words were, 'Very soon in this land, deceptive acts may occur from without and within. At that time, if we do not dare to protect our territory, our spiritual personalities including the Victorious Father and Son, the Dalai Lama and Panchen Lama, may be exterminated without trace, the property and authority of our Lakangs and monks may be taken away. Moreover, our political system, developed by the Three Great Dharma Kings, Tri Songtsen Gampo, Tri Songdetsen, and Tri Ralpachen, will vanish without anything remaining. The property of all people, high and low, will be seized, and the people forced to become slaves. All living beings will have to endure endless days of suffering and will be stricken with fear. Such a time will come.'"

"It sounds like Xi revealed her plans to him. It's terrible that so many peaceful people died due to her wrath. Too bad Altus couldn't have done more."

"They weren't as peaceful as you might think. The Tibetans

tortured and mutilated thieves, runaway serfs, and other criminals by gouging out their eyes, pulling out tongues, hamstringing them, or simply cutting off a limb. There are no truly innocent people in this world, other than young children. Besides, how many civilizations do you think Altus has seen fall in his lifetime? Even more to the point, how many people has he killed? I'd surmise tens of thousands if you throw in his time spent with Caesar. But it wasn't so much the destruction of the people that bothered Altus, it was the destruction of the monasteries and what they meant to the history of mankind, that he lamented."

They hold no regard for human life! How could I ever be that way?

Knowing that she is troubled, Abah attempts to comfort her. "If you believe in God, they're in a better place. Whether they reached heaven twenty or thirty years earlier than scheduled, is irrelevant, they made it there. Which is more than I can say for any of us. We're stuck here for eternity. And if there is a God, we'll be roasting in the fiery depths of hell longer than any of us can possibly imagine."

"I know we talked about it before, but do you believe in God?"

"Judging by the horrors I've seen in my short time, it's hard to believe there's a benevolent god."

"Does Altus feel that way?"

"Altus believes he is a god. Though he would never admit it, I feel it emanating from him. When I am at my lowest points, he projects it into me, raising my spirits. He wants me to understand how wonderful life can be if I let go of the past and embrace the gift I've been given."

Sierra is so wrapped up in the discussion, she hasn't even noticed that the horses have significantly picked up their pace. As if she were born to the saddle, her body moves instinctively, smiling as the wind blows through her hair.

"I told you this would be fun. Don't you feel better now?"

"I do! After hearing everything you've had to say, I'm not so sure I even care about Weston any longer."

"See how riding can just take your cares away," Abah muses, attempting to keep the mood light.

"Well, it's definitely more fun than I remembered it to be."

"The more time you spend riding, the better you'll become. Tomorrow you'll want to go even faster."

"I'll have to take your word, I'm not that confident yet." Looking across the rolling green hills, she sees a lake with a large house on its banks.

"Is that part of the property as well?"

"Yes, we call it the boathouse. If you'd ever like to go sailing or water skiing, just let me know."

"This is incredible." *I can't believe how well they live!*

"This is just a fraction of the estate. It's over ten-thousand acres, with more than fifty miles of riding trails. Not to mention his other homes around the world."

"I can see why you wouldn't want to leave."

Pulling on the reins, Abah stops her horse, and Sierra's follows suit. "It's all yours, you know. You only need decide what's right for you."

Daydreaming of the splendors of wealth, Sierra looks over the rippling waters of the lake. *I could live like this forever . . . I'd be crazy not to accept the disease!*

Noticing the longing look of wonderment on Sierra's face, jealousy can't help but rear its ugly head. "Don't be taken in by the beauty and money. Forever can be gruelingly long if you're not prepared."

"Can you tell me what it's like?"

"To be a vampire or to be rich?" *Should I be jealous of her? If it's not her, it will surely be another. At least I like her more than I ever did Eve.*

"Both. I want to know everything."

"Certainly," she assures.

"Are you positive Eve won't kill Weston if I take the disease?"

"Don't worry, Altus is protecting him." *Should I tell her*

truth? Does it even matter? She'll come to accept his death as surely as I accepted my father's.

"I need to know all the good and bad. Don't spare any details, no matter how painful or frightening they may be."

Watching Sierra's black hair blow seductively in the wind, her bloodlust returns. *If I don't replenish soon, I'll kill her by sunset.* "I'll gladly tell you anything you'd like to know, but it will have to be later. I must go into town on personal business."

"I really appreciate you helping me with all of this. It's been a difficult couple of days."

"Carefully consider what Altus has to offer. You may be more like Eve than you know."

Looking over the estate, a soft, confident smile crosses her face. *Could I thrive like Eve? Could I kill Eve!*

NINETEEN

Passing by the gallery, Altus catches a glimpse of Sierra, perched over Cleopatra's jewelry case. Her silky, straight hair flows onto the glass, concealing her face, and her pert butt sticks out sensually in her bent-over stance.

Complete, sexual, perfection. Does she know what she does to me?

Hearing footsteps, she looks up, greeting him with a half-smile.

"Abah informed me of what has taken place between Weston and Eve. I am terribly sorry. I never intended for anything like that to happen."

"It was definitely a surprise, but not a complete shock," she confesses.

"I have moved them into another residence on the estate. You will not see them again."

"I suppose it's for the better. Though, I was hoping to speak with him."

"You may, if you like, but do you really want to hear his lies?" *Her feelings for him linger.*

"Lies? No. Maybe an explanation as to how he could have done something like that at such a crazy time."

"Unfortunately, that is usually when one finds out who their friends and enemies truly are."

It's been a year of lies. Let it go already. "Well, Eve can have him." Focusing on the jewelry, she asks, "Did Cleopatra really wear these?"

"They were her favorite."

"The quality of the stones is amazing. I've never seen peridots radiate so much color."

"Would you like to wear them? A woman as beautiful as you deserves nothing less."

"That's very kind of you to say, but I'm not sure I'm worthy. I'd hate for something to happen to them."

"You are too beaten down by the world and your friend Weston, to know how special you truly are."

"I can't argue with that, it hasn't been easy."

"Turn around, I will put the necklace on."

"Are you sure?"

Turning, she lifts her long hair.

"You are more than worthy of such beauty." Opening the case, he removes the necklace and clasps it around her neck. "Let me look at you."

Turning, she smiles at his look of adoration. *He's nicer than I thought.*

"Your eyes shine brighter than the peridots." Reaching out, he centers the pendant so that it lays perfectly between her breasts.

Reacting to his touch, her heart beats rapidly, nipples poking at the sleeveless cotton T-shirt.

Stepping back, he takes a long look. "Magnificent." *She is perfect in every way!*

"It's not as heavy as I thought it would be."

"You are striking," he exclaims, filled with awe.

Delicately, she runs her hand over the necklace. "Is there a mirror nearby? I'd love to see how it looks."

"Yes, but first, you must put on the armband and bracelet. I want to see all the pieces adorning you."

Holding her wrist, he pushes the armband up around her bicep. After adjusting it in place, he runs his hand down her arm. "You have the shimmering skin of Cleopatra. Give me your wrist." Holding her hand, he slides the bracelet in place. "It fits as if it were designed for none other."

"They're so pretty, I have to see!" *It always feels right when he's near.*

"Come with me," he smiles, taking hold of her hand.

Weaving between the rows of artwork, he takes Sierra into the hallway, leading her to an immense antique mirror.

"It's beautiful," she gushes, gazing upon their reflection. *Damn, we look good together.*

"You truly are the most beautiful woman I have ever seen," he compliments, pushing lust.

Feeling aroused, she turns, and leans in gently.

Gliding his fingers down the sides of her midriff, he grabs her waist, pulling her close. Hands running up her back, he brings her into his kiss. Lip to lip, tongue to tongue, they hungrily accept each other's desire.

Moaning with delight, she grips his steel biceps, burning to explore more. *Kiss me hard . . . don't be gentle.* Hungry hands explore his torso, making their way down, down to his manhood. *So big!*

Letting out an appreciative groan, he unwillingly curbs his passion. *I'm pushing too hard!*

Stepping back, he confides, "I want you, Sierra, but we cannot do this."

Breathing heavily, she quickly comes to the realization that he may be transferring his emotions. *Were those my true feelings?*

"Would you like to go for a walk? The grounds are beautiful in the afternoon." *She must come to me of her own free will.*

"I'd rather lay out by the pool." *Real or not, that was hot!*

"That is a wonderful idea! You can choose whatever you like from Abah's wardrobe."

"Her clothes are a touch big, but I suppose I can find something." Holding out her arms, she pulls at the rolled-up jeans and loose-fitting shirt.

"Find a swimsuit, and Abah will take you shopping for a

new wardrobe."

Joyous at the prospect of leaving the house for even the briefest of periods, she smiles brightly, and kisses his cheek.

TWENTY

Wearing a white string bikini and sporting Cleopatra's jewelry, Sierra follows a stone path from the rear of the house to the pool. Seeing that Altus is swimming towards her, she saunters seductively toward the edge.

Breaking the plane of water, he stands, hands on hips, eyes running over every beautiful curve of her body. "I see you-, found something to wear," he stammers. *Fortuna has delivered a goddess!*

"Yeah," she smiles, fixating on his lean muscular physique. "It fits okay, just a little big on top."

"It looks wonderful from here." *By the great god Wotan, how can I resist her much longer?*

"You look pretty good yourself."

Jumping out of the pool, he lands directly before her, pulling her into his kiss.

With cool water running off his body, tingling her skin, she grabs his biceps. *Chiseled steel covered in burning flesh.* "You're getting hot from being out in the sun."

"It is a side effect of the disease," he answers, stepping back.

"Huh?" *Every time we get started, he stops. Why?*

"Our body temperatures are higher than the average human's. We average one-hundred-and-one degrees."

"Is your body trying to fight the disease? Like, with a

fever?"

Following him to a row of recliners set alongside the pool, she watches the smooth masculine shifting of his body. *They move differently than humans. Fluid, gliding, almost imperceptible. Not arrogance . . . supreme confidence.*

"That is an excellent question. It is something we have never been able to determine."

He gestures for her to sit, and rests in the adjacent recliner, putting on a pair of solid black sunglasses. "That is better, I can see you much clearer."

"What's it like?"

"To be blind on sunny days?" he muses.

"No, to be eternal," she smiles, coyly.

"It is the greatest of gifts. Time and disease are of no consequence. I move freely through the world without hindrance from anyone, or any thing. I am the ruler of this planet, and nothing can, or will, stand in my way."

Love to have that confidence! "What about others like you, could they harm you?"

"Only the ancient ones. The longer the disease resides in the body, the more firmly it takes hold. Do you recall how quickly my cut healed?"

"How could I forget?"

"Well, it would not heal as quickly for either Abah or Eve. It would take another five minutes for the wound to disappear, instead of the minute it took for mine."

"I think it was less than a minute, actually."

"You may be right. Now, think of all the cells in one's body being completely infected, and the disease requiring little to no blood to aid in the healing process."

"Are you saying the cut would have healed without the need for blood to clot?"

"Exactly, that is how it is for Khaba. Everything from his inner organs to the hair on his head are completely infected with the disease. His skin, for example, heals without the need for platelets to aid in its repair. If cut in the same manner as I had been, he would lose only a few drops of blood, the skin and muscle tissue healing instantaneously. Which also makes him the strongest of our kind, nearly ten times more powerful than the average human."

"That's remarkable. Is it possible for you to die?"

"Most definitely. But it would take a far greater force than I have ever seen. I fought among swords, catapults, and arrows well before I became what I am, and I survived those onslaughts nearly untouched."

"Nearly?"

"I had my share of arrows shot into me as well as being run through by a sword, but luckily, nothing entered a vital organ." Pointing just above his left hip bone, he discloses, "Right here, a sword ran completely through me. But the scar has disappeared with time." Fixing upon it momentarily, he becomes lost in the past. "Sometimes, it all seems like a dream. How could anyone have lived through so much and still be alive today?"

"I can see how you were injured. You took part in so many battles with Caesar it's a wonder you weren't killed. Where were you when he was murdered?"

"I was with Cleopatra, contemplating our departure for Alexandria. When told of his murder, it seemed surreal. The man that saved me from death and raised me up to unimaginable heights, was no longer. Once again, I was proven inept at protecting those I loved . . .. Upon hearing of Caesar's death, Antony escaped the city dressed as a slave, fearing Caesar's followers would be killed. Days later, after learning that Caesar's followers were not in danger, he casually returned. Shocked by his behavior, I reviled him the better part of the night before Caesar's funeral.

"After the ceremony, Cleopatra and I mourned for several days, then did as he requested, spiriting Caesarion out of Italy. Sailing for home, we contemplated who the Senate would choose to rule Egypt. Would it be Cleopatra, or her brother Ptolemy XIV? Believing it best we solidify our hold on Egypt, I strangled him and slid his corpse into the Mediterranean."

"You killed him for no other reason than to maintain control?"

"It was the will of Caesar that his son be ruler of the world, how could I possibly let someone stand in his way? Besides, history is littered with the murders of untold royals. What makes this one any worse than the rest?"

"I suppose that's true. It's just that you did it, not some historical figure." *I don't think I'll ever become accustomed to killing the way he is. Maybe that's what Abah meant about the ancestors living in different times.*

"If I had not done it, Octavius would have when he invaded Egypt. Only he would have bound him in chains and paraded him through the streets of Rome before taking his life. Which do you think he would have preferred?"

"When you put it that way, I guess his death was inevitable." *Still . . . a little hard to swallow.*

"Settling back into our lives in Egypt, we waited to see what would become of the power struggle in Rome before allying ourselves to any particular person. We hoped Octavius would succeed, but he was young, while Antony was seasoned and had much of the army supporting him. Within a matter of months, we were notified that a Triumvirate had been formed between Octavius, Antony, and Lepidus. They divided up the Roman territories with Lepidus in the West, Antony in the East, and Octavius in Italy. This was beneficial for Octavius for he was responsible for rewarding veteran soldiers with land, thereby retaining the legions loyalty. It was also significant because was able to remain in close contact with the Senate, influencing their opinions more readily than his counterparts. There seemed nothing for us to do but wait and watch.

"The next three years were spent in each other's arms, and the politics of Rome seemed a world away. That was until Antony summoned Cleopatra to Tarsus in 41 BC. As was typical of Antony, he needed money and knew none would be forthcoming from Rome. Hedging his bets, he re-established ties with the wealthiest woman in the world, hoping she would fund his military campaign against the Parthians. I tried to warn her of the implications of allying herself with him, but she reassured, 'I know this tamed man, I will only allude to my support. Should Octavius slip on his ascent, it can only benefit us.'

"I knew she was playing with fire, but there was no other who could manipulate men so easily, for none matched her sensuousness and determination." Reflecting, he grunts, "Unwisely, I put my faith in her."

"She fell in love with him, didn't she?"

"That is a myth. Did she seduce and entice him in hopes of gaining power over Rome? Yes. But what she didn't fully comprehend, was that it would look like Antony was siding with the East in hopes of wresting control of the Mediterranean from Rome. It was a minor, yet understandable error on her part to visit him, but it was a monumental error to allow him to kill her sister, Arsinoe. Once done, their alliance was cemented . . . at least in his mind."

"What was with you people? You killed her brother, and Antony, the sister. You didn't leave anything to chance, did you?"

"The power of Egypt had to stay firmly within Cleopatra's grasp. She felt Arsinoe was a threat, whereas I saw her as a mild irritant to be dealt with at a later time. That is where we differed. I learned patience from Caesar, whereas she acted whenever the opportunity presented itself. When Antony offered his assistance, she naturally took him up on the offer, not realizing the bond she was forging. He was a simpleton, a drunk, and at times a buffoon, but when he betrayed Caesar, he proved to be dangerous as well.

"After returning from Tarsus, Antony visited again, proclaiming himself a tourist, not a Consul of Rome. In his mind, he believed this would not raise suspicions of an alliance, but merely look as if he were paying a social visit to the Queen of Egypt. I tried to tell her that his actions were galvanizing Octavius's hold on the Senate, but she continued to believe Antony was our safety net.

Sighing, he utters, "From the moment of his arrival, things went poorly. He felt the way I had spoken to him before Caesar's funeral was disrespectful, and I could sense tension growing daily. Where we were once friends, he now berated me, saying, 'The power of the world is in my hands, and soon I will succeed where Caesar failed. Nor will I require Fortuna or your jaded luck to aid me.'

"He spoke of sleeping with Cleopatra in Tarsus and how she begged for more, knowing full well we were lovers. I beseeched that in his endeavor to settle some imaginary score, he was not only jeopardizing his future, but Caesarion's and Cleopatra's as well. Every minute spent within the borders of Egypt was one more grain of sand in the Senate's scale, favoring Octavius. With a forced laugh, he scoffed, 'You know nothing of Rome or politics. Return to the fields from whence you came.'"

"Wow, it sounds like there was a lot of animosity there," she observes.

"That was nothing. It only got worse. At his insistence, Cleopatra began throwing parties, and he stayed through the winter. With every passing conversation he attempted to convince her that Octavius was destined to lose, and he would soon be dictator. I longed for his departure so that peace could return, but that was not to be, for she had become pregnant with his twins."

"Are you sure they weren't yours?"

"We were fighting so much, our sex life was nonexistent. No matter, it was what she wanted. It was the same reason she gave birth to Caesar's child, she used children to secure her future as Queen of the world. The problem was, she could not see that by having his children, she was snuffing out the last flicker of his dying political flame. He was doomed, and our fortunes were tied firmly to his. It was the beginning of the end for all of us, and more painfully, for Cleopatra and me. We behaved insanely, fighting throughout her pregnancy and well into the first few months of the twin's lives."

"He really put a wedge between the two of you, didn't he?"

"Yes, and even though Cleopatra accused me of jealousy, I lied, saying I was only concerned for her future. I was unable to be honest with myself. Maybe if I had been, things would have worked out differently."

"Do you think she loved him, even slightly?"

"Not even remotely. She came to believe he would be triumphant, and in turn, we would overthrow him after he became ruler. It was insanity! I tried to explain that as foreigners, we stood no chance of ever usurping Antony's, or Octavius's title. It would have to be given to Caesarion by Octavius, just as Caesar had planned. She countered that neither Octavius nor any other ruler in their right mind would let go of such power peacefully, but I tried to convince her it was our only chance. If Octavius did not relinquish power, we would at least be left on our own to rule Egypt. But, if we sided with Antony, Octavius would consider the plans laid out by Caesar to have been abandoned, and we would be considered enemies of Rome."

Shaking his head, he angrily spits, "I may as well have been talking to the wall! After a year of bickering, we resigned ourselves to a wait-and-see policy, realizing it was the only way we could remain together amicably."

"Did it work?"

"I suppose, but only because Antony left Egypt. As weeks went by, we slowly forgave each other, and the passion returned. Over the next few years things went well, that is, until Antony returned while en-route to battle the Parthians. This time, she threw herself entirely behind him, and there was no convincing her otherwise. I knew it was foolish, but I could fight no longer, so, I agreed that if he could defeat the Parthians, there was some hope in Antony becoming the Senate's choice to lead Rome. I openly supported him as he prepared for his 'Great Triumph,' but inside, I knew we had crossed a line with Octavius. If Antony could not defeat the

Parthians, we would surely be at war with Rome. I begged Cleopatra to rethink things, but she only extolled, 'You need not worry, I have supplied him with the might of Egypt.'

"I tried to explain that even though her military forces were great, Antony was not the general Caesar had been, and it would take more than courage to win the battle."

"Did he win?"

Exhaling deeply, he mutters, "No. After a series of defeats, he began his retreat, and that is where the decimation occurred. It was the peak of the Armenian winter, so he was slowed considerably and became susceptible to raids, causing the loss of the better part of Cleopatra's army."

"Did she finally listen to you about changing alliances?"

"It was too late. She knew it as well as I did. Octavius knew who his enemies were, and no amount of pleading or justification would change his mind. And with Antony declaring Alexandria his permanent home, I felt Cleopatra had betrayed me as well. Dejected, I spent my days in the library studying the history of Egypt's Pharaohs, and nights seeking out illicit encounters. In my mind, Antony residing in the palace was not only an insult to me, but also Caesarion. Eventually, I had had enough, and mentioned that I would be returning to Rome. She thought I was aligning myself with Octavius and called me a traitor. I said it had nothing to do with choosing sides, I simply could not bear being near the two of them. In desperation, she begged me to stay at her palace in Memphis, offering me time to make sense of things."

"And did you?" she asks, running her eyes up and down Altus's tanned, muscular frame. *Had we met under normal circumstances, he'd be perfect for me. No question.*

"Yes, I lived there for a number of years. I visited when Antony was not in Alexandria, or she would visit me when weary of his drunken antics. We spent those times much as we had before Caesar died, caught up in the simple joy of being near one another."

"What about when she wasn't there? Weren't you

distraught knowing they were together?"

"At first, I spent time commissioning the construction of a Mithraic church. At one time, I was a deeply religious person. But we both know how that ended up," he snorts. "After that, I dove back into my studies, this time, at the Memphis library. If it were not for my hunger of knowledge, I would never have made it through those years. With every fact I consumed, Antony, Rome, and Cleopatra fell further into the recesses of my mind. With her frequent visits, she would tell me of current events, and how in due time, Antony would take his rightful place in Rome, but I knew it was wishful thinking. The Senate saw Antony's residing in Alexandria as a sure sign he would make it the Capitol of the world, turning Rome into a backwater, if anointed Caesar. There was only one subject we could discuss without contention, and that was Pharaonic history. From the uniting of the two kingdoms by Narmer, to her Ptolemaic lineage, we debated the greatness of Snefru, Djoser, Ramses II, Amenophis IV, and Tutankhamun."

"She was proud of her heritage, wasn't she?"

"Very much so. She was the first of the Ptolemy's to speak the ancient Egyptian language. Possessing an encyclopedic knowledge of history, there was no Pharaoh about which she did not have some knowledge. It was during one of these conversations that she mentioned the 'Damned One,' Anubis Khaba, condemned to eternal life by Anubis, Lord of the Netherworld. I was so intrigued I began researching the later third Dynasty for any scrap of information. Strangely, I found it nearly impossible to find any mention of him. Before and after him, there was a wealth of details on every Pharoah and every minute decision that had ever been made, but for some reason, his era of rule had vanished."

"How did you find any information?"

"It was an arduous task. It was only through my research of Pharaohs in the Dynasties that followed, that I found small details of information. I brought servants with me to search scrolls of the third and fourth Dynasties for any mention of his name. We combed through thousands of scrolls looking for the most minute of details but found only sightings of him moving about the palace in the dark of night. After a year of voraciously reading scrolls in the Alexandria and Memphis libraries, I knew nothing more of him than what Cleopatra originally mentioned.

"She scorned my research, demanding that I cease my madness and focus on what truly mattered, meaning Rome. Returning to Memphis, after another heated conversation about my turning into a sad recluse, I weighed her words carefully. Maybe I was hiding from reality. I had spent a year obsessing on a man that had died twenty-five-hundred years earlier, and found nothing significant, not to mention ignoring Cleopatra and Caesarion.

"On a long, rainy afternoon spent in the Memphis library, I was beyond exasperation and decided it time to end my search. My eyes tired and head throbbing, I grabbed the last papyrus on the table and unfurled it. And there it was, in bold hieroglyphs.

'Khaba! Baka! Behold, Horus is against you. He denounces your god Anubis. You are cut to pieces by the sword in his hands. He has thrown you into this fire of his serpent Uamamti of the Netherworld. He burns you with the flame which comes forth of his mouth. Your bones have perished, your names do not exist upon earth, your members are not in the Netherworld. Your bodies are given to the fishes.'

"I could not believe it! Finally, evidence that Khaba was indeed eternal. Baka lived approximately one-hundred years after Khaba's death, so the two could not have been condemned equally, and at the same time. Since it read that Horus blamed Anubis for Khaba's and Baka's faults, I instantly knew where my questions were to be answered. The city of Abydos."

"Why Abydos?"

"That was the center of the cult of Anubis. It was so simple, but I had been blind. Instead of looking for Khaba, I should have focused on the god he was said to have sold his soul to. I was so elated, I laughed aloud, rolling up the scrolls to return them to the librarian.

"Rising from my chair, a librarian with a thick beard approached, inquiring, 'Have you found what you seek?'

"'I believe I have found the path,' I replied, happily.

"'Why do you seek information on a Pharaoh that accomplished little, when there is much to learn of the greatness of Pharaohs such as Ramses II?' he queried.

"'Because he is thought to be eternal,' I justified.

"'All Pharaohs are eternal,'" he contested. "'As a foreigner you do not understand our ways. It is due to the misconceptions of men, such as yourself, that the myth of Anubis Khaba came to be. I suggest you stop wasting your time and return to the palace.'

"When he held out his hands to take the scrolls, I saw two distinctive tattoos on the inside of his right forearm. In hieroglyphs, the first one said Osiris, and the second, with its picture of a rising sun over a Jabiru bird, spelled Khaba. I pretended not to have noticed, but when catching his eye, I saw contempt.

"Crossing his arms about his chest, he directed, 'Go now, I will return the scrolls to their rightful place.'

"As I walked away, he added, 'Return to your Queen.'

"At that moment, I agreed, wholeheartedly. I made my way out of the library, thinking only about Cleopatra and how much I missed her. Stepping into a light drizzle, I felt a tug on my sleeve and turned to find a different librarian.

"Visibly upset, he scolded, 'You know that all scrolls must be returned to me, the master librarian. Return to your table this moment and gather them, so that I may put everything back in its proper place.'

"'Your bearded assistant has put them away for you,' I replied."

"Perplexed, he challenged, 'There are no unshaven

librarians here, or anywhere else in Egypt. It is a mandate that we remain free of all hair upon our bodies.'

"I was dumbstruck! After years spent in Egypt's libraries, I knew the mandate just as well as he did, yet I didn't even think to question the stranger about his beard. When we returned to the table, the scrolls were gone. Checking the shelf where they previously resided, we found it empty as well."

"Didn't you wonder how he knew you were close with Cleopatra?" she asks.

"That was no secret. I was a foreigner and had been seen with her numerous times in Memphis."

"Was it Khaba?"

"No, the tattoo alone told me that. When Khaba ruled Egypt, Anubis was the lord of the underworld, but approximately two-hundred years later, during the fifth Dynasty, the Ennead and Ogdoad belief systems merged, and Anubis became the god of mummification, standing down in respect for Osiris. It was from that point on that Osiris was considered the Lord of the Netherworld. So, I knew the bearded man was not as old as Khaba, but possibly an acquaintance, or in some type of cult worshipping him. This further justified me going to Abydos because that was the center of worship for both Osiris and Anubis.

"Before sailing for Abydos, I returned to Alexandria to inform Cleopatra of my discovery. Upon arriving, it was clear that I had been away too long. She was making plans to set sail for Greece and join Antony in battle against Octavius. Sobbing, she agonized over our inability to coexist, as well as not being as open with each other as we once were. I tried to tell her that it was her involvement with Antony that had brought us to this point, but she focused on my crazed obsession with Khaba. I tried to explain that Khaba was only a respite from Antony, and if he were out of our lives, we would be happy again.

"She yelled, 'That is exactly why I am sailing for Greece, I want an end to our trouble with Rome! You have not aided me in these five years since Antony waged war against Parthia, and I have concluded that I must take matters into my own hands.'

"'You are mad!' I shouted, 'Surely sailing to your death!'

"Desperately, she pleaded, 'This is the only way we can be together! Can you not see how much I love you? I am willing to end my life in the hopes we may be happy again.'

"I tried to convince her that winning the war would not remove Antony from our lives, but she persisted that once the war was won, he would return to Rome. And, if he ever did return to Alexandria, we could easily dispose of him, rightly putting Caesarion before the Senate as the true leader of Rome. It was a ridiculous plan, holding no place in reality, but I did not wish to argue. For if there was even a glimmer of hope in returning to the way we were, I was more than willing to try. Antony was superior to Octavius in warfare, but Octavius would have the seasoned admiral Marcus Agrippa commanding his navy, meaning, there would be no chance of winning a battle at sea. Antony would have to force them into a land battle, for that was where he was at his best. I instructed her to pull Octavius inland where they could rely on the grain supply of a friendly village, and her ships could cut off Octavius's grain supply from Rome, or any coastal towns that might aid him. I emphatically stressed this point so that she would be equally adamant with Antony.

"We made love endlessly the week before she left, both of us knowing full well we may never see each other again. Before she boarded her ship, I told her to remain in the rear with the treasury ships, where it was safe. I held her tight, pleading, 'If ever you sense all is lost, raise your sails and return to me.'

"Tears welling in her eyes, she cried, 'You always have, and always will be my only love. . .. Pray for my victory, my king!'

"Pulling from our embrace, head hung low, she boarded the ship. As it was untethered and the oarsmen began their count, I yelled, 'Follow the winds of Fortuna, for they will guide your destiny!'

"As the fleet left the harbor, I stood forlorn, leaving only after the sun set behind the Pharos lighthouse."

"Why didn't you go with her?"

"There can be only one general in battle, and I swore to Caesar I would protect his son. And that meant keeping him out of this battle, if not for the sake of preserving his life, then surely from exhibiting an alliance with Antony."

"Did you take him with you to Abydos?"

"No, I left him with his tutor and guards in Memphis. It was the safest of all her residences because it was relatively small and easy to guard, not to mention everyone believed the boy to be at the palace in Alexandria."

"How was it possible that no one would notice his absence?"

"We had a boy that looked exactly like him, a body double used in times of emergency. It was during Cleopatra's trip to meet Antony in Tarsus that she happened upon the boy and paid his mother for the adoption. It was not uncommon to have a double, or even disguise oneself during those times. Treachery was abundant."

"Couldn't people tell when someone was wearing a disguise?"

"Hannibal wore disguises amongst his troops and was never recognized, so obviously they could be quite effective. But in Caesarion's case, the double needed only be present in the palace. Of course, those close to us knew, but any attempt to kidnap or murder him would have been done by someone outside the royal family. But that was a minor concern, my foremost worry was that I had sent Cleopatra to her death. The pain was so great, I decided to travel to Abydos by horseback instead of boat. It had been years since I traveled any great distance on horseback, and I knew the endless miles would clear my head.

"I moved slowly through the towns along the Nile, sometimes staying for weeks on end. In every village, I spoke with priests familiar with Osiris and Anubis, asking if they had any knowledge of Khaba being associated with either. Sadly, none acknowledged an association beyond the myth I already knew. It took months to reach Abydos, at which point I flung myself headlong into the search. I went to the Temple of Osiris first, knowing that that would be where my greatest hope lie, but was crushed when a priest told me the symbol of Osiris Khaba was tattooed on people as a good luck charm, in hopes of everlasting life. Visiting the Temple of Anubis, the priests laughed at my inquiries, asking if I also sought the door to the Netherworld. After having fun at my expense, the Lector Priest felt it his duty to sit me down and explain Anubis's role in the afterlife. I protested that I did not care about the mummification process, because I had seen it performed many times while residing in Egypt, but he began rambling, nonetheless. He took great pride in the process for he went into more detail than I needed to hear.

"As if schooling me, he instructed, 'First the holy rod is inserted into the nostrils, drawing out the brain with its hook. What cannot be retrieved through this method is assisted by the injecting of a disintegrating drug to soften and deteriorate the remainder. With the next step, a knife of obsidian is used to open the belly, after which, all contents are removed. The cavity is then cleansed with palm wine, followed by a further cleansing with pounded spices. After this process is complete, the cavity is filled with a mixture of myrrh, cassia, and other spices before being sewn closed. The final act is to cover the entire body with natron for no more than seventy days, for that is exactly the amount of time the Dog Star Anubis takes to rejuvenate before reappearing in the morning sky, as well as the time required for one's rebirth. Upon the seventieth day, the body is cleansed, and rolled in strips of finely cut linen that have been treated with myrrh and cassia. The wrappings are smeared over with gum, and the body taken to wood craftsmen, who form a casket to be laid in the sarcophagus. Most importantly, though, are the verses that must be read to Anubis as the tasks are performed.'

"Sensing I did not hold reverence the process, he decided to bore me with a reading from the Scriptures of the Dead. I gazed lifelessly at the altar, my mind drifting to Cleopatra. Where was she? What was she doing? Was she even alive!

"After listening to what felt like hours of endless chants, I knew I had to get out of there and find news of her. I had purposely been avoiding any gossip or talk about what was happening because I feared the worst, but now I needed to know! I tried to interrupt the priest and bid my goodbyes, but he kept talking as if I were mute. I was about to forcibly remove myself when he mentioned that the mummification process changed around the year 2600 BC. He did not realize it, but that was near the time Khaba died. He explained that previously, the internal organs were never removed from the deceased's body. In fact, they had not even used natron to dehydrate the bodies, they were merely wrapped in cloth and coated with resin. Going further, he noted a terrible upheaval among the priests of the period. The Controller of the Mysteries, God's Seal Bearer, and the Lector Priest were all beheaded and left in the desert to be fed upon by jackals, and when a new order of priests was brought in, they were instructed to perform additional tasks in the mummification process. A Scribe to line the body for incision points, a Paraschistes to make the incisions with a knife of obsidian, and a Taricheutes, or embalmer, to desiccate the body using natron. The organs would then be put in canopic jars and transported along with the body to the funeral, all acts having been performed by different priests.

"Grinning, I concluded, 'It sounds as if they were trying to make sure that no one escaped death, each priest affirming the other's work.'

"Thinking me a fool, he scoffed, 'No one escapes death. Not you . . . not I . . . nor Khaba. Do not fool yourself into thinking that the mummification process changed for any reason beyond the rotting of the dead. Eternal life is a central tenet to our beliefs, and the rotting away of flesh does not appear eternal. If the populace no longer believed in eternity, it would lead to the questioning of not only Anubis, but all gods.

And without gods, we are lost to lawlessness and disorder. I tell you these things because I want your search to end here. You are alive, Khaba is dead. Do not waste the precious minutes of your life on the long departed. Life is for the living, my young friend.'

"I could not help but feel he was right. After all, wasn't that what Cleopatra was trying to tell me? Leaving the temple, I made my way to the Chancellor of Abydos' nome, or district, as it would be called today, asking if he had heard any news of Cleopatra. From word passed on, he said Octavius was sailing for Greece. With that, I placed him somewhere in the Ionian Sea, and if Antony listened, he would be far inland, an extended march for Octavius. I knew from experience with Caesar that it could be a long battle, especially if Antony played cat and mouse across Greece, waiting for the precise moment to strike."

"I thought you said he was a fool."

"When seeking greatness, yes, but with his back to the wall and left with no other option but to fight, he was ruthless and calculating. I only hoped he knew just how far backed up against the wall he truly was. Thus, with the possibility of war lasting a year or more, I decided it best to return to my search."

"You weren't worried they'd be fighting soon? You'd been gone so long."

"Time in the ancient world moved slowly. You live in the modern age of computers, airplanes, and phones. You have no idea the time it took to cross such expansive spaces, especially when tens of thousands of men were involved. Besides, I had no other choice. I could not have wasted days, weeks, or even months in the palace, wondering if she was okay. I had to keep moving . . . keep my mind on other things. And that just happened to be Khaba. If it were not for him, I do not know what would have occupied my mind during those lonely days."

"Did you visit the library in Abydos?"

"Yes, but there was not much there, only a list of priests from the temples of Anubis and Osiris. A librarian, on a hunch, sent me to the house of records, which is where I found a piece of information that would send me right back where I started."

"What was it?"

"An aerial diagram of two pyramids. Though its location was not easily recognizable, the names Khaba and Baka were clearly written below them. Judging by the course of the Nile, it was in Lower Egypt, but there were no clear reference points for me to approximate their locations. Remembering the massive aerial map of Egypt painted on the entrance wall to the library in Alexandria, I laughed at myself for having traveled so far, only to retrace my steps. I copied the diagram and went to my horse. I looked to the north end of town, with its road leading back to Alexandria, and thought of the endless days I would spend waiting for Cleopatra's return, then, without giving it a second thought, rode south, retracing my journey with Caesar to Philae Island and the Temple of Isis.

"Knowing my path would eventually lead me to Alexandria, I took every possible detour to extend my time on the road. I visited the temples of Hathor, Amun, Amenhotep, Horus, Sebek, and even the Birth Temple at Hermonthis to view the newly completed carvings depicting Caesarion's birth, whereupon I once again pledged to protect the child and fulfill his destiny. Reaching the Temple of Isis, I gazed upon the relief of Isis with her crown of horns and sun disk, thinking about her titles as Protector of the Pharaoh, Goddess of Sexuality, and Great Lady of Magic - all fitting Cleopatra so well. Thoughts of her and Antony rushed back, making me more restless than ever, so I pushed further south to the temples of Ramses II, Queen Nefertari, and finally to the last of the great temples in Upper Egypt, the Temple of Aten, in Sesebi.

"Deciding it was time to return, I ventured into the desert for my northward journey home, craving the solitude of sand and sky to ponder my life. Where I once seemed to be ascending for greater purpose, I now felt as if I were falling into a deep pit, the inevitable bottom shattering my soul. I slept by day and rode at night, solemnly gazing upon our unreachable celestial canopy. The world seemed so enormous from where I had begun, yet so small when I thought of how it all lay balanced on the precipice of Cleopatra's existence. I ran countless scenarios through my mind, each coming to the same incontrovertible conclusion. Her death was at hand.

"Extremely adept at prolonging time, I made sojourns to the Great Oasis, as well as the Little Oasis. No more than a lost Bedouin haplessly wandering the desert, I was a feather in the wind. When I finally felt it was time to venture to Alexandria, I thought it best to check on Caesarion first. Believing I was far enough south to stop at the Faiyum Oasis, I planned on resting my horse and refilling my skins with water before making the trip into Memphis. Thinking myself to be no more than a day's ride from the oasis, I came to find that I had gravely miscalculated my location and committed the ultimate blunder. I was lost in the desert. Angered at my stupidity and arrogance, I berated myself for believing that I knew better than Antony or Cleopatra, when I was the one who would soon die!

"From lack of water, my horse soon collapsed, pinning my leg beneath its carcass. With what little energy I had left, I dug myself out, and quickly wrung the last of my skins dry. I tried to sleep by day but was too thirsty to stay in one place. The sun blistered me, and I could think of nothing but the endless blue seas Cleopatra must be sailing on at that very moment. I regretted everything! My pride, my foolish emotions, my unbridled ambitions, even my hatred of Antony. But more than anything, I hated myself for chasing a ghost. I cursed the name Khaba! The only satisfaction I felt, was in knowing that I would soon be dead and would hunt him down in the afterlife. Robbing him of whatever he held dear.

"On a star-filled night, my legs gave out and I fell to the desert floor. The taste of blood filled my mouth as I landed face-first on one of the many accursed rocks littering the desert. Pushing myself up, I crawled to a nearby boulder sticking out of the sand. I lay against the rock and gazed upon the Star of Isis, thinking how the most important star in the heavens also represented the most significant person in my life, Cleopatra."

"Why was it the most important star?"

"It rose in the Egyptian new year, the beginning of July, and coincided with the flooding of the Nile, not to mention, being the foundation of the entire Egyptian religious system. It was also called the Dog Star, but is presently named Sirius, deriving from the ancient Greek word seirios, meaning the scorcher. Being that it was the brightest of all stars, along with its heliacal summer rising, the ancients believed it was responsible for the heat of summer. That is where the saying, 'the dog days of summer' originated."

"Funny. Why is it called the Dog Star?"

"The constellation of stars around it forms the shape of a dog, therefore the similarity with the jackal-headed, Anubis. You can see why my eye was naturally drawn to it in the night sky. I thought it appropriate, that star should accompany me as I lay dying, for it embodied the two people most comprising my world, Cleopatra and Khaba. As my body weakened, and breath fell short, I romantically pondered the possibility of Cleopatra gazing upon the same star at that exact moment in time. What a fitting end I thought, both of us wishing upon the same star as death neared. I whispered, 'I love you, Cleopatra,' and with dying breath, screamed, 'Khaba, I'm coming for you!'"

TWENTY-ONE

Sunlight reflecting off the lake casts a glare in Weston's eyes, as he steps onto the expansive patio of the boathouse. Lifting a hand to block the light, he walks across the limestone patio to an oversized lounge chair and drops comfortably into the thick cushion.

I should probably explain things to Sierra. But how? And would she listen? Thinking over the possibilities, he rationalizes, *Do I really want to make amends? It was never that great to begin with, and the sex with Eve is otherworldly.*

"Ouch," he smiles, caressing the raw fingernail scratches adorning his chest. *I could get used to this. Except her treating me like a little bitch, that is. . . . Oh well, she'll break. They all do. That's how women are put together. It just may take a little longer with this one.*

"What are you thinking about, lover?" Eve asks, as she sits in the chair beside his.

Damn, she's quiet! How'd she get here so fast? "I- I didn't even hear you come out. I was just thinking about Sierra."

"I wouldn't worry about her, she's in good hands."

"What do you mean?"

"Altus won't let her get lonely."

Angered, he sternly advises, "He'd better not touch her."

"Or what?" she smirks.

"He'd better not, that's all. I'm not out of the picture yet, and there's someone who knows our whereabouts." *Has Sierra dumped me? Never! She's not the type.*

"No one's coming, lover. And if someone were, they would be dead the minute they stepped on the estate."

Fuck, she sees right through me.

"That's what I love about you, West. You always like to make things fun for me. You don't mind if I call you West, do you?"

Narrowing his eyes, he attempts to stare her down, but when she leans in close, he turns away, meekly. *Don't push her. She's too strong.*

Looking over the lake with feigned interest, her burning stare quickly draws him back. "Why don't you believe me?" *For God's sake, I sound like a wussy!*

"Do you remember the call I received after your last pathetic attempt at fucking me?"

"Yeah," he responds with indignation, hurt she considers him lame, when she's the best he's ever had.

"That was the bell tolling for your relationship with Sierra, it seems she's become quite fond of Altus in your absence."

Gritting his teeth, he glares with contempt. "You must think I'm a fool to believe that!" *She wouldn't leave me. No way!*

"I don't think you're a fool, only arrogant. But the two can be indistinguishable."

"Where is she? I want to see her now!"

"From what I understand, she's having lunch with Altus. And if I know him like I think I do, he'll be having her for dessert," she giggles.

"You think that's funny?" Frustrated and physically outmatched, he furiously rubs his forehead.

"I do. But there's no need for you to be upset, you have a new friend, don't you?" Meeting his gaze, she raises a brow and grins.

"Is she really with him?"

"That's the truth, baby boy. Sierra is so upset, she needed someone to fulfill her. And believe me, Altus can fill her much more deeply than you ever could."

"I don't believe it," he retorts, angrily. "Sierra would never do that to me!"

"It seems she's feeling awfully lonely since her boyfriend cheated on her, and needed a shoulder to cry on."

"You used me!"

"I used you, you used me. Whichever way you put it, it's irrelevant. All that matters, is, you've got what you've always desired," she smiles, implying herself, "and Altus is getting what he wishes."

"He's after Sierra?"

"My, you do pick things up fast, Einstein."

"Fuck off!" he shouts, unable to fathom that he was outsmarted.

From the corner of his eye, a blurred fist strikes his face, sending him to the ground.

"Never speak to me that way." Calmly inspecting her knuckles, she looks for a cut that may be oozing a tasty drop of blood.

Face planted to the limestone, his mind races. *I have to get out of here, and fast! Play along for now - an opportunity will come. I'll kill her, and take off before the others find out.* "I'm sorry. I shouldn't have said that," he apologizes, slinking back into his chair.

"I'll forgive you this time, but you must remember your place. I don't like to punish you, but it's for your own good. Do you understand?"

Fuck you, bitch! Running his tongue along his gumline, he probes for loose teeth.

"Do you understand?" she asks again, raising her voice.

"Yes, I do!" *Did that come out the wrong way? I don't want to get hit again.*

"Good. When I ask you a question, answer me directly. Do you understand?"

"Yes, I understand," he huffs.

"That's better. I think we're making progress. Don't you?" she smiles, flipping her hair back.

"Yeah, sure," he mumbles.

Sensing that he's feeling dejected, and not wanting her spirits dampened, she matter-of-factly states, "I find Sierra to be very, very unpleasant. Let's talk about something else. What would you like to talk about?"

"Nothing."

"Not even yourself?"

"Especially not that." *Especially not with you!*

"In that case, tell me about yourself."

Shaking his head incredulously, he sighs, "There's not much to tell."

"You're being modest," she patronizes, "I bet you're very interesting."

"Okay, if you really want to talk about me, that's fine. But could you please stop ridiculing me?" *Is her whole mission in life to fuck me, then degrade me?*

"No problem, I'll stop. See how easy it can be if you ask nicely?"

"Yeah, I see. Only too well." *I kiss your ass, and you treat me like shit.*

"Don't act so pitiful, let's not forget who put you in this situation."

"I know, I know," he answers, defeatedly. *Beats jail, hands down.*

"So, tell me."

"What do you want to know?"

"Why don't you tell me how much money you make from robbing homes."

"I do okay. Not as well as your friend Altus, but I make close to a million a year."

"Not bad, I suppose. But what if you get caught?"

"I won't."

"We caught you."

"Yeah, well, I look at this as an anomaly. It's not every day you rob a house of vampires."

"True. But what happens if the police catch you? You're far

too pretty to go to prison. You'll be someone's bitch before the sun sets."

"If need be, I could hire an influential attorney to get me off."

"You have that much money?"

"I have some. But I also come from a wealthy family. Between my father's name, and money, I figure I'd get off with community service."

"Who's your father?"

"Nathan Willmar."

Eve's mouth opens in a joyous smile. "No way! You're such a liar."

"Yes . . . I mean, no . . . he's my father! You think I would lie about something like that?"

"Hmm." *Should I tell him?*

"Hmm, what?"

Smiling like the Cheshire Cat, she spouts, "I knew your great grandfather."

"What!"

"Wilson. That was his name, wasn't it? Wilson Willmar."

"Yes . . . but how!" Frowning heavily, he holds his hands out, accentuating the impossibility.

"My father and your great-grandfather were partners in more than a few business ventures." *I can't believe he's from old money.*

"I don't understand. How old are you?"

"I'm about one-hundred-and-twenty," she guesses, time holding no meaning.

Could it be true? How else could she know his name? "Did you know him very well?"

"Not really, he used to bring his children with him, but they were all very young. I never paid them any attention."

"What was he like?"

"Very serious. I believe he was good at putting deals together but lacked the money to make them happen. That's where my father came in, he bankrolled the deals, and they split the profits."

Eve sits momentarily quiet, then begins laughing.

"What's so funny?" he asks, defensively.

"You're just so different!"

"How?" he challenges, not liking her tone.

"I knew by the way he used to look at me, he thought I was unruly and wild. I think he believed my father indulged me too much. But if he could see you, he would be heartbroken. And if he knew you were fucking me, he would turn over in his grave." Laughing hysterically, she's nearly bent over in the chair.

"Why's everything so funny to you?" *I love fucking her, but the rest is pure humiliation.*

"You don't find it funny that he thought I was loose and irresponsible, and here you are, his great-grandson, a carefree and undisciplined thief, begging for my pussy?"

Frustrated and indignant, he rebukes, "Whatever you think of him, or he would think of me, doesn't really matter, does it? Because I'm still getting the lion's share of his money when my father kicks the bucket."

"Is that what you're doing? Biding time as a thief until your father dies?"

"It's more than that. It's the excitement. The money's great, but that's only to live on." He looks to the distant tree line, pondering Sierra's endless whining. "That's what she never understood."

"Who?"

Fuck, shouldn't have said that. Taking a deep breath, he confesses, "Sierra. She only wanted enough money to quit. One big score, and that would have been enough for her. But it's a way of life for me. She never understood that."

"Then why involve her?"

"I needed her." He pauses briefly, contemplates what he's about to say, then spills the ugly truth. "This may sound funny for an art thief to say, but I couldn't tell what was truly valuable and what was paint by numbers."

Watching Eve roar with laughter, he adds, "I knew that would get you."

"It's just so ironic! I take it Sierra knew the value of art and offered to help you?"

"Actually, an old friend invited me to a party, and when he started talking about how his girlfriend was an art historian, how beautiful she was, and all this other crap, I thought, she's exactly what I need."

"You stole her from your friend?"

"That wasn't my intention. At least not completely, anyway. What I really wanted was to pump her brain."

"And instead, you pumped her pussy," she smiles, wryly.

"Ha-ha, very funny. It was only after meeting her that I tried to steal her away. She was cute, and after talking most of the night, I knew she could do what I needed most. Spot valuable paintings at a moment's notice."

"She was okay with robbing people?"

"She needed money for her sick father, and I knew if I could get her to love me, she would do anything."

"She loved you that much?"

"Yeah," he chirps, casually. "Only I should have known she could never be like me. She was too strait-laced and pure. You know how everyone has a dark side? Well, with her, it was obscured by the everlasting hope of middle-class values. All she ever wanted was to fall in love and join the masses in suburbia with two-point-five kids and a minivan."

"The Booboisie," she hisses.

"Huh, what does that mean?"

"A friend of mine, H.L. Mencken coined it. Referring to the ignorant middle classes."

"Why does his name sound familiar?"

"He was a writer in the early part of the twentieth century," she answers, off-handedly. *Why is Altus so attracted to her? She's pretty in her own way, but not beautiful like Abah, or me.* "What's Sierra like?"

"She's a great girl, just not for me. Ya know the type. Down to earth, nice, pedestrian."

"Then, you don't love her?"

"Meh, not really. I care for her, but we're too different to spend our lives together. I think she knows it too. Lately, it's our differences that are most pronounced."

Knowing Altus will be thrilled to hear this, she digs deeper. "Were you about to split up?"

"Yes and no. There's no way I'm going back to school to study art, so until I find someone to replace her, we're kinda stuck together. And, even if I do find someone, I don't know if I can just let her leave."

"Why not?"

"If I let her go, and she's angry with me, she may tell other people, or worse, the police."

"I see your point. Would you kill her if it came down to it?" *Would you like me to kill her? It would be a pleasure!*

"I don't know if I'm that kinda person, but if I had to, I suppose I could. But that doesn't matter now. I'm stuck here with you, and she's off with Altus. I wish I'd never seen this place. Everything's so fucked up now!"

"I think you need to focus on what you have, not what's gone."

"And just what is it, that I have?"

"Me . . . and *only* me. I'm your whole world now, and you'd better be grateful. Because without me, you haven't even got the breath in your lungs."

Thinking they were getting close; her words surprise him. "Are you threatening me?"

"No, just telling it like it is."

Meekly nodding with affirmation, he asks, "What's your story? I think I've told you enough about my dismal life."

Smiling at his comical self-deprecation, she can't help but gloat. "My story? It's a fucking fairy tale. I was born with the masses at my feet, and I came to be a goddess in my twenty-seventh year."

"You mean, that's when you became a vampire?"

"Yes, that is when my purpose in this world was defined. I, of the most noble blood in the new world, was infused with the blood of ancient rulers. Transforming me into the modern goddess of mankind."

This bitch gets crazier with every passing second! "What do you mean by noble blood of the new world?"

"I'm descended from the Halstredge family."

"You're a Halstredge? That's unbelievable! I went to prep school with Thomas Halstredge. He was a year younger than me. What is he, your grandnephew?"

"Something like that, I suppose," she dismisses.

"Wow, that's wild! Isn't he a doctor now?" *He was so mellow. Nothing like her.*

"That's what I've read."

"You don't speak with him?"

"I haven't seen any of my family since becoming a vampire. How could I explain my youth as they grew old?"

"True. Was it hard watching family and friends grow old?"

"Yes, my friends and I were of the lost generation, coming of age during the Jazz Age. We were the Flaming Youth, surrounded by technical innovations we set new trends for social behavior."

"How so?"

"Tired of the hypocrisy and waste of World War I, we centered the world around ourselves, living for the pursuit of pleasure and enjoyment. It was the age of individualism, and Louise Brooks and I most typified that new breed of woman."

"Who's Louise Brooks?"

"She was a movie star. Along with her, Mencken, Anita Loos, F. Scott Fitzgerald, George Gershwin, and Robert Benchley, we formed the smart set of Manhattan. Vowing never to be bored, we were fast and brazen, defying all conventions of previously acceptable behavior. Especially Louise and me. With her sleek black hair cut in a Dutch bob, and mine in the daring Eaton style, we were the epitome of Lulu, Louise's character from the movie Pandora's Box. We threw away the feminine ideal of the Gibson Girl and pushed the envelope of sexuality, hosting petting parties that quickly turned into orgies."

Gazing across the lake, the memories bring out a cheerfulness not previously revealed. "God, I loved those days! There's nothing like the fire of youth!" Hair blowing lightly in the wind, she offers a bright, genuine smile.

She's actually human under all that craziness. Damn, she's beautiful! "You miss it, don't you?"

"At times, I do. Especially Louise, we were so close, up until I met Altus. I recently saw some nude photos of her taken by Alfred Cheney Johnston when she was a Ziegfeld girl, and it brought back memories of skinny dipping in William Hearst's pool at San Simeon. She was so carefree and beautiful . . . it tore my heart out when I saw her on TV in the 1970s. It seemed impossible that she could be so old when I was still so young. To this day, I watch Pandora's Box every now and then just to see her looking back at me - as if time never passed, still whiling away our days in the bar of the Algonquin Hotel, laughing drunkenly with the other members of the Round Table. All of us too caught up in our own magnificence to ever fathom burning out, after blazing so brilliantly."

"You were a flapper!" Elbow resting on chair, he leans closer, enjoying her company for the first time outside of bed.

Caught up in the moment, eyes twinkling bright, she recites a poem.

"The Playful flapper here we see,
The fairest of the fair.
She's not what Grandma used to be,
You might say, au contraire.
Her girlish ways may make a stir,
Her manners cause a scene,
But there is no more harm in her
Than in a submarine.

She nightly knocks for many a goal

The usual dancing men.
Her speed is great, but her control
Is something else again.
All spotlights focus on her pranks.
All tongues her prowess herald.
For which she well may render thanks
To God and Scott Fitzgerald.

Her golden rule is plain enough-
Just get them young and treat them rough."

"That was wonderful, did you make it up?"

"No, it was written by Dorothy Parker. Though, she did tell me I was the inspiration."

"You seem like you loved your friends. Weren't you tempted to see them again?"

Eyes losing their sparkle, she curls the edge of her mouth. "With the collapse of the stock market, our way of life ended. It's hard to be carefree and decadent when you're surrounded by poverty and misery. I watched from afar as their beauty and lust faded like the scent of a cut flower, unable to stem the tide of time."

"What about your family?"

"That was extremely difficult. Especially my father. I was his princess, and when I disappeared, he took it very badly. I read the papers for a time, but it only made matters worse. Reading about his desperation as my missing person's case grew cold, made me want to visit him, but Altus would never allow it. He said he would have to kill me if I ever did anything so foolish."

"You watched from afar as your father suffered? That must have been difficult."

"Yes," she whispers, pain as strong as ever.

"I'm so sorry." Feeling sympathy, he takes hold of her hand.

She squeezes firmly as the memories take hold. "Altus never understood what I was going through. That's why I never told him that I visited my father before he died."

"Was he a lot older when you finally saw him?"

"Yes."

"Was he shocked that you looked so young?"

"I suppose."

"He didn't see you?" he questions, slightly confused.

"He did, but I think dementia had made him less cognizant. I'd read in the papers he was near death, and I wanted him to know that I was alive. I'd always felt my selfishness contributed to his failing health."

Clenching her jaw, she exhales, "I went late one night when everyone was asleep, wandering through the old house like a ghost. I saw pictures of my younger brother and sister, who now had children of their own, and my parents . . . the lines grew deeper with every passing photo that lined the wall. My heart ached for the life I'd abandoned. How could I have left all those that ever loved and cared for me? My emotions were running wild, and I knew I couldn't stay much longer, so I made my way to my parent's bedroom. Tears rolled down my cheeks as I opened the door and saw the two frail figures sleeping in the moonlight. I sat next to my father, searching his aged face for the man I once knew. When I looked away, attempting to hold back the tears, I was confronted with a picture of myself on his nightstand, taken near the time I left. I began to sob uncontrollably, forgetting all I had become, and turned back into the little girl that adored her father to no end. Wallowing in sorrow, I didn't see him wake, only hearing the tired words, 'Don't cry, baby girl.' Startled, I turned to see his crystal blue eyes gazing at me in the moonlight. I picked him up and carried him to the pool where he used to watch me swim, long since drained and full of leaves. I set him in a reclining chair and laid close at his side. He was unable to speak, but I saw the love in his eyes."

Falling silent, a tear rolls down her cheek. Hoping Weston has not seen, she quickly wipes it away. "As he lay there, with the sun's first light turning his eyes bluer than I had ever seen,

I took his suffering, and bore it upon myself."

Feeling sympathy for the devil, he squeezes her hand gently. "I had no idea, I'm truly sorry." *Deep down, she really is a caring, lovely girl.*

"I was his angel in life, it only seemed natural I take away his agony before his body failed him. . .. The sad part is, I don't know if he knew I was still alive, or if he thought me a dream. A figment of his imagination."

"Does it matter? You were with him when he needed you most, that's what counts."

"I like to believe that, but taking my parent's lives, no matter the reason, has haunted me to this day."

"Parents!" he exclaims, startled by the plural reference.

"The thought of leaving my mother to suffer his death was unimaginable. Returning his body to the bedroom, I drained her, set his limp arms around her, and fled from the only place that ever offered me an ounce unconditional love. My lips stained with blood, and soul filled with shame, I never stopped running."

Catching sight of Weston, open-mouthed and aghast, she realizes she's divulged too much.

Shaking loose his hand, she stands, rigidly erect, and looks out over the water, proudly proclaiming, "But this was my destiny. It is my very existence that gives evidence to my mother and father's immortality."

TWENTY-TWO

In search of more clothing, Sierra makes her way from the pool to Abah's bedroom. Humming her favorite song, the sounds of a man and woman in the throes of passion brings pause. Stopping at the entrance to Abah's room, she lightly puts an ear to the door.

Is Altus in there? He couldn't be, I just left him by the pool. God . . . please don't let it be Weston!

Slowly turning the knob, she gently pushes the door open. Taking a peek, she finds Abah grinding rhythmically on top of a young man she has never seen.

"Give it to me harder!" she demands, "Is that all you've got!"

Displaying god-like finesse, her body twists and flows in fluid, sensual movements, thrusting hips but a blur to the human eye.

Overcome with lust, Sierra steps in for a closer look, unaware that Abah's transference has taken hold.

"Come closer," Abah moans, with beckoning finger.

Pulled in by lust, she saunters to the bed, her tan, shimmering skin starkly contrasted against the white bikini.

"You wanna join us?" he begs, imagining the heaven hidden beneath Sierra's bikini.

Her body aches, YES, but she can only shake her head, NO. So heartbreakingly innocent of face, she wants to grab his long brown hair, and scream, RUN! SHE'S A KILLER, but the lust permeating her soul would never commit such treason.

"Sierra," Abah purrs, pushing palpable lust throughout the room. "Watch closely, you're going to enjoy this."

Biting her lip, Sierra fights the urge to reach in the bikini, and satisfy herself. *The way she moves . . . body writhing and muscles flexing. Unbelievably sexy!*

"Relax baby, this is going to feel good," Abah whispers, slowly running a finger across his moist lips, to his chin, jaw line, then neck, ending with a gentle caress of his unblemished, throbbing jugular. With a deep kiss, tongues intertwine, and he climaxes in shuddering approval. Her kiss leaves his lips, and her tongue follows his jawline to his tender neck, where she gives him the smallest, almost imperceptible, kiss goodbye. *So hot and young, you fuck like a stud. But now it's time, to suck your blood.*

With lids falling, and a lustful gasp, she strikes with vicious accuracy. He jerks at the puncturing of his jugular, but soon writhes in ecstasy, too overcome with transference to realize this will be his last lay.

Consumed with lust with fearful curiosity, Sierra takes in the deathly throws of passion, watching his once animated body go limp.

The last wave of orgasmic pleasure washes through Abah, and she pulls away, blood dripping from her lips onto the smooth, youthful cadaver.

"Is he dead?" Sierra murmurs, heart pumping a mile-a-minute.

"Yes." Knowing that anxiety and fear may soon overtake her, she continues transferring lust as she wipes the blood from her chin, and hungrily licks it from her fingers.

"It happened so quickly . . . he actually enjoyed it!"

"It's because I pushed my emotions into him."

"God, you looked so sexy when you did it. I wanted it to be me!"

"Tell me that you want me," Abah breathes.

"I do want you," she exhales, resting a hand on Abah's

shoulder. Softly kissing her cheek, she quickly locks onto her blood-covered lips, the taste of iron filling her mouth.

Breaking their kiss, Abah climbs off the man, and tosses him from the bed with a swipe of her hand. *Dead weight.* "You never asked why you were so turned on this morning."

"Huh?" *Stop talking and kiss me!*

"This morning, when I showed you how we project our feelings, you never asked why you got so turned on."

"I didn't think about it." Her half-opened eyes gaze lustfully on Abah's full breasts and stiff nipples. *Take me . . . I'm yours! What are you waiting for?*

"Ask me."

"Okay, why-?" she exhales impatiently, yearning to be touched.

"Because I wanted you. And I want more now. I want every bit of you."

"Mmm." *Teach me to love you!*

"I wanted you from the moment I saw you. It was my lust for you that overtook your fear that first night." Cupping Sierra's breast, she licks the virgin side of her neck.

Pulling back to get a good look at her tight, athletic body, Sierra wets her fingers and reaches between Abah's legs, rubbing the foreign, familiar place.

Writhing, Abah pulls her close, close enough to feel the warm softness of her skin and surging blood. *If I seduce her, Altus will be furious. Calm her down.*

Pulling Sierra's hand from her slippery love, she sucks the fingers clean. "I'd love to go further, but I can't." *Relax, baby. Just breathe.*

Don't stop! Eyes fixed on a drip hanging from Abah's nub, thoughts of tasting a place she has never known, fade rapidly, as she removes her hand from Abah's grasp. *Why am I doing this?*

Taking a step back, she asks, "How much of that was your emotions in me?"

"Like I said, we can't make you do anything you wouldn't

normally do. I'm very attracted to you, and I would say you feel the same. It just took my transference to bring it out."

Nodding, with feigned understanding, she sits beside her. *Would I have done that without her pushing me? Oh my, God. I completely forgot, she killed him!*

Sensing anxiety taking hold of Sierra, she uses all her strength to push overwhelming tranquility. "You know if it weren't for you. I'm not so sure I'd be as happy as I am right now," she distracts.

"How do you mean?" *Is she really that lonely?*

"This last year has been tough. Having you here has really lifted my spirits."

"I suppose I'd be out of my mind if it weren't for you. You've explained so much, you feel more like a friend than a . . . a . . ."

"Let's just say friend."

Soft smile turning to frown, Sierra's eyes are unwillingly drawn to the corpse.

"Maybe you should go to your room and rest." *If she stares at him much longer, I'll wear myself out trying to keep her calm.*

"That's a good idea. I-I just came to get some clothes," she stammers, unable to look away from the body.

"Are you going to be okay?"

"Yeah . . . just thinking." *Did I really watch him die? And do nothing?*

"Remember our talk about heaven?" Moving closer, she puts a hand to her cheek, forcing Sierra to meet her eyes.

"Mm-hmm."

"Well, he's there now."

"And if there is no heaven?"

"Then it really doesn't matter, does it?"

"I don't think I'll ever be able to go through with this." *How on earth am I supposed to do something like that!*

"You will."

"Did it take long to get used to it?"

"If I had seen what you saw, I would've been hysterical."

"I did okay?" *I don't feel okay.*

"You did better than okay, you're a goddess.

TWENTY-THREE

Throwing an armful of Abah's clothes at the foot of her bed, Sierra flops down, face-first into a pillow.

How did it come to this? How could everything have gone so far astray in just a few short days! Do I really want the disease, or are they making me feel as if I want it?

"How could I have been so stupid," she cries. "Is this even me anymore? My God, I actually watched her kill him. And did nothing!"

The words leaving her mouth, bring a new realization. *I'm an accomplice to murder. I've gone from the frying pan, straight into the fires of hell! I'm gonna be sick.*

Jumping off the bed, she runs to the bathroom, dropping to her knees before the porcelain god. With gut-wrenching heaves and watery eyes, the vomit surges, over and over, followed by fatiguing dry heaves.

"Fuck." Wiping her mouth, she spits out the bile.

Stumbling to the sink, eyes flooded with tears, she takes a close look at the accomplice in the mirror. *Can't bear to look!*

Splashing water on her face, she tries to wash away the sin. *This isn't me. I'm losing myself.*

Grabbing a towel from the rod, she buries her face in it, soaking up the tears. Taking deep breaths, she gently removes the towel and turns toward the mirror. Unable to meet her reflection, she returns to bed.

Remembering the words from a book on meditation, she breathes in the good air, and pushes out the bad. *Death. Lust. Greed.* Over and over, she focuses on her breathing, filtering the soul and cleansing the mind, until eventually, sleep takes over.

Deeper and deeper, she sinks into sleep, whereupon she is greeted by the same persistent dream. Wickedly handsome and enticingly evil, his words wash over her, demanding a response. Faceless strangers surround her, but she is unable to meet their eyes, too focused on the devil's haunting stare to break the connection. *He wants me, needs me, can't live without me! Lust in my soul, burning to be set free. YES . . . TAKE ME!*

TWENTY-FOUR

Relaxing on the veranda, Abah sips from a glass of vodka on the rocks, contentedly gazing into a crushed-velvet sun hovering above the treetops. Engrossed by the swaying trees and rush of blood, she does not hear Altus approach.

"I've taken care of him," he states, matter-of-factly.

"You scared me!" she squeals, almost jumping from her chair.

"Don't lose your edge. How many times have I told you not to give in to the rush?"

"It's the rush that makes me want to live forever. I'm so high right now, I could slay an army! If I could, I would feed every day. Cut my wrists open and drain myself to the point of starvation, all to unleash myself upon some lovely, angelic soul."

"I know, my love. That is how I know you will survive."

"It felt so right with Sierra watching me. I was so turned on, I almost bit into her too! If I hadn't found him hitchhiking this afternoon, she'd be dead right now."

"You take much too long between replenishing."

"Can I be there when you do it?" she asks eagerly, eyes gleaming with desire. "I want to be a part of it."

"I will see when the time comes. She has yet to choose."

"She will, she was on the verge of asking for it this morning.

I could see it in her eyes."

"Are you sure?"

"Without a doubt. I must confess something . . .. I think I'm falling for her."

"That's the rush talking."

"I don't think so. There's something about her. She's always on my mind!"

Is she feeling more than bloodlust? "I had better check on her. How long has she been alone?"

"I'm not sure, I've lost track of time."

"Without any transference, she may be an emotional wreck."

"What happens after she becomes one of us, and realizes we controlled her feelings?"

"As I told you, only transfer enough to keep her calm. Do not make her do things she does not desire. I want her to make the decision of her own free will, just as you did. If you confront her doubts with logic instead of transferring emotions, she will make the right decision. You want her with us, do you not?"

"Most definitely. I want all of her!" *Physically, and spiritually.*

"If you give her the knowledge and time to weigh her decision, she will join us."

"You don't think she'll have any regrets?"

"Did you? Even more to the point, do you hate it so much now?"

"God, no, I loved you for it! As I love you now. It's only when I delay in replenishing that I doubt."

"That is the affliction that must be overcome. Once you pass two-hundred, it will lessen with every passing century. You must not let it overtake your need for blood."

With a soft breeze blowing her hair, he kneels beside her. "I know things have been hard for you this last century, but you must know that I love you just as much as I did in our Charleston days."

"Do you really?" she questions.

"I do. I know you felt betrayed by my actions with Eve, and it is for that reason, I have always gone out of my way to put you first."

"I know, and I've always loved you for it. But it's different with Sierra. You look at her as you've never looked at any other. Including me."

"There is more to her than meets the eye."

"You won't forget me, will you?"

"Simply because I feel that time away will do you good, does not mean I will forget you. My love for you will never die."

"Do you promise?"

"I do," he confirms, with a kiss. "Please, come in the house, we will have dinner soon."

"I'm not hungry. The rush is best at night, and if those clouds on the horizon blow in, it should be wonderfully dark."

"Will you be staying on the estate?"

"I think I'll go to the stables; a night ride sounds wondrous. All this daylight has my eyes burning."

"Hopefully, she will accept the disease soon, and we can get back to sleeping through the daylight."

"You should visit her; she's probably coming down hard."

"Enjoy the night, my love."

"I will. It's when I'm at my best."

"Aren't we all," he grins, devilishly. "Aren't we all."

TWENTY-FIVE

Knocking lightly, Altus opens the door to Sierra's bedroom. Finding her asleep, he kneels at the bedside, caressing her hair.

Waking with his touch, she rolls over, opening her sultry green eyes. Even in the dim light of early evening, he can see that she's been crying.

"Are you okay?" he asks.

"No. I'm not."

"I have asked a great deal of you; I am sorry that you had to witness Abah replenishing."

"What's happening to me? The things I've done here are not at all like me," she whispers, voice strained.

"You are simply experiencing a different way of life."

Turning, she stares at the ceiling, defeat and desperation covering her soft, innocent face. "It's a life I'm not sure I can live."

"I care for you very deeply, Sierra. I would never hurt you or make you do anything you would not want to do." *She's worse than I thought, I had better give her transference.*

Feeling her spirits perk up a bit, she turns to him, "You hardly know me, how can you say you care for me?

"Do you trust me?"

"That's a bit of a loaded question," she contends.

"Believe me when I say, you have done nothing to be guilty

or ashamed of. You have merely opened a door that has shown you a different path from the one normally taken. There is no shame in Abah or me, nor should there be in you."

Sitting up, she softly exhales, "So much has happened, I think my emotions are getting the best of me."

"When I consider everything you have dealt with, I believe you have shown greater strength than any of my progeny."

"Have I?" *I don't feel very strong.*

"You have, and that is only one of the reasons for which I care for you so deeply."

Not entirely sure of his affection, she is happy to hear it, nevertheless. "Thank you for making me feel better. I always feel good when I'm with you."

"And I, with you. Shall we go downstairs and open a bottle of wine? It will help you relax, possibly put things into perspective."

"Lately, I seem to be doing a lot of drinking to put things into perspective."

Standing, he turns to find Cleopatra's jewelry laid out neatly on the dresser, and smiles, seeing the care she has afforded it. "If you enjoy wearing the jewelry, by all means, please do."

Thinking about the jewelry, she recalls Abah's feelings of jealousy. "It's so valuable, if something were to happen to it, I would never forgive myself."

Taking a deep breath, she stands up and looks at the pile of clothing on the floor. "I have to get out of this bikini."

Randomly grabbing a pair of jeans and a white T-shirt, she heads to the bathroom for privacy.

"Are you sure you wouldn't like to wear the jewelry? You are taking excellent care of it."

"Yeah, I'm sure. Why don't we put it back in the case, I think I'd feel better if it were there." Looking in the mirror, she rolls her eyes. *I look like hell. It's a good thing that bitch, Eve, brought makeup.*

"As you wish. Should you desire to wear it again, please, feel free."

"That's a wonderful gesture, but Caesar would probably turn over in his grave if he knew you were letting me wear it."

"I think he would make an exception for you. He had an immense appreciation for beautiful women."

"I think you're flattering me, but I'll take it as a compliment anyway."

Combing her hair with her fingers, she steps back from the mirror to get a good look. *Not too bad, I suppose, for someone else's clothes and makeup.* Exhaling slowly, she breathes out the last of the emotional agony.

Walking out of the bathroom, casually sexy in a T-shirt knotted at the bottom, and rolled-up, boyfriend jeans, she gives him a soft look of exasperation. "Okay, I'm ready."

"You look more beautiful every time I see you."

Following him into the hallway and down the stairs, she looks up at the painting of the angels. "What will you do with the body?"

"I have a hidden mausoleum on the property where our victims are placed."

"A hidden building?" she probes, suspicious they may have thrown him in a ditch.

"It is more a series of catacombs than an actual building. My inspiration came from the Christian catacombs that ran throughout ancient Rome. It is much the same, only more modern in that each tomb is sealed."

"Do you mark each one with their name?"

"No. There are a multitude of religious symbols and passages in the entry hall, but the tombs remain unmarked."

"I thought you weren't religious."

"The people that have given their lives for our existence deserve the respect and honor befitting what they would normally receive upon their deaths. All of us, we are no more than links in a cosmic chain. From the air we breathe to the food we eat; we must all show reverence for the things that give us life."

"You sound a little like an environmentalist."

"I am. This last century has seen damage done to the planet that will never be reversed. Humans come and go, leaving the detrimental effects for future generations to solve, but I am the living embodiment of those future generations. Therefore, I do all I can to preserve the wonders of this planet from being destroyed at the hands of short-sighted, greedy humans."

Just when I think I'm too repelled by his lifestyle to take the disease, he says something that justifies his existence. How much could I do to help mankind if I were immortal? "You're a very complicated man."

"In what way?"

"I suppose when I think about everything I've ever read or seen about vampires, they don't usually have an agenda, other than killing people. They don't honor their victims or try to save the world."

"That is why I despise the word. While we may embody everything that folklore points to as a vampire, we are much more human than we are monsters. We do not forget the people we loved, or causes once held dear, simply because we are infected with an eternal disease."

"I can see that. You still care for very deeply for Caesar and Cleopatra, don't you?"

"Yes, but part of living an immortal existence requires one to remember, without carrying the emotional attachment that brings about the sorrow and eventual apathy for life. If I were to dwell on how much I miss them, I would be lost in emotional turmoil like Abah, my will to live, rising and falling with my moods."

Following him to the kitchen, she sits on a barstool at the immense granite island and surveys the ornate white cabinetry and extensive stainless-steel appliances.

"Are there many like Abah?"

"Unfortunately, yes. They have a hard time letting go of their pre-eternal lives. Unable to adapt to the changes of the world, they get lost in the tide of time. And for some reason, around the age of one-hundred to one-hundred-and-fifty eternal years, they beg one of us to end their suffering."

"Do you think she'll make it?"

"Abah needs a spark to reignite her passion. Who or what that is, remains to be seen. What is more crucial is the time it takes her to find it. At times I fear she is living on borrowed time."

Abah told me she's been happier since she met me. Could I be that spark?

Watching her rub her lower lip, deep in thought, he wonders if Abah's desires are being returned. *Do they have feelings for one another I am oblivious to?* "Do not worry about her, there is a fire in Abah that belies her sullen demeanor."

Suddenly, Sierra smiles, confidently. *Maybe she's already found her spark!*

Curious as to her reaction, he inquires, "Why are you smiling?"

"No reason, it just makes me happy to think you believe in her."

Uncertain if she is telling the truth, he nods, and opens a bottle of wine, letting the subject go.

"Since it will only be you and I tonight, I thought I would prepare seafood pasta."

"Where is Abah?"

"She is out for the night, and I do not expect her back until morning."

"It's not something I did, is it?"

"There is nothing you have done that could ever cause trouble for Abah or me. But Eve?" he grins, "She might think otherwise."

Sierra laughs as he sets a glass of wine before her. *Was Abah right about Eve being jealous of Altus's feelings for me? Does he care for me that much?*

Watching him prepare the meal, she looks around the grand kitchen, thinking about the small home she grew up in. *Dad could never imagine me living like this. I suppose the circumstances haven't been ideal, but he is everything I've ever dreamed of. And what about living forever? I'd never have to suffer, like dad.*

Considering immortality, she recalls that Altus once thought himself dead. "What happened after you thought you were going to die in the desert?"

"When I regained consciousness, I found myself in a small room lit by an oil lamp. There were painted reliefs and hieroglyphs adorning the walls and ceiling, but I was too fatigued to examine them. Even the door, a mere fifteen feet before me, seemed too far to venture. Rolling over in bed, I found a pitcher of water and a cup sitting next to the oil lamp on the table beside my bed. I began drinking ravenously, so much so, I threw it up in a matter of seconds. As I bent over, wiping my mouth, I heard voices at the door. Lifting my head, two men entered. One of them put his hand around my neck and stood me upright, while the other looked me up and down. They were both Egyptians of average height, with short hair, but the one who examined me, with cleft-chin and small birthmark on his left cheek, moved with greater purpose and dignity than the other. An inert quality made him intriguing and mysterious, demanding my attention. I tried to say something, but was so dehydrated, only broken sounds came forth.

"The dignified man, directed, 'Do not attempt to move, you are very weak.'

"I was in no condition to stand, least of all fight, so the quiet man set me back on the bed, where I laid down. They stood next to each other and stared at me for what seemed an eternity. When he spoke again, I did not understand a word he was saying. It was not in any language I had ever heard, but I surmised what was said after seeing his friend take the empty pitcher and exit the room.

"'Why are you here?' he asked.

"Through dry, cracked lips, I uttered, 'I . . . don't know . . . where . . . here is.'

"Deep in thought, he slowly nodded, never breaking his icy stare. When the other man returned with more water, he set it on the table, then promptly exited. I weakly reached for the pitcher, and seeing my futility, he walked to the table and filled the cup. It took all my energy to sit upright, and I nodded graciously as he handed it to me.

"Picking up where he left off, he queried, 'How did you come to be here?'

"I sipped water to cool my burning throat, but my words came out hoarse and sickly. I told him as best I could that I did not know where *here* was. Needless to say, he was not happy with my response, and clenched his square jaw.

"After a moment of thought, he said, 'I can see you have traveled far, I will give you time to heal and regain your strength. If there is anything you need, please let my servant know, and he shall get it for you if I deem it necessary. All I ask, is that you not try to escape and when I come back in a month, you will be more candid with me.'

"I was dumbstruck when I heard him say I was to remain in that cell for a month! I tried to yell but could only muster a squeal. He headed for the door, and I feebly attempted to grab him. As his tunic slipped through my fingers, I fell to the floor, knocking the pitcher off the table.

"Peering at the spilled water, he scowled, 'Where you are from, water may be plentiful, but the desert does not forgive those who do not conserve. This will be your home for some time, I trust you will keep it, and yourself clean. When I see you again, I expect to see something more closely resembling a human being.'

"As he closed the door and pulled the bolts shut, I managed to eke out, 'Where am I?' But there was no answer, only the sound of footsteps going faint. I laid on the floor for a time, wondering if I should be thankful to him for saving my life, or if I should kill him for imprisoning me. After some time passed, his servant came back with an empty bucket, new pitcher of water, and a plate of food. He set the pitcher and plate on the table, the bucket on the floor, then picked me up as if I were an infant, gently laying me on the bed.

"I asked, 'Where am I?' But once again, there was no response, not even the flicker of an eye. He simply walked out of the room and bolted the door behind him.

"Left alone with my thoughts, I retraced my steps to ascertain where I might be. Not knowing how long I had been unconscious, I considered that they may have taken me far from where I fell and could be most anywhere."

Hiding a grin as best she can, the corner of her lip raises slightly. *You know what it's like to be a prisoner. Ha!*

"The first week or so went by rather quickly for I was more concerned with recovery than my predicament. Once healed, I questioned the servant aggressively as to where I was and how I came to be there. It did not take long to realize that trying to elicit a response from him was futile. It was like having a robot for a servant. He brought me what I needed, then exited without word or emotional response. I thought about Cleopatra ceaselessly, agonizing that I may never see her again. Feelings of regret returned, and I started down the slippery slope of depression. I spent so much time thinking about what I didn't have, I forgot to realize what I did. My life. When thirty days passed and he returned, I was consumed with rage.

"When he asked, 'Why are you here?'

"I bellowed, 'Tell me where I am! Stop playing games with me!'

"To which he turned his back and headed for the door. I sprang at him, wrapping my arm around his neck, and with no more effort than that of a child swatting a fly, he pulled my arm free, and held me over his head. I was stunned by his strength, especially since I am six-foot-six, and he was but five-foot-ten. He threw me across the room, and I crashed shoulder-first into the wall, bed breaking my fall. Rubbing my aching shoulder, I studied his ordinary physique, amazed at the strength hidden within.

"With a look of dismay, he shook his head. 'It is most unfortunate you have chosen this path. I see you will need more time to fully comprehend the gravity of your situation.

In sixty days, I hope to find you more accommodating.' And with those words, he slammed the door closed. Screaming at the top of my lungs, I kicked ferociously at the bolted door, hoping for his return."

"Did it work?"

Setting dinner before her, he tops off her glass of wine. "Someone did talk to me, but what he had to say, I did not want to hear. In a monotone voice, the servant stated, 'The master has decided that sixty days is no longer adequate. He shall see you in ninety.'

"I fell to the floor, exhausted, frustrated, and despondent. As the days passed, I realized how foolish I had been, for every day spent in that cell could have easily been spent with Cleopatra. I knew that if she and Antony did not win the war, Octavius would hunt her down, and I was only cheating myself of whatever short time we had left.

"I pleaded with the servant, 'I will do whatever he wishes, please tell him that I am ready to speak with him!' But, as before, there was no response."

"Did you ever try attacking the servant when the door was open?"

"No, I had seen his strength, and did not want to add more time to my imprisonment. Realizing that anger was getting me nowhere, I took stock of my situation. With time on my hands, I thought it best to calculate how long I had been there, as well as to keep track of future days. Scanning the cell, I searched for a place to secretly mark time. Since most of the walls were covered in paintings and hieroglyphs, I reasoned the wall against which my bed was pushed, to be the safest bet. There was a painting of a Pharaoh laid out on a table, with Anubis, Sekhmet, and Isis standing nearby. The wall had a white backdrop, and my bed was situated in the center, directly below the painted table. I moved the bed away from the wall, and with relief, found a clean white space. I grabbed the knife they had given me for eating, and carved an X into the wall, signifying my first thirty days of imprisonment. I deduced that it had been another ten days since I had seen him, made ten hash marks, and pushed the bed back into place. I did not know for how many days I slept, nor did I know how many days I was lost in the desert, but I did know it was near the beginning of September when I became lost, so, I surmised it must be near the latter half of October 31 BC.

"Sitting on the bed, I contentedly leaned against the wall, finally feeling as if I had done something productive. With satisfaction, I stared at the wall to my right, examining the beautiful painting of Anubis, surrounded by hieroglyphs. Then it hit me, I had been a blind fool! Sunken so low in depression, I had viewed the paintings around me as nothing more than decorations, but once my mind was clear of fear and anger, I could see the answer was all around me. I was locked up in the annex of an ancient burial chamber, and all I need do was deduce the owner of the burial chamber, and I would know where I was. Looking over the figures of Atum, Anubis, Sekhmet, and Isis, I translated the hieroglyphs that ran vertically over Anubis's head. When I read, 'Anubis, Lord of the Sacred Land,' I knew I was in a tomb predating Osiris. All I could hope for, was that the name of the Pharaoh was somewhere in the hundreds of painted hieroglyphs."

"The story began with Atum, the creator of everything in the universe. *'I am the Lord of All, father of all Kings and life itself. I pass my son on to you, Anubis, Lord of the Sacred Land, as he begins his journey toward eternal life.'*

"Anubis answered, *'I receive this king, of great and holy stature to sail upon the solar barge of heaven. Not to sleep with the eternal dead but to remain amongst the land of the living.'*

"The lioness-headed Sekhmet, preached, *'I, Lord of Scarlet and Lord of Flame, with my lifeblood shall give unto this king the eternal force of life. Great are the number I have slaughtered, and greater yet are my powers. By command of the Lord of the Dead Anubis, I shall give this king the blood of the Gods, forging his heaven upon Atum's creation.'*

"Lastly, Isis, on bent knee, proclaimed, *'I, the Divine Mother and Lady of the West, so long as my star shines in the heavens, shall watch over and protect this King of Kings. As Uraeus's blood flows through Atum, so shall it flow through this Lord of Eternity and Eater of Blood.'*

"I couldn't believe what I was reading! It was an alliance among the gods to give eternal life to a king, but not in the usual Egyptian sense of going to the Western world to die, instead, he was to remain a living being. Sensing I was onto something, I jumped from the bed, and pushed it clear of the painting. It was the picture of the Pharaoh laid out on the table with Isis standing to the left, Anubis in the center, and Sekhmet on the right, holding her hands over the dead Pharaoh's mouth. Isis chanted, *'You will be like Ra, rising and setting through all eternity. You will be complete. You will be Justified. You will be youthful. For in truth, you are Anubis Khaba. Lord of all eternity.'*

"I was ecstatic! I had haphazardly wandered through the desert and somehow happened upon the pyramid I went in search of. I screamed with pride, having proven Cleopatra and all the others wrong. Examining the painting more closely, I found that Sekhmet was not holding her hands over his mouth, but was sticking a knife in her wrist, causing blood to flow into Khaba's mouth. Moving on, I turned my attention to the third wall and its painting of a solar barge sitting atop the table-shaped sign of heaven. The barge, with its symbol of heaven, was being pulled by four jackals and four snakes, as they rode upon a giant serpent. At the front of the barge, Anubis prodded the giant serpent with his staff, and behind him, Khaba sat in a throne wearing Pschent, the double crown of upper and lower Egypt. In his left hand, he held Atum's staff of life, signifying he was a god possessing eternal life, while in his right, he held the cartouche of Anubis, meaning he was now, Anubis Khaba. Behind him, a mummified Isis stood erect, and to the rear, Sekhmet worshipped a coiled fire-spitting serpent, while above it all, a large Udjat eye kept watch."

"What did it all mean?" she asks, comfortably enjoying

their time together.

"Anubis was prodding the giant serpent to move the barge, keeping Khaba's Ka, or life force, alive, while his servants, the jackals, helped pull. The mummified Isis kept her eternal watch over him, and Sekhmet was worshipping the serpents that represent the lifeblood of Atum. Sometimes Atum was represented as a serpent, since it was believed serpents held the key to eternal life. And the reason that neither the giant snake nor the four snakes pulling the barge resided upon the sign of heaven, was because they already possessed the blood of eternal life, as Atum did. The Udjat eye, which is the symbol of the celestial hawk god Horus, watched over and protected Khaba, keeping him in good state. Surrounding the painting were three hymns, one to each side and another above the Udjat eye. The first, to the left of the painting, read,

He who turns his face to the West of Heaven. How beautiful is Atum!

Thou risest anew being young.

Khaba has risen, thy blood is in him.

The hot breath of the Uraeus-goddess has taken hold of his flesh.

Re-Horus of the Horizon rises!

This thy barge sails with a good wind, the heart of Anubis Khaba rejoices!

"The second, set above the Udjat eye, proclaimed,

The king has risen again, and the Bodily Form shines forth,
Lord of the Land of the Glorified! He has shattered the bones of the vertebrae, seized on the hearts of the Gods;
He has dined upon blood, swallowed down his fresh portion,
to be nourished by lungs of the wise ones,
to be warmed with life from their hearts and their magic power.
The King he rises, to feast upon the red broth!
The Bodily Form it stirs! It quickens!

Their magic is working within him!
Nevermore can his heavenly glory be gone from him:
He has taken unto himself the genius of every God!
The time of the King now, it is eternity, his boundaries, they touch infinity.
Through his power to do what he will, avoid whatever he hates, concerning all things in the kingdom of heaven throughout all space and time.
Nevermore shall the power of deities be deadly,
who would hack the abode where the heart of Khaba dwells amid the living on this our earth, for ever and ever more.

"And the last, to the right, read,

Everlasting One,
who wanders through the years without an end to his existence.
Ancient One who becomes young, who traverses eternity.
When old he makes himself young.
With numerous eyes, with many years,
he who leads millions when he gives light.

"After reading everything, I felt ashamed. I had spent the last month wallowing in self-pity when I could have easily answered his questions that very first day. Mortified, I could not believe it would be nearly ninety days before I would get the chance to speak with him again. I became bereft thinking how I had spent so much time trying to find him, yet, when I did, I was so consumed by petty anger, I blocked out all sense of reason and went on the defensive. What a fool I had been! Where I had wasted thirty days not observing my surroundings, I now had months to analyze every inch of my prison. Engulfed in shame, I read the hieroglyphs on the wall opposite my bed. The first, to the left of the centered door, was a poem, it read,

A pale sky darkens,

stars hide away,
Nations of heavenly bowmen are shaken,
bones of the earth Gods tremble-
All cease motion, are still,
for they have looked upon Khaba, the King,
Whose Soul rises in glory, transfigured, a God,
alive among his fathers of old time,
nourished by ancient mothers.

The King, this is he! Lord of the twisty ways of wisdom
whose very mother knew not his name,
His magnificence lights the black sky,

his power flames in the Land of the Risen
Like Atum his father, who bore him;
and once having born him,
strong was the Son more than the Father!

The lifeblood of the Kings hover about him;
feminine spirits steady his feet;
Isis watches over his domain;
Uraei rear from his brow;
And his guiding Serpent precedes:
"Watch over the Soul!
Be helpful, O Fiery One!"
All the Mighty Companions are guarding the King!

The King, this is he! strong Bull of the Sky
with bloodlust in his heart,
Who feasts on the incarnation of each God,
eating the organs of those
Who come, their bodies fat with magical power;
fresh from the isle of Flame.

The King, this is he! his change now accomplished,
united again with his blessed Spirits.
The King is arisen, transfigured, become this great God,

Lord over acolyte Gods;
He sits on Anubis's eternal throne of blood with his eye to the heavens,
and his back toward the earth.

The King, this is he! who deals out judgement
sitting in concert with One
whose name must never be hidden,
this day when sacrifice comes to all mankind.
The King, this is he! lord of the offering meal,
he knots the sacred cord,
provides his own gifts for the altar.

The King, this is he! who drinks of scarlet,
feeds upon Gods;

Keeper of tribute victims,
he renders swift sentence.

"And to the right of the door was a painting of Anubis Khaba, chanting the 'Hymn of Sekhmet.'

Mine is a heart of carnelian, crimson as murder on a holy day.
Mine is a heart of corneal, the gnarled roots of a dogwood and the bursting of flowers.
I am the broken wax seal on my lover's letters.
I am the phoenix, the fiery sun, consuming and resuming myself.
I will what I will.
Mine is a heart of carnelian, blood red as the crest of a phoenix."

"Did you try and tell the servant that you finally had the answers he wanted?" she asks.

"Many times, but he remained silent. There was nothing to be done, except prepare for our next meeting. I tried to think of every possible question he might ask, in hopes of gaining my freedom. I read the hieroglyphs again and again, even the hymns adorning the ceiling, their redundancy seeping into my brain, making me ache for freedom."

"What was on the ceiling that was so bad?"

"It was a hymn from the Egyptian Book of the Dead, meant to be sung to a number of gods. It read,

> *Atum, this thy son is here,*
> *Anubis, whom thou hast preserved alive, he lives!*
> *He lives, this Khaba lives!'*
> *He is not dead, this Khaba is not dead:*
> *he is not gone down, this Khaba is not gone down:*
> *he has not been judged, this Khaba has not been judged.*
> *He judges, this Khaba judges!*

"Then, the next verse would replace Atum with Nut, Geb, Isis, or any of a multitude of Egyptian gods, repeating the same verse, over and over. It was meant to announce that he was immortal, but what it really did, was drive me to the brink of insanity. Where I had once yearned to read such words, I now closed my eyes, ignoring their existence. The days began to drag, and I counted the hash marks over and over, sometimes more than once a day, believing I had misread them earlier.

"Seeing that she has finished eating, he asks, "Would you like to sit in the parlor? It is more comfortable, and we can open another bottle of wine."

"Sure, I'd love to!" *What if I don't take the disease? Could I ever live without regret, knowing what I gave up?*

TWENTY-SIX

"Do you ever worry about things?" Sierra asks, soaking in his muscular frame covered in crisp designer clothing, topped off with a sexy, vampiric strut.

"It depends, what types of things are you referring to?"

"I don't know. Like money, or things not going well."

"Having money only removes the worry of money."

"Which is the biggest worry for most people," she justifies.

"That is true, but some things are much more important money."

Entering the exquisitely decorated parlor with its silk wallpaper, gilded cornices, and Viennese furnishings, he points to a piano occupying the center of the room. "Take this, for instance. There is no price that would justify me selling it."

Studying the antique piano, she attempts to ascertain its age. "Did it belong to a loved one?"

"Many years ago, when I was living in Vienna, I secretly commissioned a 'Mass for the Dead,' from the composer Mozart."

"What?" she exclaims. "You're the one that commissioned it! Not Count Walsegg?"

"Yes, it was me. The 'Requiem Mass,' as it was called, was an idea I had for the Century's Gathering, held in the year 1800."

"What is that? A gathering of vampires?" *I bet there's a lot of dead people lying around town after that party.*

"Yes, I try to monitor what is happening with our kind, maintaining a sense order, for lack of a better phrase. If there were not an elder keeping tabs on the progeny, it is likely they would do things to jeopardize our existence."

"What was he like?" she begs, flabbergasted that he knew Mozart.

"I did not know him well, but was an ardent follower of his music. I commissioned the piece in secrecy because I thought it best not to bring attention to myself. Unfortunately, he became ill around the time he began composing the piece, and according to his wife, Constanze, foolishly believed it was for his own funeral. I found it a fitting piece for a gathering of the undead but had no idea he would correlate it with his failing health. After his death, I visited Constanze and found her to be in grave financial need. Feeling somewhat to blame for the whole fiasco, I offered an immense sum for the piano so that she might once again live comfortably."

Sitting on the antique bench, she runs her fingers over the cracked, weathered keys, striking randomly to see if it's in tune. "I can't believe I'm touching the piano Mozart played!"

Watching her softly touch the keys, he smiles, warmly. *Has Fortuna befriended me, again?*

Loosening her fingers, she takes a deep breath and starts playing the second movement from Mozart's piano concerto number 21. K467.

Sitting on the couch across from her, he proclaims, "I had no idea. How long have you played?"

"Two lessons a week, from the time I was five, right up through high school." Her look of concentration slowly turns to sorrow as the familiar song brings tears to her eyes.

"What is wrong?" he asks, compassionately.

Stopping, she looks away, wiping the tears. "It's my father's favorite. I used to play it for him before he became sick."

"What ails him?"

"He has Alzheimer's. He's in a nursing home because I

couldn't take care of him any longer. I've tried to get him good care, but once the money ran out from the sale of our family home, there was nothing left to do but put him on Medicaid."

"I am so sorry. Is he in government care now?"

Wiping away the tears, she bashfully meets his eye. "Where he is now, isn't bad, but some of them were real nightmares. To keep him in a decent home takes a lot of money, so I have to cover the cost, as well as support myself. Which hasn't been so bad since I met Weston, because we make great money."

"That is why you are a thief," he notes. *Eve did well. Weston revealed the truth.*

"Yes, and because I wanted Weston to love me. Not so long ago, I would have done anything for him to say, 'I love you.' But I've come to realize I was only kidding myself. He never cared for me."

Hanging her head, she dries her cheeks. "I never dreamt I'd be so alone."

Understanding what drives her and knowing how hard it can be to watch loved ones die, his empathy pours forth. "I want to help you. Together we will find the best care that money can buy."

Shocked by his offer, her eyes open wide. "I could never accept it! I appreciate it, but I hardly know you."

"The money is of no importance; it is making you happy that matters most."

"I couldn't. Especially not after trying to rob you!"

"Had you not attempted to steal from me, I would not feel the joy you have brought to my life."

He keeps saying that! Why? "You hardly know me, yet you say you have strong feelings for me. How's that possible?"

"I know it seems like things are moving fast, but you must believe me when I say that I care for you very deeply. And, if helping your father will make you happy, then it is but a small price to see you smile."

Joining him on the couch, she hugs him tightly, tears streaming down her face.

"Then it is agreed. We will find the finest doctors available and put him in their care."

Overcome with joy, she begs, "Are you sure?"

"Yes, I am certain. The days we have spent together have brought me great happiness. It has been many centuries since I have been so enamored of a woman."

Unable to find the words to appropriately express her feelings, she wipes away the last of her tears, kisses him gently, and looks deep in his eyes. *Not just grey, flecks of blue. Soft blue, caring, accepting.*

Pushing the hair back from her face, his fingers caress her cheek, then lips. She gently kisses his fingertips, wets her lips, and grabs him by the hair, pulling his lips to hers.

Retreating from the throws of passion, he stutters, "Y-you keep surprising me. I had no idea you were such an accomplished pianist." *It is too soon. Do not rush her!*

Breathing heavily, passion burning, she licks her lips. *Mmm, still taste him.*

TWENTY-SEVEN

Sensing an honor not found in modern-day men, she gives him space, and takes hold of his hand. "What happened after the ninety days passed and you met with Khaba?"

"When the time came, I went about cleaning myself and the cell beyond reproach. Waiting quietly on the ninetieth day, when his servant brought my breakfast, he entered."

"Crossing his arms, he gazed down at me, sitting on the edge of the bed. With an approving nod, he grunted, 'You have shown great respect for yourself, and your surroundings. I commend you.'

"I blurted, 'I am ready to answer any question you have, and I hope you will answer some of mine as well.'

"Tilting his head, inquisitively, he said, 'You are bold and daring. I honor that in a man, but do not presume I will give you what you desire unless I hear the truth. Tell me, why are you here?'

"I responded, 'Hearing tales of your existence, I was so fascinated, I aggressively sought you out.'

"'Who is it you think I am?' he challenged.

"'The ancient Pharaoh Khaba. At least that is who I meant to seek, and that is whose antechamber I am in, judging by the hieroglyphs.'

"'I appreciate your honesty, so I will be honest with you. I am indeed the Pharaoh Khaba.' Analyzing my every move, he grumbled, 'What is it you desire of me?'

"'I wanted no more than to see if you were real.'

"'You have gone through much to prove my existence. Why should I believe you went to such great lengths out of curiosity?'

"Giving it a moment's thought, I replied, 'I have a great need to learn and understand. I come from a land far away, vastly different from Egypt. I have found myself fascinated by your country and people, and that, in turn, has led me to you.

"He looked at me blankly, saying, 'Perhaps I did not make myself clear. What did you hope to achieve when you found me?'

"Fearful I would give him the wrong answer and find myself confined for a greater length of time, I quickly spouted, 'In the beginning, I only wanted to prove that you were real, but as time passed, I cannot deny, a part of me desired eternal life.'

"Tilting his head again, he raised his brows. 'Once again, I appreciate your honesty. Tell me, what purpose would eternal life serve you?'

"Sensing I was not telling him what he wanted to hear, I looked to the painting of the four gods on the wall, desperately hoping something would pop in my head. Knowing I was at a loss, he commented, 'The answer is not within these paintings, it resides within you.'

"Unsure of what to say, I shifted about uneasily. After a moment or two, a thought crossed my mind, and I went with it. 'Previously, only the prospect of eternal life fascinated me. But when I consider it on a deeper level, I suppose I could save those I love from death, as well as make the world a better place.'

"For the first time, I heard his servant laugh. I was grasping at straws, and they knew it. Khaba frowned, not quite sure if I was a liar, or a fool.

"He graciously explained, 'Saving loved ones is indeed possible, though never does the love remain. In time, animosity or indifference brings eternal regret. And as for the second part of your answer, I would appreciate your honesty over answers you believe will pacify me. Even if it requires admitting ignorance.'

"Holding my hands up, almost in surrender, I said, 'I am sorry. I am only trying to answer you as best I can without raising your ire. I do not mean to offend, but our previous encounters were more than brief.'

"Regretting the words as they poured forth, I feared his response would be to stand up and walk out, but instead, he remarked, 'You carry the characteristics of your people. You are strong, both mentally and physically. Which of the Germani tribes do you hail from?'

"I was stunned that he not only knew where I was from, but the characteristics of the German people. Delighted, I told him, 'I am Cheruscan. But how do you know of my people?'

"'I have been to your land.'

"Shocked, I conceded, 'In my ignorance, I presumed you had lived your entire life within the Eastern portion of the Mediterranean.'

"Setting his hands on hips, he smiled, 'I have not only visited your land, I have also been to the other side of the world. Far across the sea, lies a land of untouched splendor.'"

"Was he talking about America?" Sierra interjects.

"Yes, but initially I believed he was talking about China, or Serica, as it was referred to in ancient times."

"Because silk was called seric cloth, right?"

"You know your history."

"I was an art history major, you know," she smiles, proudly. "Was there any connection with him and the pyramids in South America?"

"I do not know how much Khaba influenced them, but there was another of our kind that lived with the Mayans, and he was definitely the builder of at least one pyramid. But I am getting ahead of myself. When he told me there was a land far more mysterious than Serica, I became enamored of his life. I thought I had traveled great distances and seen much of the world, but I had seen nothing in comparison. I wanted to keep discussing foreign lands, but he cut me off to resume his interrogation, asking, 'You are Germani, but you live and dress as a Roman. Are you here to serve Rome?'

"I informed him how I came to meet Caesar and Cleopatra, and what had eventually become of us. He sat in quiet contemplation for an extended period, then inquired, 'If Antony and Cleopatra were to lose this war, you have no doubt Egypt would become a province of Rome?'

"I did not hesitate in answering, 'Yes!' How much control Rome would hold over Egypt, I was not sure, but I knew I had his undivided attention. From that moment on, I knew he valued Egypt's sovereignty just as much as he valued his own life. He begged for details on what has happening in Rome and Alexandria, and what I thought the inevitable outcome might be. I painted a picture much bleaker than was probably true, for I had a gut feeling I was his only link to foreign affairs. As the conversation progressed, I found that his servants were instructed to look for people inquiring about him, yet he relied heavily upon hearsay to determine what was happening in the world of politics. They had come to be living in a state of paranoia. Leaving the tomb to feed, listen to idle chatter, then rush back before being discovered. He spoke of trips around the world, but they were few and far between. After talking most of the morning, he abruptly stood up, informing me, 'I have enjoyed our conversation, but I have matters I must attend to. I will return tomorrow, and we will speak again.'

"As quickly as he had come, he was gone. I analyzed our conversation endlessly, wondering if I had been too presumptuous in thinking he knew nothing of the current political state.

"The next morning, he returned alone, carrying my breakfast. His first words were, 'I had my servants look into your story. You are the one named, Altus.'

"Terrified that he had found my tales to be false

exaggerations, I gulped, 'Yes, I am Altus.'

"To my complete surprise, he bowed, 'I am honored to be in your presence.'

"Gasping, I could not believe my good luck. Whoever his servants had spoken with, it seemed they were only able to confirm my connection to Cleopatra and Antony, not my wild tales of Rome's impending subjugation of Egypt."

"He asked, 'If I give you information on the war, can you tell me what the outcome will be?'

"I was dying for information on Cleopatra, and blurted, 'Yes, I can tell you anything you need to know!'

"He sat at my side as if we were old friends, saying, 'There was a battle at Actium several months ago. Almost to the day I found you. The outcome was not favorable for Egypt.'

"My heart sank, for I knew Cleopatra was dead. I balled my hands into fists, cursing myself for wandering through the desert when I could have been at her side.

"Seeing my anger and frustration, he consoled, 'Do not fear for Cleopatra, she survived the battle, as did Antony, but I fear the war is lost. In Antony's haste to be with Cleopatra, he left his army, and they, in turn, abandoned him to join Octavius. There is word, they are marching toward Egypt.'

"My emotions ran wild, at first I was ecstatic that Cleopatra survived, then sullen, realizing my worst fears were about to come true. I asked, 'Do you have details of the battle?'

"'Only that Cleopatra is said to have sailed off in the early stages, handing victory to Octavius by default,' he stated.

"I became forlorn. Had she taken my words too close to heart? Giving it further thought, I soon realized, if Antony quit to be with Cleopatra, he must have been nearby, which could only mean, he fought a naval battle with Agrippa. 'Damn you, Antony!' I screamed, causing Khaba to leap from the bed.

"Not wanting to anger him, I apologized profusely. 'I am sorry, it is that he did exactly what I feared. He fought the wrong battle and ended all our hopes!'

"With grave concern, he sat again, imploring, 'What is to

happen next?'

"I shook my head in disgust. 'Octavius will march into Egypt and kill Antony, take Cleopatra to Rome as his prisoner, then execute her at his Triumphal celebration.'

"The words alone made me sick. I had to get out of there, fast! Thinking quickly, I formulated a plan to shock him into thinking I was Egypt's only chance of salvation. I spun a tale of Rome's armies going city to city, temple to temple, and tomb to tomb, plundering Egypt to its core. I informed him that I was friends with Octavius as well as many senators, and that if anyone were able to save Egypt, it would be me. In desperation, I brazenly commanded, 'Set me free, immediately! I must return to Rome and put a halt to this war!' It was a desperate ploy, but I hung onto it by the skin of my teeth.

"Rubbing sweaty palms together, he balked, 'I . . .. I fear that is impossible, you know too much about me.'

"From that momentary hesitation, I knew he was desperate. I pushed further, magnifying the destruction the Roman armies would inflict. Describing in detail the sieges I had partaken in with Caesar, I explained how it would be tenfold worse due to Egypt's riches. I could see his mind racing, he could not stomach the idea of his homeland being pillaged.

"Visibly agitated, he rubbed his chin pensively, then nodded briskly, confirming his thoughts, as he spoke. 'I shall let you leave to prevent this war, but I will accompany you. I can protect you better than any of your soldiers.'

"Hiding my exuberance, I expressed only the urgency with which we needed to move. I knew the quicker he ran about, the less time he would have to think, limiting the possibility of a change of heart."

"'Follow me,' he commanded, exiting my cell.

"Anxious to be free, I traced his every step. Up a stairway and down a long hallway, we went, until we reached an intersecting hallway. Turning right, there were rooms dotting the right-hand wall. Reaching the end of the hall, he called out in his ancient tongue, and the servant from my prison and two other men promptly came out of three different rooms. One of the servants took me into the last room, while the other two followed him back down the hallway. Sensing something familiar about the man, I studied him as he grabbed a tunic from an open chest. Then it hit me. 'The library in Memphis!'

"Locking eyes on me, he confessed, 'Yes, it was me. Please remove your clothing that I may offer you a clean tunic.'

"No sooner had I thrown on the garment, than Khaba entered the room. With the motion of his hand, I followed him to the bottom of a staircase, where the other two servants waited, one holding a bag of food and the other, skins of water. Khaba uttered a command, and one of the men ran up the stairwell. Looking up, I could see nothing in the dark recess. I heard him grunt, then suddenly a ray of light ripped down the stairwell, blinding my vision. He had pushed a massive stone block off the entrance to the stairs, and once removed, I ran up to greet the blinding rays of the sun. I held my arms wide, guzzling air as I stepped onto the welcoming desert sands. Eyes closed tight, the sun's rays enveloped every ounce of my being in sweet, burning love. My soul rejoiced, *I'M ALIVE!*

"As Khaba spoke with his servants, I turned from the burning orb to study the incomplete layer pyramid from which I had just exited. 'Why it is unfinished?' I interrupted.

"'My reign was short,' he explained, 'I died prematurely and was buried in a mastaba tomb, north of here.'

"Unable to comprehend why he would be buried elsewhere, I argued, 'But the interior is finished, covered in hieroglyphs.'

"'That was done long after my mortal death, by my progeny. When I first came to reside here, it was no more than rough stone walls.'

"Turning his attention back to the servants, I thought, Caesar was right, Fortuna does indeed watch over me. I stared down the sun until nudged by a servant, handing me a skin of water. Slinging it over my shoulder, the servants went back down the stairwell and yanked on a rope that was affixed to the bottom of the massive stone, pulling it back over the stairs, concealing the opening.

"Khaba looked at me soberly. 'I am trusting you with my secret. Need I say more?'

"Putting my hand on his shoulder, I promised, 'I shall never betray you. You saved my life as surely as Caesar, and for that, I will always be indebted to you.'

"With a look of gratitude, he reciprocated, putting his hand on mine. 'Good, we understand each other. I am taking an enormous risk by venturing out among humans in this manner.'

"Wrapping his face in a traditional bourque, we passed a large boulder near his pyramid. 'That is where I found you,' he pointed. 'It is the unfinished pyramid of Baka.'

"I shook my head in disbelief, thinking, what a strange hand destiny deals me. Asking where we were headed, he answered, 'We will be in Memphis by nightfall. There is a village in the valley just beyond here, we will purchase horses to hasten our journey.'

"It turned out that I had traveled further north than I believed, missing the Faiyum oasis completely."

"But if you had made it to Faiyum, you wouldn't have met Khaba. Or me," Sierra smiles.

"You are right, for even if I had found his pyramid, I would never have found the stairwell. And by chance, if I had, he would have undoubtedly killed me." Considering the possibility, he thinks aloud, "It is strange how destiny steers me in the most opportune of directions."

"Maybe it's not destiny, maybe you're Fortuna's favored son. Did you ever think Caesar saw it more clearly than you?"

"While that may be possible, I would never be so bold as to admit it aloud."

"Because of superstition, or because you still believe in your ancient Pagan gods," she jests.

"I believe that if I affirm either, you will delight in accusing me of being a hypocrite," he grins, happy that she challenges him so comfortably. "Instead, I will tell you that we did indeed arrive in Memphis by nightfall."

Softly smiling, she throws her leg over his, and cuddles close.

Putting a hand on her thigh, he rubs gently. "We rode to Cleopatra's residence, but it was vacant. Caesarion and his guards had most likely been summoned back to Alexandria months ago, upon Cleopatra's return. I told him we would spend the night there, and sail for Alexandria in the morning. After such a long period in captivity, I longed to soak in a bath and sleep in a comfortable bed. When I awoke the next morning, I found him anxiously waiting to embark. We went to the docks and procured passage on a small barge setting sail for Alexandria. Watching him reach into a bag about his neck and pull out a handful of coins, I asked how he went about attaining money.

"He guided me to a quiet area on the barge where we could be alone and explained that they did not require much, and what they did, was stolen from temples and palaces. As the words rolled off his tongue, my mouth fell open. He was nothing more than a petty thief! The visions of him in the palace were nothing more than sightings of a burglar at work. It was pathetic! The man who possessed the greatest gift in the universe, was spending eternity as a two-bit criminal. I grew quiet, staring at the shores of the Nile as we sailed downstream. The waters were below the banks, and I envisioned the fields of grain ready to be harvested and sent off to ports throughout the Mediterranean. I looked back at Khaba with contempt, thinking, the poor farmers of this land have more dignity than this immortal Pharaoh.

"Unexpectedly turning, he saw the look on my face, demanding, 'What is it that goes through your mind!'

"'Nothing,' I mumbled, looking away.

"'Because you have yet to serve my purpose, do not be so brazen as to think I need you,' he threatened.

"Hoping to calm his boiling anger, I explained that one of such high standing should not be stealing from nobility, but instead, be using his gift to help others.

"'I have tried many times to pass my gift on to rulers I felt worthy,' he argued, 'but they have either passed away in the acceptance of my blood, or turned evil. Making it necessary to end their lives.'

"'Why rely on others to do great things, when it is you that possesses greatness?' I implored.

"Looking over the rippling water, he exhaled, 'I thought I could rule for eternity when I accepted this gift, but whence I reappeared from my tomb, I was looked upon as a devil. Forever cast out of society.'

"Curious, I asked, 'How is it that you died and came back to life?'

"He informed me that the Lector Priest from the Temple of Anubis offered him eternal life, and in return, all he need do was shower the priest with riches. He laughed at the man as if he were a fool, but the priest went on to tell him of Sekhemkhet, the Pharaoh that preceded him. It seems that Sekhemkhet accepted the offer of immortality, but once dead, no longer possessed the palace riches, and thus became a tomb raider to pay off the priest. Khaba expressed that if he could prove as much, he would gladly meet the terms of his agreement. Weeks went by and he thought he would never hear from the priest again, then, one day, he was summoned to the Temple of Anubis.

"When he arrived, the priest escorted him to a secluded room in the back of the temple, revealing the fully animated Sekhemkhet. Before Khaba could say a word, the priest lunged at Sekhemkhet, plunging a knife into his stomach. Khaba jumped back in horror, but Sekhemkhet merely laughed, lifting his garment to reveal a miraculously healing wound. The priest informed him that by drinking the blood of the Goddess Sekhmet, it would forever guard his body from aging, but that a deathly sickness takes place upon the mixing of human blood with that of a god's. Khaba boldly said he feared no sickness, so, as a final warning, the priest explained that only those seen righteous by Anubis are granted eternal life. Undaunted, Khaba said he would accept the blood of the gods, and when the time came, he should be taken to the Temple of Anubis, so that the priest may pray for his salvation.

"The priest agreed, and Khaba began thinking things through. He wanted eternal life, but he saw a terrible flaw in the way they went about arranging Sekhemkhet's death. The Lector Priest, along with two fellow priests, had sealed Sekhemkhet's empty sarcophagus so that all believed him to be entombed, which left him free to carry on with his life, in secret. But that was not what disillusioned Khaba, it was giving up being king that dismayed him. He had great plans for his country, and if he were to die, real or imagined, none of those plans would ever come to fruition.

"Instead of pretending to be dead, like Sekhemkhet, he treated the sickness as if he were dying, telling court officials he felt his death at hand, and that they should begin preparing for his funeral. It was then that he implemented the genius of his plan. He told the court officials to spread word throughout the kingdom that he would confer with Anubis when he reached the sacred land and offer an abiding allegiance if granted eternal life. By doing this, it would confirm his status as an eternal god if he happened to live, and if he died, nothing was lost.

"Halfway through the sickness, the priests proclaimed him dead, carried him in a casket to his mastaba, and placed him in the sarcophagus. He resided in the burial mound until overcoming the sickness, then dug himself out, and for all appearances, looked to have been granted immortality by Anubis.

"Everything went perfectly according to plan, except for the one unaccounted intangible. The reaction of the people. After digging himself out of the tomb, he returned directly to the palace instead of consulting with the priests. Upon entering, everyone was shocked. Rightfully consumed with fear. He beckoned his courtier with open arms, and the man hesitantly made his way to him. In what can only be described as fate, or incredibly bad luck, the man had cut himself shaving that morning, leaving the smallest of nicks above his lip. Lusting for blood, Khaba was carnally drawn to it as the men embraced. The onlookers thought he was merely kissing the man, happy to see him after being reborn, but when bloodlust took over and he ripped into his throat, the people screamed, and soldiers drew swords. Realizing he had committed an incredible atrocity, he threw the courtier to the floor, and sprinted from the palace in disgrace. From that moment forward, he was viewed as an abomination, not a god. People ran from him, screaming *Anubis Khaba*, fearing he would bite them with the Jaws of Anubis, sending their souls to the netherworld. The story spread throughout the Eastern world, leaving him no choice but to hide. And where better to hide, than the unfinished, abandoned pyramid that bore his name. The horrified court officials wasted no time in condemning him, erasing his name from every monument, plaque, and scroll. It was forbidden to speak or write the name Khaba, and he was scratched from the official list of kings, as if he never existed."

Expressing pity, Altus continues in a somber tone. "The sad part is, he only wanted the best for Egypt. He had monumental plans for his country and its people but was never able to lay the foundations. It was then that Sekhemkhet informed him as to the true predicament of their situation. The Controller of Mysteries, Gods Seal Bearer, and the Lector Priest were all immortal, and their demands for riches were beyond sense and reason. Khaba refused to dig up burial chambers and suggested they steal from the royal palace. Sekhemkhet agreed, and they began sneaking into the palace, as well as homes of royalty, removing whatever items of value they could find. After months of robbery and increasingly exorbitant demands by the priests, Khaba felt it was time to leave Egypt."

"Is that when they sailed for America?"

"Yes, that was when they discovered South America. Sekhemkhet knew the priests would never have imagined such a land existed, so, he stayed and made himself a god."

"Where is he now?" Sierra asks.

"Certainly dead, but he is without doubt the reason you see pyramids there today. Shortly after Sekhemkhet proclaimed himself a god to the natives, Khaba became disillusioned and returned to Egypt, desperately longing for home. He knew he did not stand a chance against the priests when they were together, but if he could behead them one by one, he felt his problems might be solved.

"Upon his return, he found that his departure with Sekhemkhet had caused an unanticipated chain of events. Someone had apparently seen Khaba and Sekhemkhet sailing on a barge bound for the Mediterranean, and rightly pointed a finger at the priests who were supposed to have buried them. It seemed the court officials had tired of bogus funerals and rightfully wanted their dead to remain that way. When they went to interrogate the priests, they quickly found they were not dealing with normal human beings. What started out as a simple process of arrest, quickly escalated into a full-blown battle. The fifteen soldiers accompanying the officials, drew their swords, hoping the priests would back down, but one of the priests pulled a knife, and with preternatural speed, killed a court official. This prompted retaliation from the soldiers, and they vigorously began stabbing the priests, finding much to their horror, the priest's wounds healed as quickly as the swords were withdrawn. After a prolonged battle, during which many of the soldiers were killed, the priests were slowly bled down to human strength, at which point, they were beheaded, and fed to a pack of jackals in the desert."

"Ah, that was the reason for the shake-up in the Temple of Anubis, and the removing of the organs of the dead!" Sierra realizes.

"Yes, they were found to be immortal and creating more of their kind, so, a new ritual was created where the dead would be gutted. And since all parts of the body were considered sacred, they created Canopic Jars to hold the internal remains, placing them in the tomb so that the body was essentially still whole."

"Wait . . . I just thought of something! If the blood of the priests had the disease, what became of the jackals?"

Exhaling loudly, Altus hangs his head. "Somehow, during the frenzy of feeding, blood was intermixed. The jackals became infected, and after conquering the disease, attacked anything that moved. Humans included."

"Were they able to pass the disease on to people?"

"If blood was exchanged, the disease passed on. Only this time, jackal blood was mixed in. They were wild creatures! The disease demands a new infusion of blood approximately once a month, but, whereas we choose one victim carefully, they were ravenous. When bloodlust came on, they changed from humans into animals, viciously ripping people to shreds. Sometimes drinking only drops from each kill."

"Werewolves!" she declares, "And since you need blood once a month, and there's a full moon every month, that's how the correlation originated!"

"Most definitely. For years we attempted to exterminate their species. Because they would never drain a person completely, some of the victims lived through the attack, causing the disease to spread like wildfire. It seemed every time we killed one, two more would pop up. It was a vicious war that lasted for centuries! Because they were part animal, they were stronger than us, not to mention they had claws. In the year 1473, I was nearly killed by a pair of them in Venice. Leaving a party thrown by one of my progeny, I was attacked in the dead of night. Without a sword to fight, I thought myself dead. I kicked in the door of a blacksmith's shop, grabbed an axe, and as I turned to fight, one of them jumped on my back. I grabbed it by the fur of its neck and threw it to the floor, burying the axe in its head. The next leaped on me before I had a chance to gain my footing and pinned me to the floor. As it clawed at my throat, I stuck the axe head in its mouth to keep from being bitten. Using all my strength, I broke free, got to my feet, and saw a partially completed sword lying on a nearby forge. Diving to grab it, the creature saw my intentions and leapt for me. As I fell to the floor with sword in hand, it landed on me just as I was able to point the sword in its direction. Landing cleanly on the point, it pierced its heart. I pulled the animal to me, constantly twisting the sword to keep its heart from healing. Blood poured over me, and I rolled to one side, attempting to keep it from entering my wounds. After it died and returned to human form, I returned to my progeny's villa and waited for my bloodlust to return, hoping beyond hope I would not change into an animal. Once I was found to be human, we decided it best to increase our numbers and kill them off for good."

"That's scary! Were you able to get rid of them?"

"It has been over a century since the last sighting. The last infestation was in Charleston, and that was eradicated just before the Civil War. The problem is, there is never just one. To this day, whenever I read about someone being viciously torn apart, I look to see if a pattern is forming. What starts with one mutilation, multiplies rapidly."

"This is all so crazy! What's next, witches and goblins?"

"Let us hope not," he laughs. "To get back to the instigators of the problem, the priests, they had been disposed of, leaving Khaba free to pursue his goals. Since he could no longer be Pharaoh, he decided to try the next best thing, turn the current Pharaoh into his puppet. That Pharaoh was Baka, a newly ordained king that spent most of his time in orgies, ignoring the plight of the people. When Khaba offered him eternal life in return for becoming his mouthpiece, Baka jumped at the chance. Everything was lining up well for Khaba, and it seemed the only problem would be concealing the sickness. You see, once the court officials realized that both Sekhemkhet and Khaba were sick before their so-called deaths, everyone became suspicious of those that recovered from a near-death illness. Hoping to conceal the sickness, Khaba decided it would be best for Baka to go on a trip up the Nile with as few people as possible, thereby limiting witnesses.

"Baka put the plan into motion, telling the priests and officials he needed a respite from his duties and would be sailing to Abu, or Elephantine Island, as it is known today. He would be gone for three weeks, a month in modern times, as the ancient Egyptian week had ten days. More than enough time to take the blood and recover from the sickness.

"Everything went just as planned. He became sick on the trip up the Nile, recuperated in Abu, and sailed uneventfully back to Memphis, with no one the wiser. It was perfect! Khaba had his puppet, and though some spoke of Baka being slightly ill, no one suspected a thing. Then Baka did something irrational, he had his pyramid built next to Khaba's. With hundreds of workers living within a few-hundred yards of Khaba, it would only be a matter of time before someone would see him. He was all too soon finding out the problem with puppet rulers. If anyone was so stupid as to be told what to say and do, they were also foolish enough to make ill-conceived decisions. The workers had barely finished the substructure when rumors ran rampant about Anubis Khaba stalking the area, harvesting souls for the netherworld. The workers became so frightened, they quit in droves. This in turn, upset Baka, for he felt his pyramid would never be completed if Khaba lived nearby."

"Why would he care about a pyramid? He was eternal," she justifies.

"Pride. I suppose he wanted his pyramid to last forever, just as he thought he would. Even though he would have to fake his death one day, he wished to see the pyramid completed in his *lifetime*, possibly to enjoy the ceremony upon its dedication."

"How would he fake his death without anyone finding out?"

"Fire, it was the easiest and surest method. Find someone of similar stature, kill him, and throw the body in a burning building. But that was years away for Baka. As construction on the pyramid slowed to a snail's pace, Baka demanded that Khaba stay out of the area until it was finished. With nowhere else to live, he sent messages through his progeny to reason with Baka. After months of no compromise, Baka refused to continue meeting with the progeny and demanded to see Khaba, face to face. It had been about one-hundred years since Khaba left with Sekhemkhet, but there were still drawings of him everywhere, the cleft-chin and dot birthmark on his cheek making him easily recognizable. Playing it safe, Khaba requested a late-night meeting in a small garden near the royal palace.

"Upon entering the garden, he found Baka sitting on a bench, throwing crumbs in a fishpond. He tried to convince Baka that it was in all their best interests that the pyramid be finished as soon as possible, but it was impossible for him to live elsewhere. Baka listened intently, then grabbed hold of Khaba's wrist. Thinking it strange, he tried to pull away, and that's when Baka screamed, 'Attack!'

"From every bush around them came soldiers with bows and arrows, and swords. Breaking free of Baka's grip, the swordsmen circled around him as Baka jumped clear, yelling, 'Kill him now!'

"As fast as the swords penetrated Khaba, the wounds healed. Terrified, one of the soldiers dropped his sword and ran. Picking it up, Khaba began swinging with such speed, it was but a blur of silver cutting through the air. Sensing they could not match his prowess, the swordsmen backed off, allowing room for the archers. Unable to dodge arrows, Khaba broke through the line of soldiers and grabbed Baka around the neck, placing the point of the sword in his back.

"A soldier screamed, 'Anubis Khaba has hold of our Pharaoh, stop in place!' and they all froze. Khaba gazed warily at the soldiers, and ripped the robe off Baka, loudly proclaiming, 'I am not the only evil spirit among you, look closely, your Pharaoh does not die!' Running the sword through Baka's midriff, it protruded out of his stomach accompanied by a shower of blood.

"Removing it, he watched the soldier's faces to gauge their reactions. Expressions turned from shock to horror, as the wound healed before their eyes. Khaba hoped they would freeze in terror, to make for an easy escape, but before he could run, a sword was plunged into his back, piercing his lung. As he dropped to the ground, spitting blood, another sword entered his midriff. No sooner would one wound heal than he would receive three more. Through the fury of blood and steel, he saw Baka being assaulted in the same manner, only an arm's length away. Nearly bled out and lacking the energy to move, the soldiers threw them both in a cart and wheeled them to the banks of the Nile.

"Dumping them at the water's edge, Khaba played dead, whereas Baka crawled to his hands and knees. This would be Baka's final mistake. The captain of the regiment raised his sword to the cheers of the soldiers, and brought it down swiftly, separating Baka's head from his body. Holding his sword upright once more, the captain took a side-swing at Khaba's neck, but the tip stuck in the ground, preventing it from going more than a couple of inches into the side of his neck. The soldiers screamed with victory and set the bodies afire. Luckily for Khaba, his tunic burned off, and the fire ceased, leaving him only partially burned.

"Sensing they were dead, the soldiers threw the bodies into the Nile. But Fortuna favored Khaba. It was a dark night with a fast current, and he was able to grab hold of a small boat fifty yards downstream. Drifting with the boat, he eventually came upon a small village and crawled up the banks to discover a drunken fisherman, passed out, thus giving him the blood he required to get back on his feet."

"If your head is separated from your body, there's no chance at survival?" Sierra queries.

"No, we cannot live. And that is the quickest and most painless way for us to die. Being killed with a stake through the heart is also possible, but not as simple. Like all living things, blood must continually flow through our bodies to survive. But what makes dying by a stake so difficult, is that I or any of my kind can easily remove it, and the heart will heal. You must never fear dying in such a manner."

He's offering it to me. Immortality! "And that's why Khaba survived," she gleams. "Nothing stopped his heart from beating, and his head wasn't severed."

"Yes, he was extremely fortunate. But after that horrific incident, he retreated to his pyramid and grew reclusive. He also became more selective about who he passed the disease onto, especially if they were powerful. As time went by, his pyramid was said to be haunted, his ghost lingering about the area, killing those who wandered near. It became accursed ground, and no other Pharaoh ever dared build a pyramid in the area. Where he once hated the court officials for erasing his name, he now took up their quest. The less information there was to be found about him, the safer he was. His progeny cleared out the libraries and public record houses of all mention of his name and hunted down those that went in search of him."

Altus's voice softens, conveying his understanding of Khaba's plight. "I came to look upon him differently. I no longer saw him as a pathetic criminal existing on the outer fringes of society, but instead, as someone who desperately wanted to be part of society but was denied the opportunity. I felt obligated to help him, for without his assistance, I would have died in the desert. As we sailed, my thoughts turned to the endless fields of grain from which the farmers made their livelihood. I thought about the grain merchants who sail the Nile, selling the precious grain to merchants in Alexandria, who then ship the cargo to a multitude of cities throughout the Mediterranean. With exasperation, I thought, 'There is no one more familiar with Egypt than Khaba, yet the simple captains of these barges are wealthier than he is.' That is when it came to me. I asked, 'How much money have you?'

"'Enough to get us to Alexandria,' he answered, 'but I can

easily acquire more. Why do you ask?'

"Amused, I thought of him creeping into palaces and temples to steal more valuables. I narrowed my eyes, and with conviction, announced, 'You are going to become the wealthiest merchant in all of Egypt.'

He looked at me quizzically. 'What do you mean by this?'

"I pieced the plan together as I spoke, more assured with every word that passed my lips. He would start by purchasing a barge and a small ship. Buying grain from the Nile farmers, he would use the barge to transport it to Alexandria, then load the ship and sail to the Roman port of Ostia. The abundance of merchants there would make for an easy sale, and the lions-share of the profit would remain with him.

"It was brilliant! If his progeny were unable to sail, he could hire a captain and stay contentedly behind the scenes, a financier, so to speak. He could live in Alexandria, Memphis, Thebes, or wherever he chose, his days of hiding would be over. I was thrilled with myself and the plan, yet he looked at me as if I had lost my mind. He was sure he would be recognized moving so brazenly among humans, especially if he were to take up residence in one place. I argued that with such great wealth, he could have homes all over the Mediterranean, moving every fifteen or twenty years to conceal his immortality. He and his progeny would rotate through these residences within defined periods, all the while selling grain. With only four homes, it would take him eighty years to make it back to any one residence. Far longer than most people lived. I tried to impress on him that with a myriad of progeny and employees, he could be the wealthiest man in the world, and no one ever need know his name.

"Looking at me defeatedly, he muttered 'I appreciate your advice, but you do not understand my situation. In time, I would only be betrayed. Much like with Baka.'

"It was then I realized what a detrimental effect that one incident had had on him. He was terrified not only of the human world, but also by the betrayal of his own kind. He saw himself as an eternal pariah. I explained that it would be different this time because his progeny would be indentured servants for a period of one-hundred years, and during that time, he would support them in luxury, then, after having paid their dues, they would be free to trade grain in any city of their liking. It was a win-win for everyone!

"Gazing over the Nile, I could see he was considering it, but just when I thought I had him, he shook his head. 'Forget such nonsense. You will never understand!'

"I relented only slightly, asserting, 'When we reach Alexandria, if you are recognized, only then will I forget my plan.' And with those words, we did not speak again until reaching the palace."

Looking into Sierra's tired, half-open eyes, he stops talking.

"What happened in Alexandria? Was he recognized?"

"It is late, you are tired. We shall continue tomorrow."

"I suppose I should sleep, but I'd rather have another drink." *I don't think I can handle that dream anymore.*

"Sleep is best," he advises, rubbing her leg. "Tomorrow you will feel much better about what has taken place today."

Taking hold of his hand, she softly confides, "I appreciate you helping me with my father. I wish there were a way to show my thanks."

"I should be thanking you. You have brought a vigor to my life, not felt in centuries."

Leaning close, she kisses him lightly, whispering, "I don't want to be alone tonight."

Looking deep into her eyes for confirmation, he refrains from transferring any emotions. "Is this truly what you want?"

"Yes, more than anything," she confirms.

TWENTY-EIGHT

Following Altus into his bedroom, Sierra is surprised to find modern decor instead of the luxurious French style that adorns much of the home. The walls are wood-paneled, with a painting by Modigliani above the bed, and a sleek black sofa faces a fireplace surrounded by bookshelves. With a fifteen-foot ceiling and wall of expansive windows, there is a panoramic view of the estate, with distant clouds passing a nearly full moon.

"Why did you decorate this room differently?"

"I prefer the clean lines of modern furniture in my bedroom, it is more masculine."

"I agree." Looking about the room, she focuses on the wall of built-in bookshelves opposite the bed. Finding scrolls, artwork, and old books filling every inch, she asks, "Do you collect old scrolls?"

"They are parts of my journal; the rest reside within my vault."

"Can I take a look?"

"You may look at anything you wish."

Meandering slowly along the shelves, she admires the assorted statues and collectibles. Reaching the end, she focuses on a small bronze figure of Michelangelo's David. Inquisitively, she stares at the figure, attempting to judge its age. "May I?"

"Please do." Sitting on the end of the bed, he lovingly watches her examine every detail.

"What is this? I've read about a figure such as this commissioned to Michelangelo to be given to Pierre de Rohan, a military commander of Charles VIII, but there was a falling out, and it ended up in the hands of the King of France, before ultimately disappearing. But this can't be it because it isn't anatomically correct with the statue."

Raising a brow, he is once again impressed by her knowledge of art. "It was indeed commissioned to Michelangelo, but he was unable to fulfill the contract. Benedetto da Rovezzano cast the one you hold in your hands, fulfilling it in his stead. The reason it is not anatomically correct, save the head and hands, is because it was cast from Michelangelo's original model for David."

"The head and hands of David being larger because the statue was to be placed on top of the Santa Maria del Fiore Cathedral in Florence, and they would not be clearly visible if they had been scaled to proportion, right?"

"Very impressive," he compliments.

"But what about the dick, it's huge!" Turning the figure from side to side, she stares with wonder at the appendage. "It looks like the Greek Fertility God, Priapus!"

Unable to control his laughter, he finds it hard to comment beyond, "It is not that big!"

Turning it over and about, she continues in wide-eyed examination.

Seeing the same, cute look of determination on her face as when she played the piano, he basks in her beauty. "Did you know that Priapus was used as a scarecrow, and thought to scare away thieves? Epigrams were written where he threatened transgressors with sodomy."

"No, there wasn't," she smiles, happily. "Now, I know you're lying to me."

"Listen, I will tell you one. 'I warn you, my lad, you will be sodomized; you, my girl, I shall futter; for the thief who is bearded, a third punishment remains. . . . For if I do seize you . . . you shall be so stretched that you will think your anus never had any wrinkles.'"

"So, what is this, the Fertility God David?" she laughs.

"The man that modeled for David had much larger genitalia than was proper to exhibit at the time. At least that is what the Operai, or overseers of the Duomo told Michelangelo when he first completed the statue. They made it mandatory to scale down the proportions before being seen in public."

"Really?"

"That is the truth. You are looking at the model himself."

"No, you can't be! I mean, you look like him, but the statue appears younger. More boyish."

"That is because David was but a boy when he killed Goliath, my features were softened to appear younger. Late in the summer of 1501, I was fighting the tide of builders tearing down ancient Roman structures to use the blocks in new construction, and was seeking famous artists and architects in the hopes they might help me. I already had Raphael aligned to my cause, that is, until he was appointed the architect of St. Peter's, but prior to that, he thought it wise to get Michelangelo's support, since he was closely connected with the church. The prime offender of such building projects.

"Michelangelo had recently agreed to complete a project started 40 years earlier by Agostino di Duccio, carving David for the cathedral of Santa Maria del Fiore, and I was instructed that I could find him in his workshop behind the Duomo. Upon entering, I accidentally interrupted his study of nudes, begged his forgiveness, and requested to speak with him another day. Narrowing his eyes, he looked me up and down, and asked if I would remove my clothing.

"Startled, I asked, 'For what purpose?' and he pointed to the huge block of marble behind him, saying, 'I am looking for the man worthy of representing David.'

"I replied, 'If you listen to my pleas, I will gladly disrobe.' With a firm nod, he agreed, then sketched me in numerous poses."

"That's it? That's all it took?"

"I wish I could tell you it was a more daunting or involved process, but it went rather quickly. Upon finishing the sketches, we discussed my fear of the Roman ruins being pillaged for churches and government buildings, and I asked for his assistance in stemming the tide. He assured he would do all he could to help and asked that I return in three days to view the clay models. When I returned, he informed me that the Operai demanded the genitalia be shrunken before being seen in public.

"Outraged, he wailed, 'They only see the physical presence of your form, not the spiritual ardor that emanates from within. They are ignorant of the correlation between physical beauty and God's divine creation.'"

"Was he as bad-tempered as they say?"

"Oh yes, possibly worse. He was a consummated perfectionist. If he saw even the most minute of imperfections in any piece, he abandoned it. Never to return."

"I'd read that."

"His personality made it nearly impossible to carry on a friendship. He once told me that he did not want friends of any sort, for he barely had time to eat, least of all entertain. I tried to stay in contact with him over the years, but I moved too frequently, and he rarely returned my letters. When I heard of his death, all I could think about was how he saw a spiritual intensity in me."

"I know what he meant," she moans, huskily, "I feel your intensity whenever you're near." Returning the statue to the shelf, she saunters before him, removing her shirt and standing between his legs.

With a wicked grin, he pulls her close, sucking one nipple as he delicately pinches and twists the other. Switching from breast to breast, her nipples stiffen, yearning for his touch.

"Mmm, that feels so good," she pants. Running her hands through his hair, she pushes him down.

Grabbing her plump ass and squeezing tightly, he traces her stomach with kisses, before stripping the jeans from her legs.

No panties! Was she planning this? Love that!

Going to his knees, he dives into her sweetness, expertly working her nub with his burning tongue. Entering one finger, then another, and another, drips turn to a gushing flow.

"Ooh, yes!" *He's getting me ready for that magnificent cock.*

Tongue, lips, and face, dripping with sex, he slowly licks and kisses his way up her trembling stomach, to her pert nipples, and vulnerable neck. Eventually meeting her hungry, longing mouth.

Pulling at his shirt, she rips the buttons free, revealing his chiseled torso. *So pumped!* Running her hands down his abs, she hungrily grabs for his manhood. *Feels even bigger than I remember!*

"God, Sierra. I have longed for this day!"

God, huh? Now you're religious? Stepping back, she stares at him with lusting eyes and drops to her knees. *Let's see how big you really are.*

Undoing his pants, she lets the massive shaft free. "Oh. My. God! I've never seen-" *Can this be real?*

"I'll go slow, so as not to hurt you."

Grasping the huge rod, she licks the underside of the massive pink head, his hips jerking with approval.

"Take me," he commands.

Spitting on it, for extra lube, she opens wide, accepting the hot, engorged head in her mouth. *Mmm . . . so sweet!*

Slowly working her way down, it grows in girth, demanding her to open wider than she ever imagined possible.

"Fuck, Sierra! Yes . . ., take it all!"

Moving slowly, with controlled rhythm, she accepts his challenge, swallowing every inch.

Prick throbbing heavily with his heartbeat, she pulls back, and wraps both hands around the pulsating shaft. *Whoa, it keeps getting bigger, and harder!* "You'll have to go easy on me, I've never had anyone near this big."

Picking her up, light as a feather, he throws her on the bed. "You continually surprise me. I want to give you everything you have ever dreamt of, and more!"

Kneeling over her, his touch takes command of her body, and lips meet in a deep, lust-filled kiss. Running his hands over her soft, responsive curves, he makes his way down to her sex, burying a finger inside to massage her swollen G-spot.

"You taste so sweet. I want every drop of you!"

Burying his face between her legs, he sucks, licks, and flicks at her clit, wetness flowing as a heat builds within her soul. Unable to contain the passion, it runs through her body, exploding between her legs in a mind-numbing climax.

"God, yes! Fuck me now!" she pleads.

Eagerly complying, he stands, pulls her to the edge of the bed, and spreads her wide. Stroking himself roughly, he yearns to experience the unknown sweetness of her love.

Damn, he works it hard. He's going to have me begging!

Rubbing his engorged head between her swollen lips, the excessive wetness allows for easy entry.

"Oh, my God! Whoa!" she groans, girth spreading her open as never before.

With every thrust he goes deeper, and his moans become louder. *So tight. Must make it last!*

"Damn baby, you're way back there! Never . . . felt . . . so . . . full!" *Fuck! I'm gushing!*

"How I've waited for this!"

"Damn, baby! Are you all the way in?"

"Not even close. You'll never want another after I am through with you."

"Yes! Make me yours!"

Taking control of her body, he spins her about, changing positions at will, contorting her to his wanton desires.

"Holy fuck! Can't . . . take . . . more," she cries. *I'm gonna explode!*

Picking her up, she wraps her legs around him, as tongues intertwine in a battle of passion. Taking hold of her waist, he raises her gently before slamming her down on his fiery shaft. Sweaty, glistening abs, flexing with every insertion.

In between the rush of orgasms, she sees that while one of his hands is pulling her hair, the other is pinching her nipple, and it is the strength of his cock alone that supports her weight. With thrusting hips, and vein-bulging thighs sending her up and down his juice-covered pole, her arms and legs fall loose, a rag doll to his lust.

"Look me in the eyes," he commands, "I want to see those green eyes sparkle when you cum."

Sensing her complete surrender, he takes hold of her wrist and pierces it with a fang.

"Yes, drink from me!"

Shaft thickening, and extending further than he ever dreamt possible, he explodes inside of her.

Unable to believe the intense heat of his load, her sex tightens in a climax that sends spasms through her entire soul, causing her to fall blissfully unconscious.

Laying her softly on the bed, her eyes flutter open, just as he whispers, "You are mine for eternity."

TWENTY-NINE

Ambling from the stables to the main house, the early morning mist shrouds Abah. Riding boots in hand, her bare feet glide through the dew-covered grass, heightened sensations soaking up the cool kiss of every blade. With the intensity of the blood-rush fading, she settles into the soul-consuming lust, confidence, and strength that make being a vampire so wonderful.

I could live like this forever. With Sierra and Altus by my side, I would never doubt again.

Daydreaming of a blood-fueled threesome, her concentration is broken by the sound of a car coming up the drive. Watching it clear the encompassing trees, she steps onto the cold cement of the driveway, waiting for the black limousine's arrival. The headlights cast a glow through the purple haze of morning, and she takes a deep breath, preparing for what appears to be the arrival of Xi.

What could Xi want that she would fly to the other side of the world to speak with Altus?

Thinking back on her abrupt departure from Shangri La, she mulls over the tension in their relationship. *Why does she have problems with me, but get along so well with Eve? Is it my disregard for her religion, or that I asked Altus to intervene in Tibet?*

Coming to a stop as it pulls beside her, the tinted rear

window rolls down, revealing the unmistakable face of Xi. With long black hair and black eyes set in softly sharpened features, she is exotically beautiful and self-assured. An easily identifiable goddess or dominatrix, whichever best serves her purpose.

"Abah, you look wonderful. How are you?"

"I've never been better. And you?"

"As always, I am at my best," Xi smiles. "You look as if you've been communing with nature. Would you like a ride?"

Is she starting with the derogatory comments already? "No thanks, I'll walk."

"How is Altus?"

"He's been busy with someone new."

Surprised, she inquires, "I did not know he was looking for more progeny. Is he replacing you?"

Sensing Xi is trying to irritate her, she condescendingly retorts, "I suppose it happens to all of us. After all, how many times has he replaced you?"

Smile fading, she narrows her eyes. "I understand that you may not be fit for eternity. Had you stayed to learn more of The Way, you would not be questioning your existence."

"You judge too quickly. I'm only beginning my second life as we speak." Looking at the house, a mere hundred yards away, she turns her back and starts walking, leaving the limousine to complete its journey. *Is it really that insulting that I didn't believe in The Way? Or that I didn't want to see a people's way of life destroyed? Or could it be that Altus's love for me brings out her animosity?*

Enjoying the brisk morning air, she confidently approaches the house as Xi's progeny unload the luggage. Finishing their duties, two progeny stand on each side of Xi, waiting for the next command.

Abah examines the four women, all with hair pulled back tight, wearing white, see-through kimonos. *Ugh, I hated wearing those!*

On Xi's left are Asian twins, both skinny and small breasted, with large pert nipples. On her right, is a tall, striking Caucasian girl with blonde hair, blue eyes, killer curves, and abnormally large tits that make Abah's seem average by comparison. Next to her is a taller than average Indian girl that is without doubt, the most beautiful woman she has ever seen. With hazel eyes, jet black hair, and a red jewel set upon her brow, her thin body has the symmetrical curves of the perfect female figure. Her breasts are larger than average, and there is a sultry sense of perfection to her, making it hard to look away. Xi, wearing a red silk kimono, is taller than the twins and has a nearly identical build to the Indian girl, only with more substantial tits, and large, erect nipples.

"Has your walk refreshed you?" Xi asks.

"Yes, it allowed me the time to reflect upon our conversation, giving me greater insight."

"I am glad," she replies, assuming she is giving The Way a second thought.

"Come with me, I'll let you in the house," Abah gestures.

As Xi and her progeny follow with the luggage, Abah asks, "How long do you plan on staying?"

"Not long, I am but a courier of news."

"Good or bad?"

"You shall know when the time is right," she answers, coolly.

"Is it so important that it couldn't be sent encrypted or done over the phone?"

"Had you taken this much interest in The Way, you would be a stronger woman. Like my disciples."

Let it go already. I'll never be your pawn!

Abah touches a finger to the security screen at the front door, and with a click, the door pops open.

"Please, make yourselves at home. I'll get Altus." Taking a couple steps up the stairway, Abah stops to look back. "Do I need to forewarn him of anything?"

"You are doing all that is needed." Xi blinks, condescendingly.

THIRTY

Reaching Altus's bedroom, Abah finds the door ajar. Swinging it open, she finds Sierra and Altus sleeping in each other's arms. Even with the recent feeding, her confidence is shaken.

Is there anything left of Altus and me?

Shuffling to the bed, her thoughts return to a time when he loved only her, and the two required nothing but each other's presence. With a firm push of her hand, she nudges his shoulder. "Xi has arrived."

Rising gently, so as not to wake Sierra, he whispers, "Thank you, I will be down shortly."

Awakened by his movements, Sierra opens her eyes.

"Xi has arrived. Go back to sleep," he suggests, with a kiss.

Why, so I can be haunted by the same old nightmare?

After watching Altus enter his closet, she eagerly turns to Abah. "Xi is downstairs?"

"Yes."

"Should I meet her?" she inquires, wondering if it would be okay.

"Well, if you're in a good mood, which I would guess you are, I wouldn't. She may put you in a bad one."

"Why is that? Is she in a bad mood?"

"It's not her mood. It's her attitude. Do you enjoy being talked down to?"

"No," she warily answers. "But I am curious."

"Then come down. Just don't ask a lot of questions, she's much more private than Altus."

"Hmm, what should I say?"

"How about. Hi, it was nice meeting you, goodbye."

"Can't be that bad," she giggles, "I'll be down in a minute."

"Closing the door as she leaves, Abah peers back at Sierra jumping out of bed, and headed toward Altus. *Now that he has her, does he still want me?*

* * *

Entering the great hall, Abah senses Xi's condescending glance but decides to play nice. "Would you like something to eat or drink?"

"Tea would be wonderful. Show my girls where it is, and they will prepare it." With a slight nod of her head, the twins jump up, following Abah to the adjacent kitchen.

After showing the twins where to find everything, she returns, finding Altus entering from the hallway.

"It is wonderful to see you!" Xi smiles, standing to greet him.

"It has been too long," he gushes.

"I miss the days when it was only you and me, and time moved slowly."

"The world has changed, but our love remains." Kissing her softly, he embraces her tightly.

Stepping into the room, Sierra is surprised to find Altus in the arms of another woman. Visibly uncomfortable, she looks away, only to find the blonde and Indian progeny eyeing her with bloodlust. Unsure of how to react, she sits next to Abah on the loveseat, wondering aloud, "Why are they staring at me?"

"They are Xi's servant girls, who have yet to learn their place," Abah announces, loudly.

Turning from his embrace, Xi demands, "What have they done?"

"It's nothing I can't handle," Abah affirms, putting a comforting hand on Sierra's leg.

Xi speaks harshly to the two in Chinese, causing them to hang their heads.

Not since she has arrived, has Sierra felt so uncomfortable. Sweat trickling down her temple, she wants to look more closely at Xi, but fears catching her eye.

Sensing Sierra's fear from ten feet away, Xi glares at her, sternly. "What is your name?"

"Sierra," she timidly replies, "and you must be Xi."

"You are correct," she answers disdainfully.

Sierra nervously pulls at the neck of her T-shirt, looking away from Xi's cold gaze to the warm safety of Altus.

Seeing her discomfort, he firmly instructs, "Need I tell you to know your place?"

Breaking her gaze, Xi turns back to Altus. "I am very curious about the girl. I did not mean to stare."

"Her name is Sierra, not, the girl. You will give her the same respect you give me."

"I am sorry," she complies, bowing her head.

Abah turns to Sierra, grinning, as if to say, *You won that battle.*

Sierra looks at Altus and senses the reverence that everyone holds for him. *I'll always be safe with him. There's nothing he can't handle. And, he wants me for eternity!* Feeling confident with her place in Altus's life, she confidently asks, "Abah and I are going to make some coffee. Would you like some, darling?"

"I would love that," he replies, a slight curl of his lip breaking into a smile. *Strong. Beautiful. Mine.*

"Xi, are you sure we can't make you coffee instead of tea, we are in America, after all," Abah sarcastically spouts, getting shots in while Xi is down.

As they head for the kitchen, Xi continues examining her every movement. Slowly shifting her gaze back to Altus, who stares at her with contempt, she hisses, “You fool yourself!”

“Not another word.”

“I am sorry,” she bows. “I did not come here to act in such a manner. I come with urgent news from Khaba.”

“What is so important that he sends you as a messenger?”

“We must speak in private. It is for your ears only.”

“We will speak further, after breakfast.”

Xi and Altus sit in chairs at opposing ends of a large coffee table. The couch, where Xi’s progeny sit, is directly across from the loveseat where Abah and Sierra sat, forming a square around the table.

The twins walk into the room, one holding a platter with cups of tea, while the other holds a bowl of sugar. After the first girl sets the platter on the table, the second hands a cup to Xi, bowing after it is taken. Sitting down next to the other two progeny, they partake only after Xi begins drinking.

Altus takes a close look at the four girls sitting on the couch, and comments, “They are all exceptionally beautiful. What are their ages?”

“They have longed to meet you," Xi divulges. "If it pleases, they would like to introduce themselves.”

Nodding to the women, he sits comfortably back in the chair. “Please do,” he nods.

With an outstretched hand from Xi, the first of the twins walks before him.

“I am Bai, and it is thirty years since I gave my soul to The Way of Xi.” Bowing slightly, she removes her kimono and turns slowly so that Altus can inspect every inch of her naked body.

Following her lead, her sister comes to her side. “I am Lai, and it has also been thirty years since I gave my soul to The Way of Xi.” Bowing, she lets the kimono slide to the floor and spins gracefully in a circle.

The tall blonde steps nervously next to Lai, and with a heavy Russian accent, purrs, “I em Natalia, et ees thirty-five years I geev soul to Ze Way of Xi." Letting the kimono slip off, it hangs up momentarily on her enormous tits, before falling to the floor.

After witnessing the first three girls' attempts at seduction, the last rises slowly from the couch, sauntering beside Natalia. Seductively removing her kimono, she runs her fingers up her swaying hips, then cups her breasts while twisting her nipples. "I am Lyla, it has been sixty-five years since I gave my soul to The Way of Xi." Hungrily eyeing Altus, she turns and squeezes Natalia's breasts.

"They are all of incomparable beauty. I commend you on your selection."

"They have heard much about you," Xi tells him proudly. "They have waited with great anticipation for this day."

Lyla sensually licks her lips. "I especially, have longed to meet you."

The girls circle Lyla, kissing, licking, sucking, squeezing, and penetrating her to moans of lusting approval. Writhing to their touch, she gazes lustfully at Altus, never once breaking eye contact.

Entering the room with a cup of coffee in each hand, Sierra stops dead in her tracks. "What the-"

Abah gently nudges her with an elbow. "It looks as if the show has begun."

Forcing a laugh, it comes out as an exaggerated breath, far too shocked by the sexcapade to take it in stride.

"This is nothing," Abah mutters, "you should see what happens at Shangri La. It may seem crazy now, but you'll come to love this. The lust we feel is much greater than anything you've ever known. After you take the disease, you'll experience sex more deeply than you've ever dreamt possible."

Following Abah to the loveseat, they sit, watching the girls passionately make love.

Every time I think I've heard, or seen it all, they take it to another level. No wonder I've been drinking so much lately!

Without being fully conscious of what is taking place,

Sierra becomes wet from the transference of lust permeating the room.

Taking hold of Sierra's wrist, Abah brings it to her mouth, licking the fresh puncture wound.

Overcome with lust, Sierra moans, "Kiss me."

Before things can progress further, Altus jealously interjects, "Sierra is not ready. Please take her to my room."

Rising from his chair, he turns his attention to Xi. "Follow me to the study so that we may discuss what brought you here."

THIRTY-ONE

Resting atop Altus's disheveled bed, Sierra pulls his pillow close, breathing in his scent. Could I still be here in a thousand years? Never knowing fear again.

A smile crosses her face as she rubs her head in the pillow, giddy at the very thought.

Surprised by the opening of the door, she finds Altus entering with a look of noted concern.

"Something has come up that requires I travel to Egypt," he apologizes.

"When are you leaving?" *How can you leave me now!*

"I have already scheduled my pilot to meet me at the airport.

"When will you be back?"

Sitting beside her and caressing her thigh, he looks softly into her eyes. "I want you to come with me. But before you give me an answer, I must know that you are certain about joining me in eternal life. I had not planned on asking you so soon, for I believed there would be more time to consider the ramifications."

The thought of not being near him or ever seeing him again makes her ache, glassy eyes revealing her dismay. "I don't want to lose you. Whatever it takes, I'm willing to do."

Exuberant, he smiles, "You will not regret your decision!"

"As long as you love me, I will never regret it," she ardently tells him, taking hold of his hair and pulling him into her kiss. *God, I want him!*

Fighting the urge to make love, he pulls away. “We must prepare for the trip. Go to your room and bring back what you need. Anything you do not have; we will purchase in Egypt.”

“Cairo?”

“Luxor.”

“Love me?”

“Forever!”

Leaning in, she kisses him firmly. “Muah.”

Watching her leave, he grabs the phone and calls Eve. “Xi is here, she will be visiting you soon.”

“When?”

“Tonight, or tomorrow. If you like, you can call the main house and inquire with her. Do not leave Weston alone, I want you with him at all times. I have also spoken with Xi about you visiting Shangri La. One of her progeny, Lyla, will be staying here for the next year, leaving you free to travel.”

Fulfilling her wish of being free, she gushes, “I would love that. Thank you!”

“All I ask is that you dispose of Weston before you leave. Drain him and put him in a tomb so deep in the tunnels, Sierra will never find him.”

“I will, you have my word.”

“You have great strength for one so young, I know you will prosper. I appreciate that you have always respected my wishes and been such a willing progeny.”

“Anything you ask of me, I do my best.”

“I know, and I love you for it. Enjoy your time in Shangri La, and I look forward to your return.”

Pausing before making the next call, he takes a deep breath.

With the ringing of the phone, Abah pulls herself free of the bloody, sexual onslaught of Xi’s progeny. “Yes?” she pants.

“I have an emergency in Egypt that I must attend to. I would like you to stay and watch the house. If you like, you may call the servants back.”

"Won't that be a problem with Sierra?"

"She will be coming with me."

"Oh," she replies, empty and disappointed. "How soon are you going?"

"We are leaving immediately, and I do not know how soon we shall return."

"Okay . . .," she half-heartedly replies.

"I also want to inform you that Eve will be traveling with Xi to Shangri La, and Lyla staying with us. Please make her feel welcome."

"Is there anything else you need of me?" she whimpers, feeling hollow.

"No, but I will call if anything arises. Stay steady with replenishing and remain strong. Take care, my love. Goodbye."

Softly setting down the phone, she stares at it as if it were the embodiment of a dead dream. *So, this is it . . . I never pictured it ending this way.*

THIRTY-TWO

The Manhattan skyline leaves Sierra's view as the elegantly appointed private jet heads out over the Atlantic Ocean. Tilting forward in her seat, elbows on knees, she reaches out to Altus, sitting across from her, and takes hold of his hand. "I've never been to Egypt. Is it pretty?"

"At one time, it was the most beautiful nation in all the world. Although you will be impressed by its ruins, the splendor has long since disappeared."

"Is Alexandria like Rome, ruins scattered throughout the city?"

"The Alexandria of ancient times is underwater. Earthquakes and tidal waves rendered it non-existent. On July 21, 365, Cleopatra's palace and the entire waterfront fell victim to a Tsunami, and a succession of earthquakes over the next one-thousand years relegated it to history."

"What about Memphis?"

"Little remains of Memphis. Much like Rome during the Renaissance, the monuments of Memphis were torn down, and the stone blocks used to build modern Cairo. At Luxor, you will find the most impressive ruins, along with the Valleys of the Kings and Queens."

"And Khaba's pyramid? Is that still there?"

"Though nowhere near as impressive as those on the Giza Plateau, it still stands in Zawiyet el-Aryan."

“Did he end up taking your advice and become a grain merchant?”

“During the last days of our journey, I could see he was thinking about my plan, so I thought it best to give him space. When we reached the palace, I desperately shouted Cleopatra’s name, unable to contain my exuberance.

“When I heard her call out, ‘Altus!’ I couldn’t believe my ears. We kissed for what seemed an eternity until her attention was drawn away by Khaba, glued to my side, watching as if he had never seen a couple kiss.

“With a derogatory glance, she asked, ‘Who is this?’

“‘This is the man that saved my life,’ I replied, gratefully. “He found me near death in the desert.’

“Looking like he had been living in a cave, she apprehensively eyed him up and down, before embracing him. ‘You are a most welcome guest in my palace, anything you wish for, shall be granted.’

“‘Thank you, my Queen. It is an honor to be your guest,’ he bowed.

“Calling servants forth to take him to his room, she grabbed my hand and pulled me to the bedroom. We made love for hours, lounging about her bathing chambers, before she eventually inquired, ‘What is your friend’s name?’

“I clearly could not say Khaba, and we had not discussed an alias, so I turned away, looking at a vase of flowers encircled in the smoke of incense. They reminded me of my readings on the famous gardener Nakht, the Gardener of the Divine Offerings of Amun, so naturally, I answered, ‘Nakht.’

“‘You were extremely fortunate,’ she remarked, then a look of confusion crossed her face. ‘Why were you in the desert?’

“I mentioned everything up to the point of collapsing by the rock, saying, ‘That is where Nakht found me.’

“Angrily, she snapped, ‘I thought you were dead! You have no idea how many nights I laid awake crying.’

“I explained that I had long since realized my foolishness and given up on the search for Khaba. When I asked where

Antony was, she told me he no longer lived in the palace.

"Solemnly, I asked, 'What happened at Actium?'

"Looking away, almost in shame, she let out a long sigh, 'It seemed not meant to be, for it went poorly from the start. Before Octavius and Agrippa even arrived, malaria struck the camp, decimating the oarsmen. It was so bad, we had to burn many of the ships so that they not be commandeered by Octavius. When they appeared on the horizon, it was frightening to behold, for we were clearly outnumbered. Agrippa blockaded our ships in the harbor, while Octavius held the upper peninsula with his troops. In the same manner you said to cut off their grain supply, Octavius cut off ours, and the troops became weary. In early September, we decided to draw them into battle, thinking, if things went poorly, we could simply retreat, the navy to Egypt, and Antony marching inland. Agrippa formed an arc around the harbor, and Antony felt we could be successful if my ships drew them into battle on his northern line. Unfortunately, before the battle even began, General Dellius committed treason and joined Octavius, informing him of our plan. When Antony pushed north, Agrippa would only sail further out, leaving it up to us to initiate the fight. By midday, there was nothing left to do but engage Agrippa's fleet on the northern end. That is when something strange happened. Do you recall how you told me to obey the winds of fortune? Well, a great Northwest wind blew across the harbor as the battle commenced, and I remembered your words, *Follow the winds of Fortuna*. So, that is what I did . . . Agrippa's lines were stretched so wide, I sailed easily between his ships and headed for home. I believed Antony to have joined his troops and retreated inland, but later in the day, a small vessel sailed next to mine, and he boarded. I asked him why he abandoned his soldiers, but he would not speak a word. Storming below deck, he locked himself in a cabin. That night, I gazed upon the Dog Star Anubis and wished I had gone with you in search of Khaba. When I returned to Alexandria, I was told that you had traveled south over a year earlier, and no one had seen you since. With every passing day, I feared you dead. . .. You have no idea the torment I have been through!'

"I told her that she filled my every thought, and that I too looked upon the star of Isis, only I thought myself to be dead as I called her name.

"Interrogating me, she barked, 'That was so long ago, surely it did not take you this long to heal!'

"I was stuck. I could not say that I found Khaba, and was locked in his tomb, so, after a moment of silence, I meekly voiced, 'I was sicker than you can imagine.' It was a terrible answer, and concerned it would only bring about further inquiry, I quickly changed the subject, entreating, 'What has become of Antony?'

"Coldly, she buzzed, 'He is playing the role of the misanthrope Timon, he lives in a small home near the Pharos lighthouse, seeing no one. He is a broken man, replaying his errors in judgment. He is no longer the man you remember.'

"A part of me felt he deserved as much, but it was impossible to gloat when our destinies were intertwined. Dispirited with future prospects, I asked if she had any news of Octavius.

"'He is coming by land,' she grunted, looking away. 'My spies have informed me that he is gathering his legions in Syria. It will be months before he begins his advance.'

"I breathed a sigh of relief since he was not on the march but had no clue as to what our next move should be. As I pondered, she queried, 'Tell me of Nakht.'

"Fearing I may be found in a lie, I replied, 'The sun is setting, it is best we prepare for the evening meal. Nakht must be starving.'

Wrinkling her brow at my obvious covertness, she hesitantly agreed.

"Throwing on my clothes, I told her I must make certain that his needs were being met. Sprinting through the palace, asking servants where he was to be found, I was directed to the grand balcony, overlooking the Royal Harbor. Informing him of Cleopatra's suspicions, I told him he was to be known as Nakht, a grain merchant from Memphis, and that I was not only dehydrated, but sick beyond reason when he found me.

"We had barely sat down to eat when Cleopatra started digging for information, asking, 'Tell me Nakht, how did you come to find Altus?'

"'He was not far from my fields in the valley,' he explained. 'Near the pyramid of Baka.'

"With a tilt of her head, she frowned, 'Where is that? I am not familiar with its location.'

"'It is on the plains near Memphis, almost completely buried.'

"She looked confused, so he continued, 'Near the unfinished layer pyramid, north of Saqqara.'

"'Yes, I should have known!" she lit up. "They are the only pyramids so close to the Nile Valley.' Bright acceptance quickly turned to suspicious glare. 'That is strange . . ., I have studied the history of many pyramids, but never have I known of the Pharaoh Baka's.'

"I spurted, 'He is a resident of the valley, so it is most likely conjecture. What is important, is that he found me. And for that, I owe him my life!'

"'We are both indebted to you,' she added, 'I trust you will be staying with us for some time?'

"Before he could say anything foolish, I answered, 'He will, the flood is months away, and I insisted he stay.'

"'Excellent, I look forward to getting to know you.'

"To my complete surprise, he asked, 'Let me know if I am out of place, my Queen, but what is happening with the war? I understand all is not well.'

"I nearly spat up my wine. She was so stunned by his impudence; I could practically see a storm cloud brewing above her head. I cut in, 'Nakht fears not only for his future as a merchant but also for your safety.'

"She softened, slightly, 'Do you not remember my triumphal entrance upon returning from Actium?'

"'Unfortunately, I was not here to witness it,' he remarked, 'but I did learn of its magnificence. I congratulate you on your great victory, and I am sorry if I have offended. I only ask because there is rumor that Roman Legions are marching toward Egypt as we speak.'

"Before Cleopatra became enraged by a simple merchant questioning her acts of governance, I noticed the servants bringing our meal, and loudly proclaimed, 'At last, the meal has arrived!'

"It only broke the tension momentarily, for once we began eating, she interrogated, 'Why does a simple merchant concern himself with such rumors?'

"I blurted, 'He fears for his family.'

"That is correct, my Queen,' he agreed.

"But it was clear she was not pacified. After a deep breath, she slammed her fist on the table, roaring, 'The affairs of the palace are not to be questioned or scrutinized by one such as you!' Then, upon seeing my face aghast, she took another breath, and calmed herself. 'But, since you saved Altus's life, I will tell you this. I will not involve the people of Egypt, nor her military, to take upon themselves a burden which is mine to bear. . .. Besides, as a grain merchant, you would be least affected if such an event were to take place. Rome is too reliant upon Egypt's grain for survival. Even if something were to happen to me, you would most likely prosper from Rome's increased piracy protection on the seas.'

"I placated, 'We are all tense with the current state of affairs. I think it best we discuss other matters.'

"I looked over at him, hoping he would concur, but he was lost in thought. Attempting to pacify, I turned to Cleopatra. 'He is a simple and honorable man, not accustomed to dealing with royalty. Please, forgive his manners.'

"'This is true, my Queen, forgive me,' he begged, returning to his thoughts.

"The look on her face softened, and she murmured, 'Altus is correct, these are tense times for all. I forgive your intrusiveness. . . this once.'

"'Thank you, my Queen, I am terribly sorry,' he acquiesced, staying silent for the remainder of the meal.

"I tried to lighten the mood, but a dark cloud had formed between them, and I was unable to lift it for the remainder of Cleopatra's life. Fortunately for me, it was entirely Cleopatra that harbored the animosity. He was ambivalent about her anger and preferred to confer with me on political matters, allowing me to twist the truth enough to stay alive. Oddly enough, it was a seed planted during that conversation with Cleopatra that would bond him to me. When he heard from her lips that the grain would always flow from Egypt, regardless of who controlled the country, he started inquiring further into my plan.

"Days not spent with Cleopatra, I showed him the city as well as the homes of the Jewish merchants. I explained how these men imported and exported so many items, it was necessary that they travel to other countries quite frequently."

"Why did you single out Jewish merchants?" Sierra questions, leaning back comfortably, putting her legs between his. *I must be dreaming. A week ago, I was miserable, and now, I'm starting a new life. A life that knows no end.*

"While holding a monopoly on the river trade in Alexandria, they also ran trade through every city in the known world. They were a prolific and hard-working race, skilled in matters of business, so much so, their profit inevitably benefitted whichever city they resided in. Every city of the ancient world had a Jewish population, and they played a significant role in international trade. It was their tenacity as a people that helped all cities grow and prosper, not just Rome and Alexandria. In fact, it was due to their ingenuity that they were not persecuted to the extent of the Christians during the early years of the Roman Empire.

"The more I informed Khaba about trade, the more he opened to the idea, realizing that moving about would not be seen as suspicious. We went to the docks to find the cost of barges and ships, how much they could carry, and the cost of a captain to sail such vessels. As winter turned to spring, he became more convinced of my plan with every passing week. During that short period of time, it seemed that all was not lost. Cleopatra and I were happy, and we were foolishly optimistic that a truce could be reached with Octavius.

"It was also during this time that I came to notice a change in Khaba. While he was still concerned for the future of Egypt, it was equally apparent that he enjoyed living like a king, for the life of splendor he was becoming accustomed to in the palace made him hunger for wealth. Unfortunately, it also was during this period that one of Cleopatra's most faithful maidservants went missing. It seems he was so smitten with the girl, he could not keep from draining her as they made love. And since Cleopatra had seen him making advances toward her on several occasions, she naturally thought he had something to do with it. I tried to cover for him, but by that time, Cleopatra had taken all she could of his insolence. Whereas Antony had come between us before, it was now Khaba. She felt he had been duly repaid and was taking advantage of our hospitality.

"When he was near, she would say things, like, 'Throw gems at him and he will scurry back into the desert where he belongs,' just to let him know he was not wanted.

"It seemed that whenever Cleopatra and I could finally be happy, someone was standing in our way. I made up reasons for him staying, but since I could not tell her the truth, she discounted my answers as trivial. With every day that passed, he became more of an issue. Finally, in the act of spite, she invited Antony back to the palace. From that point on, it was chaos. Antony knew his life was over, so he was doing the utmost to enjoy what little he had left. He began drinking more heavily than ever and throwing parties for the 'Society of Partners in Death,' a reference to Cleopatra and himself. He stumbled drunkenly about the palace, gibbering endlessly about what could have been.

"Justifiably, Khaba became even more concerned about the future of Egypt, for Cleopatra had joined Antony in his partying ways. He demanded we visit the Senate immediately, hoping reason might save the day, but I did not have the heart or courage to tell him that I knew no senators beyond a friendly introduction, nor that I would be seen as an ally of Cleopatra and taken for a traitor.

"Eventually, between Antony's partying, Cleopatra's need to be rid of Khaba, and his desire to sail for Rome, the tension grew so great, I decided it best to visit the Senate. I knew from Cleopatra's spies that Octavius was about to depart Syria, so I had more than enough time to speak with the Senate and return to Alexandria before his arrival in Egypt.

"During another emotional, tear-filled parting with Cleopatra, I instructed, 'Send envoys to meet Octavius with your scepter and diadem. Ask him to crown Caesarion Pharaoh, he may still hold Caesar's wishes close to heart. If he does not, you will need to start peace negotiations. In the meantime, pray that I can sway the Senate to peace by telling them you are willing to capitulate.'

"Breaking our embrace," she caressed my cheek, asking, 'What has become of us?'

"I held her tight, faithfully assuring, 'Soon, we shall be happy forever, and nothing will stand in our way.'

"Hanging my head in despair, I made my way to the docks. Upon boarding the ship, Khaba said, 'Antony was not fit to rule an army, least of all a kingdom. You should have killed him years ago when he spoke of such things.'

"Surprised by his comments, I rebuked, 'I could not kill one of the Triumvirate leaders of Rome, that surely would have brought an end to Egypt!'

"Scowling, he implored, 'It is every man's duty to put an end to destructive leaders. Just as I have tried to give eternal life to great kings, I have also struck down bad rulers. You must understand, if people and society thrive, we thrive. A return to chaos, with people living as barbarians, suits neither mankind nor myself. In time, you will come to understand that the destinies of all living beings are intertwined.'

"I agreed wholeheartedly, but at the time, all I cared about was the destiny of Cleopatra and me, not society's inconceivable return to barbarism. During the voyage, I set upon achieving two goals. First, to convince Khaba to become a merchant, and second, gain his trust so that he may grant me eternal life. I set the time frame for achieving the first goal to be our departure from Ostia, knowing that if I could not accomplish that, the second was most likely unattainable. I knew he had a desire to change his life, I just had to give him the push that would make him take that first step.

"Before docking in Ostia, I repeated over and over that all power now lay with Octavius and his legions, preaching, 'Do not expect much to happen here.'

"When we docked, he took hold of my arm, confiding, 'I was unaware of the sad state of affairs in Cleopatra's Palace. You alone hold the future of Egypt in your hands. All I ask, is that you do your best.'

"I felt as if a death sentence had been lifted! We got rooms for the night and went about finding merchants in the morning. We found the need for grain so great, that top dollar was always to be paid. He tossed numbers about, estimating what could be earned if he had two, three, even four ships, and I encouraged his high-flying dreams, sensing he was close to making a favorable decision.

"But my happiness was to be fleeting, for as we entered Rome, I felt my stomach sink. I had never been there as an absolute outsider. With Caesar as my guardian, I moved about freely, but now, I was considered a foreigner. Even worse, a foreigner with alliances to Egypt.

"I stood outside the Senate entrance, nervously looking to see if I recognized any of the senators I was once friendly with. I did not know what I was more frightened of, having to speak my intentions to a senator I barely knew, or telling Khaba I recognized no one, and that we should return to Alexandria."

"I thought he said it would be okay if you did your best?" Sierra queries, still basking in the afterglow of the previous night's sex.

"He presumed the best I could do was speak to members of the Senate, not linger on the steps, then set sail for home. I hoped I would find one of the senators that Caesar had placed when he increased the number of Senate seats from six-hundred to nine-hundred and I kept an eye out for just such a man, his name was Telonius, and I had become friendly with him during a feast at Caesar's Gardens. As the Senate came close to convening, my fears took root. It had been fourteen years since I left Rome, and there was sure to have been a great deal of turnover among the senators. Too nervous to look at Khaba, I swung my head from side to side, scanning the crowd for Telonius or anyone else I had ever known. There were so many new faces I began to lose hope. I spoke aloud, 'This is not good,' to forewarn him, and hoped he would reply favorably, but instead, he remained silent. Eventually, the stream of senators turned to a trickle, a few stragglers, then no one. The Senate had convened. It seemed hardly enough senators had walked past to hold session, but I thought, in my anxiety, I did not comprehend the great numbers passing me. I thought about going to the Senate floor and blindly pleading my case, but knew a centurion would forcibly remove me before a word left my mouth. I informed Khaba that since they were in session, all senators would be inside, and we would have to wait until they left before having another opportunity. He looked about, hoping more were yet to come, but I thought it best we leave for a time, and began walking down the steps.

"He grabbed my arm, demanding, 'Wait! We have come so far, and the Senate is just convening. Surely, some are late.'

"I started to wonder what he would do when he realized I had been lying. I became fearful we were not as close as I believed, and he would drain me on those very steps. How ironic, I thought. Caesar lost his life here fourteen years earlier, and I was about to lose mine in the same place.

"A minute passed, and he exhaled in desperation, rumbling, 'We will return later.'

"Upon reaching the bottom step, I heard someone call out, 'Altus!' I gasped and turned to see Telonius, waving his hand as he trotted down the steps. I could not believe my good luck! His hair had gone entirely gray since last seeing him, but he was much the same regal figure. Never so happy to see anyone, I hugged him tightly, as if he were pulling my head from the chopping block.

"He cheered, 'Sellius told me he caught sight of you, but I could not believe it. I had to come see for myself!'

"I had no idea who Sellius was, but responded, 'I did not even see him, so much time has passed I do not seem to recognize anyone anymore.'

"'We have all grown older, my friend. I have not seen you since Caesar's time, where have you been keeping yourself?'

"I glanced at Khaba, who looked hopeful, then back at the long, friendly face of Telonius. 'I have been in Alexandria, with Cleopatra.' I searched his expression for a negative reaction but saw none. 'That is why I am here. I am trying to find out the state of affairs concerning the war.'

"He turned sullen, explaining, 'The war is nearly over, and the Senate, along with the people of Rome, are tired. After years of civil war and the defeat of Antony, the people have united behind Octavius. Some say Egypt may not even fight, the people turning over Antony and Cleopatra to save themselves from destruction.'

"Almost pleading, I asked, 'Do you think the Senate could prevent this war if Antony were turned over to Octavius, and Cleopatra agreed to your terms of surrender?'

"Telonius eyed me with pity. 'The Senate can do nothing for Cleopatra. Octavius will not stop until Egypt, and her treasuries belong to Rome. I could be killed for treason telling you this, but in honor of our friendship, I feel it necessary. The veterans have not been paid, and they are close to revolt.

Agrippa pacifies them at this very moment with the promise of Egyptian gold. You must understand, Octavius's future rests upon the riches of Egypt, and the Senate supports him fully. No one can stop Octavius's advance but Octavius, and he would never forfeit his opportunity to rule the world.'

"No longer concerned about Khaba killing me, I now feared for Cleopatra's life. In desperation, I pleaded, 'Is it possible to present my case before the Senate?'

"Looking at me as if I had lost my mind, he implored, 'I watched Caesar die by the sharp end of a sword in that very building. I will not watch you go down the same way! If not for our friendship, then for the love Caesar held for you, leave this place and forget such foolishness.'

"Setting my jaw, I nodded slowly, meeting his earnest brown eyes with a sense of defeat. I told him it was wonderful seeing him again, and as he made his way up the steps, we waved goodbye. Mournfully, I looked about the streets of Rome, wondering what could have been, had Caesar lived.

"Khaba abruptly ended my daydreaming, declaring, 'We have no time to lose, we must return to Egypt and seek out Octavius.'

"I agreed with the rushing home part, especially since it was a three-week journey, but meeting with Octavius seemed more than slightly foolish. Aghast, I thought, if he does not kill me, he will surely push Octavius to do it for him.

THIRTY-THREE

"A week into our journey, I considered my two goals and felt it time to put my plan into motion. Inquiring into his thoughts on buying and selling grain, he agreed that shortly after arriving in Alexandria he would purchase the needed boats and go in search of a captain for the trips to Ostia.

As days passed, and I considered tactful methods by which to ask for his blood, I noticed a pensive change in his mood. Curious, as to his thoughts, I asked, 'Are you worried about the Roman's destroying the temples and palaces?'

"'Yes, but that is not my only concern.'

"'What is it then?' I asked, fearing he had an issue with me.

"Earnestly, he declared, 'There is something we must speak of. I am grateful that you have helped me find a new way of life, but I require something else. You have put my feet upon this new path, but I am afraid I cannot walk it alone.' Lowering his voice, he looked me in the eye, and said, 'I want you to join me as a partner in business, as well as immortality.'

"With purposeful apprehension, I replied, 'It is a great honor that you ask me to join you in business.' Then, hanging my head, as if deep in thought, uttered, 'But I must give serious consideration to your offer of eternal life.'

"'Whatever your decision, I will honor it,' he exhaled, with an uneasy expression.

“I was exuberant but did not want to show my true feelings. When he told me that he wanted me to consider the ramifications, I knew that if I happily responded, yes, he might have had doubts to my intentions all along. Thus, I pretended to be cautiously thinking things through, asking such questions as, ‘Do you ever wish you were mortal again, or, do you miss loved ones?’ I played him masterfully! Waiting until he feared I would say, no, I warmly put a hand on his shoulder, and smiled, ‘I gladly accept your gift. But, promise me that you will guide my feet along the path of eternity, as I guide yours through the land of the living.’

“‘You will not regret your decision!’ he yelped, wrapping me in his embrace. ‘We will learn much from each other!’”

“Did he give you his blood right away?” Sierra asks.

“No, we were too close to landing for me to be sick, and I wanted to purchase the boats before he had second thoughts. When we arrived in Alexandria, Cleopatra informed me that all attempts at negotiations with Octavius had been futile. I likewise told her of my failure with the Senate, to which she groaned, ‘I fear our lives are to be lived in another realm.’

“I tried to tell her that all was not lost, and that I would soon have an answer to our problems.

“Perplexed, she muttered, ‘You were right about Antony, and I believed you to be wrong, so now, even though I fear you to be mistaken, I will put my faith in you.’

“I told her I needed to attend to matters with Nakht, then, ‘All would be right.’

“She couldn’t believe I would spend time with him, instead of her, but acquiesced, ‘Do what you must. All I ask, is that you keep me from Octavius’s chains.’

“Octavius was about a month away from Alexandria, so I still had plenty of time to help Khaba find boats, take the disease, then go about saving Cleopatra and Caesarion. I moved methodically along the docks, not wasting any time. We quickly found two barges, then went in search of a ship. While walking the docks, he stopped and asked how far Octavius was from Alexandria. When I replied, 'Thirty-five days,' he stressed that we must hurry and put his remaining money down on a ship, so that we may ride to Octavius. I thought he had forgotten about such foolishness. But, in reality, he was so blinded by his love for Egypt, logic had taken a back seat. I tried to reason with him, reiterating the words of Telonius, but he would not take, no, for an answer.

"Where I once believed I had enough time to perform all the tasks I had set out for myself, I was now hopelessly short of time. Informing Cleopatra of my plan to meet Octavius, she thought me mad. Antony thought I would surely be killed, but graciously said, 'I commend your actions. I wish I possessed your courage.'

"It was strange hearing such things from him, for he always exemplified the utmost courage when I rode with him under Caesar. Looking upon him, in his vulnerable state, I said, 'It was at your side where I learned such courage, old friend. Never forget the steel from which you are made.' And with those words, I shook his hand, kissed Cleopatra goodbye, and rode off for what seemed to be, my death."

"Why were you so nice to Anthony after everything he'd done? Wasn't he still sleeping with Cleopatra?"

"No, he was not. Since the battle at Actium, Cleopatra no longer needed him, and was cast aside. As for being nice to him, during the Battle of Alesia, when my fellow tribesmen harbored nothing but hate for me, it was Antony who informed Caesar of their discontent. It was also Antony that trained me in the use of the Roman half-sword, not to mention opening my eyes to the religion of Mithraism. It was his, as well as the other soldier's devotion to the god Mithra that turned me from the Germanic god, Wotan."

"I thought most Romans believed in gods like Mars and Venus, not in Eastern religions."

"All soldiers were deeply religious, and it was believed that Mithra was real, due to Mithraism's monotheistic principle, unlike the many polytheistic religions of the time. That being said, gods such as Fortuna were still worshipped due to deeply held superstitions."

"The soldiers believed in more than one religion?"

"I know it sounds strange today, but in that era, it was commonplace to switch religions throughout one's life. That is why the similarities are so numerous between all religions, including Christianity."

"Similar to Christianity? How so?" she questions.

"During my early years in Constantinople, there was a man named Eusebius of Caesarea. He is now referred to as the father of church history and was ordered by Constantine the Great to assemble fifty of the world's first Bibles. During his study of all scriptures, primarily those pertaining to Christianity, he wrote, 'The religion of Jesus Christ is neither new nor strange.'

"Celsus, in the second century AD wrote, 'Are our Pagan beliefs to be accounted myths and the Christians' believed? What reasons do the Christians give for the distinctiveness of their beliefs? In truth, there is nothing at all unusual about what the Christians believe.'

"For further proof, I will give you examples of the actions of Jesus compared with those of other ancient gods, then you may decide for yourself.

"First, the gospel of Luke records that Jesus was visited by three wise men after his birth. Mithra was also visited shortly after birth by three shepherds. Both trio of visitors bringing gold, frankincense, and myrrh. There is also a Pagan belief from the sixth century BC that these are the exact materials to be used when worshipping gods.

"Second, Jesus is recorded throughout the gospels as healing the sick and restoring the dead to life, as was Asclepius, a Greek god. Many Pagans, as well as early Christians of the time, debated as to who was the more effective healer.

"Third, both Mithra and Jesus healed the sick and mentally ill, as well as raising a person from the dead.

"Fourth, John 21:11 records that Jesus performed a miracle which enabled Simon Peter to catch 153 fish. The Pagan,

Pythagoras, considered 153 a sacred number. The ratio of 153 to 265 was referred to by Archimedes as the 'Measure of the Fish.' That ratio is also used to generate a fish-like shape using two circles, and that same sign was later used by early Christians.

"Fifth, Jesus's dead body was wrapped in linen, and anointed with myrrh and aloe, while Osiris was wrapped in linen and anointed with myrrh.

"Here are similarities that Jesus, Osiris, and Dionysus all share. God for a father. Virginal human woman for a mother. A birth prophesied by a star in the heavens. All performed the miracle of converting water into wine, yet were powerless to perform miracles in their hometowns. Each rode triumphantly into a city on a donkey as the inhabitants waved palm leaves upon their entrance. They were all born near the Winter Solstice, December 21, and killed near the time of the Vernal Equinox, March 21. Though there is one exception to this. Jesus was born on January 6, but the date was changed to compete with the mass audiences of Pagan religions. There is more, they all died as a sacrifice for the sins of the world and were either hung on a tree, stake, or cross when killed, before returning to life a few days later. And the caves or tombs where they were buried, were all visited by three female followers, with each eventually ascending into heaven."

Disillusioned, Sierra murmurs, "They're all so similar. I had no idea." I*t just gets worse and worse. Is Christianity just a bunch of fictional stories? The ten commandments written by someone trying to the stem the tide of moral degradation in a barbarous world*?

"I have not touched on the similarities with Krishna, or the falcon-headed god Horus. Would you like to hear more?"

"Are those religions older than Christianity?"

"Hundreds to thousands of years older. It was only the tenacity and physical violence of the Christians that extinguished the competing Pagan religions. Before the Christians, people were, for the most part, very accommodating of other religions. But the Christians viewed themselves as separate and distinct from society. They were usually poor, or outsiders, and very quick to riot, causing a great deal trouble. That was the main reason the Romans fed them to the lions, their propensity for making trouble. Even today, they speak more of suffering in hell than the rewards of heaven. What does that tell you?"

"Since meeting you, I've learned so much about religion, I've come to doubt nearly everything I once held dear."

"Is that entirely bad?"

"In some ways, no, in others, yes. To tell you the truth, I'd rather not talk about it anymore. Why don't you continue where you left off with Antony." *I've put a lifetime of faith in a myth!*

Sensing that she is struggling with her thoughts, he squeezes her hand. "As I was saying, despite everything that had come between us, I still felt as if Antony were a good friend. When Khaba asked what my plans were for Octavius, I rightfully responded, 'To leave the encounter with my life.'

"Shocked, he countered, 'You hope to accomplish nothing? This is no time for appeasement!'

"I wanted to scream that this was *precisely* the time for appeasement because our lives hung in the balance, but he was too focused on the destruction of Egypt to be concerned with anything else. It was then I realized that I had to make it seem as if I could save Egypt from destruction during my talk with Octavius, or my life may be over. So that I could speak in private and not be found a liar, I instructed Khaba to remain outside Octavius's tent, watching for soldiers who might attack.

"'I will protect you from whatever arises,' he assured.

"Though he was powerful, I knew it would take a hundred of his kind to escape Octavius's legions, but nevertheless, I gratefully replied, 'I know I can rely on you.'

"As we approached the encampment, four scouts rode out to escort us in. I told Khaba, 'Only by the grace of Fortuna will

Egypt's temples and our lives be saved.' I hoped for my own sake he would repeat the words, 'All I ask is that you do your best,' as he said in Ostia, but he was eerily silent.

"The soldiers took our swords and escorted us to Octavius's tent, whereupon I looked at Khaba and pointed to the ground twenty feet outside the entrance, meaning for him to stand there, keeping guard. Pulling back the entrance flap, I found Octavius standing in the center of the expansive tent, a Centurion to either side. The war table was empty of plans, and with open hand, he motioned for me to sit in a chair that had been set away from the table. Pulling a chair in front of mine, he sat directly across from me, with both Centurions taking their place to my rear.

"Octavius spoke first, saying, 'It has been many years.'

"'It has. You are no longer the boy I remember,' I proudly commented. His hair was now short and wavy like his Roman brethren, and his youthful exuberance had been replaced by a look of confident manhood.

"'Much has changed. The wheel of life has scattered our paths,' he said, eyeing me suspiciously.

"'It has indeed. But that does not mean our paths may not converge again.'

"He confidently replied, 'I never diverted from the path you allude to. My eyes stayed straight, feet firm. It was you and your whore that chose to cast away Caesar's wishes.'

"I bristled at him calling Cleopatra a whore but kept my focus, conceding, 'I will grant that Cleopatra's judgment was swayed by Antony, but Caesarion and I always remained true to your cause.'

"Angered, he raised his voice. 'You abandoned my cause when you chose to live in Alexandria. Had you remained in Rome with Caesarion, things would have been different.'

"I came to understand what Cleopatra had been telling me all along. Once he had a firm grip on the Senate, he would never relinquish it. We had been foolish to believe in either him or Antony. We should have remained neutral, preserving the life we had, instead of trying to rule the world. I attempted to find common ground before it turned into a screaming match, saying, 'Let us speak truthfully. I believed Antony to be a fool and was angered when Cleopatra joined his cause. I insisted we stay with you and honor Caesar, but she believed you would never hand over such power. And now that I have come to speak with you, I believe she was correct.'

"Before I could say another word, he roared, 'Do not bring accusations against me! The reason I am the man I am today is due to the betrayal of Antony, Cleopatra, and yourself! We were to unite! Do you not remember that day in Caesar's Garden? I made an oath to abide by his wishes. As did you! If you were not sided with Antony, then why did you not come to me and explain your predicament? You were no stranger to the streets of Rome!'

"He was right, and we both knew it. I should have contacted him at least once during my many years in Egypt, if for no other reason than to keep a line of communication open. I raised my voice, trying one last time to convince him, loudly proclaiming, 'You are right! I should have come to you and did not. But that does not mean I forfeited your cause! I was stuck between my love for Cleopatra and my duty to Caesar, merely passing time until you beckoned Caesarion to Rome. I know I should have remained in contact with you, but that is a mistake I cannot correct!' Sensing the futility of arguing, I softly pleaded, 'All I ask, is for the life of Cleopatra and Caesarion. The treasuries are yours to empty. Just let the three of us find a new land, and the world is yours to rule.'

"He arrogantly spouted, 'The world is already mine to rule! Sides were chosen, and you chose poorly. Do not come to me now and ask for mercy, because if Antony and Cleopatra had won this war, you would not be seeking me out to offer mercy!' He paused for a moment, taking a breath to calm himself, and continued, 'It is over Altus, I have given you too much time already. My destiny awaits. In keeping with the love Caesar held for you, I will let you leave here with your life. But should

I ever see you again, I will nail you to a cross before the Temple of Fortuna, where your luck failed my father so long ago. . .. Now go!'"

"Do you think he really would have let Caesarion fulfill his birthright if you had sided with him from the beginning?" she asks.

"Definitely not. He exaggerated our betrayal, but that is not to say he did not feel its sting. I do believe on some level he thought we betrayed not only him, but Caesar, and for that reason, he gave no mercy to Antony or Cleopatra.

"As Khaba and I mounted our horses, I uttered, 'Turn back your head, and gaze upon the new master of Egypt.'

"He looked at Octavius, then me, commenting, 'A new day is dawning. By the grace of Atum, I pray it is a favorable sun that shines upon us.'

"I was speechless. Not only had Octavius confirmed my worst fears, but I had also wasted more of the precious time that could have been spent with Cleopatra. I told him there was no time to waste and that I needed to take his blood as soon as we returned.

"Upon reaching the palace, I informed Cleopatra that I was wrong, Octavius was indeed the man she thought he was, and that time was brief. Then I told her the truth about Khaba, saying he had offered me the gift of eternal life, and that she could have it as well.

"She looked at me as if I were insane, screaming, 'Khaba speaks with the forked tongue of Uraeus, he is not to be trusted! You lost your mind in the desert! If you had put your energy into helping Antony and me, instead of finding Khaba, we could have defeated Octavius! Then, after his defeat, the two of us could have easily manipulated Antony.'

"I countered that we never stood a chance with Antony. His drunkenness, substantial expenditure, and debauchery would forever cripple his ambitions, no matter the endeavor.

"'It was more than that, it was jealousy!' she shouted. 'You let your foolish notions of love stand in the way of our happiness. Do you not believe it hurt me to be with Caesar and Antony? I told you the first day we met, be patient, and your dreams would come true. Why did you have to let your petty jealousy stand in our way?'

"I lied, saying that had nothing to do with it, and that it was Antony's faults that I was trying to protect us from.

"She wept, 'I love you, Altus, you were always the only man in my heart. I even told Caesar of my love for you, why do you think he let us spend so much time together? It was always you! But now we need so much more than love.'

"I tried to convince her that Khaba was our only answer. I beseeched, 'All we need do is survive the sickness, and we can be happy forever!'

"'And what of Caesarion?' she begged. 'Do we curse him as well? What if I survive and you do not? What good is eternity if you are not with me! And what of Octavius, he will surely continue his search for me. And if he catches me, then what? Will he burn me alive, only to find that I cannot die? Turning me into a tortured freak in Roman amphitheaters? Set afire one night, only to be shot by arrows the next! I cannot bear the thought of it, please stop this madness and help me find a logical solution!'

"'There is no logical solution,' I fomented, 'can you not see that! Egypt is no longer yours to rule! Octavius marches this way as we speak, and he will only let you live long enough to be exhibited in his triumphal parade before ending your life! Do you not understand? Khaba is our only chance!'

"She looked away, tears streaming down her cheeks. 'I cannot do what you ask of me. If I am to die by Octavius's hand, then so be it. But I will not put to chance an eternity without you, or Caesarion.'

"Wiping her tears, I pressured no further, apologetically whispering, 'I will be back for you, please understand.' And with those words, I joined Khaba for our journey to Memphis."

"Why didn't you do it in the palace? Maybe if Cleopatra had seen that you survived, she would have done it as well."

“Khaba had to get money for the boats, and he said that a ritual ceremony must be performed when intermixing the blood. Ironically, the ceremony was performed in the same room he held me captive. Where I once thought I would die, I was now giving myself over to immortality."

THIRTY-FOUR

"During the ritual of accepting his blood, I realized the room was not a burial chamber, as I previously believed, but a ceremonial chamber where progeny were given the disease. While giving me his blood, one of the servants, dressed in the mask of Anubis, covered me with blankets for the inevitable cold that would penetrate my body, as another chanted the hymns that covered the ceiling, substituting my name for Khaba's. Over and over, he repeated the hymn, changing the name of the god with each new verse.

> *'Atum, this thy son is here,*
> *Anubis, whom thou hast preserved alive, he lives!*
> *He lives, this Altus lives!'*
> *He is not dead, this Altus is not dead:*
> *he is not gone down, this Altus is not gone down:*
> *he has not been judged, this Altus has not been judged.*
> *He judges, this Altus judges!'*

"Waiting for the sickness to take me, I thought it funny the hymns that once seemed so repetitive and ridiculous, now soothed my mind and comforted my soul. He chanted continuously until I fell asleep, then, once again, they locked me in the room.

"Why did they lock you up?"

"In the middle stage of the disease, one becomes crazed, attacking everyone, and every thing. The pain that fills the body and mind sends one into fits and convulsions, nothing you see or feel, makes sense."

Concerned about the physical struggle, Sierra considers death. *Maybe I should have thought it through before telling him I would take the disease.* "What are the early and late stages like?"

"The early stage is much like when you have a fever, with the exception that you do not get hot, you have terrible chills, the body shaking uncontrollably. Then you go into the middle stage, which some find to be the worst, because of the dementia and convulsions mixed with body aches."

"Ugh, that does sound pretty bad."

"With the onset of the final stage, depression sets in, and the body stiffens, as if rigor mortis is taking hold. Every fiber of your being screams with pain, especially one's head, due to the canine teeth becoming mobile. A muscle develops in the gum line to push your teeth out when you desire it, or hunger demands it. Some beg to be killed during this stage, unable to endure the pain and depression. This is where you must be strong. Though your muscles scream with agony at the slightest movement, you must move your limbs to keep blood circulating. If you do not, blood will clot in your veins, bringing on death. This is when many die. In too much pain and too depressed to move, they lie still in their agony, slowly succumbing to death."

"The final stage scares me the most. How long does the whole sickness last?"

"On average, ten to fourteen days, with the last stage being half of the total duration."

"How about the other stages?"

"The mania of the second stage is the shortest, it lasts two days at most. That is when the disease begins taking over the body's cells."

Worried, she hangs her head, fervently rubbing her lower lip.

Realizing he may have instilled too much fear, he becomes more upbeat. "It sounds bad, but if you are strong, you will survive. The key is to focus your anger on someone or something you hate. Let anger be your salvation."

"What did you focus your anger on?"

Altus laughs, "I thought of everyone I ever knew, and every injustice ever done to me, nurtured the hate, and focused my revenge."

"And did you follow through after becoming a vampire?"

"Of course not. I simply used my mind to create hate where there was none, much like I would use my hand to pick up an object. Your mind is simply a tool you must learn to use if you are to survive for any length of time."

"How does the disease end, does it slowly slip away like the flu?"

"Yes. As you near the end, depression lessens, and the pain is not so acute, making it easier to move your limbs. Once you are able to walk, the sickness dissipates within a few days. Then, the hunger sets in."

"What was it like the first time?"

"The first time comes naturally, there is no fear or hesitation. After that, some get caught in the moral struggle of taking another's life. In time it is overcome, becoming almost like a dance, or sex. That is why many of our victims are attractive people. There is a physical attraction, and when close enough to feel their surging blood, you want to rip their clothes off, making love to them as you suck them dry. The blood and sex," he lustfully moans, "it is like nothing you have ever experienced!"

"Has anyone ever survived the sickness and not changed into a vampire?"

"Of the tens of thousands that have survived the sickness, only a handful did not become vampires. You must not worry about that. The odds are infinitesimally small."

"What happened to them?"

"They turned mad, logic and reason wiped from their

consciousness. The disease never took hold, their canines never became mobile, and the sickness did not end in fourteen days, it drug on for another week, fever cooking their brains. We ended all their lives, save one. Caligula. He was a just and noble emperor, and we felt he was lucid enough to continue acting rationally. We were wrong."

"Oh my God! Are you sure it won't happen to me?" *This gets scarier all the time!*

"We have given much thought as to why it happened to those people, and we believe it was due to underlying health conditions. In Caligula's case, he had epilepsy. Please do not worry," he reassures, hand on her knee, "I will be with you throughout the sickness."

"Did Khaba stay with you during the sickness?"

"He required more money for the boats than he currently had stashed, so he and his progeny were off robbing homes and temples. They would check on me once or twice during the day, but once the sun fell, I could not count on them until morning. When the sickness finally ended, it was the middle of the night, and I ached to be set free. The hunger grabbed hold of me, and I came to thirst for blood! The door was locked, and I began pounding, but with my newfound strength, I unintentionally broke the bolts that held it closed. I climbed to the boulder that covered the stairwell and easily pushed it free, making my way into the night. My eyes could see with the clarity of daytime, ears picking up the slithering of a snake, and legs giving me the speed of a lion. I climbed the pyramid and surveyed my surroundings, king of the desert!

"When I found them to be nowhere in sight, I rushed back into the pyramid, bathed in a bucket of water, and threw on one of the progeny's tunics. Anxiously waiting for their return, I passed the time by reading the hieroglyphs lining the hallways. They were the names and stories of all the vampires Khaba had ever created, or known, and I read every one, until reaching the end of the hall. There, I found a room full of scrolls dated over two-thousand years prior, telling the history of mankind. It was Khaba's journal, and I read until I heard them approach.

"Finding me sitting on the floor, Khaba asked, 'How do you feel?'

"'Like a god!' I shouted.

"'I expected as much,' he smiled, then solemnly told me that during my sickness, Octavius had entered Alexandria, and Antony was dead.

"Filled with remorse, he said, 'There was a battle near the Hippodrome and Antony routed Octavius's advanced cavalry, but at the decisive battle the next day, Cleopatra's navy and cavalry deserted him, joining Octavius. Antony screamed of treachery, and Cleopatra locked herself in her mausoleum, fearful of Antony's wrath. As the news made its way to Antony, it became misconstrued, and he received word that she had died, her body lying in state in the mausoleum. Distraught, sensing all was lost, he asked his servant, Eros, to kill him. When Eros killed himself instead, Antony was said to have uttered, 'Well done Eros, you were not able to do it, but you teach me what I must do,' and fell upon his sword. Not long after, a servant informed him that Cleopatra was alive, and he had his servants carry him to the mausoleum, where Cleopatra's servants pulled him up through a window, and he died soon after.'

"Grabbing Khaba's tunic, I yelled, 'We must leave immediately!' and together we ran to the nearby village to buy horses. We pushed our horses to the point of collapse, arriving in Alexandria on the afternoon of Sextilis the twelfth, or August, as it would come to be known after the death of Octavius. Riding straight to the palace, we saw Octavius walking down the steps with several soldiers. Hoping Cleopatra may still be residing in the mausoleum, we rode there before attempting to enter the palace. Approaching the mausoleum, we saw guards outside the door, and knew she must be within. We walked slowly by the entrance to get a good look at the two, six-foot-tall, clean-shaven, short-haired

Roman soldiers in battle dress. As we passed, we heard them talk of the arrival of Cleopatra's evening meal and how their replacements would soon be arriving.

"'We can easily overpower the two guards and rescue her,' Khaba urged.

"'There may be more guards inside,' I cautiously replied. 'If that is the case, they will alarm the others, and a whole legion will be upon us in minutes. I need to see what we are up against before we act.'

"I looked at the people walking among us, wondering if they could somehow create a diversion, when he said, 'They spoke of Cleopatra's evening meal. You can bring it to her.'

"'That is a wonderful idea,' I agreed.

"We went to a nearby market to purchase food, but it was late in the day, most stalls closed except for an old woman selling figs. We put some in a basket and covered them with leaves to make it look like a larger meal. Approaching the guards, I became anxious, thinking they would look at a meal of figs suspiciously. Khaba, preparing for the worst, surreptitiously walked a few yards away from the soldier on my left and waited for any sign of trouble.

"When I stood before them, the soldier on my right asked, 'What is it you have there?'

"I answered, 'The evening meal for the Queen.'

"Consumed by fear and bloodlust, I sensed the blood surging through their bodies as the soldier on the leftt pulled up the leaves to look at the figs. Bloodlust pushed my fangs out, making my gums bleed slightly upon first extrusion, and the heavenly taste made my head swirl. Clenching my jaw, I hung my head, secretly begging him to challenge me so that I may quench my thirst. But instead, he glanced at the figs, saying, 'Not much of a meal. Octavius must plan on starving her.' Laughing, he opened the door and motioned me through.

"There was no one on the first floor, so I ran to the second, finding Cleopatra with her faithful servants, Eras and Charmion. She embraced me, and with tears in her eyes, cried,

'I thought I had lost you forever!'

"Seeing cuts all over her chest, I protectively asked, 'What have they done to you?' all the while, fighting the urge to rip the wounds open and suckle the blood from her breast.

"She breathlessly answered, 'It is of my own doing. As Antony lay dying, he said you returned and vowed to fight to the death for my honor, but unfortunately, were killed.'

"Confused as to why he would say such a thing, I reasoned, he must have thought Cleopatra dead soon too, and wanted her to believe that I had not abandoned her. I felt remorse at having said so many bad things about him, and ashamed for not having fought at his side through any of his recent battles.

"As I hung my head, mourning his death, Cleopatra looked at me closely, gushing, 'You have done it! The beauty of youth shines from you!'

"'Yes! And now I need only to give it to you and we need never part.'

"'It is too late for me," she reasoned. "My answer is as it was before. I will not run, nor hide from my duty as Queen. You must understand, I beg of you!'

"I yelled, 'I can free you from this tomb! There are but two guards, we can easily escape!'

"'There is nothing to be done now but save Caesarion,' she directed. 'He is traveling to India by way of Ethiopia. Find him and protect him.'

"I begged her to listen to reason, pleading, 'We can all go to India and begin our lives anew! What is my life without you!'

"Not listening to a word, she continued, 'His twin is with him, send him back, and take Caesarion far away. When the twin returns, Octavius will kill him, forever freeing Caesarion.'

"I continued my pleas, but she begged, 'I cannot! Please do not ask me further.' She took hold of my hand and guided me to her chaise, confessing, 'Do you remember the Chapel of Amun? Did you know I planned on seducing you there? Caesar planned to go with me that day, but I convinced him his writings were more important. When I told him that I wanted you to escort me, he became suspicious, but I had no choice. I had to be with you!'

"As she spoke, a tear ran down my face.

"Drying my cheek, she softly smiled, 'It was I that begged him to let you stay in Egypt. Guaranteeing that if you stayed, he would surely have a son, and only then did he acquiesce. I could not bear the thought of you being away from me, especially if it were to be in a war that could take your life!'

"Her words became choked as she dried my eyes. 'Do you not see? From the moment you held your sword over me, that first day, you have held my heart in your hands. There has never been another in my heart or soul. It was destiny that Caesar found you on the other side of the world and brought you to me. We had the world in our hands, my love, and none have ever known the sweetness of love as we did for so many years. Remember me as the woman that laid beside you as we sailed the Royal Harbor, not the shell you see before you now.'

"Kissing me with those soft, full lips, she whispered, 'This gift of eternal life. It has granted you eternity to find me. By the grace of Anubis, I shall return!'

"Tears poured down my face, and though I tried, I could not muster a word.

"'Promise me you will find me! Promise me, my love!'

"Never would I agree to such madness! But somehow, the words, 'I will,' came forth, as my fangs pushed outward. Clenching my teeth in anger, I futilely attempted to push back the bloodlust.

"'Hold my soul within you,' she pleaded, 'Ours is a love that cannot die!'

"Laying back, she held out her arm. 'Take me now, so that we may be together forever.'

"The uncontrollable fury of bloodlust overtook any sense of reason I once possessed, and with fangs fully extended, the jaws of Anubis acted as intended. I dove in, satiating my body's desire and her subservient wish to be harvested. I felt her love, lust, soul, and everything else that made her unique, flowing into my body. Intoxicated with her sweet blood, my body and soul felt more alive than I had ever known! Only when her arm fell loose did I realize she was gone. Looking upon her lifeless body, I became enraged. I turned to run, but Eras and Charmion were both on bended knee, arms held high. Consumed with anger, I picked up Eras, and drank till she fell limp. Grabbing Charmion, she embraced me as I bit into her neck. Following Anubis's wishes, I sent soul after soul to the netherworld as payment for my eternal gift.

"Returning to Cleopatra, I kissed her softly on the lips, and whispered, 'Goodbye, my love.'"

THIRTY-FIVE

With a wide smile, Eve throws open the front door of the boathouse, letting in Xi, her progeny, and the mid-morning sun.

The home, nearly an exact copy of the Petit Trianon on the grounds of the Palace of Versailles, emits shameless opulence, with inlaid marble floors and an exceptionally grand staircase.

Getting an eyeful of the scantily clad women, Eve bounces, "You brought me presents!"

"Yes, but I'm afraid the most exotic of your gifts, Lyla, has yet to return from her night in the city with Abah," Xi regretfully informs her.

"Oh, that's too bad. The more, the merrier!"

"You will fit in very well in Shangri La, of that I have no doubt." Taking Eve by the hair, Xi kisses her roughly, expertly controlling the level and momentum of passion.

Pulling back with a smile, and a lick of her lips, Eve shoots a condescending look at the three progeny. "How soon do we leave?"

"Tonigh-" Xi replies, her attention drawn away by Weston, swaggering down the swooping staircase.

Seeing the attraction in her eyes, Eve smiles, "This is Weston, Sierra's ex-boyfriend. Once he saw me, he forgot all about her. Isn't that right, baby?" she boasts, extending a hand to bring him near.

"We've gotten pretty close," he nods, examining Xi's progeny in their sheer kimonos.

"You two make an attractive couple. Your features are so similar, you could be brother and sister," Xi observes, looking from Weston to Eve.

Weston, not acknowledging, can only gawk at Natalia's enormous tits beneath the see-through fabric.

"Do you like her?" Eve asks, recognizing the look of lust.

"Yeah! I mean, no. It's just that her clothes are so-"

"Revealing?" Xi smirks.

"Yeah, but I didn't mean to stare," he apologizes, afraid to create any jealousy that may end up with him lying on the floor. "I'm just surprised to see all these women here."

"Would you like to see more?" Xi asks.

Unsure, he looks to Eve.

Giving him a knowing grin, she raises a brow. "Let's have some fun!"

Receiving all the approval he needs, he happily proclaims, "I would love to see more of all of you."

"You will," Xi replies, "but first, we want to see what you have to offer."

Unbuttoning the top of his jeans, he arrogantly spouts, "Sure, I'll whip it out. If one of you sucks it."

Running her hand down his torso, Eve undoes his zipper. "Oh, we'll do much more than that."

God, Eve is amazing! She's everything I ever wanted in a girl.

Removing his T-shirt, he throws it to the cold marble floor, and pulls down his jeans to reveal his thick rod, growing quickly. "How do you like that?"

"Well, he's no Altus," Xi retorts, causing the girls to snicker.

Feeling less assured, he shifts about uneasily, bending over to pick up the jeans from around his ankles.

"I did not tell you to pick them up," Xi scolds. "Stand up straight."

Speaking to her progeny in Chinese, the twins promptly remove her red kimono. Sticking her chest out proudly, she asks, "Have you ever seen better tits?"

Enthralled by her perfectly shaped tits, he finds it impossible to take his eyes off her incredibly large nipples. Standing out well over an inch, and thick as a finger, his cock rises in appreciation. "My God, your nipples are fucking huge!"

"Would you like to suck them?" Eve teases.

"Hell, yeah!" *You don't need to ask me twice.*

"Maybe we should take him to the ceremonial chamber," Eve suggests.

"Perfect idea," Xi confirms, relishing his awe.

Too caught up in the idea of having sex with all five women, only after they enter the lower level, does he think to ask, "What's the ceremonial chamber?"

"It's where I became who I am," Eve reveals.

"You ask too much," Xi spits, "we will tell you what you need to know."

Entering the chamber, he looks around the sparsely furnished room, seeing only a four-poster bed made of steel, two chairs, and a small kitchenette next to a door that leads to a bathroom. Looking more closely at the bed, he warily notices leather straps attached to each corner post. "Why don't we do it outside? It's a beautiful day," he sheepishly suggests.

"Sit," Xi commands.

Knowing better than to fight, he plops onto the edge of the bed.

"Relax, you're going to have the time of your life," Eve giggles. "Hold tight, I'll be right back."

Watching her leave the room, he momentarily wonders where she's going, before becoming too preoccupied with the girls removing their kimonos to care. Lining up before him, the twins stand on each side of Xi, hungrily sucking her engorged nipples, while Natalia stands to the side, squeezing her massive tits, and lustfully gazing down at him.

Laying back on an elbow, he strokes himself vigorously. *This is gonna be fuckin' great. Eve is the best thing that ever happened to me!*

Baring her fangs, Xi smiles, looking like the devil's mistress, preparing to harvest a soul with the assistance of her sex-crazed minions.

Nudging back, fear pushes him to the center of the bed, until the sight of Eve entering the room with a duffel bag gives him solace, then concern. "What's in the bag?"

"Open your mouth and swallow," Eve instructs, putting two pills in his mouth, followed by a chaser of water.

"What is it?" he asks, after swallowing.

"Viagra and Molly. We want you to be all you can be." Biting her lip, she runs a fingernail beneath his balls, making his cock to jump to attention. "Lay flat, spread your arms and legs."

Assuming the spread-eagle position, Eve and the progeny strap down his wrists and ankles.

Xi reaches into the duffle bag and withdraws a paddle, whip, dildos, alligator clips, and a flogger, handing them out like candy to the women.

"What the fuck," he exclaims, causing them all to giggle.

Xi holds a finger to her pursed lips. "Hush, or I'll tie a horse bit in your mouth." Straddling his stomach, she hangs her tits in his face.

Sucking them gently, lust erases his fear of fangs and toys.

"Harder," Xi demands, as Natalia climbs on behind her, guiding his upright shaft into her sex.

With the wet, burning sensation of Natalia grinding him, he loses focus on Xi's nipples, making her shout, "Bite it!"

Sinking his teeth lightly into one of her nipples, she lets out a joyous scream.

Pulling away, she spins around, and straddles his face, grinding fiercely on his mouth, as she sticks her chest out to Natalia.

Without hesitation, Natalia opens wide, sinking a fang into her thick nipple, before hungrily sucking up every crimson drop that pours forth.

With the pain of her nipple being pierced and the sucking of her nub by Weston, Xi gushes into his mouth in orgasmic delight.

Sweeter and wetter than Eve, he gulps at the flow of juice pouring into his mouth and over his face. *Holy fuck, this is heaven!*

Hips shaking from the intensity of the climax, Xi climbs off, and Natalia moves onto his face, as Bai jumps on for a ride.

One by one, the girls take turns riding his cock and hungry mouth. When Lai pivots onto his face and the time arrives for Eve to jump on, she feels his shaft isn't as hard as she'd like it to be and grabs the flogger for incentive.

Whipping his proud member, she yells, "Make her cum, baby!" until Lai lets loose, gushing at the sight of the throbbing vein on his inflamed, beaten shaft.

Red, swollen, and tender from the whipping, Eve gets an ice cube from the freezer and runs it softly over his abused dick.

Pushing Lai off, he cries, "Oh, my fuckin' God, that feels good!" As spasms of relief jolt through his throbbing cock, and nerve jerking hips.

Biting her lip seductively, Xi clips alligator clamps onto her own nipples, causing blood to flow. Yearning for more of Weston's adept oral skills, she commands, "Make me cum in two minutes, or Eve will take the paddle to that sorry excuse of a cock."

Climbing onto his face, she glances down to get a good look at his pain-revealing eyes as Eve strikes his cock with the flogger.

"Ooh, that's it, baby," Xi coos. "Keep doing that, right there, and I'll cum way before your two minutes are up."

His tongue is weak, straining to meet Xi's rigorous demands, and the more time passes, the more worried he becomes. *Please cum fast, baby! Please! My tongue is aching!*

Having used up his catalog of moves, he throws in a few new ones for good measure. Xi's closed eyes and open mouth make it look as if she's close to climaxing, so he pushes harder, hoping to get her over the edge. *Come on, baby, cum! CUM!*

Running her fingers up her tits to wipe the dripping blood,

she hungrily sucks them clean, taking her to the precipice of orgasm. Abruptly, she lets out a deep breath, and relaxes. “Oh, you were so close!”

Eyes wide with fear, he tenses every fiber of his being in fearful preparation of the paddle. With a solid thud, the studded paddle smacks his girth cleanly, the home-run swing causing welts to rise on impact.

Xi cackles with glee, as a pained tear falls from his eye to the accompaniment of a torrential scream.

Laughing uncontrollably, Xi plants herself firmly back on his wailing mouth.

Eyes bugging-out further with every ensuing smack, his tongue slowly goes numb from over-exertion. After ten whacks of the paddle and a ferocious working over of her entire pussy, Xi reaches her climax, and rolls off of him with a satisfied smile.

Looking down at his pained manhood, he is aghast at the swollen head turned purple, and yells, "Get more ice!"

Going to the freezer for another ice cube, Eve sucks it seductively, making it wet and smooth. Gingerly touching it to the underside of the bulbous head, his hips, shaft, and stomach, jerk with spasms from the otherworldly, cooling sensations.

“You look so yummy, fucking all of us,” Eve purrs. “Aren’t you glad your mine?”

“You know I am! Just keep rubbing ice on it. My cock’s on fuckin’ fire!”

As Eve rubs the rapidly melting cube over his burning shaft, Xi sucks him intermittently, making for a tantalizing rhythm of hot and cold sensations.

The sweet ride of pleasure to pain has him writhing, and he lustfully cries, “Damn, this is the best fuckin’ sex I’ve ever had!” only to be answered by the excruciating pain of Xi’s fangs sinking into his tortured prick.

Pain turns to exquisite pleasure as each of the girls take turns on his pole, sucking him harder than he ever imagined possible. With every girl, his moans of pleasure become fainter, until finally, the loss of blood causes his eyes to roll back into his head, and he sinks into the pillow, unconscious.

"Stop!" Eve yells, causing Lai to pull her blood-covered lips from his shaft.

"Why?" Xi questions.

Eve, looks down at her passed-out boytoy, and shrugs, "I don't know . . . there's just something about him I find irresistible."

"You should bring him to Shangri La. He would fit in perfectly," Xi suggests.

Altus's command to 'Dispose of Weston,' runs warily through her mind, but his boyish good looks and distant connection to her family take control of her heart, when she proclaims, "Altus did say he was mine to *dispose of*."

THIRTY-SIX

Strolling hand-in-hand across the heat-soaked tarmac of Luxor International Airport, Altus and Sierra walk toward a black Mercedes sedan. As they approach, an Egyptian man with cropped hair, wearing a white tunic, steps out, opens the rear door, and prepares for their arrival.

"Master Altus," the man bows politely. "I trust you had a pleasant flight."

"Thank you for coming, Khamir." Shaking his hand, he gestures his head to Sierra. "I would like you to meet Sierra. Sierra, this is Khamir, he is Khaba's most loyal progeny."

Holding up one hand up to block the sun, she shakes his hand. "It's nice to meet you."

"Please, let me help you in the car," Khamir offers, holding her hand.

After placing their luggage in the trunk, Khamir jumps in the driver's seat and turns up the air conditioning. "It is so wonderful to see you again, master Altus. Will you be staying in the City of a Thousand Gates very long?" he asks, big brown eyes and soft complexion looking at Altus in the rearview mirror.

"It is nice to see you as well, my old friend. I am not certain yet as to how long I will be staying."

"However long, I do hope your stay is a pleasant one." Running a hand across his forehead, he wipes away the sweat and begins driving.

Thrilled to be in Egypt, Sierra eagerly asks, "How far are we from the Valley of the Kings?"

Moving close, Altus takes hold of her hand. "It is just across the Nile, a mere forty-five-minute drive."

"Would your friend like to drive by Luxor Temple?" Khamir asks, "I am sure she would find it fascinating."

"That is a wonderful idea, please do," he smiles, basking in her glow.

Driving down el-Nil Street, parallel to the Nile, she stares out the window at the simple architecture of Luxor city until a unique structure captures her attention. "That's a pretty building, what is it?"

"It is the Old Winter Palace Hotel, where Howard Carter proclaimed his discovery of Tutankhamun's tomb, and the Thief of Cairo, King Farouk, had an apartment."

"Why's he called the Thief of Cairo?"

"He was a kleptomaniac. Even though he was king, he used to walk among the commoners and practice his skills as a pickpocket. Notably stealing a priceless pocket watch from Winston Churchill, and a ceremonial sword from the Shah of Iran."

"You can't be serious," she chuckles, returning her gaze to the Nile. "It was so beautiful from the air, the river bordered by green vegetation, then the starkness of the desert stretching as far as the eye could see."

"On your right, Miss Sierra, is the Luxor Temple," Khamir points out.

"It's beautiful!" Taken in by the impressive Colonnade of Amenhotep III, and the two colossal statues of Ramses II, she asks, "Will we go there?"

"Yes, after meeting with Khaba, we will do anything your heart desires."

"Pardon me, sir, but Master Khaba was not expecting you so soon. He is in Abydos presently, returning this evening. If the lady wishes, I would be more than happy to wait in the car while you tour the temple."

"Most tourists visit the sites in the morning or evening due to the intensity of the sun," Altus advises, "but I suppose we would have the ruins much to ourselves. Are you sure you can bear the heat?"

Too excited to be deterred, she happily exclaims, "Let's go! It doesn't look that big, and if it gets too hot, we can leave."

"Your wish is my desire." Swiping her hair back over her shoulder, he kisses her softly. *So much beauty and zest for life! She fits me well.*

Stopping in front of the temple, Khamir tells them, "I will purchase bottles of cold water and have them waiting on your return."

"Thank you, Khamir." Stepping from the car, Altus pauses at the sight of the temple, faded figures passing through his mind. Shaking his head to clear the memories, he follows her eager gait to the imposing entrance.

Pointing at two rows of sphinxes that extend away from the temple, he tells her, "These are the remains of the Avenue of Sphinxes. They used to line the road to the Karnak Temple Complex, approximately a mile from here."

"Can we go there?"

Eyes lit up; he grins at her contagious exuberance. "Karnak is a much larger site than this, but if you feel you can stand the heat, we will go."

Holding his hand tightly, she rubs up against him, heart fluttering with every brush of his touch. "Tell me what you know of this temple."

"There used to be six statues of Ramses II here at the entrance, as well as two obelisks, instead of the one. The baboons on the obelisk are meant to greet the morning sun, and the reliefs that adorn the pylon tell the story of Ramses II victory over the Hittites at the Battle of Kadesh. The temple was started by Amenhotep III, then completed by Tutankhamun."

Progressing through the Colonnade, into the Sun Court of

Amenhotep III, through the Roman sanctuary, and into the Sanctuary of Alexander the Great, he explains, "Alexander rebuilt this chapel by removing the four original columns and opening it to the north and south. There was once a gold statue of Amun here, if you look carefully, you can see the relief."

"Is that the same one painted on the wall in Khaba's pyramid?"

"That was Atum, a more ancient god from the Ennead belief system, Amun is from the Ogdoad belief system centered here in Luxor, or Thebes, as it was called in ancient times."

Sierra gives him a quick kiss, eyes twinkling. "See, this wasn't so bad. I think I can handle Karnak."

"I hope Khamir has brought a great deal of water," he smiles, with adoration.

"How much bigger is Karnak?"

"At least ten times larger," he warns, wiping the sweat from her brow.

"Then we'd better get moving!"

Exiting the temple, they find Khamir parked nearby, bottles of water spread across the front seat. Grasping bottles from Khamir's outstretched hands, Altus declares, "Sierra is feeling adventurous, and would like to visit Karnak as well."

"It is fortunate I purchased so much water, you will be thankful for every drop," he stresses, driving away from the temple.

"Is it always this quiet?" she asks, noticing the empty streets, save for the horse-drawn carriages sitting idly along the sides of el-Nil.

"Only in the middle of day, Miss Sierra. The heat is too much for most people, but I can see, you have the heart of an Egyptian to venture out in such temperatures."

Smiling, she looks out the window at two young tourists riding past on bicycles. "They must have the heart of Egyptians as well."

"They are backpackers, Miss Sierra, too poor to hire a taxi. They will collapse from exhaustion when they reach their hotel, never again to venture out in the mid-day sun," Khamir laughs, knowingly.

"I was once a backpacker too, only in Europe. I know the feeling," she exhorts.

"Here we are," Khamir announces, pulling up to the Temple Karnak. "It is empty, no tourists will block your path. Only beggars, requesting baksheesh."

Frowning inquisitively, she looks to Altus.

"It is akin to a handout. It is believed that the fortunate should help the less fortunate, especially if a favor is performed."

"For tourists, there is no favor, only an outstretched hand," Khamir jokes, handing them water as they exit the car. "Stay cool, for there is not a cloud in the sky."

"Thank you for the water, Khamir. I'll try to stay in the shade," she reassures.

"It is my privilege to serve such a beautiful woman. Enjoy yourselves!"

Stepping away from the car, she chimes, "You were right, it's huge! I didn't expect it to be this grand."

"This is but the entrance, it stretches far beyond." Reminiscing, he gazes at the ruins. *So much has changed, yet so familiar.*

Starting at the gate of Nectanebo I, they pass statues of Ramses II before entering the Great Hypostyle Hall with its forest of papyrus shaped columns. He reads the many hieroglyphs before exiting through the pylon of Amenhotep III, at the rear of the hall. They walk past the pylons of Thutmose I and III, through the courtyard of the Middle Kingdom and into the Akhmenu, where the great warrior Thutmose III had columns shaped to resemble the poles that held up his tent during battle campaigns.

Looking up at the stone trusses between the columns, she thinks aloud, "I can't believe the paint from the artwork is still here, after so many years."

Leaving the shade of the ruins, he takes her to the sun-drenched bleachers overlooking the Sacred Lake, where they sit, hand in hand, admiring the panoramic view of the temples.

"The lake before you is where the priest would bathe as many as eight times a day. The water was thought to be sacred, purifying him, and subsequently blessing his prayers."

"It must have been amazing in ancient times."

"Indeed, it was. Egypt's beauty was only matched by Rome. And that was only after Octavius became known as Augustus, building the Roman cities of marble, rather than brick."

Hoisting a bottle of water, she sucks down the last gulp. "How did Octavius come to be known as Augustus?"

"Let us return to Hypostyle Hall, where we can sit in the shade."

Taking her hand, they walk back to the ruins. "Octavius being named Augustus, would happen a few years after I left Egypt, so I was not aware of it for some time. After leaving Cleopatra in the mausoleum, I informed Khaba that I could no longer remain with him but must go in search of Caesarion. He was dismayed, but I expressed that the foundation had been laid, and all he need do was take the first step. Telling him I was bound for India via Ethiopia, he informed me that only in the land of Serica would we be safe. He instructed that India was too dangerous and we must go through Parthia, tracing the caravans that brought seric cloth from the land of Serica, and there we should reside in the capitol city of Thinae."

"Is Thinae still standing?"

"Yes, it was the ancient city of Ch'ang-an, or Xi'an as it is known today. He warned that it would take over a year to complete the journey, and that it was far too perilous to venture without the aid of a caravan. Knowing that time was of the essence, we hugged, and he said, 'You have done much for me, and I have yet to repay your kindness. When Octavius perishes and those that know you have fallen from this world, I will send for you.'

"Not knowing what to say, I gritted my teeth in determination, spurred my horse, and moved on. I headed south to Ethiopia, finding Caesarion, his double, and tutor en-route with servants. I told Caesarion to take a horse from one of the treasure wagons and fill two bags with the most valuable of items. Then I gave his tutor, Rhodon, and the rest of the servants the remaining treasure, telling them it was theirs to keep if they kept their silence, and if they didn't, I had allies in Egypt that would end their lives. I instructed Rhodon to tell Caesarion's double that Octavius wanted to crown him king, and that I was taking Caesarion to meet with Cleopatra in Abu before we would all rendezvous in Alexandria. I stressed to Rhodon, if need be, deliver the boy personally, for the Romans must believe they have Caesarion."

"Didn't you feel guilty?" *I should the know the answer to that by now. Will I ever accept killing as he does?*

"I was fulfilling a promise to Caesar, and if Octavius had not found Caesarion, he would have searched the ends of the earth to find him."

Reaching Hypostyle Hall, they sit on the raised footing of a column, huddled close, enveloped in shade.

"It's hard for me to deal with death the way you do."

"You will come to accept it. It is but a natural part of life."

I hope you're right. "Did anyone see either of you leaving Egypt?"

"None that could recognize us. We rode to Jerusalem, then pushed on to Palmyra and the beginnings of what would later be called the Silk Road. We traded our horses for camels and joined a caravan of over three-hundred wagons carrying coral, incense, and glassware to Serica, where it would be traded for silk."

"What did the Chinese want with coral?"

"The red coral of the Mediterranean was highly valued for its special powers. It was thought to lose color when placed on the skin of those who would be seriously ill, as well as to protect from danger."

"How old was Caesarion then?"

"He was seventeen and eager for adventure. The harsh

climate and marauding Huns posed no threat to him, for he was young and supremely confident in his fighting abilities. Much to my disliking, he would ride ahead and scout the terrain for bandits. I felt as if I had just pulled him from the teeth of a lion, and he was now courting a tiger. Though, while I was concerned for him, my greatest worry was my hunger for blood. I waited as long as I could before replenishing. Instead of the typical three to four-week period, I replenished every five to seven weeks. Luckily, there were over one-thousand men on the trip, so the disappearance of only a dozen was not a significant cause for alarm. After taking my second victim, a rumor spread through camp that it was most likely the cannibalistic shepherds that haunted the Silk Road, which was of significant relief to my anxiety. The only time I encountered a problem was when we slept by day and traveled at night, using the stars as our guide. Fortunately, that was only for the briefest of periods.

"From flat dry lands to rocky ridges, and gorges where sudden rainstorms were said to have swept away entire caravans, we made our way. Until one morning, with the break of dawn, a yellow mist rose on the horizon. It was the undulating sand dunes of the Taklamakan desert, or more aptly translated, *Go in and you will never come out.* At its very edge was a rope-like column of stone, much different than the man-made Stone Tower in Daraut-Kurghan, which marked the halfway point of the Silk Road. This column stood like a beacon, over eighty feet tall with a narrow pathway twisting around its exterior. Feeling adventurous, Caesarion and I walked the treacherously thin path, examining the indecipherable, yet intricate carvings that covered every surface. Reaching the flat-topped pinnacle, where there was barely enough room for two people, I held Caesarion tight as fierce winds whipped our tunics. With the traders cheering below, and the wild gusts trying to push us from our steeple, I swore to Caesarion, on my life, that I would one day fulfill his parent's wish of crowning him king of the world.

"Determinedly raising his fist to the heavens, he shouted, 'When that time comes, all shall bow before me! Trembling with fear in my presence!'"

"It sounds as if the exhilaration of climbing the tower went to his head," she comments.

"It was a terrifyingly impressive experience, I suppose he was justified. The tower was not wide at its base like most ancient structures, but a narrow pole, a mere eight feet in diameter including the foot-wide spiral path."

"Who built it?"

"No one knows. It was there even before Khaba's time. What made it so impressive was that it was made of one solid piece of stone, and the carvings impossibly precise. There were images of pyramids, as well as a myriad of other strange objects, that had such detail, only modern tools could imitate them today. There was also writing that surrounded the images, and it was like nothing I had ever seen. Then, or since." Shaking his head lightly, he stares at the stone slabs that make up the floor of the great hall. "I have seen many things come and go in this world, but that still mystifies me."

"Is it still standing?"

"Vanished, without a trace."

"Is it buried in the sand?"

"While it is possible that the Sea of Death swallowed it whole, it is unlikely. It stood for more than two millennia, unmarred. One of the progeny who randomly traveled the silk road, said it disappeared within the span of three centuries."

"Strange." Rubbing her lower lip, she ponders the possibilities of its disappearance.

"You look adorable when you do that."

Looking into his grey eyes, framed with long, black eyelashes, she smiles at his look of adoration. "Do what?"

"Rub your lip like that. You look so cute, it makes me want to kiss you."

"What's stopping you?"

With the touch of a finger to her lower lip, he leans close, kissing her lower lip, upper lip, then a full kiss of passion as he moves in closer, bodies creating more heat than the Egyptian sun.

His lips fit perfectly. So effortless . . . like we're one.

"Baksheesh . . . baksheesh!" a beggar pleads, hand stuck out, smiling widely to display what little remains of his yellowed teeth.

"Why now?" Altus moans, pulling away from her sweet lips. Reaching into a pocket, he hands the man two one-hundred-dollar bills.

With a joyous smile, the man bows. "Grace be upon you and your beautiful wife."

"We're not married," she reveals.

Smiling, Altus turns to her. "Not yet, anyway."

"Ahh, yes. I can see for myself that you two were made for each other. There will be much happiness in your future!"

Sharing a laugh, Altus takes hold of her hand. "Thank you for the kind words, sir. Please enjoy the rest of your day."

Watching the man walk away, she raises the corner of her mouth in a wry grin, "Are beggars known to be prophets in this part of the world?"

"Let us hope so." *So sensual, so loving. . .. Different than what I expected. Better. Yes . . . much better!* Sensing romantic thoughts running away with him, he gets back to his story before daydreaming gets the best of him. "To return to my story, pushing deeper into the desert, I thought I saw a heavenly mirage. There was a massive lake with a grand city on its shores. Caesarion, thinking we had made exceptional time, asked one of our guides if it was Thinae. The guide laughed at his ignorance, howling, 'It is Loulan, our destination. You have far to travel before you reach Thinae.'"

"Why does Loulan sound familiar?"

"You may recall it being referred to as the Oriental Pompeii, since it was swallowed up by the desert and rediscovered only a century ago, or, more likely, you heard news of the Loulan Beauty, a mummy of European descent that was dated as far back as the bronze age."

"Yeah, that's it! And the Chinese government didn't want to release DNA samples because it proved that Europeans were there before the Chinese."

"Precisely. The city had a remarkably diverse population because it was a central exchange point on the Silk Road, and that is where the coral, glassware, and incense of our caravan was traded for silk. We bade our Persian guides goodbye and joined a caravan of Chinese traders headed east with the cargo of Western goods. Not knowing the Chinese language, I found it difficult communicating with our new guides, and therefore, impossible to ascertain if they believed in the cannibalistic shepherds. Nevertheless, we plodded along, day after day, oasis to oasis, until the road before us became defined, and we split from the caravan. After well over a year of traveling, we finally arrived in Thinae."

THIRTY-SEVEN

Evenly spaced palm trees line a private road leading to a compound encircled by a wall of sand-colored stucco. An abundance of varying trees can be seen over the fifteen-foot wall, partially hiding the extensive roofline of the large Moorish home within. Driving through the iron gate, an expansive lawn with trees, bushes, ponds, and flowers, fills the landscape.

"Wow, it's beautiful!" Sierra proclaims. "The house is so big, it looks a little like the Old Winter Palace Hotel, only more intricate with the arches and Moorish details."

"Yes, it is the style of the desert, Miss Sierra," Khamir remarks. "The brown stucco is reminiscent of the ancient stone monuments you visited today."

Pulling up to the house, Khamir stops at the ten-foot, double-doored entrance. Two male servants in white tunics exit the house and open the car doors for Altus and Sierra. Bowing as they exit, they each hold out a hand, gesturing towards the house.

Altus takes Sierra by the hand, and as they walk up the short flight of steps, a tall, thin, Nubian woman greets them at the door. Wearing a white, form-fitting, sleeveless dress, her long black hair flows to her waist, swinging gently with her graceful movements.

"Welcome to the house of millions of years," she smiles,

hazel eyes shining like gold against her dark skin.

"It has been many years Marhib, your home was new when I last visited."

"Yes, I believe you came when Howard Carter unearthed Tutankhamun."

"Is Khaba still angry about that?" Altus muses.

"I believe he has calmed down with the new century," she smiles. Looking at Sierra, she asks, "Who is the goddess you grace us with?"

"This is Sierra, she has come to meet the great Pharaoh Khaba."

Blushing, Sierra smiles politely, holding out a hand to Marhib. *She's beautiful too. Is there some kind of beauty contest to be a vampire?*

Marhib looks on her with gentle eyes, insisting, "That will not do," and opens her arms, hugging Sierra.

Feeling the intense warmth of her body and the smoothness of the silk dress, Sierra feels comforted and welcomed. *So nice. I like her!*

"Khaba is very anxious to meet you. He has talked of you continuously since speaking with Xi." With outstretched arm, she tells them, "Please, come inside."

Why would Xi talk about me? Is she trashing me?

As if Sierra voiced her concerns aloud, Marhib gushes, "Xi had only the kindest things to say. She said you were a classic beauty, and now that I've met you, I agree."

"Thank you, you're too kind!" *Is she covering for Xi? Why would Khaba have any interest in me?*

Marhib escorts them through the two-story entry, into the main living area furnished with Persian rugs, Moorish furniture, and arched windows that look onto the lushly landscaped estate. They follow her through a key archway, down a long hallway that ends with a set of double doors, and she swings them open to reveal the expansive bedroom where they will be staying. The walls are covered in silk wallpaper with an intricate blue and gold Moroccan print, while a coffee table surrounded with chairs sits at one end of the room, and a large bed at the other. The tan fabric of the chairs and bed are a pleasant match to the wallpaper, and a wall of arched windows looks onto a pool, with rushing waterfall.

"You have a beautiful home," she tells Marhib.

"Thank you, I hope you will enjoy your stay."

"So far, it's been wonderful. The sites are fascinating!"

"She has already seen Luxor and Karnak since arriving this morning," he boasts.

"I see why Altus favors you, you possess much energy."

"When will Khaba return?" he asks.

"I expect him any moment. You have had a long flight, and after being in the sun all day I expect you will want to clean up before dinner. Take a break for once, Altus, I will send someone for you after dinner has been prepared."

"That would be wonderful. Thank you."

Sierra smiles as Marhib bows, and watches her leave, before asking, "Do you have hyperactivity issues or something?"

Altus laughs, explaining, "Khaba and Marhib believe I work too hard. They think we have achieved as much as possible, and now is the time to relax and enjoy our lives."

"And what do you think?"

"I believe we are at a crucial point in our existence, the technology of man is growing at a rate that threatens not only us, but all of mankind."

"You mean nuclear weapons?"

"That is but one concern, there are other advances I fear may reveal our existence. The cataloging of humans, being my foremost worry."

"How so?"

"With the ever-increasing threat of violence and terrorism. I believe it is only a matter of time before people are inserted with microchips at birth."

"Do you really believe people are that frightened of violence and terrorism that they would want something like that in them?"

"I do not think the average person cares much about being monitored. Look at Edward Snowden, he sacrificed himself to let the people of the world know they were being spied on, and did anyone care? No. Now, think about a chip being marketed as an answer to child abductions, followed as a means to monitor vital signs, so that in the event of emergency, the police or paramedics could immediately be dispatched to a person's precise location. Governments will slowly convince enough people to get one until it is seen as suspicious or unpatriotic not to have one. Then, as an appeasement to the activists that do not want it, laws will be passed that require only newborns be inserted with the chip. Thereby quieting the activists and achieving their goal simultaneously."

"What about the rest of the world? Everyone can't do it."

"America's power and wealth will enable all humans to be fitted with such a device. If they spend billions on wars over oil, imagine what they will spend to monitor every human being. And communist countries such as China and Russia could easily make it a law. Not even having to convince the populace."

"I suppose that's true." Looking around the room, the emotional whirlwind of the last few days brings pause. *It's all happened so fast. And what about Weston? Is he safe with Eve?*

Watching her blankly stare out the window, he asks, "Are you okay?"

"Raising her brow and curling her lips, she meets his gaze. "I don't know if I'm having doubts, or I just need more time. I know I want to be with you, but the truth is, we really don't know each other very well. And I worry about the sickness and my ability to survive."

"It is only natural to have doubts. You are taking a giant step into a new world, but I will always be here for you. When you are low, I will pick you up. When you question, I will supply the answer. When you hunger, I shall feed you. And when you burn with desire, I shall fulfill your demands. You will never doubt my love."

With soft eyes, she hugs him, and he wraps her tightly in his protective embrace.

"Will you really be there for me always?" she begs.

"I will love you for eternity."

THIRTY-EIGHT

Retracing her steps, Marhib walks down the hallway, passing through the Moroccan tiled foyer, with its blue and white design. In a moment of perfect timing, Khaba enters the house, wearing grey dress pants, and a white, half-collared shirt.

"Have they arrived?" he asks, anxiously.

"Yes, they are preparing for dinner as we speak."

"Did you see the girl?"

"I did, she is lovely."

"And!" he bursts, frustrated with her casual observance.

"It is true. She resembles the painting."

"It is as Xi warned," he exhales, a sense of worry in his voice.

"What will you say to him?"

"There is nothing I can say that will change his mind. And I fear to dissuade him will only aggravate matters. All I can do is warn him of the dangers." Wringing his hands, he briskly walks away. "I will be in the library, please call me when they arrive for dinner."

The immense library would be considered a ballroom in most mansions, and it's filled with bookshelves and tables, all burgeoning with artifacts, books, and scrolls. Paintings of ancient Pharaohs cover the walls, and sheer, red drapes accent large arched windows looking onto a blooming garden. In the center of the room resides a large wooden desk, with four, well-worn leather chairs placed in front, and a larger one behind.

Sitting behind the desk, Khaba kicks up his feet, and casually rests them on the desktop. Staring at a faded, ancient painting of a Pharaoh, he asks aloud, “Could it be?”

THIRTY-NINE

Marhib instructs the servants to inform Altus that dinner is ready as she makes her way to the library. Stepping through the doorway, she finds Khaba transfixed on a painting, and comments, “I hope you’ve been doing more than staring at that this whole time.”

“I have done nothing but,” he admits.

“You’ve had enough time to think. Come join our guests.”

Khaba swings his feet off the desk, nervously rubs his hands, and follows her.

The dining room is large and sparsely decorated. A rectangular wood table fills the center of the room, and it’s surrounded by fourteen chairs, with two iron chandeliers hanging above. The walls are beige with no decorations, and a wall of glass looking onto a blooming garden provides a spectacular burst of color.

Finding Altus and Sierra standing beside the table, he smiles warmly, “How was your trip, old friend?”

“It passed quickly.” Walking to Khaba, Altus gives him a hug.

Breaking their embrace, Khaba looks at Sierra. “With such a beautiful woman accompanying you, I am not surprised.”

“I would like you to meet Sierra,” he smiles, looking in her direction.

Sierra sticks out her hand, but instead of shaking it, Khaba holds it softly, bows to kiss it, then stands upright, examining her every feature.

"Incredible!" he proclaims.

Never having had a man give her this type of reaction, she looks at Altus from the corner of her eye. *Is this how men greeted women in ancient Egypt?*

"Sierra is very impressed with both Luxor and Karnak," Altus casually mentions, hoping to break his analytical gaze.

Marhib, seeing that he has not gotten the hint, puts her hands on his back, pushing him toward the table. "It is time to eat. Altus, Sierra, please sit down."

Khaba's concentration finally broken, booms, "Yes, we must eat!"

More comfortable with vampires every passing day, Sierra studies their fluid movements and gestures. *Do they realize they look so elegant, and refined? The blur of their movements when excited or agitated is like watching a superior race.*

Khaba sits in the sole chair at the end of the table, with Sierra and Altus to his left, and Marhib to his right. The servants bring the meal to the table and begin filling their plates with kushari.

Everyone is silent as the food is served and glasses are filled with wine, yet Khaba's stare remains unbroken, firmly fixed on Sierra.

He's giving me the same look Altus did. Are they both so old, they don't know that eyeballing a woman isn't proper etiquette? Attempting to break his gaze, Sierra starts a conversation. "Altus has told me much about you, you've led a fascinating life."

"Altus flatters me, it is he, that has lived a wondrous life."

"I will agree with that," Marhib confirms, hoping to end the silence, once and for all.

"Altus's determination and drive has taken him many places, not to mention making us very wealthy," Khaba elaborates.

I see what Altus meant. Though he is not as striking as the other vampires, he has a dignified and powerful presence. He moves like Altus. Supremely confident. "He told me how you directed him to the land of China, long before most Westerners even knew what Asian people looked like."

"Yes, that was just prior to Octavius taking control of Egypt. I did not know at the time it would have such a positive effect on me."

"Altus leaving, or Octavius taking over?" Marhib jokes, hoping to keep the mood light after the inauspicious beginning.

Eyes lit, Khaba smiles, "Octavius, of course! Under his rule, Alexandria quickly grew in population and became more prosperous than ever. The Nile became the granary of the Empire, and it was not long after that, that the Roman Senate decreed Octavius's name be changed to Augustus, in reverence to a religious ring in Roman history."

"I'm assuming you sold a lot more grain after the Romans took control of Egypt," Sierra remarks, watching a servant top off her half empty glass of wine. *Damn, these vampires like to drink!*

"Grain was only a starting point, I quickly added African ivory, amethysts, and emeralds. But the real fortune was made in silk."

"True," Altus nods, "when I arrived in China, it seemed only natural after having traveled the Silk Road, I send a shipment of silk to Khaba. Like most Westerners, I believed it grew from a special tree, but was amazed to find that caterpillars spun the fine thread for their cocoons and that the diet of the caterpillars was of the utmost importance. I was shown the various stages of their growth from one tenth of an inch to two inches, all the while being fed a high quality of mulberry leaves. Then, when the time was right for spinning their cocoons, they were put on trusses in a location where the heat could be controlled for five days, assuring a constant quality and long thread. But the key to the process was plunging the chrysalis into boiling water before it could rupture its cocoon and break the thread, which was normally about three-hundred yards long. After learning the process, I started a silk farm and sent caravan after caravan to Khaba."

"Once we realized the money to be made by cutting out the middlemen, namely the Parthians, Persians, and Kushans, it was a windfall," Khaba regales. "We sucked Rome dry of every piece of gold it plundered."

"But it was Caesarion conducting business affairs through the treacherous Middle East that brought us real wealth,' Altus interjects. "It was also his dealings in India that gave us a stranglehold on the spice trade."

"You are too modest, spice was an open commodity to any trader, it was silk that was difficult to export," Khaba objects.

"I suppose you are correct," Altus admits, "all shipments out of China were done by the government at that time. I smuggled it out successfully for decades during the Han and Xin Dynasty's before eventually being caught."

"What happened when they caught you?" Sierra asks.

"I told them I was from the distant land of Ta-Ch'in, or Rome as we know it, and that I could fulfill their dreams of bypassing the An'hsi, the Persians. You see, the Chinese knew a distant land existed far beyond Persia, they just did not know how to make contact. And the Persians, being the middlemen, were in no way going to inform them and cut off their own livelihood."

"Thus, Altus told them he would introduce them in exchange for his life," Khaba informs her, examining her features just a touch too long, before turning away.

"And did you?" *He keeps looking at me, followed by the quick blur of his head as he turns away. Does he think I can't tell?*

"I could not do that. There was a fortune to be made, and I saw no sense in handing it over so easily. I told them I would take them, but the weather upon the seas that led to Rome would be at their worst if we departed immediately. Knowing the fear the Chinese held for the sea, I knew they would agree, and the trip was postponed indefinitely."

"Did they lock you up in prison?" Taking a sideways glance at Khaba, she looks over to see if he is still staring.

"To my incredibly good luck, they did not, for if they had, I would surely have been found not to be human."

"They had him move into the palace, at the behest of the Empress Xiaoping," Khaba smirks.

"Yes, it seems the Empress became very fond of our Altus, so much so, his bedroom was only doors away from hers," Marhib adds, winking at Altus.

"Fortuna again?" Turning to meet Khaba's eyes, Sierra glares boldly, starting a staring contest, until he looks away. *Hopefully, he got the hint.*

"Yes, but in a way I had not realized. You see, the Yellow River had changed course twelve years earlier, causing tens of thousands of people to flee from their homes, and they, in turn, went to nearby towns and villages for sustenance, drawing heavily upon the already low grain supplies. Famine spread year after year, until the peasants banded together in a large, loosely organized army, albeit a strong one, called the Red Eyebrows, due to a red streak they painted on their foreheads. The emperor at the time, Wang Mang, having already inflamed the populace over governmental actions in which he devalued currency, and stripped large estate owners of their property rights, was in extremely poor standing, thus when the peasants began starving, it threw fuel on an already smoldering fire. Eventually, civil war broke out in China and Wang Mang was forced to confront the Red Eyebrows. Fortunately, for me, this occurred during the time he was holding me against my will."

"I would not refer to orgies with the Empress in the Imperial Harem as being held against ones will," Khaba jests.

"Well, that's it! There's nothing left to shock me anymore," Sierra announces, shaking her head in disbelief, much to the amusement of everyone.

"I will admit it was not entirely against my will," Altus chortles. "For the short time I had known her, I felt very deeply for her. And when the Red Eyebrows marched on Ch'ang-an, overtaking the Imperial Palace as well as the city, I naturally saved her from her father's fate of beheading. I killed one of the concubines, dressed her as the Empress, and threw her into the flames that engulfed the palace. Dressing the Empress in peasant clothing, we went to the only place I could safely send silk to Khaba, and that was Loulan. Once there, the Empress shortened her name from Xiaoping to Xi, and took over the transporting of silk to Rome."

"And that is when we owned the world," Khaba announces, proudly. "With Xi in China exporting silk, Caesarion in Persia and India exporting spices, perfumes, and dyes, myself in Egypt, and Altus in Rome importing all of the goods for Roman consumption, we owned every trade route in the ancient world."

Leaning back, elbow on chair, Altus rests his head in hand. "But it was the opening of the sea route between China and India that enabled us to continually move goods when the Huns and Persians prevented caravans from traveling over land. Once the sea routes were established, they proved infallible. Our progeny manned the ships, and if pirates attempted to steal the cargo, they were drained, and their ship added to the fleet."

"How did they replenish themselves on the open sea when it was only vampires?" Sierra asks, curiously.

Altus looks at her, wondering if he should tell her the truth, then decides she must know everything. "We sailed along the coasts, for the most part, allowing them to pull into port and replenish themselves, and for dire emergencies, we had a prison below deck, with feeders."

Marhib, picking up on Sierra's uneasiness, attempts to comfort her. "It sounds worse than it is."

Chiming in, Khaba attempts to change the subject. "You may be interested to know that Altus wrote a book. It was a manual for our progeny to study the ancient sea routes. It was called the Periplus of the Erythraean Sea, and it documented all routes as far as the land of Thys, or Southern China, as you know it."

People as feeders! Will I end up having the doubts that plague Abah? Burying shock, and fear, she pretends not to be fazed, inquiring, "When did you return to Rome?"

"In the year 27 AD. Augustus had been dead for thirteen years and Xi was comfortable with her position in Loulan, and I thought it time to return to Rome and begin importing the goods that were flowing so successfully out of the countries we inhabited. I purchased a residence in the Groves of the Caesar's amid the royalty and aristocracy of Rome, near where Cleopatra and I once visited Caesar, and I also purchased residences throughout the Mediterranean, namely in Pompeii for relaxation, Lake Nemi to escape the summer heat, and Ostia, to monitor shipments coming into port.

"Much had changed since I was last in Rome. New marble buildings graced the old avenues that once seemed run-down. The Senate was now a marble structure, and there were new temples along with an extensive network of roads. I tried to find fault with Augustus's projects, but even I had to admit that a police force to monitor the brutish youths, and fire brigade to extinguish the common fires of the wooden tenements were exceptional ideas. His only great failure seemed to be at the Battle of Teutoburg Forest in Germany, against a tribe of Cherusci. He was defeated by a man named Arminius, whose father was none other than my onetime friend Segimer. I thought it poetic justice that my people dealt him the one blow he could not overcome, for Romans were never again to attempt the conquest of my father's lands. And regardless of Augustus' successors being maniacal, they built impressive monuments with wondrous technical achievements, along with symbols of vanity, such as the one-hundred-and-thirty-foot-high bronze statue of Nero, the Colossus Neronis. Unfortunately, during the Middle Ages, the Colossus was melted down, piece by piece, and the bronze refashioned for some inexplicable mundane use. Much the same way the marble of Rome was burned to make quicklime or used in construction projects during the Renaissance and Baroque eras."

"Quod non fecerunt Barbari, fecerunt Barberini; What the Barbarians weren't able to do, was done by the Barberinis," Khaba sadly proclaims. "How many wonders of ancient Rome went into the building of St. Peter's Basilica and the Barberini Palazzi alone? It boggles the mind."

"I know where the copper roof tiles of the Pantheon are, adorning the Baldachin of St. Peters," Altus confers, sadly.

Sensing that Khaba has realized he was staring too much, Sierra relaxes, resting her arm on the chair, holding Altus's hand. "What was the Colosseum like?"

"It was magnificent! The podium, being the first level of seating, was for Roman senators. The Emperor's marble encased box, adorned with purple silk cushions, was located on this level as well. Above the podium level was the maenianum primum, for Roman aristocrats, which is where I sat. From there, I witnessed the myriad of games between animals, the killing of prisoners by animals, gladiatorial combat, and naval battles. When it opened, the first one-hundred days of celebration was an event beyond imagination! Nine-thousand wild animals were paraded before the spectators, then assembled in a magnitude of games, the likes of which this world will never see again."

"Were they all killed?" Sierra cringes, appalled at the thought of such needless slaughter.

"In this era of extinct animals and conservation, it seems cruel, but you must remember this was near the dawn of civilization. The world's resources seemed limitless. One-thousand years from now, your generation will be criticized for pillaging the earth's resources and global warming. Which is worse in the context of man's ultimate survival?"

He's right, I suppose we should be intelligent enough to know better.

"But not all acts done during those times were bad. The

technology was fairly advanced, and it would be fifteen-hundred years before man would repeat many of those same accomplishments."

"Why didn't you and your kind keep technology apace?"

"What if the Industrial Revolution had taken place one-thousand years ago, and the advent of nuclear weapons not long after? Would the world still be here after the likes of Genghis Khan, Napoleon, or Hitler?"

"True," she concurs.

"Many great things were accomplished during those times, though. I even went so far as to sponsor an expeditionary trip across the Atlantic, or the Green Sea of Darkness as it was called by the Arabs, to North America, where we traded the Indians silk and glass for maize. I sent it to Caesarion in hopes he could grow and harvest the corn in India, but it was a short-lived venture, never finding its niche in the Mediterranean."

"Whatever happened to Caesarion?" Sierra probes.

A hush falls over the table, with Altus looking warily to Khaba. After a long pause, he flatly states, "He still lives."

"Let's go out on the patio," Marhib announces, attempting to change the subject. "We are done with dinner, and I am sure Sierra would love to experience the cool peacefulness of the desert in the evening."

"That sounds lovely!" Sierra agrees.

A servant opens a sliding glass panel in the wall of windows, and they exit onto the patio, each taking a seat around a flaming, stone fire pit.

"When was it that you moved to Constantinople?" Marhib asks, hoping to end any talk of Caesarion.

"After living in Rome for more than two centuries and witnessing the incredible boom in population and building, Rome began to falter. It was the most beautiful of all ancient cities, with wonders like the Colosseum, Forum, and the Baths of Caracalla, but with no new lands to plunder, and its citizens taxed beyond reason, its military might fell, and the population decreased with every barbarian invasion. In the latter part of the third century, Diocletian split the Empire in two, and it was then that I moved to Byzantium, which was soon to become Nova Roma, or Constantinopolis, when Constantine declared it the capital of the Eastern Empire in 324. Whereas prosperity had run its course in Rome, it was just beginning in Byzantium. As my fortunes grew, I watched Rome fall to pieces with the invasions of Alaric in 409, and its complete looting in 455 at the hands of Gaiseric, King of the Vandals. I always imagined Hannibal looking down from heaven, watching Gaiseric doing exactly what he had attempted to do almost seven-hundred years earlier, shipping Rome's treasures off to Carthage by way of Ostia." Hanging his head in thought, he pauses briefly. "In retrospect, it does not seem quite the tragedy I once thought it to be. The Western Empire was effectively dead after the invasion of Alaric, even though its symbolism lived on until Odoacer deposed the Emperor Romulus Augustulus in 476."

Pausing again, he stares into his glass of wine as he swirls it slowly. "Founded by Romulus in the year 753 BC, it came to an end over a millennium later with a less than god-like Romulus in the year 476. The civilization that had taken me in, cast me out, then wrapped its arms around me with unimaginable riches, was dead. . .. At the time, I didn't realize it, but I was in mourning for myself, my city, and all those that once inhabited it. If it had not been for Xi leaving Loulan to live with me in Constantinople, I don't know if I would be here today. It was fortunate for me that the Tarim River, which fed lake Lop Nor, slowly changed course, forcing Xi to abandon Loulan, and in turn, bring us closer than I ever imagined."

"How long were you two together?" Sierra asks, with a note of jealousy. *That's why Xi looked at me like that! They have a history no woman can surpass.*

"Until 1193, when the Buddhist University of Nalanda was attacked by Muslims. Xi went to India with the hope of rebuilding the university and stopping the Turkish Muslims from wiping out Buddhism in India. Which proved to be an impossible task, even for her. I, meanwhile, remained in Constantinople until the arrival of the Fourth Crusade in 1204. The looting of the Hagia Sophia church, libraries, and Byzantine art treasures, coupled with the precarious political state of the city, convinced me to relocate to Venice.

"I felt reborn in Europe! The Great Clearances were taking place, which was essentially the clearing and cultivating of vast forests and marshes throughout Europe, thus causing the population to grow exponentially with the abundance of food. This was also during the time of the Medieval Warm Period, so people as far north as Scandinavia and Northern Britain were growing wheat, and their populations grew in turn. With the explosion in population, it was only natural that trade burgeon with it, so, what was originally planned as an escape, became a fortuitous venture for all.

"Being close to my old home, I naturally visited Rome for extended periods, attempting to protect architectural treasures from being destroyed in favor of new building projects. But when I found the ears of the Popes, architects, and artists, deaf to my pleas, I gave up on Italy and centered my shipping fleet in Lisbon. From there, I brought in as much as Xi and Caesarion could send from the Orient and India. After Spain conquered Portugal, and their colonies became divided amongst the English, French, and Dutch, I made London, Amsterdam, and Saint Petersburg my main places of residence, frequently traveling to check on progeny and the state of political affairs. By the middle of the eighteenth century, we were wealthy beyond belief. We held power over governments, and to the best of our abilities manipulated them to our benefit, as well as mankind's."

"Sometimes with disastrous results," Khaba adds, somberly.

"Only when actions were pursued outside the approval of the Triumvirate, were the results catastrophic," Altus protests, feeling Khaba overstated the problem. "And that is why, in the last century, we came to the conclusion that it was best not to interfere with the ways of man unless they directly cause harm to our kind."

"How does technology fit into that?" Sierra probes, touching on previously discussed concerns.

"That is something I have yet to decide upon. America and China are leading the world into an unknown and possibly dangerous realm for our kind. How far we will go to prevent that, depends upon the actions of the people. When I first moved to America to extend trade routes, I found Americans to be an intelligent, forthright, and brave people, willingly fighting for their beliefs. But they have become greedy and arrogant, much like the later generations of Rome. It is a bleak future, and only the common people of this world can change its course, and they are too busy defining their existence on social media outlets to care about anything except themselves."

"We're greedy for material goods, that's how we value ourselves in America," Sierra admits, forthrightly. "Was that also true of Romans?"

"Yes."

"You're not going to start on politics and technology again, are you Altus?" Marhib teases.

"It is late, Sierra needs to sleep. She has had a long day," Khaba tells him. "The moon is high, and we must speak of the matter that brought you here."

"Perhaps you are right," Altus agrees, gently squeezing Sierra's hand. "It is best that you sleep. I will join you after speaking with Khaba."

FORTY

With a slight frown and analytical glance, Altus studies a painting on the library wall. "It has been many years since I laid eyes on this."

"Do the memories haunt you?" Khaba asks.

Longingly gazing at the portrait, Altus recites a poem.

"She looks like the rising morning star,
At the start of a happy year,
Shining bright, fair of skin,
Lovely the look of her eyes,
Sweet the speech of her lips...
With graceful step she treads the ground,
Captures my heart by her movements,
She causes all men's necks
To turn about to see her;
Joy has he whom she embraces,
He is like the first of men!"

"I have not that heard that since it was first written over three-thousand years ago!"

"I read it in the library at Alexandria. It was the epitome of what she meant to me. It is funny how some things remain in the soul. Never losing their vibrancy."

"Would you like to take the painting with you?"

"I appreciate the gesture, but I could not bear to look

at it every day," Altus laments, gazing upon the painting of Cleopatra.

"What do you intend to accomplish with Sierra?"

"You know what I hope to accomplish," he answers, locking eyes with Khaba.

"When Xi first told me of this girl, I thought either her, or you to be insane. But I will admit, the resemblance is uncanny. Not only the physical features, but in both voice and mannerism. In all my years, I have never seen two people so alike. But you must realize, she is no more Cleopatra than Eve is Laura de Noves."

"You need not tell me things I already know."

"And what will happen when she remains herself after the disease has taken her?"

"I have come to love her in our short time together. I admit, it was her uncanny similarity to Cleopatra that drew me in, but there is a softness to her that I love and cherish. I will not cast her out."

"Not immediately, anyway. But in time, you will. You will come to resent her for everything she is not. Which is not her fault. It will be your broken dream brought back to life, more painful than ever. Earlier, when you spoke of your time in Byzantium and how Xi helped you through it, it was not Rome you wasted all those years lamenting. It was Cleopatra and Caesar. As Rome crumbled, you feared their memories would too, and you spent centuries fixating on them, not even aware of the events surrounding you. And Xi handling business only made it worse! Her love and understanding gave you the time you craved to caress your sorrows. It was only her leaving that forced you back into the business of trade, thus joining the land of the living. The only time you forget about Cleopatra is when you are focused on business. This girl is dredging up your past and polishing rotted memories. You speak of forgetting the past, but you carry it with you like no other!"

"It does not get the best of me! I am still alive, am I not?" *Who are you to judge me! Living like a frightened rabbit in the ground for centuries!*

"Yes, you are alive. But the only thing that makes it so, is a promise made eons ago to a woman ranting at death's door. You carry it as the mythical Jesus bore his cross."

"Stop! I will hear no more of this!" Altus bellows. "With or without your understanding, I will give her the disease!"

Khaba closes his eyes, solemnly bowing his head. "If you are able to live with the repercussions, then I agree with your decision."

Altus relaxes and settles back in his chair before turning the conversation to the real reason he came to Egypt. "What has Caesarion done now, that it demands my presence?"

"He is here, in Egypt. He knew you would not come to him, so he asked that I summon you."

"What is it that he wants?"

"He wants our support."

"For what?"

"He has many of the same fears you hold about the future. He has devised a plan that will not only ensure our continued existence but also guarantee our prosperity."

"It sounds as if you believe in his plan. I hope you are not so foolish as to support another of his *world domination* schemes."

"I am not saying that I blindly support his plan, what I am saying, is that it is worth listening to."

"And if I disagree with it?"

"You know my answer. Caesarion is not a member of the Triumvirate, whereas you are its leader. You have always done what is best for us, and because of that, we will abide by your decision. But as our leader, you must listen to the words of our people. He gains support among the young progeny. Not only in the Middle East, but worldwide."

"The progeny that exist today will no longer be among us two-hundred years from now. Their thoughts and opinions are meaningless."

"As I said, your decision shall be the decision of the

Triumvirate."

"Where is he?"

"He is in Aswan, at the Old Cataract Hotel. Khamir may accompany you if you wish."

"No, I want to go alone. Besides, I want Khamir to take Sierra to the West Bank tomorrow and show her the Valleys of the Kings and Queens."

"I shall have Marhib accompany them. With an early start, they should see most everything by day's end."

"Thank you," he breathes, returning his gaze to the painting.

"She was the most beautiful of women," Khaba confesses, trying to atone for earlier comments.

"She still is my friend . . . she still is."

"Any man is blessed to have such a woman once in a lifetime."

"And I have lived countless waiting for her return."

"What if Sierra comes to find she is merely a copy of Cleopatra? How long do you think it will take her to resent you?"

"That is but one of the thoughts that plague me. I know I am venturing into treacherous waters, but it is my promise that you so callously trivialize, that made my decision for me. What if it is her! What if, by some random fluke in the universe, she has indeed come back to me? Is it possible that people are reborn constantly? Could Caesar or Baka have come back hundreds of times, only they never crossed our paths?"

"There is no reincarnation, and there are no gods. To believe in such things will only bring about your demise. Tell me, your progeny Abah, does she still struggle with religion?"

"Yes, and I fear it may bring about her end."

"You must fully appreciate that the mythology of God is but a burden to our people. Since the spread of Christianity and Islam, nearly all our progeny have failed to live past one-hundred-and-fifty. Belief in God poisons the mind, haunting modern man as surely as his shadow follows in the light of the sun. We were taught the fable in its crudest form, far before it was refined, and that is why only the four of us still exist. Do you really believe Sierra is any different?"

"I know she is of the modern age, but you must understand, if I do not act on this, I cannot last another two-thousand years, believing I let her go twice."

FORTY-ONE

The afternoon sun is at its zenith as Altus pulls up to the Old Cataract Hotel. The valet smiles happily as the driver's door pops open, and Altus tosses him the keys to the McLaren F1.

Walking through the lobby, he approaches the front desk as a hand grabs his shoulder from behind. Expecting to see Caesarion, he turns to find two Arab men in tunics. Both are of average height and looks, with short hair, and no distinguishing traits.

Perfect spies.

They bow to him, and the man to his left performs introductions. "I am Abdul, and this is Barama," he turns his head, gesturing to his compatriot. "We are your escorts."

"Lead the way," Altus grunts, following the men through the Moorish door-key arches of the 1902 restaurant, then outside to King Faoud's corner, a patio built on an outcropping of rocks that overlooks the Nile, and Elephantine Island. Seeing a tall, striking man, with long black hair, he immediately recognizes Caesarion.

"It has been too long," Caesarion smiles, giving Altus a heartfelt embrace. "Please sit down." After unbuttoning the jacket of his grey Italian suit, he sits across the table from Altus.

Looking back at the escorts standing guard, Altus

comments, "If privacy is required, let us sail a felucca down the Nile."

"If you wish, my yacht is docked below, but I prefer we stay here. The tourists have all left for Abu Simbel or the Temple of Isis, so no one will intrude. Besides, the view is lovely. I understand why King Faoud spent so many evenings watching the sunset from this patio."

"If you feel it safe, we will stay."

"How have you been these last many years?"

"I have been well," Altus replies, brusquely.

"And your trip here?"

Sighing, he quickly tires of the formalities. "If you needed to speak with me, why did you not come to America? Why was it necessary for me to come here?"

"Because this is where it all began. Civilization, Khaba, you, and me! This land is our home, no matter where our pursuits take us."

"That is true," he agrees, with a tip of his head. "But what demands such urgency?"

"I am uniting freedom fighters to form an army."

"The terrorists you speak of are too fragmented and volatile to ever be more than a nuisance," he scowls. "If this is the basis of your plan, you should have not wasted my time. You know of our edict on interference, it could bring about your beheading if Khaba and I determine your actions to be dangerous to us, or mankind. You, of all people, should know that. It was because of your actions that we enacted the edict."

Caesarion scoffs, not caring about laws or edicts for beings such as themselves. "If you had not convinced Peter III to refrain from invading Germany when he had them at his mercy, I would never have guided Napoleon or Hitler."

"I admit, it was for my love of homeland that I acted independently of the Triumvirate. But I was not looking to conquer the world, only to save my country and the thousands of men who would die fighting for it."

"And when Khaba asked that you not interfere, what did

you say?"

"I told him he did not understand," he meekly groans, knowing what is coming.

"How could he not have understood? He lived under Persian rule for two-hundred years."

"I understand that. But I did it to help mankind, just as Khaba's interferences have also been to the benefit of man. Your acts of interference are done to benefit no one but yourself."

"And how did the death of Alexander the Great benefit mankind?"

"Khaba had no idea he would not live through the disease. Besides, it was a risk Alexander agreed to."

"And had he lived, how would his conquering of more nations have benefited mankind?"

"Khaba believed he was a far-sighted statesman that would unite the world in peace, not a bloodthirsty conqueror like Napoleon, or Hitler."

"One man's terrorist is another man's freedom fighter. You bore me with rhetoric. Besides, if Alexander had lived, Rome would never have risen to such power, and my father would not have idolized Alexander and tried to emulate his accomplishments. Therefore, you and I would be no more than the dried-up decoration Ramses II has become." Caesarion pauses for a moment to consider the implications and has an epiphany. "And Alexander, after being crowned Pharaoh, and declared a god by the oracle at Siwah, would still be ruling the world today. No mortal being would dare question him as the supreme being. It would have been perfect in its execution!"

"Hyperbole! He could not even conquer the sickness, what makes you think he would have lasted two-thousand years?"

"Because we have."

"I will not talk of it any longer. It is the present and future for which I am concerned. And your interfering may cause a great deal of harm to us, as well as mankind."

"Yes, back to the matter at hand. Your interference with

humans."

Altus's anger begins to boil. "It was only once that I acted independently of the Triumvirate! One act in more than two-thousand years!"

"One act? Please!" he snickers. "Then why did you stay with Catherine the Great for so many years after Peter was gone? You loved the power of influence you held over her, as well as the commanding of her army. It was your hunger for power and greatness that kept you at her side. Would she have even thought to capture the Black Sea, or bring culture to Russia if it were not for you? Admit it, you loved the power!"

"Maybe I did enjoy the power. But I did it to help the people of Russia, not conquer the world," he rationalizes, converting accusations to altruism.

"If you cared so much for the people, then why did you not push to emancipate the serfs? You are no different than me, my father, or my mother. We are all of great power and destiny. We are gods among men!" he exclaims, throwing his arms above his head. "This disease, as you call it, is no such thing. Somewhere in time, the blood of the gods was mixed with humans, and we became the glorious beneficiaries. Tell me this is not true! We are no different than any of the multitude of gods worshiped throughout time, with the exception that we are real. Mankind can reach out and touch us!"

Caesarion pauses to examine his surroundings, before resuming in a subdued tone. "We can answer their questions, giving them solace that their prayers will be answered. We can grant everlasting life at whim. What god has ever done so much for man?"

"What is it you hope to achieve?"

"To fulfill my birthright as ruler of the world, just as my mother and father intended."

"What you speak of is impossible in this day and age." *Same old Caesarion. Crazy as ever!*

"It is not. For you see, this time, I will be the messiah. I will be in no need of puppet rulers or their nations, I alone will command mankind for eternity. A common religion will be the flag under which I unite the world in peace."

"And what of the religions that are not messianic, such as Buddhism?"

"I will decree a tolerance for all religions. And my angels, or progeny as we know them, shall come to teach all men of the God of Abraham."

"You will be considered a heretic. You cannot be all things to all religions." Rubbing his forehead, he can't bear to look him in the eye. *I cannot believe Khaba had me fly across the world to listen to this madness!*

"I will fulfill the Yaum al-Qiyamah judgment day prophecies of Islam, purporting to be the Mahdi. Another of our kind will play the part of Issa, or Jesus, as the Christians refer to him. I will twist the two largest religions into one, giving everyone just enough reason to believe. And the doubters? They shall be forced to convert or be singled out as heretics and infidels."

"And what do you plan on doing with those that resist you?"

"When the few denounce me, I shall call out to the people that they are the false prophets spoken of in the Bible and Qur'an. For all those that follow my teachings and worship me, there will be an eternity of peace and prosperity."

"How do you plan on bringing prosperity to everyone?"

Caesarion holds up his arms, pretending to preach, "It is a world of evil and sin I come forth unto, it took thousands of years to bring about such evil, and it will take many years to extinguish. In time, the righteous shall prosper, and the evil will be cast out."

Shaking his head, Altus is unable to believe what he is hearing. "It is impossible . . . your hunger for power blinds you to logic and reason. Have you learned nothing of the religious wars of the past? What happens when this war starts, and nuclear missiles are launched? When the whole of earth is covered in darkness, and all mankind dies, what is it worth to be ruler of that world? Where even we cannot survive!"

"You greatly exaggerate."

"I consider all scenarios, just as your father taught me. You possess the self-confidence and self-absorption of your father, yet you lack his intellect and compassion to rationalize and balance your actions. You confuse what is good for you, as being good for the world!"

"I have our interests and mankind's best interests at heart. After all, what does man yearn for more than peace? After I implement random attacks throughout the world, mankind will hunger for it!"

"Have you forgotten what happened the last time you interfered?"

"There is no need to remind me. That circus of freaks and their fixation on anti-Semitism, they could never focus on what was truly important. If only I had had Napoleon with me in 1939, things would have been much different!"

"All of us! Khaba, Xi and me, were sickened to see that the purpose of that war was to annihilate the Jews. Not to mention my personal disgust at how you infused the German army with symbolism from the ancient Roman military."

"I know, I know! I tried to halt the massacre of the Jews by setting up the assassination of Reinhardt Heydrich, but it was too late, things were already too far in motion. As for Roman symbolism, I only wanted to show the world that the greatness of Rome could live again. Admittedly, I was foolish. I did not think things through as I should have. Any government ruled by hatred and ignorance can never stand the test of time. Besides, Hitler was an unwilling puppet. He would not listen when I told him he needed long-range bombers to reach deep into Britain and Russia. And of course, that was his downfall. I came to understand the frustration you felt with Antony so many years ago."

"That is your regret! That he would not build long-range bombers to destroy England's airfields and the armament factories in Eastern Russia?" Furious with his callousness, Altus becomes enraged. "This is exactly why I have not spoken with you since the war! You have no understanding or compassion for mankind! I will not allow your caustic ambitions to bring about the end of the world!"

"This time, it will be different! I will follow the prophecies of the Bible and the Qur'an. I will use their false prophecies against them, and best of all, no one will doubt the Mahdi being eternal. I will rule this planet until the sun grows great in the sky and envelopes the earth, and by that time, it may be of no consequence. With mankind's rapidly increasing technology, I will have expanded my rule to other inhabitable planets. Think of it, Altus! No more hiding in the shadows, switching names on bank accounts, homes, and all the other hoops we jump through every sixty to seventy years. This technology they are creating will ensnare us one day, and you know it! Cameras line the streets of cities across the world. How much longer before facial recognition software picks one of us out as being immortal? With the Five Eyes alliance, half the world is already under common surveillance. Will we have to live in the shadows as Khaba did for centuries? Terrified of humans, taking shelter in the earth? What if they create a global currency, requiring all funds be converted into a new form of legal tender? And what if the conversion process requires a retinal scan? We'll either have to abandon fortunes or be instantly famous for being so wealthy. Neither sounds like a good option to me. And that is just the tip of the iceberg. What of artificial intelligence?"

"You know of my concerns for these issues but having mankind stare down the barrel of a religious gun is not the solution."

"You do not realize how quickly technology moves forward. Hitler and I both believed the enigma code would easily protect messages throughout the war, but Alan Turing proved us wrong. Are you familiar with Turing's associate, Irving Good?"

"It has been many years since I read his theories on artificial intelligence, but I do recall his concerns."

"Then you know that even the most basic of AI will see our

patterns of moving about the world, business transactions, communications, and who-knows-what-else, that is unique to our species. Now, take Good's example of this basic form of intelligence, creating an ultra-intelligent machine that mankind cannot control, then follow this with his theory on an intelligence explosion. What will stop this super intelligence from seizing control of the entire world? Will all of mankind be counting on the grace of this supreme intelligence for survival, much as animals on the verge of extinction rely on mankind's benevolent nature? Mankind is moving too fast into the realm of AI. They are so taken with their own technological advancements, they see only the comfort and riches that come from it, not the destruction that lay ahead."

Viciously angered at the very thought of his life being ended by a machine, Caesarion slams his fist on the table, and through gritted teeth, snarls, "I'm sick of it! This planet belongs to us! We have been its caretaker for thousands of years. They come and go like the seasons. Never changing! Can you say that man is any more intelligent today than he was two-thousand years ago? They are still as petty and frivolous as ever. More concerned with money and fashion, than their brothers starving in the streets. They don't deserve to be our leaders . . . we should be theirs! Think of it. Together, we can rule the universe, just as we were meant to. I as the messiah, and the rest of our kind, angels, sent from heaven above, worshiped for eternity as the gods we truly are! You can rule the Americas, Khaba would want no more than Africa and the Middle East, Xi in Asia, and I will make Rome the center of the world once again, the Vatican being my palace. I will unite all people and put an end to the religious fighting. Do you not see? It is destiny! Where Khaba failed with Alexander, he will have succeeded through you, in granting me eternal life."

Elbow resting on chair, Altus rubs his brow in frustration. Not wanting it to turn into a screaming match, he speaks calmly. "I understand your feelings, but I fear you are going about it the wrong way. I will grant you this. If, in time, technology does become our adversary, I will consider your plan more seriously, but until then, I cannot."

"Time is short! Man needs God less and less as his lifestyle becomes more opulent. With every technological advancement, more of them become atheists. I fear that with further advancements in technology, mankind will no longer need God and our time will have passed. You can see it for yourself in America. In another one-hundred years, the majority of men may be so content with themselves that they render all gods mythical. At this moment, all vampires are either on the precipice of glory or facing extinction. You speak of me starting a nuclear war, but what if these nations start a war we cannot control? Or even worse, artificial intelligence decides that man is no longer deserving of life and launches a war that is akin to a bad science fiction movie? Do you really want to put our future into the hands of these greedy, self-serving, feeble-minded humans? If we take over now, we can dismantle the weapons, saving ourselves and mankind. Can you imagine the money available to help people when we do away with the military-industrial complex? We can offer healthcare, food, housing. No ordinary man could want for more. A universal basic income so that homelessness is relegated obsolete. It is our time, that is why we are here! We are not the *diseased freaks* you make us out to be. We are gods, here to protect mankind from its inevitable self-destruction. It is only fitting they worship us!"

"I will be perfectly honest with you. I do not agree with your plan, but the reasons for it are more than valid. I am concerned with these very same issues, but I have yet to find a solution."

"There is time for you to think it over, but I believe that within a century our time will have passed. I am currently setting up sleeper cells of liberators all over the world. In time, they will attack with greater and greater frequency, causing unrest among the people."

Altus nods in dejected affirmation, knowing he is right about the timeline, when a disturbing thought comes to him.

"Were you involved in the 9-11 attacks?"

"No, it was because of those attacks, mixed with the nuclear ambitions of Iran and North Korea, that I began to see the necessity of my plan."

"That is understandable," he confirms.

"If you like, speak with Khaba and Xi about modifying my plan, but I do not believe any other course of action will suffice."

Altus sits quietly, looking at the Nile and the abundance of feluccas sailing the tranquil waters. "I could not bear to see it all end."

"You have been more than a father to me these many years, and like most fathers and sons, we do not readily see eye-to-eye. But I value your opinion and advice. Please do not dwell on past errors, letting them cloud your judgment."

"You have always been my only family Caesarion. From the moment you were born, I raised you as my own. I will agree that there are times I am much harder on you than Khaba or Xi, but it is only because I see the greatness from whence you came."

"It is not my bloodline that makes me great, it is by your guidance that I became the man I am today."

"That is a very honorable thing to say, but I am not sure I am willing to accept that kind of blame," Altus jokes.

Caesarion laughs, cheerfully asking, "Can you stay for the day? We will sail to the Temple of Isis, if you like."

"I cannot. I promised Khaba I would speak with him about your plan, and I must return to someone that has accompanied me."

"The girl, Sierra."

"Khaba told you?" Leaning back in the chair, he bites his lip, trying to hide his surprise.

"Do not be angry with him. I look favorably upon her. I know what you are attempting, and I agree, wholeheartedly. You see her as fulfilling a lost love, whereas I see her as a portent of our destinies being fulfilled. If my mother's soul does indeed reside within you, as prophesized, I ask that you grant my parent's wishes, and stand aside as I implement my plan, fulfilling my birthright."

Caesar's words fill his thoughts. *'When the time is right, fulfill Caesarion's birthright as ruler of the world, for his future is brighter than the Star of Isis.'* With that ancient directive, he half-heartedly nods, letting out a sigh, and barely audible, "Agreed."

Happy that Altus will not stand in his way, he confidently proclaims, "This girl is the embodiment of my mother's prophecy. If she returns, we shall prosper!"

FORTY-TWO

Arriving at Khaba's home, Altus heads for the library to discuss the details of his conversation with Caesarion. Finding him in the same chair he was in the previous evening, he sits across the desk from him.

"I have heard what he had to say," Altus announces.

"What do you think?" Khaba asks, pensively.

"His cause is just, but the plan is flawed."

Khaba stares at him for a moment, waiting to hear if he will elaborate, before saying, "I believe his plan is flawed as well, but likely for different reasons than you."

"In what way?" he asks.

"I believe that it will take one man to unite and save this world. Many believe it to be a preordained religious messiah, whereas I believe it to be something quite different. I think the genetic makeup of this *disease*, as we call it, is mankind's messiah. This messianic blood, so to speak, was meant to be passed on, much as it has been, until it came to reside in the individual that possessed the strength, wisdom, and courage to rule the world. I also believe that this has already taken place, and it is time for that chosen person to take that responsibility upon himself, saving mankind, as well as his own species. These thousands of years spent creating and arguing over religion was but a necessary step for all humans to accept their subservience to a messiah. Unfortunately, with scientific progress, man is losing faith in the very religions that promised him a savior. That is why I believe Caesarion is correct with his plan." He looks at Altus, wondering if he will respond harshly to his admittance of believing in the plan, then continues when there is none. "I have stared at this painting all day, and I have come to the realization that Sierra was sent to us as a sign, or prophecy, that the messiah's time is at hand."

"Are you saying that Sierra is the messiah?"

"No, I am saying that you are the chosen messiah, not Caesarion. His plan is not flawed, it is his choice to appoint himself as the messiah that is in error."

Looking at him blankly, Altus bellows, "You want, *ME*, to go through with his plan? You have gone mad! I will not deceive the people of this world into thinking I am the messiah."

"But you must! It is for their own good that you lie to them. They have been lying to themselves for thousands of years, putting their faith in ancient fairy tales. Why not give them what they desire most?"

"I agree that the world is in trouble and that our kind are within the crosshairs, but to put ourselves upon the throne of God, whether real or imaginary, is not to the benefit of mankind. In time, man will grow and come to realize that in helping his fellow man and eliminating warfare is where his salvation lies. But until then, interfering in that process can only set him back thousands of years in intellectual growth. Do you really want mankind throwing themselves at the feet of a bogus messiah?"

"No, I expect you to nurture mankind. Promoting the exploration of everything scientific, he will no longer need to fight his fellow man, nor struggle with religion. You will educate mankind to give to others, as well as giving reverence to mother earth. You will teach that only by performing such acts will they gain entrance into the kingdom of heaven. It can only come to fruition with you! Caesarion lacks the compassion and understanding, not to mention your intelligence and hunger for righteousness. If you do not go forward with the plan, then no one will."

Exhaling heavily, Altus rolls his eyes, not knowing how to respond.

"This girl, Sierra, we will give her your blood and nurture her through the sickness. As she recovers, you are free to read the Bible, Qur'an, and all the scrolls I possess of religions throughout history. I even have ancient Jewish writings that modern man is completely unaware of. Perhaps, from these fables, you will find what man has been seeking for so long, and that the name of Altus is no different than the names Jesus, Mohammed Mahdi, or Mithra. With one crucial exception . . . you exist! And therefore, you, and you alone, can benefit mankind through your benevolence."

Looking randomly about the room, Altus is unable to make eye contact, feeling shame for what he is about to reveal. "I will read through the scriptures and whatever else you so desire, but I have already given Caesarion my word, that if Cleopatra returns, I will acquiesce and grant his father's wish. So, you see, only if Sierra dies, or remains herself, can I do what you ask of me."

Visibly shaken, Khaba lunges forward, looking as if he is about to jump over the desk and strangle him. "You should never have agreed to such terms with Caesarion! You know his unpredictability and egomaniacal behavior better than any of us!"

"Do you genuinely believe Cleopatra's prophecy, that it warrants such a reaction? I was a fool to entertain it myself!"

Khaba takes a deep breath, leans back calmly in his chair, and runs a hand through his hair. "You know my answer to that. My fear is that Caesarion will twist her very survival to justify that his destiny is being fulfilled. He is very adamant about his plan, so much so, if it were up to me, I would rather kill the girl, than have him move forward with the plan."

Shocked, Altus narrows his eyes to slits, casting a deadly gaze.

Khaba raises a hand, waving lightly. “I have no desire to do any such thing. It is only my way of saying how much I dread the possibility of Caesarion becoming the messiah.”

Altus tilts forward in his chair, elbows resting on knees. *Maybe he’s right. If she lives, she will only resent me . . .. Even worse, Caesarion will twist her survival into being the impetus that launches his plan. It may be better for everyone if I kill her.*

FORTY-THREE

Intently looking out the window of Xi's helicopter as it circles around the impressive Potala Palace in Lhasa, China, Eve declares, "It's beautiful!"

"It was commissioned by the fifth Dalai Lama in the seventeenth century. It is nearly one-thousand feet long, with one-thousand rooms. It took over fifty years to build," Xi informs.

"How big is Shangri La?"

"It is less than a quarter the size of Potala, but is every bit, if not more beautiful."

Eve turns to Weston, sitting beside her, and smiles, resting a hand on his leg. He feebly smiles back, too drained to give any significant physical reaction. To raise his spirits, she kisses him on the cheek before turning her attention back to the world below.

Flying away from the palace, the terrain changes, becoming more mountainous as they head toward Shangri La. The rugged, dramatic mountains make for stunning scenery, and Eve gently lays her head against the window, soaking up the natural beauty.

After two hours of jagged mountain peaks and stunning ravines, a highly detailed monastery perched on the edge of a cliff comes into view. The helicopter circles the U-shaped complex, slowing its speed, before landing in the courtyard at the center of the monastery. Six handsome young men run to the helicopter wearing the national dress of Tibet, the Chuba, a black cloak wrapped around the body, fastened at the waist with a red sash. Opening the door, they bow to Xi, and stand rigidly at attention, three to each side of the steps.

Xi exits the helicopter, and Eve escorts Weston, followed by Natalia and the twins. Holding onto Weston's hand, Eve helps support him as they walk toward the entrance of the monastery.

The main building, making up the bottom of the U shape, rises four stories high and represents the legendary Mount Meru. With its flared rooftops and golden steeples, the upper two stories bear striking similarity to the ancient Samye Monastery. The attached side buildings are both white, matching the lower structure of Shangri La, and the two-story structures frame the expansive courtyard, extending out to the cliff's edge.

Xi pulls Eve to her side as they cross the grassy courtyard. "The streams of yellow flags you see flying about the monastery represent a prayer. As the wind blows, the prayer is released, bringing luck and prosperity to those devoted to the Way of Xi. The two wheels you see on each side of the courtyard are prayer wheels, each time a wheel is spun, the spinner is blessed."

"That's fascinating," Eve replies, then wrinkles her brow. "Why is there a brass swastika on the facade of the main building?"

"Swastikas are a Buddhist symbol of good fortune when shown clockwise. They existed in ancient times, far before the symbol became associated with the Nazis. The main building is where the prayer halls, library, ceremonial hall, and primary residences are located. The smaller building to your right, is where the servants live, as well as being the location of the kitchen. The building to your left is where all ancient scriptures and artifacts are located. That building is strictly off-limits to servants, and only open to progeny upon request.

When you enter the main building, you will see a shrine, or chorten, as it is properly called, holding the remains of my father, the Great Emperor Wang Mang. Every morning, prayers are given at the shrine. When you hear the gong ring four times, your presence is required."

Eve nods, raising an eyebrow. *Sounds a little odd, but If you say so, I'm game.* Looking about the grounds, she asks, "Why is there only one tree in the whole courtyard?"

"It is singular in its representation of the Way of Xi. It is from the Eastern Ocean, where it was fed by the waters of Ardevisura, meaning, those who eat from it, become immortal."

"I like that!"

"The fir tree is not only considered to be life-conferring and health-restoring but also closely related to the crane, the bird of immortality. Cranes are also considered to be the souls of old fir trees."

"I have a lot to learn, don't I?"

"Yes, and you will find everything to be intellectually stimulating and life-affirming."

Stopping at the fir tree, near the steps to the main entrance, Xi, Eve, and Weston wait for the five servants carrying their luggage. The sixth servant walks before a five-foot round gong set beside the tree, picks up a wooden staff with padded end, and swings it into the gong three times. As the sound reverberates throughout the courtyard, forty-four men run from the servants' quarters and line up before Xi, with the five men that retrieved the luggage falling into line as well. They wear the same chubas with red belts and bow in unison as the servant that rang the gong, announces, "The Dalai Lama has returned!" Striking the gong twice, Natalia and the twins form a line in front of the men, facing Xi. As the notes echo, twenty women exit the main building and join Natalia and the twins in line, whereupon they all bow in unison.

Xi studies the line of women, instructing, "A new disciple has joined us, her name is Eve. You will do all you can to help in her learning the Way of Xi. What she demands of you, I demand of you. What she asks for, she shall receive."

Turning to Eve, she explains, "The women are my progeny, whereas the men, as I am sure you have surmised, are no more than servants. They are never to taste our blood, never to speak without being spoken to, and most importantly, never to leave Shangri La."

"I like the sound of that. Will they do as I command?"

"To the letter," Xi responds, proudly.

Softly biting the tip of her finger, Eve reveals an impish grin. Confidently strutting behind the progeny, she lustfully examines the row of men that look more like male models, than helpless servants. With hands on hips, and a narrowing of her eyes, she shouts, "Disrobe!"

In unison, the men untie their chubas, letting them fall to the ground. She saunters along the line of ripped, muscular men, consisting of all races and sizes, judging them as she makes her way. Stopping randomly, she runs a hand over the men she finds more attractive or well-endowed. Reaching the end of the line, she walks back to Xi, smiling, "I'm going to like it here!"

Feeling faint, but not missing the opportunity to get an eyeful of the beautiful women, Weston checks them out one by one. Turning his gaze to the row of men, he notices a common trait, a bond shared, puncture marks on their cocks. *Holy fuck, we're feeders!*

Xi turns her attention to the servant that rang the gong, instructing, "Stand front and center."

The bald, black man willingly takes his place before Xi and Eve. Standing over seven-feet-tall, he dominates the view with his muscular physique, huge rod, and prominent bone structure.

Xi sternly commands, "At attention!" to which the men respond by stroking themselves fervently.

Eve watches with joy as the tall black servant abuses his enormous shaft, coming to full erection within seconds.

"Would you like to try?" Xi asks, holding out a hand before the massive cock.

Eve happily disrobes and walks before him. His dick comes to her forehead, and she strokes it with both hands, futilely attempting to encircle its girth. She commands, "Fuck me," and jumps high in the air, spreading her legs to accept him.

Catching her mid-air, he guides her down his shaft, and she wraps her legs around him.

As the line of men stroke themselves, Xi calls out, "Replenish!" and the women kneel instinctively before them, fangs penetrating the erect rods.

Weston watches men fall randomly as they are drained to unconsciousness, only to see the women move wantonly onto the next upright tool.

Always loving to break arrogant men, Xi glares at Weston, lips curling into a sneer. "Bare yourself!"

Removing his black jeans and T-shirt, he cautiously strokes himself, careful not to rub the healing puncture wounds. *I should have listened to Sierra . . . God, I miss her!*

"Move quickly, or I will cut your throat open," she hisses.

Still dazed from the loss of blood, he mumbles, "I'm moving," as he walks fearfully closer.

Kneeling before him, Xi bares her fangs, and laughs maniacally.

In another time, he lived for women in such a position, but now, all he can do is close his eyes and look away, accepting his fate as the weaker sex.

FORTY-FOUR

"Lie down and relax," Khaba instructs, motioning to the lone bed in the barren room.

Resting on the edge of the bed, Sierra eyes the leather straps attached to each corner of the metal frame. "Are these to tie me down during the madness of the middle stage?"

"Yes, you will be glad they are there when you reach that point," Altus confirms, with a kiss.

Looking at the painted hieroglyphs and pictures of ancient gods adorning the walls of Khaba's ceremonial chamber, she comments, "I feel like I'm in one of the tombs we visited today."

"These are the same paintings that decorated the walls of Khaba's pyramid when I took the disease."

"Are the hieroglyphs on the ceiling the same hymns that comforted you during your sickness?"

"Yes, Marhib will chant them as the first stage takes hold."

"Have you come to accept the end of your life as a human?" Khaba asks, softly.

"Yes, I have. Altus has proven that there are probably no greater gods than your kind."

"Probably?" Marhib asks, compassionately. "That does not sound very definite. Are you sure you wouldn't like another day to think it over? It is a monumental decision."

"I'd rather do it now. If I think about it too long, I'll only dwell on the sickness and become more anxious. Plus, I have everything I'll ever need," she smiles, looking into Altus's eyes.

"Then it is time," Khaba proclaims, putting the ancient mask of Anubis over his head, as Marhib dons Isis' crown of horns with sun disk.

Wrinkling her brow, she turns to Altus. "Do we really need the costumes?" *It's difficult enough without these guys freaking me out.*

"Do not worry, Khaba believes in tradition. Lie down and relax." Gazing into her eyes, Altus gently arranges her hair, then runs his fingers over her defined eyebrows, and down across her cheekbone, to her full moist lips. *She is too precious, I cannot kill her.*

Parting her lips, she kisses the tip of his finger, adjusts her head in the pillow, and takes a deep breath as Marhib begins chanting.

"Atum, this thy daughter is here,
Anubis, whom thou hast preserved alive, she lives!
She lives, this Sierra lives!
She is not dead, this Sierra is not dead:
she is not gone down, this Sierra is not gone down:
she has not been judged, this Sierra has not been judged.
She judges, this Sierra judges!"

Standing on the opposite side of the bed, Khaba reaches across, handing Altus a knife of obsidian.

Eyes wide, Sierra watches the exchange of the polished black knife.

"Do not fear," Khaba comforts, "close your eyes and Anubis shall replenish your soul."

Altus kneels beside the bed, instructing, "Open your mouth wide and stick out your tongue when Khaba commands, 'Open your Ka to the blood of Sekhmet.'"

Fearfully anticipating what's to come, she props herself up on an elbow, giving Altus one last kiss. "Love me?"

"Forever," he assures, staring deep into her glittering eyes.

"See you on the other side," she blinks, a touch of concern crossing her face.

Sensing her apprehension, Altus stresses, "You must hold my blood in your mouth as long as possible before swallowing."

Taking a deep breath, she falls back in the pillow, and closes her eyes. The rhythmic chants of Marhib fill the room as she concentrates on the melody, breathing out fear and breathing in serenity.

Having been sung to the ancient gods of Atum, Shu, Tefnut, Geb, and Nut, she relaxes, letting the ancient melody soothe her anxiety.

Khaba holds his hands to the heavens, proclaiming, "Great is the number Sekhmet has slaughtered, and greater yet are her powers. By command of the Lord of the Dead, Anubis, open your Ka to the blood of Sekhmet!"

Eyes squeezed tight, she opens her mouth and sticks out her tongue, anticipating the flow of Altus's blood.

As Marhib chants, "Isis, this thy daughter is here!" Altus slashes the knife across her tongue, sending a shower of blood across her face amid screams of pain.

Swallowing the rush of blood, she clenches her tearful eyes and reopens her mouth.

Gritting his teeth, Altus buries the knife in his wrist. Holding it directly over her mouth, blood follows the wave of his knuckles to the base of the knife, pouring onto her tongue, and filling her mouth. With the wound healing and stream lessening, he mercilessly twists the knife in his artery to keep the gash from sealing.

With blood dripping from the corners of her mouth, Altus removes the knife, and stresses, "Close your mouth and let our blood mix as long as you possibly can."

Lips pressed firmly together and tears streaming down her face, she fights the urge to swallow.

"Open your Ka and accept the blood of the gods!" Khaba commands, throwing his arms wide.

Wanting to get the vile taste out of her mouth as quickly as possible, she clenches her teeth and gulps it down, all the while, twisting her head in the pillow to alleviate the pain of her half-severed tongue.

"You will be like Ra, rising and setting through all eternity," Khaba chants. "You will awaken gladly every day, all afflictions expelled. You will traverse eternity in joy. You are complete. You are justified. You are eternally youthful. For in truth, you are Isis Sierra, Goddess of all eternity!"

FORTY-FIVE

Escorting Caesarion into the library, Marhib gives Khaba a tight-lipped smile, followed by a cautionary look to Altus.

"I see that you have been doing some research," Caesarion observes, joining them at a desk covered in scrolls and religious artifacts.

"Mostly within the Qur'an, since that is where your plan is centered," Khaba informs him.

"What is your plan exactly?" Altus probes. "Religious prophecy can be vague, but believers will be in search of precise details."

"Please, let me start from the beginning. Then, as I go, you may ask anything you feel relevant." Acknowledging their acceptance, he takes a deep breath, preparing for his presentation of Armageddon. "As written in the Qur'an, with the arrival of Yaum al-Qiyamah, or Judgment Day, people will be reprimanded for their acts of disobedience by a fire in the sky that swallows up Baghdad, and turns the sky red. Blood will be shed, houses destroyed, and a fear will come over Iraq from which there shall be no rest."

"You are planning a nuclear strike!" Altus snaps.

"Please, let him continue," Khaba insists.

"It is foretold that the ground will cave in, and fog will cover the skies for forty days, and a night three nights long will follow the fog. After the night of three nights, the sun will rise in the west, and the Beast of the Earth shall emerge, marking the faces of people. It is also written that a breeze from the south shall cause sores in the armpits of Muslims, from which they will die, and the Qur'an will be lifted from the hearts of the people."

"Most of that will be fulfilled with the nuclear strike," Khaba affirms.

Caesarion, fully aware of Altus's look of discontent, continues unabated. "This Beast of the Earth will take its shape in the prophecy of a revolution by the Sufyani, a descendent of Abu Sufyan. Abu Sufyan was said to have been one of Mohammed's greatest enemies, along with his son, Muawiya I, and Muawiya's son, Yazid. The Sufyani's revolution is said to start in Palestine, and eventually span the Middle East. After the strike on Baghdad, my Sufyani army will start striking throughout the Middle East, partially fulfilling the Islamic prophecy, as well as fulfilling the Christian prophecy of the land of Gog attacking Israel, foretold of in the book of Revelations."

"What you are saying, is that your army will be Gog to the Christians, and Sufyani's to the Muslims," Khaba states, making it clear in his mind.

"Will these liberators you are currently training, make up your Sufyani army?" Altus frowns, crossing his arms brusquely.

"Yes, when the time comes, they will be assimilated into one fighting force. Though they are not now, nor will they ever be under my command, for they will be under the command of one of my progeny. My face cannot be known to them, for I will not make my presence known until I sound a loud trumpet in the sky above Mecca, proclaiming myself Mohammed al-Mahdi, the Islamic messiah. Upon my emergence, my army of progeny will miraculously come out of the desert to meet me in Mecca, and we will march off to fight the Sufyani army, or Gog, depending on your religion."

"Thereby fulfilling the prophecy of a cry from heaven upon your arrival in Mecca," Altus interjects, "and because you will be commanding an army of progeny to defeat the Sufyani forces, it will also fulfill the prophecy of your soldiers having the strength of forty men. Being that the leader of the Sufyani's, this so-called descendent of Abu Sufyan, is one of your progeny, I assume he will arise after being killed and proclaim himself the messiah. Thereby fulfilling the Christian prophecy of the Antichrist, as well as his Islamic counterpart, the Dajjal, all within this one individual. Correct?"

"Yes," Caesarion confirms, "and upon his resurrection, he will be adorned with a mark on his face, a tattoo, that he and all his army will put on their foreheads. This will fulfill the Christian prophecy of the mark of the Beast, as well as the Islamic prophecy of the Beast of the Earth marking the faces of people. But here is where I will need your assistance, Altus. Not long after I have proclaimed myself Mahdi, the prophecy tells of sinful opposers that will join in the fight against me. I believe this may come in the form of troops from the United States, for once I proclaim myself messiah, the U.S. will not only attack the Sufyani army but quite possibly my Mahdi army of progeny as well. This is when the prophecy of Issa, or Jesus, will come to pass. From the Mount of Olives, you will proclaim yourself Jesus, fulfilling the Christian prophecy, as well as the Islamic, of Issa and the Mahdi working together to fight evil and cement justice on Earth."

Jaw clenched, Altus looks incredulously from Caesarion to Khaba.

"Please, let him finish," Khaba reiterates.

"Then, in the battle of Aqabat Afiq in Jerusalem, you will behead my Sufyani progeny, the Dajjal, or Antichrist to the Christians, and end the war, fulfilling the Qur'an and Christian prophecies."

"And what of the Islamic prophecy that Jesus dies in forty years, being buried next to Mohammed, in Medina?" Altus protests.

"He cannot and will not! Without you, or Jesus, I should say, I would lose control of the Christian world. That is why we will alter some of the prophecies after we are crowned messiahs. It is a minor detail."

"A minor detail!" Running a hand through his long hair, Altus shifts about uneasily. "Even if things go as planned right up through the battle of Aqabat Afiq, you will lose followers when you start altering prophecies."

"Once the war begins, many of these details that have not been worked out may become moot points," Khaba reasons. "Altus, you know better than any of us the confusion of war, you cannot expect everyone to believe in the accuracy of the prophecies down to the last letter. People by their very nature do not require much convincing."

"What of the materialism of Western Civilization? I cannot bring an end to the materialistic ways of the West!"

"Yes, you can!" Caesarion emphatically retorts. "Once you are found to be Jesus, the entire Christian world will heed your words, and you will preach of becoming more spiritual, thereby changing the Muslims' negative view of Western Civilization. We will twist the religions of Christianity and Islam just enough to satisfy both faiths."

"You make it sound simple. What if we cannot find that middle ground? Then what . . .? Do not forget, we still have Hindu's and Buddhist's to deal with, do not assume Xi can convince Buddhists to suddenly change a lifetime of beliefs," Altus rebukes.

"Those are issues that will work themselves out as we progress. With the two largest religions under our control, we will have the power of numbers, and popularity behind us. Never underestimate the compliancy of humans. Once the Buddhists and Hindus find these religions to be the true religions, they will naturally join the Islamic or Christian faiths. Thereby fulfilling the Islamic prophecy that reads, *A large number of non-believers will convert to Islam once they see that the signs of the prophecy have come to pass.*"

“And what of the Jews?” Altus declares.

“You, or Jesus, more correctly defined. Will confirm the belief that when you appeared in ancient times, you were the Suffering Messiah, Mashiach Ben-Yosef, that Daniel spoke of in the second temple period. And now, you have returned as the Glorious Messiah, Mashiach Ben-David, who has returned to reign over his people.”

“Well, I am glad you have done some research on the matter,” Altus scoffs, sarcastically. “But how will you fulfill the most important prophecies of all, making each religion the true faith of mankind? Christians will never turn to Islam, nor Muslims to Christianity. Not to mention Judaism!”

“That is something that will be worked out when the time comes. Do not forget, we are the messiahs, thereby speaking what God truly desires of all mankind. Maybe he will desire a combination of all faiths?” Caesarion spouts, confidently.

Unable to believe his ears, Altus argues, “That is a huge problem to be worked out later! It leaves enormous possibility for failure! Do not be so quick to assume the Jews will forget about the building of the third temple. It is a cornerstone of their belief! And if you satisfy the Jews by building the temple, you will outrage Muslims by tearing down Masjid al-Aqsa and the Dome of the Rock.”

“These are problems that can be solved as they arise,” Caesarion dismisses, with a wave of his hand.

Mouth open, eyes wide, Altus cannot believe there are so many holes in the plan. “And what about the Qur’an prophecy that Jesus will return and deny that he ever claimed to be Lord? You cannot fulfill that because you will lose the Christians. And what about the promise of Israel being eternally restored under the Jewish and Christian faiths, whereas it is eternally destroyed in the Islamic faith? There is far too much room for error! And if it all falls apart, we will be hunted down and found to be immortal. Thereby risking our species’ future, not just yours and mine!”

“You greatly underestimate the compliancy of humans!”

Caesarion snaps.

"I may, but you overexaggerate!" Altus screams. "Why is it you must start this campaign of terrorism if you only need to create an army under the name of Abu Sufyan?"

"Because this army needs a purpose before it will march, and America, Israel, and the rest of Western Civilization serve that purpose in the metaphorical form of the Dajjal. Though most believe him to be a man, much like the Christian Antichrist, there is a segment of the Muslim world that believe his physical attributes to be a metaphor for Western Civilization. The fair complexion of the Dajjal is thought to mean Caucasian people, while the right eye being blind, is metaphorical. You see, in the Qur'an, it is written that the left side of the body is hell, and the right, heaven. This is thought to mean that white Westerners are blind to spirituality, while the left eye gleams with the luxury and comfort of earthly treasures. Thus, while the Dajjal will appear as an actual person once the battle begins, the metaphorical aspect will be the impetus that starts the war."

"And what will become of these Islamic militants you train under the name of the Sufyani army, when the war is over?" Altus begs.

"None will survive the war, my progeny, and all of mankind will see to that. You forget that they will bear the sign of the Beast on their foreheads, thus making for easy targets."

"Think about it," Khaba pleads, "that is all we ask. Sierra is only beginning the middle stage of the disease, and there is much time to make the plan better.

"Will you at least do that?" Caesarion pleads, a son before his father.

"I will consider the plan while Sierra accepts the disease, and though I do not believe in its plausibility, I will do all I can to make it better. Even though I do not believe it can be made better, since there are far too many unknowns." Tired of arguing, Altus snarls, "Please excuse me, I must check on Sierra."

FORTY-SIX

Sighing loudly to let out his frustration, Altus walks down the curved iron staircase to the ceremonial chamber in the lower level of Khaba's home. I should have never agreed to Caesarion having his way if Cleopatra returns!

Approaching the chamber, he finds Marhib closing the door, muffling the agonizing screams coming from within the room.

Softly smiling as he approaches, she asks, "I heard the screaming up there, is everything alright?"

"No. But truthfully, I am more concerned with the screaming down here. She does not sound well."

"It's always the same at this stage. Complete lunacy."

"I thought I might look in on her, but she would most likely not even recognize me."

"You should rest, it's late. Soon, Sierra will tire, and fall asleep."

"I would love to rest, but I have too much on my mind." Staring at the door, his inner voice commands, *Drain her! End the madness!*

"What is it about the plan that bothers you?" she questions. "The possibility that God exists?"

"That is the least of my worries, it has more to do with our survival."

"And if there is a God, would that make a difference?"

"You cannot ask me that. You know as well as I do, it is

a fabrication. Khaba has told us over and over that there was no Jewish exodus from Egypt, and he was there, so he would know! Not to mention the scrolls clearly showing the story's growth over time, and the borrowing from different religions."

"I know. But what if?"

"Then it would be quite obvious that we could never do such a thing. And it would also mean that you and I are no more than the devil's pawns." Curious as to why she pushes the subject, he suspiciously probes, "Why do you ask such a thing?"

"No reason. I only thought it might make a difference, that's all."

Not satisfied with her answer, but too exhausted to dig deeper, he exhales, "In that case, I'm going to bed. I sense a long day tomorrow."

FORTY-SEVEN

Frustrated by the likelihood of arguing with Khaba and Caesarion, Altus lies listlessly in bed, wasting away the early morning by channel surfing on the TV. Hearing a knock on the door, he responds, "Come in."

With perpetual soft confidence, Marhib brings him breakfast.

Happy to see her, and not Caesarion or Khaba, he smiles appreciatively. "You did not have to do that for me."

Craning her head back into the hallway, she looks for signs of life as she closes the door. Satisfied that no one is near, she asks, "Feeling any better this morning?"

"I suppose. But it is only because I am not thinking about what the day has in store."

Setting the tray on the bed, she takes a backward glance at the door. Convinced of their privacy, she reaches underneath the tray, pulling forth a stack of tattered papyrus. With a strained whisper, she implores, "You must read this! For better or worse, I believe we are at a point in time where the truth must be known."

"What is it?"

"I can't explain, there's no time! Please, read it as quickly possible. I'm sending Khaba and Caesarion to Abydos under the guise that you need time to think over the plan, which should give you the better part of the day to comprehend what this means to us. And I'm not just talking about our species, I mean all of mankind!"

"What could be that important?" he inquires.

"It is the journal of Beronike, one of Caesarion's earliest progeny. You only need concern yourself with the latter years, from 780 onwards. It is dated before the time of Dionysus Exiguus's altering of the years to Anno Domini, making it approximately 27 AD."

"That is near the time I returned to Rome. What is written?"

Avoiding his question, she holds a finger to her lips. *Quiet!* "That's fine. I'll tell Khaba of your wishes," she announces loudly, head turned toward the door, so that her voice might carry into the hallway. Leaning close, she whispers, "Read! When you're done, bring it to me!"

Dashing to the door, she takes a breath and swoops back her long hair. Giving him a tight-lipped smile, she exits the room, and pulls the door closed.

Setting the tray aside, he flips through the layers of papyrus until he finds the faded numerals 780, written across the top of a page.

15 Mars 780

With the blackness of night, I was able to replenish myself from a passing caravan. While he was unkempt, smelly, and ugly, his blood was as the nectar of pomegranate. How I miss the beautiful boys of Palmyra.

25 Mars 780

After replenishing last night, Caesarion took me into the Judaean Desert while the caravan camped. We made love upon an outcropping as the moon lit our bodies, then slumbered until the sun's rays opened our eyes. Walking back to camp, we saw a tired and disheveled man resting against a rock, just below the outcropping where we slept. Noticing him near death, I asked if he wanted food or water. When he replied, he had no need from man, for he was 'The Son of God,' we laughed hysterically.

Having fun with the deluded fool, Caesarion joyously taunted, 'If you are the son of God, command these stones to become loaves of bread.'

Not fazed by our laughter, he looked deep into Caesarion's eyes, calmly saying, 'Man shall not live by bread alone, but by every word that proceeds from the mouth of God.'

Caesarion smirked at his ignorance, hoping to continue the assault, but I longed for civilization and a decent meal, urging, 'Let us leave this wanderer to the beasts of the desert, so that we may continue our journey.'

IT CANNOT BE! Wide-eyed, and mouth aghast, Altus reads the passage again. Unable to fathom the implications, his breath becomes short. "IMPOSSIBLE!"

He reads the next entry but finds only trivial details of her life. Day after day, page after page, he continues to read, until finding further relevant entries.

24 Mars 781

Strangeness born of the most unholy!

Jerusalem is in full festivities with the Day of Firstfruits celebration, and my love was here to spend it with me. While at the temple completing the sale of seric cloth, the carcass from the desert appeared and made trouble. Abreast with vigor, he flipped the trade tables over as he chased everyone out but the priests, screaming, 'It is written, my house shall be called a house of prayer, but you make it a den of thieves!'

I was shocked at his audacity, yet Caesarion only grinned as he consulted with Caiaphas and the other priests. When I approached Caesarion, the priests looked at me with the lust reserved for any common harlot. The fools! If only they knew my power!

Caesarion, angered that business would not be completed, sought to make an example of the troublemaker named Yeshua. Holding Caesarion's hand, we approached the inciter as he stood stoically on the portico of Solomon's temple.

When his eyes met mine, my soul grew cold, strength leaving my body. But where I shrank, Caesarion stood bold, demanding, 'If you are the son of God, throw yourself down; for it is written; He will give his angels charge of you, and on their hands, they will bear you up, lest you strike your foot against a stone.'

Once again, Yeshua calmly met Caesarion's gaze, stating, 'Again it is written, You shall not tempt the lord your God,' then walked away to meet the throngs of sick and decrepit that came to lay eyes on him.

As we left the temple, among the poor's cries of, 'Hosanna to the son of David!' I asked Caesarion how he knew of such words from the Torah.

Frowning, he uttered, 'I am not certain. I have read little of the Torah, yet words fill my mouth.

Gasping for air, Altus furiously flips the fragile, cracked papyrus, sheet by sheet, scanning every line for further mention of Jesus. Days of entries, turn to months, until finally, he comes upon the name Yeshua.

11 December 782

Upon leaving the priests of the temple this morning, I happened upon Yeshua. He was standing alone, as if waiting for me as I turned the corner. After our last meeting, I was determined that he not get the best of me again. From first gaze, I pushed my lust into him in. But it was to no avail. The harder I tried, the more compassionate he became. Witnessing my frustration, he softly asked, 'Why do you choose the widest of paths to walk? You need only ask for forgiveness that I may cleanse your soul.'

HOW IS IT THAT HE KNOWS MY SINS?

Terrified, I turned to run but could manage no more than a step before his hand fell upon my shoulder.

Never can I mention this to Caesarion, but I felt the love of his God encapsulate my entire being. Such depth of compassion! As tears of shame poured down my face, staining my finest seric dress, he tenderly spoke, 'So you may know the love of God, as opposed to the concupiscence of Satan.'

Confused and ashamed, I ran with all my might. Only now do I wish I had stayed. The emptiness I feel since shunning his touch is like nothing I have ever experienced. I dare not think it, but is this man truly the messiah people believe him to be?

"What did he mean by cleansing her soul! Was he offering to cure the disease?" Altus asks, aloud. *Could we become mortal again by an act of God? What about Caesarion's plan? Will God take away the disease and make us mortal? Punishing our mountainous sins with an easy tap of his finger!*

Panting for breath, he reads on.

2 Mars 783
I am pale, weak, and aging rapidly. I cannot go on replenishing myself with the small drops I take from the homeless filling the alleys of Jerusalem. Pecking at their legs and arms as they drunkenly sleep, I am no better than a starving rat. I fear my guilt over taking another's life will surely bring about my end.

3 Mars 783
I have hidden my religious readings in preparation for Caesarion's arrival. If he were to find me studying such things, he would consider me the ultimate fool! I can only hope he does not notice my lack of replenishment. If he were to learn of my recent contact with Yeshua, I am certain he would put an end to me.

4 Mars 783
Caesarion arrived in high spirits telling me he had once again come across the 'Son of God,' while en-route from Jericho. When Yeshua finished preaching to a crowd of followers, Caesarion beckoned him to meet upon a limestone outcropping so that they may be alone. Laughing as he recounted the story, I fell more ill with each passing word.

Repeating their exchange, he said, 'I asked what kind of God would send him among the wretches of society when a man such as myself could promise him the wealth and might of all the kingdoms of the world. But instead of replying, he only stared at me with that same resolute firmness. Then, I stretched my hand across the horizon and told him, To you I will give all this authority and their glory; for it has been delivered to me, and I give it to whom I will. You only need fall down and worship me, and it shall all be yours.' Yeshua stood strong, yelling, Begone Satan! You shall worship the Lord your God, and him only shall you serve.'

As he gleefully recounted the story, I fell to my knees, vomiting. Sick to exhaustion with his evil words!

I know not what to do. Even the smallest drop of blood carries the heaviest of sins. I fear my end is at hand.

Breathing in spasms, Altus leans back into a pillow. *IT IS ALL TRUE! And Caesarion filled Satan's role in the Temptations! What does that make me?* Slapping his forehead with the palm of his hand, he tries to rub away the agonizing thoughts. *It is destiny . . . all of it! From the ancient drought that sent me into the lands of the Belgae, to Sierra breaking into my home, I have been played as a pawn in the celestial revelations bringing forth the Kingdom of Heaven!*

Staring blankly at the ceiling, he contemplates the implications of the time of God being at hand.

Suddenly, his inner voice brings forth an answer. *Kill Sierra, thereby preventing her from becoming Cleopatra and fulfilling Caesarion's plan. That would change everything! Or would it . . .? Is it more likely that after two-thousand years of destiny playing its part, I will only be confronted by a never-ending stream of Sierras until my will is broken, and I end up here again, stuck amidst the triad of my love for Cleopatra, Caesarion's plan, and my promise to Caesar.*

Thinking over the options, his thoughts flip from slicing Sierra's throat, to letting the hand of God control his fate. Until it comes to him. *It does no good to prolong the inevitable. Right or wrong, good or bad, I must play the hand destiny has dealt!*

Climbing off the bed, he clenches his fists, proclaiming, "Maybe there is enough free will incarnate that I may twist destiny. Picking which side I play for!"

Determinedly walking through the house, papyrus tight in hand, he goes in search of Marhib. Nervous that he may run into Caesarion or Khaba, he listens for voices, peaking into each room before entering.

Pumped full of adrenaline, he glances into Marhib's bedroom and finds her sitting in a chair, staring out the window like a statue.

"Where did this come from!" he demands.

Jumping at the sound of his voice, she lets out a breath. "It was left with Khaba after she came to visit him in Alexandria. And the last entries, what did you think?"

"I could not finish it! What else could possibly matter than the fact that God exists?"

Thinking he may be premature in talking with her before he has read all of it, she fills him in on the details. "Beronike rarely fed in the last months of Jesus's life. She became a wraith and spurned Caesarion. Jesus happened past her in the streets, and she grasped at his cloak, hoping once more to feel the love of God before withering away. As it slipped through her fingers, the disease was removed, and she became human again."

Falling into the chair next to her, he stammers, "I-I cannot believe it! How?"

"Because he was the Son of God," Marhib justifies.

"I realize that. It is just impossible to believe! What became of Beronike?"

"She followed Jesus as he bore the cross, giving him her veil to wipe away his sweat. After he died, she used it cover his face on the way to Joseph of Arimathea's sepulcher, honoring the Jewish tradition of covering any form of harm or disfigurement. Then, she rolled it up and put it under his head, softening the hard slab of stone as he was laid to rest."

"The Sudarium!" he exclaims.

"Yes, the Veil of Veronica, or Beronike, in ancient Greek. She wrote that after the stone was put in place covering the tomb, she stayed with Mary Magdalene. Upon witnessing the empty tomb days later, she took the veil and shroud that Joseph put over Jesus, and headed for Rome, while Mary sought out the apostles' John and Peter."

"I assume the winding sheet she took was the Turin Shroud, bearing the image of Jesus."

"Yes, but there's more. On her way to Rome to present the veil and shroud to Tiberius, she was visited by Jesus. He told her to preach the word of God to the souls afflicted with the blood disorder he had cured in her, and because she knew Caesarion would kill her if she went to him, she came to Khaba, hoping he would help spread the word of God to our people."

"Why did Khaba never tell any of us?"

"If he had, how many of us would still be alive? Would you?" she asks, soberly.

Fully aware that God and sin has always been the greatest burden to his kind, he grits his teeth. "It would have made my life harder, without doubt."

"Think about this for a moment. Since there is a God, are we Satan's imps and God's angels are secretly living among us? Or are some vampires Satan's imps, and others God's minions? Our roles predefined. Have you ever considered that the lives you have taken may well have been preordained by God?"

"There are so many lives I have ended; it is impossible to believe that they were all evil."

"You told me once, that you go with an inner sense when you choose your victims. Have you ever considered that your gut feeling is simply the will of God?"

"I find it easier to believe that there are angels among us, and we have never seen them."

"After two-thousand years, do you really believe there are angels walking among us? You have lived much longer than me, you know there is nothing besides humans and vampires."

"Are you trying to insinuate that God approves of our killing? Nonsense!"

"What do you think the reason could have been that Khaba hid this journal from you? You have known him for over two millennia. Is he good or evil?"

"You know the answer. He is altruistic beyond measure! From the day I met him, he has been trying to make people's lives better. He has always tried to end wars and ease suffering, not to mention donating billions of dollars to more causes than I can keep track of."

"Maybe Khaba didn't tell you of this journal because he sees the evil in Caesarion, and knows that there must be one of our kind to stand against him when the time is right. Who fills that role better than you?"

"It is too much to fathom. Vampires fighting the war of good and evil?"

"How could a disease exist that grants eternal life? Who, but God, could create a disease to fill his world with eternal angels and demons? It's almost biblical in design, isn't it?"

"Then which of our kind are good? Or evil? Are all vampires preordained one way or the other, or are we judged the same as humans? By our actions?"

"I don't know," she shrugs. "Maybe sides will be chosen when all vampires witness the opposing ideologies of you and Caesarion. It's possible that those who kill for pleasure and amusement are preordained to join Caesarion, and those that kill to survive, will side with you. Maybe God tells us who to kill with our gut feelings, and when we deviate through lust, anger, or pride, we go against the will of God."

"It is all too much to comprehend."

"It's all I've thought about for years. . . . And when I laid eyes on Sierra, I knew it was all coming to a culmination."

"Does Khaba know that you have knowledge of Beronike?"

"No, I found the journal in his vault almost twenty years ago, while admiring artifacts of Hatshepsut. If I had seen this when I took the disease over three-hundred years ago, I don't think I would have lived more than forty or fifty years. The burden of guilt being far too great."

"Then it is best that neither of us admits to any knowledge of it for the time being. Does Caesarion have knowledge of the journal?"

"I don't believe so, but I think it best you be wary of Caesarion. I have never told you this, but he holds a great deal of animosity towards you."

Altus squints his eyes, wondering if there is more bad blood between them than he is aware of. "Tell me more."

"Despite the fact that he always resented you for placing Xi in the Triumvirate instead of him, I believe he harbors a substantial amount of anger for taking his mother's life."

Altus looks away, blankly gazing out the window, replaying Caesarion's acceptance of Cleopatra's death. "That is very strange, he always told me he understood my actions."

"He is not like you and me. He is controlled by hate. The anger of his parent's death laid a bitter foundation he has only built upon with every passing century. I probably shouldn't tell you this, because it's just a feeling I get from things he has said in the past, but I think he harbors a great deal of hate for the Jews. Do you recall how closely he allied himself with Napoleon and Hitler? "

"Are you saying it was him that prompted the Final Solution?" he blurts, shocked at the very thought.

"It's a feeling I get from bits and pieces of conversations with him, over the years."

Analyzing past actions, he comes to a realization. "I wonder if that is why Napoleon's attitude towards the Jews was so perplexing. One moment supporting them, the next, virulently opposing them. Like when he promised a homeland for the Jews in Palestine, then shortly after, dismissed the whole plan. Perhaps Napoleon wasn't anti-Semitic at all, he was only being influenced by Caesarion." *That would explain it!*

Feeling his pain, she hates to load too much upon him, but feels the time demands it. "I think in the early years he spent in the Middle East, especially Jerusalem, something happened that hardened his heart toward the Jews. I don't know if it was Beronike, or the whole business of trade in general, but being that the Jews controlled so much of it, I think that may be where it all started. His hate and anger run so deep, I fear he may be setting you up as the Antichrist with his plan. Think about it, one of the Islamic prophecies is that Jesus only lives forty years from the revelation of the Mahdi. Do you really believe he is leaving so much of his plan to guesswork? I think he is concealing his true plan of action because he knows you will behead him."

Leaning back in the chair, he closes his eyes, and sighs.

Knowing her words are hitting home, she continues. "At this very moment, he is attending to one of his many groups of militants. He fosters their hate and educates them in the wicked ways of the West. Do you really think he will wipe out his devoted army of militants after you proclaim yourself Jesus? I think they are more akin to Nazi SS troops, than stooges set up for a fall. And here's another thing for you to worry about. He has a group of scientists working on portable nuclear weapons, and from the pieces of information I've put together from conversations with Khaba, he's awfully close to outfitting trucks with these nuclear devices. He could strike anywhere, anytime."

Rubbing his unshaven face, Altus exhales, "He could easily wipe out Jerusalem, which would solve the issue of building the third temple by the Jewish messiah, as well as eliminating the Dome of the Rock and Masjid al-Aqsa in one fell swoop, thereby building something later to satisfy all religions. It is clear . . . he does indeed have every minute detail of his plan worked out; he is simply leaving me in the dark as to the details that will cost me my life."

"And he's not worried about the Jews," she continues, "because after he blows up Jerusalem, he will hunt down the remainder, just as he orchestrated in World War II. It wouldn't surprise me if has the numbers 666 somewhere on his body."

"The numbers are actually 616," Altus explains, feeling she must understand everything at this point in time. "It was misread years ago due to the poor condition of the papyrus it was taken from. It was assumed to be all sixes because the number of God is seven, thereby being one less, 666, making it evil. Much like left was thought to be evil and the side of women, and right to be good, the side of men. I can only assume that women were associated with evil due to the snake in the Garden of Eden, or possibly, because it is a man's world."

"The *man's world* version I have no trouble believing, but what is the significance of 616?"

"It was during the time of Nero, and the numerical symbolism added up to Caesar Nero, who we all know was evil, by his very nature."

"But were they just trying to make it fit, altering the true 666?"

"No, because Nero was also known as Caesar Neron, which also added up to 666. That is why during the 1980's, when people fingered Ronald Wilson Reagan as the Antichrist, six letters in each name, Republican scholars quickly pointed out that the true numbers were, in fact, 616."

"I suppose none of that really matters now, does it?"

"No, for it seems that very soon we may see the appearance of Jesus Christ, regardless of the happenstance of numerical symbolism."

"I'm not so certain, Altus. I can't help but wonder if all the players aren't already on this earth, and in their assigned places."

"What do you mean?"

"You know how Khaba believes in messianic blood, and individuals' lives being predetermined?"

"Yes," he answers, suspiciously, looking into in her round hazel eyes, wondering what she might be getting at.

"I think it may be possible that Caesarion was influenced by God, or Satan, to choose you for the role of Jesus."

"You cannot say that!" he scoffs. "Not after reading Beronike's journal. Jesus truly existed, and for that very reason, he shall return!"

"Think about it for a moment. While it is true Jesus existed, is it really a matter of fact that he is coming back? Isn't it more plausible that the disease we carry was created by God, and we are the very demons and angels that will play out Armageddon? Just look at Caesarion's interactions with Jesus! I believe we carry the blood of angels in our veins, touched by divinity, yet human enough to care and be shaped by the world of man. These very traits making us the most adept at seeing both the beauty and ugliness of man, thereby making us the most adept at condemning or saving mankind."

"I do not believe I am Jesus. No matter what you say or do to convince me!"

"If you believe it was destiny to bring Sierra here, at this exact point in time, what makes it so impossible to believe that you would be doing no more than fulfilling your preassigned role, acting out the part of Jesus?"

"There is more than a slight difference between delivering Sierra as a pawn, which I am, than assuming the role of Jesus Christ!"

"And what if Caesarion takes over the world, annihilates the Jews, and tortures his opposers, but the true Jesus or Mahdi never returns? Will you not stand up against Caesarion for the benefit of mankind? Even it means going by the name Jesus?"

FORTY-EIGHT

The mania has passed, and depths of depression lessened, yet the throbbing headache and stiffness in Sierra's limbs persists. Instead of focusing her hate on other people, she directed it towards God and the world around her for filling her head with lies. God's existence has been thoroughly disproven, believing that if he truly existed, he would not allow good people, like her mother and brother, to die senselessly, nor make people suffer, as her father has for so many years. With the burden of God's morality lifted, she yearns to begin her life anew.

Turning to Altus, who is sitting in a chair beside her bed, she smiles as widely as her cracked, parched, lips allow.

"You are progressing better than any I have ever seen," he whispers, lovingly.

She tries to speak, but her tongue is swollen, and her upper jaw aches from the canine teeth becoming mobile. So instead, she closes her mouth and lifts an arm, signaling she'd like to walk again.

Scooping her up as easily as a small child, he sets her on her feet, wrapping his arm around her waist. They move with careful steps, Altus carrying only as much of her weight as she cannot bear. After a few minutes, she falls loosely into his arms, and he lays her gently back in bed.

With thoughts of Cleopatra's ambition returning ever more

frequently, he thinks, *She is so much more compassionate and caring than Cleopatra ever was. Is she everything I ever wanted? The beauty I lust for, without the impassioned determination for godly status that tore us apart. The world has changed . . . I've changed! Does Cleopatra belong in my past, and Sierra my future?*

Tenderly pushing the hair back from her face, he watches her fall asleep. *How could the destiny of all mankind be held within this fragile girl . . .? And what if Cleopatra returns? Will she side with her son, or me? Will I have to battle Caesarion and Cleopatra? Has my whole existence really been nothing more than to be a vessel carrying this love, thereby bringing about Armageddon?* Considering the implications, the same thought that has plagued him for days, creeps back in. *Cut her throat! End the madness!*

Jumping from his chair, he anxiously paces about the room. Lapping the perimeter, over and over, a gut-wrenching command fills his head. *KILL HER! KILL HER!*

The opening of the door stifles the inner voice, demanding his attention. Khaba and Marhib come to his side, as Caesarion walks to the far side of the bed.

In awe of the sleeping figure, Caesarion marvels at the uncanny resemblance. Lifting his head, he declares, "It is a miracle!" as a tear falls down his cheek. "She looks exactly as my mother did so many years ago. I feel as I did, when I was but a child, watching her sleep!"

"It is amazing, is it not?" Khaba confirms.

"How is she today?" Marhib asks, soothingly.

"She is near the end. Never have I seen the sickness come on so quickly, nor leave so abruptly. It is only seven days, and already her teeth extend fully. Left to her own means, she would be walking on her own tomorrow evening. Completely healed by the eighth day."

"And if she drank now?" Caesarion prods.

"It is too soon, I do not believe she even feels the hunger yet," Altus rebukes.

"But if she feels even a trace, can you imagine how soon she will recover with even one drop of your blood?" he counters.

"All will reveal itself in time! After two-thousand years, you can wait two more days!" Altus shouts, eyes searching the room for an answer his thoughts cannot provide.

Sierra, awakened by the sound of Altus's bellowing, opens her eyes to find Caesarion standing over her. Unable to believe what she is seeing, her lids open wide. *It's him! The man from my dream!*

"It is time, Altus!" Caesarion hungrily demands. "Cut yourself and let her drink! Let us find if the hunger is within!"

Filled with fear and anticipation, Altus balls his hands into fists, squeezing tightly as a command fills his soul. *TAKE THE KNIFE!*

He turns to Khaba, who holds the knife of obsidian, and snatches it from his grasp. Holding a wrist above Sierra's mouth, he trembles with anticipation at the insertion of the blade, and the unforgiving future.

"Do it now!" Caesarion cries.

With burning angst and fearful trepidation, he gazes down on Sierra, thoughts racing wildly from eternal love to eternal damnation, and all points in between. Agony and anxiety ruling the moment, he thrusts the blade upward, into his waiting wrist. Wincing slightly, he twists the blade in his artery. Gliding down the blade, the blood moves preternaturally slow, caressing each knuckle with its scarlet glow before kissing the base of the knife. He longs to stop the flow from encompassing the knob at the bottom of the handle, knowing it will soon form into a drip, but destiny has played its hand, and he is helpless to its whims.

With a gasp only perceptible to himself, a drop breaks free. Twisting and twirling through the tense, stale air, the small crimson dot falls carelessly onto Sierra's plump lower lip, as if given the volume for just such a purpose.

Suddenly, everything moves more rapidly than Altus could have ever imagined. The taste of blood brings out Sierra's fangs, and with vampiric speed, she grabs his wrist, pulling the open wound to her ravenous mouth.

Desperately watching her suck from his throbbing wrist, Cleopatra fills his every thought. From the moment she rolled out of the rug, to the day he ended her life in the mausoleum, they flash before his mind's eye, a torrent of emotional visions.

Feeling every corpuscle of the sweet nectar flow through her veins, a burning heat, growing deep within, brings on orgasmic sensations, and her lust demands more. *MAKE THE FEELING GROW!*

Caesarion, joyously smiling at her ardent vigor, begins chanting,

"Hear me, O Re, Falcon of twin horizons,
father of gods!
Hear me, you seven Hathors
who weave fate with a scarlet thread!
O Hear, all you gods of heaven and earth!

Grant
That this girl, true child of noble blood,
pursue life with undying passion
Follow upon those ancient steps
so purposely laid out before her so very long ago,
fulfilling those many days of lost hope,
as a sun that never sets!

We beg of you, O Great Anubis!
That the Queen of Queens,
shall once more reign upon her throne,
nevermore to taste the bitter sting of death!"

Feeling the beautiful and mysterious man's words wash over her, every nerve begins to tingle, and the godly-blood fills her with an energy she has never known.

Drinking more than any before her at such an early stage, Altus becomes weak, and rips his arm free. Depleted, he drops into the chair behind him, only now aware of the mystical connection between Sierra and Caesarion, glittering green eyes locked helplessly onto each other's.

A cosmic force fills Sierra's soul, and she begins speaking in a language she does not comprehend. As the foreign words leave her mouth, she is taken by the familiarity of the scene, realizing it to be the fulfillment of her dream. With her tongue moving strangely, forming unfamiliar words, her vision goes blurry, then dark.

Hearing the ancient Egyptian language pour forth, Altus jolts upright in his chair.

The words fill the room with heart-wrenching amazement, loudly proclaiming, "I am complete. I am justified. I am youthful. For, in truth, I am Isis Cleopatra, Goddess of all eternity!"

Amid the ecstatic screams of Caesarion and Khaba, Altus drops his head, clasps his hands, and prays, "Father, forgive them, for they know not what they do."

Made in the USA
Columbia, SC
14 March 2023

13742137R00238